Season
of
Change

**Center Point
Large Print**

**This Large Print Book carries the
Seal of Approval of N.A.V.H.**

ॐ श्री गणेशाय नमः

Season of Change

Lois Battle

Center Point Publishing

Thorndike, Maine

This Center Point Large Print edition
is published in the year 2001 by arrangement with
Jane Rotrosen Literary Agency.

The text of this Large Print edition is unabridged.
In other aspects, this book may vary from the original
edition. Printed in Thailand. Set in 16-point Plantin type by
Bill Coskrey.

ISBN 1-58547-052-X

Library of Congress Cataloging-in-Publication Data

Battle, Lois.
    Season of Change / Lois Battle.
        p. (large print) cm.
    ISBN 1-58547-052-X (lib. bdg. : alk. paper)
    1. Large type books. I. Title.

PS3552.A8325 S3 2001
813'.54--dc21

00-055505

Chapter 1

esamine Mallick was rearranging a bouquet of flowers on her dining room table. She had intended to take out only the narcissus. They had clearly had too much refrigeration at the florist's and had begun to wilt very quickly. But as she plucked them from the crystal vase and placed them neatly on the pages of an old magazine, she noticed that some of the roses were fading and that the fern had become dry as tissue paper.

She looked at her hands and saw that the veins were beginning to become prominent through her delicate and almost translucent skin. Then the hands started to pull out the less-than-perfect blooms with increasing speed. She stood back to see what was left. Her large gray eyes, trained for over twenty years to take in line, color, and composition, were shocked to see the two remaining pink roses and a tuft of baby's breath droop to the rim of the now-too-large vase in exhaustion and disarray. She propped them up, thought of getting a smaller container. They fell back over the rim of the vase. The faint odor of the decaying stems drifted to her nostrils. A feeling of hopelessness came over her. Tears began to sting her eyes and roll slowly down her cheeks. "A grown-up woman doesn't cry because flowers die," she thought. But the tears kept coming.

She moved back from the table and stared at the carpet. She could not bring herself to raise her eyes and gaze upon all the objects she had accumulated in this room—the antique sideboard with the silver and fine china, the brocade chairs, the carefully chosen paintings—they all seemed to be closing in on her, weighing her down. She backed into the living room and felt her way down to a sitting position on the couch. Her friends were right. She must move out of the apartment. It held too many memories. It was too large for a woman alone.

Her hand touched the small, roughly hewn table next to the couch. Ed had made this when they first lived together. Later, when they had more money, they had bought the huge glass and chrome coffee table, and Ed had said that they should throw this little clumsy one into the trash. But she had not been able to part with it. It reminded her of the early days of their marriage, when all their leisure time had been spent together at home. When talking and cooking and making love had been a part of their daily life— when living was a simple pleasant thing like warm water or the color of pale green—when she didn't have to think about things or ask questions, when she simply took things into herself, as she had taken Ed time and time again.

She remembered the night he had finished making the little table. She had designed it and chosen the wood and he had taken great care with it, since it was his first attempt at carpentry. They had sat on the floor of their first apartment and rubbed walnut oil into it. They had been drinking a bottle of Chianti, and she had spilled some on the table and had begun to cry because she thought she'd ruined the surface. But the

6

real reason she was crying, which she only discovered when Ed held her and told her she was silly, was not the destruction of the surface of the table, but something much deeper. She confessed to him that she had discovered she had no deep feelings for her life as an artist. It wasn't just that she'd realized that she wasn't really talented, she had sobbed, it was that she got no satisfactions from painting that were even comparable to her pleasure in fixing a meal or shopping for bargains, or putting lotion on her body before she came to bed with him. He had listened to her with a quiet concentration that brought a furrow to his forehead even when his face was young and without lines, the same look he had when he was sitting at his desk and going over blueprints. It always flattered her that he listened to her with such absorption. He had rocked her and smoothed her hair and said that he didn't care if she did or did not go out into the world and do things. He did not care if she was a great artist. That was only an option. She had felt so deeply happy to have him accept her like that. Accept her pleasures as important, not trivial. To assure her that her existence in the world was enough for him and that she did not have to prove her worth. It was, she reflected, the first moment in her life that she had felt truly loved.

Her sense of thankfulness for such acceptance had never deserted her. On their last anniversary, the eighteenth, she had given a party for a large group of their friends and had presented him with a gold bracelet that had the words "With gratitude, Jesa" engraved on the back. One of the women present had given a little

7

smirk when Ed showed it to her. She remarked that it was a strange inscription. Jesa was surprised at the woman's response, since the engraving expressed exactly what she continued to feel. She knew that without Ed she would never have been able to achieve the ordered, comfortable, and loving existence that she enjoyed.

From the beginning he had charted their "Five Year Plans" and with her help and encouragement, they had never failed to realize their goals. He had graduated from architectural school. He had gone into partnership. He became not only affluent but widely praised for his work. Ultimately he had formed his own company and expanded his interests from architecture to the ownership of a building company. Jesa had been less than enthusiastic about that choice—it meant that he would be more burdened with responsibility and away from home that much more often. But she never really questioned his decisions since they had always been so successful. Instead, she cajoled him into a promise of a very long vacation when his current project, a cultural complex in Arizona, was completed. She bought them both jogging shoes and elicited yet another promise that he would exercise more and ease up. He never wore the shoes. A week after their eighteenth anniversary, he died of a heart attack at the Arizona construction site.

Everyone marveled at what they described as Jesa's strength of character and control. At the funeral she was, as usual, beautifully groomed and gracious. She consoled the friends and associates who collapsed into

8

her arms in tears, while her own face remained impassive. She performed all of the terrible tasks connected with a death with a quiet and steady demeanor. Only Sally, her best friend, saw that she was a robot, as zombielike as a Hiroshima survivor. And after the public responsibilities were concluded and the shock wore off, she would sit for hours in the dark and wonder what had become of her life.

Months afterward she still experienced disorientation, sudden fits of tears, and, worst of all, bouts of incurable insomnia. She thrashed about, hearing noises. Sleeping pills gave her only a few hours of relief, and she would wake reaching for that familiar body. One night her own scream had wakened her. She turned on all the lights, but she still had to hold onto the walls and grope her way into the bathroom. She splashed water on her face and looked at herself in the mirror as she dried herself. Her face was haggard. The well-cared-for skin had started to sag and she noticed new lines around her mouth. She clung to the sink and breathed deeply, looking down at her breasts. They seemed surprisingly flaccid inside of that ridiculous, low-cut satin nightdress. Who wears such a thing when they sleep alone, she asked herself. Why do I have lines on my face? Why can't I sleep? She turned on the stereo for comfort. She drank scotch and warm milk. She crawled back into the double bed and stared at the ceiling. I'm dying, she thought. I'm slowly dying.

"I must get help." She said it aloud. The sound of her voice jarred her ears. She crawled out of the bed and dialed Sally's number, sobbing. The next day she had gone to a psychiatrist who was a specialist in "grief."

He asked her about her family history. He took notes, mostly with a detached grunt and an occasional nodding of the head, but sometimes there would be a glint in his eyes, as though he were a rookie detective who had just come across an important clue.

"I can't believe you still get excited about these scraps of information I tell you," she said.

"It's my vocation," he smiled in an avuncular, yet seductive, way. "Now why do you find it difficult to believe that anyone would be interested in you?"

"But I'm paying you to be interested," she replied, surprised at her bluntness.

He cleared his throat. "That's certainly true."

Thinking that she'd answered the question, she relaxed momentarily and took in the paintings on the wall, wondering if she could ever trust a man of such dubious taste. She could feel his quizzical eyes still boring into her and noticed that his fountain pen was poised, impatient for more information.

"No one but my husband ever seemed to be really interested in me," she continued.

"What about your parents?"

"Since I was only five when they were killed, I can't really say. It's difficult to separate my aunt's propaganda from the truth—she always claimed that mother and father weren't much interested in being parents. The story is that father inherited the looks of the Smythes, but none of their thrift and industry. Mother was a dancer of questionable background, so

10

the family never accepted her. And after their marriage they apparently did their best to squander what was left of the family fortune. In fact, they were vacationing on the Riviera and had left me in the care of my nurse when the car crash took place."

"And your aunt?"

"Oh, she saw to it that I attended the best schools, but that was more of an attempt to save face with her peers and redeem my father's profligate existence than out of any genuine concern for me. It was always of paramount importance to her to do 'the right thing.'"

"How did she feel about your decision to become an artist?"

"When I told her that I was coming to New York to study she was sure that it was a manifestation of the 'bad blood' she'd been trying to suppress in me. She even threatened to cut off my little annuity until I told her that I'd get a job at Macy's to support myself. Then she relented. I suppose the notion of a Smythe being a shop girl was more than she could tolerate. But even then I could see that all that society business was a sham. No. It wasn't until I fell in love with Ed that I knew that someone could really be interested in what I thought and felt."

She turned her eyes back to the wall. The moments ticked by. Realizing that her hour was almost up, he explained that it was quite normal for a woman with her history to be inordinately affected by her husband's death. She wondered what "inordinately" meant in this context, but decided not to ask. He reached across the desk, patted her hand, and pushed

11

a prescription toward her.

"I think that these pills will help you to get some rest. Next time you come, we'll talk about . . ."

But now, after a year of pills and analysis, she was still erratic in her sleep. She said she renewed the prescriptions only because the little bottles on the bathroom shelf gave her a sense of security "in case" . . . but the bottles emptied all the same. And the pills did not stop her from waking in the night and reaching for the flesh of that familiar back. And it wasn't there. He would never be there again.

She dug her nails into the tiny coffee table until the skin around her cuticles showed white. She must get rid of the apartment. Sell the bed. Move. Give everything away. But how could she give everything away? What would she do with the little table? She could neither destroy it nor trust it to any living creature. She closed her eyes very tightly. She could feel the wrinkles being forced into her soft skin, but she couldn't open her eyes.

She sat there, clutching the table, squeezing her eyes shut, hoping for a solution. Finally opening her eyes, she looked into the dining room and saw the silly, sad flowers that remained in the vase. She walked toward them, yanked them out of the vase and threw them onto the opened magazine. Then she quickly walked into the kitchen and deposited it all in the trash container. She leaned against the polished tile of the sink and breathed heavily. Why should she try to go on living when her entire being was wracked with pain? When she had no purpose? She could, after all, make a choice to end it. She was surprised that she had not really thought of it before, but then she had made only two real decisions in her life—to go to art school and to marry Ed so she had no practice in decision making.

The thought of ending it all calmed her. She felt warm and content and private. She did not have to be that terribly public figure: the lonely widow. She did not have to force herself to go through that degrading dredging up of almost forgotten and recently felt pain on the psychiatrist's couch, that charade that was supposed to relieve her grief. To make her whole again. She did not have to see the look of concern that barely concealed a perverse curiosity on people's faces. She did not have to pretend in order to assure both them, and herself, that she was feeling better. No more going to bed with the stereo on, or touching her own body in the night to make sure it was still alive. She could sleep forever. She turned the thought over in her mind and felt the muscles around her mouth form the tiny Mona Lisa smile that she had been known for in her younger days. She was a private person once again.

"St. Aloysius preserve us!" Sally muttered as the phone jarred her out of sleep. She groped her way out of bed, tossing Rebecca's small furry body onto the floor. Rebecca shook herself, blinked at Sally in annoyance.

"Sorry, sorry, sorry . . . didn't mean to startle you."

Sally hoisted the dog under her arm and groped her way into the living room. The curtains were drawn

13

over the huge windows so that the room was still in semidarkness. Finally she tripped over the phone cord and followed it to the couch. She fumbled in the overstuffed pillows and located the receiver.

"Who the hell is this?"

"I'm terribly Sorry to disturb you, Sally. It's after eleven and I assumed that you'd be up by now," Ellman Smith's voice dropped to an apologetic whisper.

"No, no. I'm the one who should say sorry. I didn't mean to be rude, but I always am for at least the first few hours when I wake up. And in the winter I never want to wake up at all."

"I share your sentiments entirely. This time of year it seems to be an act of faith to think that the sun will ever shine again. I was wondering. . . ."

"Hold on a minute, will you? You know I can't talk without a cigarette."

Sally threw the receiver on the dilapidated couch and stumbled over to her large worktable. Pushing aside paintbrushes, magazines, an overflowing ashtray, and a half-empty carton of salmon salad, she located her pack of Camels and knocked over a jar of muddy water. She wiped her hand on her floral pajamas and plopped herself down on the couch again.

"Now, where were we?"

"I was just going to ask if you were going to the Friends of Young Artists this afternoon, and if so, perhaps I could come by and pick you up."

"Sure, sure. I'm going."

"Do you think that Jesa will be there?"

14

"Yeah. I talked to her yesterday and she sounded very good. There was a wonderful calm in her voice."

"I'm so glad to hear that. Shall we say two o'clock then?"

"Damn it, don't do that! . . . No, Ellman, I wasn't talking to you. Rebecca just knocked over her food bowl. I really must hang up. I'm over deadline on this damn children's book. Last night I was so anxious that I dreamed there were little fairies romping all over my body—no, darling, not the sort we know—little elves. So I have to finish *Troillina and the Wejams* today or they won't pay me. See you at two. Bye."

Sally hung up and walked over to the windows, flinging back the huge curtains and letting the gray winter light into the cluttered living room. Poor dear Ellman, she thought. Still hanging around asking about Jesa. Jesa could be a widow for the rest of her life and she still wouldn't look at Ellman. She needed more enticement than a pleasant manner and a hefty bank account and looks that could charitably be described as "average." Jesa needed someone who was more than trustworthy and protective. She needed someone with style, but not flash. Fortyish, but still youthful in outlook and appearance.

"If there was such a man and I found him, I'd tie him up and have you guard him, right, Rebecca? But I can't be thinking of men now. I have to get some work done."

She shuffled through the sketches on the work-table and discovered to her dismay that the spilled water had trickled down onto a finished watercolor

15

of one of the Wejams.

"Shit, I hate kids' books," she cursed and walked into the kitchen. After feeding Rebecca and making herself a pot of coffee, she sat down at the worktable and started to sketch. This was her fourth Troillina book, and since Troillina looked a bit like Sally herself, with huge brown eyes in a broad, freckled face with tufts of bright red hair, Sally usually had no trouble drawing the creature. But this morning her hand was unsteady and her mind was preoccupied. She crumpled up another sheet of paper and poured a shot of scotch into her coffee cup. Rebecca trotted over and made herself comfortable in her pillow next to the worktable and waited for Sally to talk to her.

"One of life's little ironies that I should end up the queen of the kiddie-book market, huh? I mean, you'd have thought that something like that would be more in Jesa's line. She was the one with the innocence and the flowers."

Her mind went back to the time, almost twenty years ago, when she and Jesa had become friends. She would never forget that day, because it was also the first time that she had seen Hugo Bridgeman, first love of her life, in a naked state. It had been toward the end of the semester at the art school. The summer weather had been so enticing that, even though she usually enjoyed the class, Sally felt sorry for herself for being indoors. She had unpacked her things and was sitting at her drawing board waiting for the model to appear.

She'd been disappointed with the models so far. The

females had, without exception, been lithe and in excellent shape. They had a look of boredom and narcissism that made Sally full of envy and wonder. But the males had been a sorry lot—flabby and old. There they sat or stood, all flaccid and hairy, as though they wanted it to be over so they could pick up their fee and buy a bottle of cheap wine. Sally thought they must have been recruited on the Bowery. But this particular day, a serious-looking young man with muscular shoulders and long legs walked to the front of the class and began taking off his clothes and folding them with a grim precision. Sally fancied him a gladiator preparing himself for combat. He was adding his socks to the neat pile of his belongings when the teacher appeared with a guest speaker.

"Dr. Rossman, who teaches anatomy at Columbia University, is our guest today. Dr. Rossman will explain . . ."

The young man, now completely naked, was looking at her. She pretended disinterest and began smoothing the paper in front of her.

"When the knee is straight, its bursa, or water mattress, forms a huge bulge on either side. Would you flex your knee please?" The young man obliged.

"Quick sketches first," the instructor put in.

Sally kept looking at the young man's penis and wondering what it would be like when erect. She didn't think they were going to demonstrate that. She had only seen one man undressed at this point in her life, her cousin Lenny, and that had been in a car so she couldn't really see much. She and Lenny had been

17

friends for years. The previous autumn when he was getting ready to leave for college, he'd had an older friend buy a bottle for them. They'd parked in the Palisades, sipped gin and shuddered, and talked about what they wanted to do with their lives. As Lenny became drunker he had started to cry. Sally had never seen Lenny cry before.

"I'm sure you'll be a great mathematician," she comforted him.

"It isn't that. It's that I haven't . . . I mean, I'm still . . ."

She kissed him.

The union had been clumsy and messy. Lenny had promised to write to her, but he never did. But the reality of that first encounter had not diminished Sally's sexual curiosity in any way. She was still sure that the earth could move if you weren't with a relative in the back seat of a '58 Buick.

"The spinal furrow becomes deeper as it reaches the lumbar vertebrae. . . ."

Thank God the young man had turned his back to the class. The teacher moved between the drawing boards. Sally regained a more objective attitude and sketched furiously. The teacher paused behind her. She could feel his breath on her neck. He bent forward and took her hand in his.

"The mass first, then define the line," he muttered, and released her hand.

Even though she liked the class, this particular teacher always made her feel queasy. He was pompous and brutally critical, especially with the female students. He straightened up and murmured something that sounded like grudging approval and moved over to the girl sitting next to Sally.

Sally had watched this slim girl with the fine cheekbones and the ash-blond hair all during the semester. Her combination of reserve and classic good looks made Sally suspect money and privilege, and in order to cover up her prejudice against such types, she had been more than her usual chatty self. She'd talked about the weather, made jokes, offered to loan her brushes and pencils, but the girl had never reciprocated her overtures, so Sally had turned to more receptive classmates for conversation. Even the girl's name, Jesamine Smythe, suggested someone who rode horses or went to debutante balls.

The teacher paused behind her and stood absolutely still. Then he said, in a sneering voice that was loud enough to be heard by all the students at the back of the classroom:

"Miss Smythe, even if you are ignorant of the male body in your personal life, I should have thought that you would have enough of an eye to render a recognizable buttock. This looks like a plate of apples. The lateral masses of the waist muscle . . ."

There had been a few stifled sniggers and an embarrassed turning-away of heads. Sally focused her attention on the dais, but as the teacher moved on to another unfortunate, she stole a glance at Jesamine Smythe. The girl was frantically erasing the drawing pad, so that the paper began to tear. She was struggling to control her tears. She saw Sally looking at her and a blush suffused her pale skin. Sally came to her

19

aid in the only way she knew how: she pulled a face
and rolled her eyes first toward the teacher and then
up to the ceiling.

The body on the dais relaxed. Students began to
pack up their equipment. Sally craned her neck to see
if the young man was putting on boxer or jockey
shorts, but there were too many people moving in
front of her to allow her a good look. She turned to
Jesamine.

"Let me talk to you after class."

Jesa nodded and left the room. The teacher was
shaking Dr. Rossman's hand and thanking him for the
lecture. Most of the students scurried out, but Sally
was still packing up her things. The young man walked
past her.

"I'm a bit slow," she grinned apologetically.

"That's okay. I'll be back tomorrow. Name's Hugo
Bridgeman."

"Sally Gold, thanks."

She hurried into the hallway. Jesa stood near the
door, holding a portfolio against her chest and swallowing again and again.

"Hey, don't be put off by that old lech of a teacher.
He's not even going to be here next semester."

"How do you know?"

"He's got some sort of sabbatical to do restorative
work on an old church in Europe. That's about all he's
good for, touching up someone else's stuff. That's why
he's such a shit. And he's particularly mean to anyone
who's good-looking. Has he put the moves on you?"

Jesa blushed again. Sally could tell that it wasn't

20

because the answer was yes, but rather because of the tough language. She did want to make Jesa feel better, but since she'd been rejected by her for most of the semester, she couldn't resist making her support a little hard to take. And she loved to shock people with the slang she'd picked up at the restaurant where she worked.

"No," Jesa said quietly. "I've never even talked to him outside the classroom."

"But you can sure tell from his beady little eyes that he'd love to touch your buttocks, can't you? Hey, you want to go to Inato's and have something to eat?"

"I brought my lunch."

Jesa held up a brown paper bag that had been crushed to her chest along with the briefcase.

"Forget it. I'll treat. They put so much garlic on everything at Inato's that nobody will dare to lean over your shoulder for the rest of the day.

"Say, what do you think of that model? His name's Hugo." Sally felt a special sense of pride in penetrating Jesa's reserve. She drew her into the group that had appointed themselves the movers and shakers of the art school. She took her to parties in apartments with mattresses on the floors and candles stuck into wine bottles. Engaged her in heated arguments about the virtues of Jackson Pollock and De Kooning. Badgered her into leaving the residence hotel where she lived— "Who ever heard of an artist living in a 'Lodging for Young Women'?"—and helped her to paint the bathroom of her new Village apartment a bright crimson. She shared all the details of her affair with Hugo and cried on Jesa's shoulder when he was "a beast." She gave her the name of a gynecologist and urged her to take a lover.

But Jesa never shed the shyness that uncharitable souls put down as the haughtiness of a provincial debutante. It was her only protection. Sally began to see that she couldn't lead her friend into the free-spirited, unconventional attitudes that she associated with the word "artist." Without the veneer of her manners, without the help of conventions of behavior, Jesa was an obvious victim. Avaricious landlords, lascivious men, sharp-eyed panhandlers could smell her vulnerability as quickly as a shark smells blood. She had neither the gift nor the training to survive alone. So Sally abandoned the role of liberator and styled herself as Jesa's advisor and protector. She even managed to be less than honest about Jesa's painting, convincing herself that the pale still lifes that her friend executed were lovely, that the treatment of sunlight was exquisite. And Jesa was equally enthusiastic when Sally, infatuated with Mexican artists, did whole walls of bloodshed and rapine. To the outside world it was a strange alliance indeed. "As though Grace Kelly and Elsa Lanchester were cast as sisters," someone had joked. But for two years Sally and Jesa had the giggling, completely trusting and adoring crush of preadolescent girls. Some gossiped that they were lesbians, but Sally's affairs with every bizarre man who crossed her path gave the lie to that rumor. Then Jesa met Ed.

Sally never felt quite as alone as she did in the company of Jesa and Ed. He was, of course, disposed to like anyone and anything that Jesa liked and he was attracted to the bubbly chatter and colorful histrionics that Sally could be relied upon to provide. It was only when she engaged Jesa in lengthy phone conversations or overestimated her own capacity for liquor that Sally exhausted Ed's patience. But Ed and Jesa had an intimacy that excluded all others. Though too gracious to make a show of their attachment, they had only to look at each other over a table to make everyone else present feel as though they were interrupting something very private.

Sally had rushed to her friend's side when Ed had the fatal heart attack. She had helped to arrange the funeral and had provided whatever comfort she knew how to give. After a time she had tried to reunite Jesa with the world. She had poured out invitations, arranged dates. She had suggested a shrink. She had all but forced Jesa to volunteer to teach an art class to disadvantaged teenagers. But none of these ideas had helped. The therapy seemed to make Jesa even more introspective: she began to discuss her childhood and talk about the pathological nature of her depression, but she did not improve. The kids at the alternative school had frightened her with their hostility and their slang and had made her feel inadequate. She had stopped teaching after only three sessions. She had become, if possible, more withdrawn over the last six months.

"No," Sally said aloud as she put the finishing touches on a painting of Troillina being chased by a

Wejam, and downed the last of her spiked coffee, "I haven't been much help at all." A quick look at the clock told her that she didn't have time to dwell on her inadequacies.

"Oh, Lord, it's after one and I still have a case of the morning frumps. Let's see if a shower and a dab of makeup can make this piece of mutton look a bit more like a lamb."

Rebecca trotted into the bathroom with her to watch the toilette. Sally had showered, rummaged in her closet, put on a tent dress and was rubbing Egyptian Mocha rouge onto her already ruddy cheeks when the buzzer rang. Ellman was always deadly punctual.

"Ah, Ellman, always the gentleman." Sally kissed his cheek and asked him to sit down.

Ellman surveyed the chaos of the room from behind his glasses, unbuttoned his vest, and looked around for a place to put himself.

"I don't know which I hate more, cleaning up or working," Sally yelled from the bedroom. "I still have about another six drawings to do before Friday, so I 'spose that will encourage me to wash windows or something. Anything would be preferable to those damn Wejams."

"I don't know why you denigrate your work, Sally," Ellman called out. "Gustave Doré illustrated fairy tales."

"Stop trying to lift my spirits and just help me with this zipper. Do I look all right?" Sally emerged from the bedroom and surveyed herself in the mirror above the bar. "Don't answer. I look terrible. I look like a bundle of rags tied in a hurry. I hate going to these meetings. It's more of a fashion show than a discussion."

She poured herself another slug of scotch and drank it quickly.

"Oh, Ellman, may I offer you a drink?"

"No, my dear."

Even though Ellman had declined in the most polite voice, Sally felt that he was reprimanding her. She threw back her head and laughed.

"Sorry, Ellman. I'll just be a minute. I just don't think I can face that crowd without fortifying myself."

"You don't have to face anyone. It's only a meeting."

"That's what you think. Why is it that even the most intelligent men can miss what's really going on at these things?"

"I'm sorry but I don't know what you're talking about," Ellman pushed his glasses back onto the bridge of his nose and looked at her inquiringly.

"Oh, I mean Bettina Fanshaw and that crowd. I just don't fit in with them. I always feel as though my slip's showing. Even when I'm not wearing one."

"Nonsense. You've been invaluable to the group. I simply don't understand how you can work yourself into a snit over something as simple as a meeting."

"That's because you've been trained since childhood to button your collar and your lip. You probably knew parliamentary procedure and how to use a finger bowl when you came out of your mother's womb."

"Actually I didn't master the finger bowls until I was

25

three or four."

Ellman came 'round the bar and hooked the back of Sally's dress. He gave her a fraternal pat on the shoulder.

"Come along now, dear. We don't want to be late. You did say that Jesa was coming, didn't you?"

"Yes, I talked to her yesterday. She sounded very good. Unusually calm. But I'm not going to get too excited about it. I've thought she was coming out of her depression before and she's slumped right back in, so who knows. I'll talk to her today after the meeting."

"Perhaps you'd like to come 'round to the gallery. I've just purchased some work of an artist called Severio Euzielli. Really quite remarkable stuff. As a matter of fact Bettina recommended him to me."

"Then he must be 'divine.' " Sally winked, and she picked up her coat and kissed Rebecca goodbye.

The Friends of Young Artists were meeting that afternoon in Bettina Fanshaw's apartment near the Metropolitan Museum. It was only the absence of uniformed guards that made you know that the apartment was not a wing of the museum proper. Sally didn't think that such an accumulation of objets d'art had survived in a private residence since the robber barons had been cleaned out. She wondered where Bettina ate and slept, though, knowing Bettina, she probably thought those mundane activities were beneath her.

Since the meeting was about to begin, they were ushered into a huge library. The twenty or so guests were

26

chatting among themselves and Cameron Henner had to strike the gavel on the oak table several times to call the assemblage to order. Cameron's nasal voice was irritating even in casual conversation, and when he announced that the first order of business would be the reading of the quarterly budget, there was much sighing and shifting of chairs. Sally did her best not to look toward the oak doors of the room. Bettina was seated directly behind her and gave her a look of strained tolerance whenever she turned around. Ellman inclined his head toward Sally's left ear, smoothed his thinning sandy hair, and breathed sadly.

"It's not like Jesamine to be unpunctual. Perhaps she's not coming after all."

Just then the doors were opened quietly. The maid ushered in a tall blond woman in a tailored green dress. She moved unobtrusively to a seat near the rear of the room and put on her glasses. Sally craned her neck, nudged Ellman, and whispered,

"She's here, and she's wearing green . . . that's a good sign."

Cameron Henner cleared his throat, shot a reprimanding glance at Sally, and proceeded with his never-ending list of figures.

When the meeting was finally over, Sally rushed back to Jesa, almost colliding with the waiter who was bringing in the hors d'oeuvres.

"Jesa, you look wonderful. So springlike. I expect to see vines growing out of your hair."

"But Jesamine always looks divine," Bettina Fanshaw enthused as she joined them. Jesa smiled

27

vaguely. Sally looked at Bettina's teeth and wondered how much the dental bill would be to bring a mouth that close to perfection. Bettina smoothed the hair back from her forehead and glanced at herself in a nearby mirror. Sally thought Bettina looked a good deal like the wicked queen in Snow White, and half expected her to intone, "Mirror, mirror on the wall, Who is the fairest one of all?" Instead, Bettina tore herself away from the comfort of her own reflection and took Jesa's hand. "It's so good to see you after all these months. Sally here was sure you were 'round the bend, but I said, 'I know Jesamine, she's a thoroughbred, she'll pull out of it.' "

Sally distinctly remembered that it had been Bettina who'd made remarks about Jesa falling apart, as though she were some sort of inferior product. Sally was always amazed at betrayal. Bettina can't understand love or grief, she thought. All she can understand is power. Even in her position as fund raiser for Young Artists, a job that didn't seem to necessitate connivance, Bettina was as wily as a general at peace negotiations. She was the perfect committee woman, and the committee could have been Parents and Teachers or the OPEC Trade Commission. As long as she could manipulate, she was in her element. Bettina's husband, O.W. Fanshaw, had made a pass at Sally several years ago. At first Sally had been shocked to think that a man who had such an impeccably chic wife would want her as a bedmate. But O.W. told her that sex with Bettina was like making it with a traffic cop.

"I'm feeling much better, thank you," Jesa said.

God, thought Sally, Jesa's a sheep among the wolves. She'll never be able to see through anybody who's on the make. She broke her resolution to diet, as she did whenever tension took hold of her, and reached for a canapé.

"Listen, my dear," Bettina continued, doing her best to ignore Sally's presence, "you really must come 'round for drinks next Friday. The budget is just a morass. I'm desperate for a few level-headed people. We're going to have some bright young man who works for the governor come and tell us about matching contributions. Say you'll come."

She's after money, Sally thought, stuffing another hors d'oeuvre into her mouth without realizing that it was an anchovy. She looked around for a napkin that she could discreetly spit the salty mush into, but Bettina, predictably, had linen napkins, so there was no getting rid of it. She swallowed hard and looked for some punch to wash it down.

"I can't promise. My plans are . . ." a smile played on Jesa's lips again, ". . . indefinite."

"Well, if you can't reach me at home, I'll probably be at the salon. I'm really being disciplined about my exercise, and there's a new boy there who gives the most wonderful massages . . ."

As she talked on, Bettina's eyes flitted around the room. She was capable of keeping up a line of chatter when all of her antennae were quivering for the next move. Suddenly she broke off and waved at a man who was just coming into the library. Sally didn't think that she'd ever seen him before, but even if she had he

29

was worth more than a second look. Even under the conservative suit you could see the lines of a well-kept, muscular body. His curly dark hair was worn rather longer than was acceptable in present company, and his dark eyes flashed around the room with a cunning, intelligent expression that Sally called "street smarts." He looked like a *condottiere* who was crashing a Renaissance court party.

"Severio finally came," Bettina gushed. Her enthusiasm, for once, did not sound strained. She flashed the perfect teeth again, excused herself, and wafted across the room to offer the man her cheek.

"That one looks too wild and untamed to be part of Bettina's menagerie," Sally whispered, "and he's sure giving you the eye."

The man was staring at Jesa with intense interest, barely acknowledging the people who had started to cluster around him.

"I'd like to go home," Jesa said, dropping her eyes.

"Good. Let's down this fruit-fly punch and go over to my place for a real drink. I haven't seen you in over a week, and as our hostess would say, you look divine."

Jesa allowed Sally to steer her through the crowd of nodding faces. They smiled and touched her hand and cooed out their greetings and complimented her on her appearance. She responded in kind, feeling a claustrophobia bordering on nausea that caused her to hurry toward the foyer. Ellman came up behind her and helped her on with her coat. Through the library doors she could see Bettina, arm in arm with the handsome stranger asking a little knot of guests where she had gone. She pretended not to hear and started toward the door. She had to stop and wait for Sally, who had dropped her gloves and was cursing under her breath as she bent to retrieve them.

"Would you be able to go to dinner with me on Saturday night?" Ellman asked her again as he held the door open for her.

"I'm sorry, Ellman, I really don't know what my plans are yet."

"Perhaps I'll call later in the week, if that's all right. I would love you to come to the gallery and see what I've picked up recently. I think this Severio Euzielli is remarkably talented. In fact I'm going to give him a showing. Wouldn't you like to come back in for a moment and meet him?"

"I'm sorry, Ellman, but I've been feeling a bit fatigued today. Perhaps some other time."

Ellman smiled sympathetically, kissed Sally on the cheek, and walked back into the library.

"Nobody could accuse him of lacking persistence," Sally said as they walked out into the chilling breeze. "I know he's not really your type—I guess Ellman isn't really anybody's type. He's sort of the best friend, extra man type. But you know he's quite a decent sort really. How bad could it be to go to dinner with him?"

"Stop matchmaking, Sally. Why don't *you* go out with him?"

"He hasn't asked me. Besides, he's such a connoisseur of the arts that he probably finds physical beauty mandatory in a woman.

"Why do you have such a silly inferiority complex?"

31

"Because I have a mirror in my bathroom." Sally laughed and darted onto the street to hail a taxi.

They got out of the cab and climbed the three flights to Sally's apartment. Sally rummaged in her huge purse and Rebecca started to yap excitedly on the other side of the door.

"Shut up, you're not a Doberman."

As she pushed the door open, the dog scampered up to Jesa and made ridiculous leaps of excitement, hurling her tiny body against Jesa's legs.

"Don't let that mutt con you, she gets plenty of attention. Just push all that shit on the couch onto the floor and make yourself a place to sit. What'll it be?"

"Just a little vermouth, if you have any."

Jesa pushed aside some newspapers and a robe and sat on the couch and picked Rebecca up. The dog's rough tongue licked her hands. Some dozen years ago Sally had made the mistake of subletting her apartment to a doleful-looking art history student at Barnard while she went on a holiday to Italy. When she returned, having gained a deeper understanding of Florentine artists and ten pounds, she discovered a houseful of dead plants, a mound of unemptied garbage, and a note offering a "present" in exchange for the unpaid utility bills. The present was Rebecca, whimpering in a pile of soiled newspapers. Sally called Jesa in alarm. She couldn't take the responsibility of a pet, she said. She hated women who had diminutive, cutsie dogs. Would Jesa come and take it to the pound with her? When Jesa came she had looked at the quivering puppy and said, "Rebecca of Sunnybrook

Farm." So she and Sally had made a trip to the super-
market to buy dog food and a leash and a toy, instead
of leaving Rebecca to the mercies of the kennels. The
dog continued to lap her hands, as though it remembered that she had been responsible for its deliver-
ance.

"So what do you think about it?"

"I'm sorry, Sal, I wasn't really listening."

Sally handed Jesa a glass and sat down on the floor
in front of her.

"You're always thinking. Too much. Clogs your
impulses. Put that mangy coquette down. She'll get
hairs all over that good dress."

She grabbed the dog and nestled it between her
legs.

"And no barking, you creep. Now, I was talking to
you about getting away from town. It may be a bit premature, but why not go up to Connecticut and open
up the summer house? I could come up with you as
soon as I've finished the book, and we could paint and
take walks in the country and make jam . . ."

"Make jam? From what? It's March."

"Okay, make snowmen. I don't know. It's just so
dreary sitting around waiting for the ice to melt. I
mean, this weather is bound to affect your state of
mind. I feel like I've been in an Ingmar Bergman
movie for the last three months. Being in this apartment has really given me cabin fever. I'd just like to
close the door and leave it and they could open it up
in about fifty years. You know, sort of a time capsule:
'Museum of a Slob, Circa 1980s.' "

33

"You know I've left you my apartment in my will."

"Oh, God, Jesa, now you *sound* like an Ingmar Bergman movie. Do stop being so morbid. Besides, you'll outlive me by a hundred years. As my doctor told me at my last check up, 'I cannot predict the health of someone who embraces so many forms of self-abuse'—at first I thought he was talking about my sex life."

Sally threw back her head and laughed. She knew that the laughter sounded forced, but she couldn't help it. She felt like a comedian that was trying to loosen up the audience. She took another sip of her drink.

"No, really, Jesa, it would do you such good to get away. I don't see how you can stand to be in that apartment. You haven't changed anything about it since Ed died, and it's bound to have a negative effect on you, living there with so many shared things to remind you."

"I agree with you. I just don't know what to do with everything. There's the paintings, the furniture, the . . ." Jesa began to feel dizzy. The possessions seemed to appear before her, to push her down and make her feel small. The thoughts became physical sensations, as though she were Alice Through the Looking Glass. The color drained from her face and she sank back into the pillows of the couch and closed her eyes.

"Are you all right? Jesa, I beg you not to think about all of this. Just close up the apartment and go somewhere else. You'll be able to deal with it when you return."

"You're very dear to me, Sal."

" 'Course I am. I'll get us a refill."

As Sally refilled the glasses she looked at her reflection in the mirror above the bar. She wiped a smudge of lipstick from the corner of her mouth and allowed the smile she had put on for Jesa's sake to fade. Why couldn't she just shut up and stop goading her friend, even if she did think it was for her own good? It wasn't as if she had managed to solve any of her own problems, so who was she to dispense advice? What a clown I am, she thought, as she squinted at her slightly mottled face.

" '*Après un certain age un homme est responsable pour son visage. . . .*' Do you 'spose he meant women too?"

"Who?"

"Camus. He said, 'After a certain age you're responsible for your face. . . .' Bettina would probably think that was an advertisement for Elizabeth Arden. . . . I don't mind the sags so much, it's the expressions that frighten me."

"Your face is fine, Sal."

"I'm trying to get at something else. Remember that series of Rembrandt's self-portraits—he starts out cocky as hell, and then in the middle he just sort of breaks down—there's so much worry on that face that it hurts you to look at it. Then when he's old there's dignity and humor—he looks out of his eyes and sees the whole crazy world with acceptance and curiosity."

"Yes?"

"We're in that bad middle part now. You especially, because of losing Ed. But if we can just get through this then life might be even better. The point is not to give up. Shit, remember what I was like at twenty—I thought I was gonna be the first female Picasso, with fame and lovers and kids—so here I am, living alone and drawing purple Wejams. But I still feel, you know, excited about the possibilities and if we could just hang in there. . . ."

Sally's voice lost its confident tone. She inhaled deeply and stared at the ceiling.

"What I mean is, I think I'll be a great old lady, but I sure as hell don't know how I'm gonna make it through middle age."

They sat in silence for a few moments. Rebecca jumped up next to Jesa and put her head under her hand to be stroked.

"I see you have given this animal comfort training."

"She knows what's going on all right."

Jesa put down her glass, gave Sally a hug, and stood up.

"I must go. I really must. I'm very tired."

"Consider what I suggested—about going to the country. Of course I'll have to juggle a crowded social calendar, but for you, anything."

When Jesa had gone, Sally picked Rebecca up and walked over to the window. She watched Jesa walking slowly down the street, shivering and buttoning up her coat with trembling hands.

"Oh, this god-awful winter. Maybe when she sees the flowers come out it will give her a lift. She's a great one for green things. And then I'll take you to the park, if you promise not to piss on the May buds.

Now, coffee and a cigarette and then it's back to the damn Wejams."

Chapter 2

As she walked toward the gilt doors of her building, Jesa noticed that the winter sky had already turned dark. O'Hara, the doorman, rushed forward to open the doors for her.

"Terrible cold still, isn't it, Mrs. Mallick?"

"Yes. Thank you, O'Hara."

She moved toward the elevators as quickly as possible. She had neither the strength nor the inclination to discuss the weather, O'Hara's chief topic of conversation. She wanted desperately to sneak into her apartment and not have to deal with anyone. She pressed the button and focused her eyes on the elevator.

There was a draught of cold air as the front doors were opened again and she heard the familiar sound of Mrs. Moss's voice. She prayed for the elevator to arrive. Sophie Moss had been their downstairs neighbor ever since she and Ed had moved into the building. Sophie was already a widow when they had made her acquaintance, though it took Jesa months to realize that "dear crazy Abbie," whom Sophie constantly talked about, had been dead for many years. Sophie had come by their apartment on the least pretext: to ask if they liked the new wallpaper in the lobby, to give them her own inimitable reviews of shows she'd seen, to share a cake she'd baked. Jesa had been patient and tolerant with her, because she'd seen that Sophie was lonely and needed conversation. But since Ed's death she felt an aversion toward her that she didn't understand.

"Hold the elevator, will you, dear?" Sophie piped across the lobby.

She bustled over, carrying a small box with "Viennese Pastry Shop" written on the side.

"My dear, how nice to see you. I just ran out to the store to pick up a few cookies. The girls are coming over tonight for a game of Mah-Jong and I just didn't feel up to cooking anything. Of course my doctor, you know I told you about Dr. Webster—oh, he's such a sweetheart—he's always flirting with me—well, Dr. Webster has told me that I simply must keep my weight down, but how many pleasures are left in life, I ask myself? Now when I was younger, I know you wouldn't believe it to look at me now, but I had an absolutely stunning figure. Poor crazy Abbie! You know he actually didn't want to take me to the beach because be didn't want all those other men looking at me."

She opened the pastry box and took out a cookie and offered the box to Jesa.

"No, thank you, Sophie."

"But with you, my dear, it's the opposite problem. You haven't put on flesh. In fact, you look as though you're just wasting away. I know what it's like when you have only yourself to cook for all the pleasure goes out of it. But you do have to eat to keep your strength up, and let's face it, men don't really like skinny women. I don't mean that you're skinny. Just that I've noticed that you have lost some weight. Well, it's only natural, I suppose."

Finally the elevator doors opened and they stepped inside. Sophie kept talking.

"Why don't you come into my apartment and have a cup of tea with me? Better yet, stay for supper and then meet my friends when they come over. It's only a hen session, but it's better than sitting alone."

"Thanks very much, but I have other plans for this evening."

"Going out on a date? I think that's just marvelous. You're still young. You should be going out. I can't wait for the spring to arrive—I just love to walk around and see all the young couples together. I went to see *The King and I* last week—oh, it's a lovely show, you really should go—and when they sang that song 'Hello, Young Lovers' I just burst into tears. My granddaughter Sylvia was so embarrassed. She said you could hear me sniffling all over the place. But I do love that song. It's strange, isn't it, how a song can just unravel you? Are you sure you don't want one of these cookies? They're just delicious."

Jesa shook her head and mustered a polite smile.

"My dear, did I tell you that the Coblentz's—you know that good-looking couple on the fourth floor—well, I think they're splitting up. Such a pity. But that's life nowadays. Married one month, divorced the next. I wanted to go up to her and ask her if she knew what she was doing—of course I don't know her well enough—but as Sophie Tucker would say 'A Good Man Is Hard to Find'—I know I don't have to tell you that."

The elevator stopped at Sophie's floor and Jesa put out her arm to hold the door. She was afraid that the door would close before Sophie Moss could make her exit, and she would be stuck with her for another ten minutes.

Sophie stepped out of the elevator and looked at Jesa. Her eyes blinked several times and she moved her head back and forth sagely and made a small clicking sound with her teeth.

"Remember, my dear, you're always welcome to come down and chew the fat. As Abbie used to say, 'What are friends for?' "

Jesa said thank you yet again and leaned against the wall of the elevator in relief once the doors had closed. She fought her anger toward Sophie Moss. Why should such a harmless, well-meaning woman upset her? Because, she realized, Sophie seemed to be some sort of a threat of the future. Her future. She still had friends of both sexes, still had a connection to the out-side world and still had her figure, but how long would it be before she drifted into a world of "hen sessions" and gossip and hypochondria? No, she would never be like that, she assured herself. She would never be like that. But only because she was too shy. She was a dif-ferent type, so her decline would have a different man-ifestation. She would undoubtedly waste away instead of getting plump. She would sit alone and talk to her-self instead of taking solace in the company of neigh-bors and women friends. The spectre of herself in fif-teen years appeared before her: frail and fearful, reclu-sive and full of imaginings of the past. She wouldn't even be as healthy emotionally as Sophie; she would probably try to commune with the spirit world instead of going to the bakery or the beauty parlor.

She let herself into her apartment. She could smell the faint odor of cleansers and soaps. Maggie, the cleaning woman, had been there and had left her a note on the kitchen table asking if she could change her next day of work from Thursday to Friday because she wanted to babysit for one of her grandchildren. Maggie had spelled "Fryday" with a *y*.

Jesa marveled at Maggie. At sixty she was still going strong and always seemed to be in good spirits. But she had her grandchildren. She had already put one of them through college and had grandiose plans for the other five, or was it six? But Jesa had no such connections with the future. She was sorry that Ed had resisted her plans to adopt a child when she had gone through her second miscarriage, but he had told her that he didn't think that he could have any real feeling for a child that was not his own flesh and blood, and despite her feelings, she'd been reluctant to press the issue.

She turned on all the lights, paused in the bathroom long enough to swallow the last three tranquilizers in the bottle, and walked through the apartment. Yes, everything was in perfect order. She walked into Ed's study and stared blankly at the paintings adorning the walls. There were a few watercolors of flowers and scenes of their Connecticut house that she had done and the large Winslow Homer that had been such a find. She closed the door and turned on the stereo. She listened to Brahms's Fourth several times, lying on the leather couch with her coat still on and her eyes closed. She began to feel very calm and detached. Then she got up and walked through the apartment again, checking everything to make sure it was in order, in much the same way she always did when she and Ed were going away on a holiday. She pulled the front door shut behind her and went down in the elevator. O'Hara put down his copy of the *Post* and opened the front door for her.

"It's gotten very nippy, Mrs. Mallick. I'd take an umbrella if I was you. The weather report predicts . . ."

She walked into the street. The sky was blue-black with clusters of dark clouds above the orangy glow of the city lights. She turned toward the river. Winds howled down the corridors made by the tall buildings and whipped her coat against her legs. Her eyes started to water and her face became pained with the cold. As she approached Riverside Drive, the gusts became so powerful that she had to move slowly to maintain her balance.

She saw drunks cowering in the doorways of the grand old buildings that were now dumping grounds for derelicts and welfare people. She thought that they must be cold. But they didn't frighten her. A young black man rushed up from a basement stairway where two or three other tough-looking kids were lurking.

"Spare some change, lady?"

She looked into his eyes. They were frantic, despite the broad grin on his face. One tooth was missing.

"I didn't bring my purse."

"Sorry to bother you," he called after her, with no

sarcasm in his voice.

"She's flipped," she heard him tell his companions.

Strange, she thought, as she clutched the front of her coat to her, she was usually terrified to walk in a neighborhood like this, but she felt very calm, almost as though she were watching herself in a movie. Maybe not caring about living had given her a detachment that others mistook for courage and authority, when all she really felt was that she was incapable of feeling at all.

She was close to the river now and the winds lacerated her face and body. There was no one about. She walked closer to the boat basin. She and Ed had come here often. In fact whenever she started off on an aimless walk, she invariably ended up at some location that they had frequented together. Only last week she had started walking with no particular direction in mind and had found herself in front of a restaurant where they had been regular customers. She was greatly embarrassed when the maître d' had smiled and waved at her through the window, because it was only then that she realized that she must have been standing in front of the restaurant for some time. Now she mysteriously found herself at another of their haunts. She recalled all the summer trips, lugging picnic baskets, getting seasick, Ed yelling to "come about" and laughing at her confusion about nautical terms he'd told her time after time.

She stood near the railing and looked into the black, choppy waters. There was something floating there. A jellyfish? Not in the Hudson. She peered closer. A

43

cluster of prophylactics had caught against a pole that poked out of the water. She looked beyond them. In the distance the water no longer seemed polluted. The full moon and the lights from the Jersey shore were reflected on its surface. She could imagine the warm, secret tides and eddies at the bottom. Imagine being rocked to sleep in a world silent, comforting, and secret. She closed her eyes and leaned forward on the railings.

"Jesamine?"

A figure loomed behind her, blocking off the wind so that she felt warmer almost instantly. She tried to open her eyes and focus on the body that was only a foot or two away from her.

"Jesamine? It is you, isn't it?"

She felt a hand take hold of her arm.

"Who are you?" she gasped.

"Severio Euzielli. I didn't mean to startle you. Are you all right?"

"I'm fine," she lied. Her heart was pounding and she felt unsteady on her feet. "Who are you?"

"I'm a friend of Bettina's. Actually I knew you, too, but many years ago. It's terribly cold standing here talking. May I walk you home?"

He held out a hand which she accepted.

"Oh, Jesamine, You don't have any gloves on."

He took her hand in his and rubbed it gently and started to lead her back toward the street. He was talking to her but the wind was so furious that most of his words were lost. She told him her address. Or thought she did. She felt as though she were coming

44

out of anesthesia. She had surgery after one of her miscarriages and this was the same sensation— coming to and drifting away and coming to again with no control. She tried to surface into consciousness and ask him who he was, but her teeth were chattering so badly that she couldn't speak.

They reached the doors of her building, so she must, she reasoned, have told him where she lived. O'Hara opened the door and looked at her in a peculiar way. His face, distorted like a Weegee photo, came close to hers. His eyes were rolling and bulging with concern.

"Is Mrs. Mallick all right?"

She opened her mouth, but no words came out. The man released her hand and steered her toward the elevator.

"I'm afraid she's caught a chill. I'll take her up. Top floor, isn't it?"

"Yes, the penthouse. You're Mr . . . ?"

"Euzielli. I'm a friend of Mrs. Mallick's."

O'Hara's eyes narrowed and he looked at Jesa again.

"You sure you're okay, Mrs. Mallick? Okay for this gentleman to take you up?"

"I'm . . ."

"Shivering," Severio supplied with a grin.

"Yes, shivering. I'm all right. Thank you, O'Hara."

She leaned against the fleur-de-lis wallpaper and stared at the elevator buttons. The doors closed.

"Now where are your keys, Jesa?"

"I don't think I brought them."

"Oh, you really must be more careful."

45

He pushed open the unlocked door and guided her into the living room. As he helped her to sit down on the couch she began to shake violently. She tried to form words, but her throat felt as though it had closed over.

"Now just sit back. I think you must be in shock. Have you taken any pills or anything?"

She shook her head.

"I'll get you some blankets."

He disappeared into the passageway. She tried to lift her arm and point him to the linen closet, but she was still shaking too badly. She felt herself drifting out of consciousness again. The room tilted and it was dark.

In the dream there was a little child. It had been hiding underneath a house. It was damp and very dark there. She was scared of crawly things coming up her legs. She put on her socks and crouched very still. She could hear the sound of the ocean, and she crawled out from under the house. There was a beach with flowers growing all around. She picked the flowers and took them to a man sitting up on a sand dune. He picked her up and threw her high into the air. She laughed and squirmed. He tossed her higher and higher and she was afraid to fall. The flowers scattered in the sand.

Jesa opened her eyes. A man in blue jeans and a fisherman's sweater was sitting in Ed's chair, turning the pages of one of her art books. The light from the reading lamp shone on his hair, which was dark and quite long. The large book hid his face. His hands looked powerful, but were beautifully shaped.

She started to move and realized that the satin comforter from her bed was tucked all around her, tight up to her chin. She was still in her dress and could smell the faint odor of perspiration on her body. She must have passed out and he had covered her up. And here he sat, totally relaxed, perusing the pages of Monet prints as though this were his living room, as though her conduct had not been extraordinary. She tried to think of what she could say to him by way of explanation, but found no words. But he must have sensed that she was awake and looking at him, because he lowered the book almost immediately.

"You're finally awake. How do you feel?"

He put the book down carefully and walked over to the couch and crouched on the floor next to her.

"I thought you were all right. I've seen a few shock cases, so I didn't bother to call a doctor after I checked you out."

The idea of being "checked" while she'd been passed out embarrassed her, but the look of concern and friendliness in his eyes seemed so genuine that she thought a frank answer was more appropriate than an apology.

"I don't really know how I feel."

"You probably don't need that cover now. How about a cup of tea, or would you prefer a drink? I already helped myself to your bourbon—I hope you don't think that's impertinent."

"I'd hardly be in a position to judge anybody's manners. My behavior . . ." Again she felt the muscles in her throat constrict.

"Don't try to explain anything now. In fact, explanations are not in order at all as long as you're feeling better. May I get myself a refill and pour you a brandy?"

"I'd appreciate that. I think I'll just go into the bathroom for a moment."

He helped her up and she walked unsteadily down the hall and into the bathroom. She had expected to look terrible, but the image that stared back at her from the mirrors was one she usually saw after a good night's rest. Her hair was disheveled, her face slightly puffy under the eyes, but the skin was smooth and unlined. She splashed cold water on her eyes, patted a dab of moisturizer on her face and ran a brush through her luxuriant hair. It was remarkable that she looked so well, she thought.

When she reentered the living room, he had folded the comforter and was sitting on the couch sipping his drink. He got up and handed her a snifter of brandy.

"Have a drink of this. You hadn't taken any pills, had you?"

"Only a couple of tranquilizers and that was around . . . what time is it?"

"I guess it's about two or three in the morning."

"Oh, my goodness. And you've been sitting here all that time?"

"I didn't want to leave you alone."

"I can't imagine that I slept all that time. Actually I've been rather insomniac lately. I suppose I was just exhausted."

He nodded politely and took another sip of his

drink, but she could see that he wasn't taken in by this casual explanation. His dark eyes were far too intelligent for her to continue to play any social games.

"The truth of the matter is that I've been very depressed."

"I know."

"You know?"

"Yes. I heard that your husband had died, and putting that together with what I know about you already, I assumed that you must be in pretty bad shape."

"But how do you know me?"

"I told you. We went to art school together. Well, not exactly together. I was a couple of years behind you. I'll try not to let my male ego be shattered by the fact that I obviously made less of an impression on you than you did on me. All the men at school thought you were so beautiful. I always wanted to paint you. I thought that you were the reincarnation of Botticelli's lady love, but in those days I was a shy one myself and I could never get up enough nerve to approach the lovely St. Jesamine."

"I'm sorry, but I really don't remember you."

"As I said, I'll try not to be crushed by your indifference."

"But after all those years . . . to run into you again, well, not exactly run into you."

"I suppose I'd better make a clean breast of it: I came here to your building tonight just as you were leaving and I followed you to the river. Please don't be angry with me. I was supposed to meet you today at that Friends of Young Artists meeting, but you'd left before Bettina could fulfill her promise to introduce us. In fact I watched you leave, and it was pretty clear that you weren't in a very receptive mood."

They looked at each other for a long time, she searching her memory for some recollection of him, he studying her reaction. She was surprised that she felt no trouble in holding the gaze. It was Severio who broke the eye contact and placed his drink on the table.

"Thank you for the drink. If you're feeling all right to be alone now, I'll be getting along."

"Do you have to? Of course, you must be very tired."

"Not tired so much. Usually I work late into the night, but to tell you the truth I'm hungry."

"Please let me fix you something."

"That would be very kind of you, but I doubt if you feel up to it."

"No, I'd like to. I just realized that I'm hungry myself."

She hadn't been cooking recently, but she knew that there were eggs and cream in the refrigerator. She scrounged around in the pantry and found some canned paté and marinated mushrooms. As she beat the eggs and fixed coffee, Severio sat at the table with another bourbon and watched her.

"I walked around a bit while you were resting. You really have a fine collection. Eclectic, but all in wonderful taste. Not many people have everything from Picasso to Winslow Homer. It says a lot about you."

50

"I can't take credit for the Homer. That was a coup of Ed's. We found that in a junk shop while we were on a business trip to New Mexico. God knows how it got there. I remember the owner was afraid he wouldn't make the sale. He kept assuring us that the frame was worth forty dollars. Last time it was appraised I think they said it was worth $300,000."

"So you can always sell a few paintings if things get tight."

"Oh, no, I could never get rid of anything," she heard a tension come into her voice. "What I mean is, I'm not worried about money now, but even if I were, it would be impossible for me to think of these things in monetary terms. Their value is that they have memories."

"Sometimes too many memories make it hard to live in the present. I used to get a lot of satisfaction out of accumulating things a couple of years back, but when I walked away from everything in Mexico City I really felt liberated."

"That sounds enviable in some ways, but I just don't think it's in my nature to live like that."

"Who knows? Maybe your nature will change. I don't know if it's true, but I've heard that Picasso would live in an apartment for years and when he decided to move, he'd just turn the lock in the door and leave everything. Maybe it's not in an artist's nature to be attached to material things. Of course a woman's body is material—but that's another matter. Anyway, my idea of the good life now is to enjoy things, use them, but not be attached to them."

When he mentioned a woman's body, she could feel his eyes on her. She managed to flip the omelet without breaking it and poured the coffee. They sat at the table and ate in silence, relishing the simple food. She thought of all the expensive dinners she had been treated to in the last months, when, at the urging of friends, she'd tried to go out again. Escorts who had smoothly appraised the vintage of the wine, when their eyes told her that they were really assessing her availability now that she was "on the market" again. How she had agonized about those evenings, wondering for the first time in years if she had chosen the right thing to wear, if she could keep the conversation going, if she would be able to handle a fumbling pass or a direct proposition when the evening drew to a close. When, on a first date, one man had asked to spend the night with her, she had felt dumbfounded and somehow insulted. But when another, in whom she had no interest, had failed to ask her out again, she felt strangely rejected. She had begun to think that she would never have any comfortable relations with men outside of O'Hara and the grocery boy. But here she sat at her kitchen table in her stocking feet, playing with the eggs on her plate and feeling very much at ease. She was so relaxed that she had to stifle a yawn.

"Excuse me. My aunt used to tell me that yawning was a sign of ill manners and boredom, but I don't feel bored in the least."

"It's emotional exhaustion. You must be going through a difficult period just now."

"I'm not so sure it's just a period. At least I can't see

any end to it."

He took her chin in his hand and looked into her eyes.

"You're a very sensitive woman, Jesamine. The capacity for feeling makes you equally vulnerable to pain as well as pleasure. It is true that Ed is irreplaceable. But you are also irreplaceable. Surely the best way for you to honor your love for him is to try to reach out for those things that will help you to live again."

She had heard these sentiments before, but somehow the directness of his gaze and the warmth and lightness of his touch made it seem that he was uttering a truth instead of mere words of comfort. He looked out of himself and into her, and she felt as though his energy was pouring into her being. He lifted the hair from the nape of her neck and pressed his lips there. She could feel a vein in her throat begin to pulse. She shivered and froze. He released her, walked into the living room, and picked up his jacket and moved quickly to the front door. She came into the hallway and he placed his hands on her shoulders.

She was standing so close to him that she wanted to melt into his body, not out of desire but simply out of gratitude and fatigue.

"You've been extremely kind to me tonight, Severio. You haven't pried or given me any advice. You've just been here for me. I'm very grateful."

"And I have wanted to kiss you for many years, Jesamine. I can't tell you what a rush it gave me. There are so many things I want to find out about you. But there will be time."

He caressed her hair for a moment, then released her abruptly and opened the door.

"Don't forget to lock it after me." He smiled and was gone.

Jesa leaned against the door and breathed deeply. She felt so exhausted that she could have curled up on the floor, but she walked through the apartment methodically turning off the lights. She turned back the bed covers and began to take off her clothes. She thought of taking a bath but she was too drowsy and she enjoyed the faintly musky scent of her body. Without bothering to put on a nightdress, she crawled in between the sheets and felt their coolness on her naked skin. She shifted into a comfortable position, automatically staying on the left side of the bed. Even though she now slept alone, years of marriage had conditioned her to sleeping on "her side."

Some hours later a pale winter sun began to shine dimly through the batiste panels of the draperies. She stirred and opened her eyes and realized that she was sprawled in the middle of the bed clutching a pillow to her. She remembered how, as a teenager, she had kissed and stroked her pillow as an imaginary lover, making the material moist as she practiced how to kiss. Again she buried her face in the fabric. Her fingers stroked the pillow and her mind, half conscious, imagined that her fingers were tangled in those long, loose curls. My God, she realized with surprise, I'm thinking of Severio. She moved away from the pillow and lay very still. A deliciously tingly sensation was sweeping through her body. It had been so long since she'd felt such excitement that she was overcome with a feeling of wonder. It was immediately supplanted by a shadow of guilt. How could she be lying in the bed she had shared with Ed and allow herself to have such vivid fantasies of another man? She tossed the pillow onto the floor, drew back to her own side of the bed, and curled up in a fetal position.

Severio Euzielli walked for several miles after leaving Jesa's apartment. The prospect of an affair with a beautiful woman always gave him the same surge of adrenaline an athlete feels when he hears the whistle for the big game. And this time the burst of energy was buoyed up with a sense of accomplishment: he had finally attained a position where Jesamine Smythe was within his reach.

The first time he'd ever seen her—oh, so many years ago sitting on the lawn outside the art school, he'd been filled with frustration and anger because he knew he couldn't approach her. Sure, he was successful with the girls in his old neighborhood as the only son in a large Italian family he'd had constant female adoration since childhood, and almost as soon as he'd hit puberty this confidence, plus his good looks, had made it easy enough to find willing women. But Jesamine Smythe was something se. Her grooming and carriage spelled money and WASP tradition. It had taken him years of careful self-molding to gain the prestige and polish that allowed him to approach such a woman.

As he pulled off his sweater, poured himself a

brandy, and glanced around at the chic, spare furnishings of his loft, he remembered the dingy tenement he'd shared with his family. As a young man he would take his sketch pad and sit out on the fire escape, happy to be away from the worn furniture and food smells and continual arguments. He would sketch furiously, his mind filled with sharp images of "those" women: the beautifully manicured hand that closed the door to the limousine, the head that magically arranged the silky hair with a single toss, the slim legs in leather pumps that disappeared into expensive stores when he was aching just to look at them, the eyes that peered over the upturned collar of the fur coat. What the hell did his art professors know when they cautioned him about all the years of patience and labor it would take for him to bring his talent to fruition? They were dreaming of some tacky production of *La Bohème*, relishing an artsy notion of poverty while they drew their regular paychecks. He already knew that the road to success was not strictly dependent on ability, even though he was sure he had plenty of that. He had no intention of grubbing out an existence, living in a fifth-floor walk-up, frying sausage, and drinking cheap wine while he perfected his art. He'd figured out that the glorious life-after-death that his mother got down on her knees and prayed for every night was only a myth to keep people like himself in their place. He wanted his rewards now.

His first real opportunity for advancement came, not unremarkably, through a woman: Manuela Tenorio Avitia had persuaded her father to bring her to New York on one of his extended business trips. Feeling that his daughter might get into trouble if she had too much time on her hands, Señor Avitia had allowed her to enroll in an art class. While she had no abiding interest in painting, it was at least an opportunity for the twenty-eight-year-old virgin to have a small taste of freedom. It was only a week from the time Severio offered to help her carry her equipment to the waiting limousine to the afternoon when he went to her hotel to present her with a bunch of flowers, and finding her unattended, managed to give her a sample of the sensual delights that the nuns at the Convent de Rosario had warned her against. The next day she told Señor Avitia that she was in love. Being a highly strung young woman, she announced that she would take her own life if he did not allow her to marry, because the fact that suicide was a mortal sin no longer deterred her. It was the one lapse from social and religious rectitude that ever marred Manuela's life of devotion to church and family.

The first years of the marriage went rather well. They returned to Manuela's homeland and Señor Avitia set them up in a comfortable home within walking distance of his own mansion. Severio was happy in his role of gentleman expatriate and put his time to good use. He tried to improve his work and took advantage of the Avitias' social connections to market it. He was relatively attentive to his wife's needs and only rarely deviated from his role as model son-in-law. It was only after Señor Avitia's death, when Manuela lapsed into a morbidity of a severely religious

57

caste, that he began to more or less lead his own life and disregard her. After all, life was for the living. He had become a sought-after guest for yatching parties and glittering dinners with amusing companions and if, as Manuela had once screamed at him in a jealous rage, he would have served his muse better had he spent less time in the pursuit of pleasure and more at his easel, he was, nevertheless, satisfied with his life.

When Manuela had become so pious that she had a small chapel built in the house and began to refuse to go out with him, let alone sleep with him, he had asked for a divorce. It took her several years to overcome her religious scruples and grant it to him. By that time his reputation in Mexico City had earned him enough introductions to start selling in New York almost immediately, and his association with people like Bettina Fanshaw ensured that it was only a matter of time before his name started to appear in the gossip columns, if not the art section, of the newspapers.

But his plans for further success in his career had no hold over his imagination as the early morning light came through the windows of the loft. He pulled down the shades, settled into the pillows of his bed, and sipped his brandy, imagining the joy he would feel when he finally took Jesamine Smythe Mallick. The fact that it would not be easy to gain the love of such a woman made the prospect even more intriguing. He could not simply rely on his looks and charm as he could with some experience-hungry widow. Jesamine was made of much finer stuff than that. He knew he would have to be gentle and patient and intelligent, taking time to understand her character, easing his way into her trust, before he could gain access to that secret place of vulnerability. He imagined her pale blond hair on the pillow next to him and immediately dropped off into a sound sleep.

Chapter 3

Sally shook the last drops of liquid from the thermos into the plastic cup balanced between her knees. She swallowed the contents of the cup in a gulp and peered through the windshield of the car at the late afternoon sky. The sun, which had made a brilliant appearance after fighting through the overcast morning, seemed to be giving up the attempt and disappeared behind some dark and threatening clouds.

"I think it's going to rain again."

"Don't worry. We'll be there in another half hour," Jesa replied. Her eyes behind the tinted glasses seemed to be concentrated on the road, but Sally could tell from Jesa's expression that her mind wasn't only on her driving.

"Listen, I don't care if it comes down in buckets. As long as I'm away from the city I'd feel relaxed in a blizzard. I can't tell you what a relief it is not to be looking at that goddamn drawing board. When the messenger came to pick up all that Troillina crap yesterday I felt as though I'd been given a reprieve from the electric chair. I was jumpin' for joy when you called and said you were going to take my advice."

"You were right. It was a good idea to get away."

Jesa didn't want to tell Sally that her advice wasn't the only reason behind her decision to visit the country house. The morning after her encounter with Severio she had walked around her apartment in a state of expectancy. She wasn't even conscious of waiting for a phone call until the ringing caused her to jump. She paused to pick up the receiver so that she wouldn't appear to be anxious. The moment she heard Severio's deep voice she was overcome with a case of nerves. He asked how she was feeling and suggested that he come by and take her out to dinner that evening. She quickly demurred, saying that she had made other plans. When he pressed her for the following evening she said that she was going to the country for the weekend with a friend. Until that moment she'd had no intention of making the trip. Severio rang off after promising to call her upon her return. Once she had said that she was leaving town she felt an obligation to do so. She didn't want to appear coy, but the fantasies she'd felt after he'd left the previous evening made her fearful of another encounter, even though her thoughts had been on him ever since. She wanted to talk to Sally about it, but was afraid to unleash Sally's matchmaking imagination.

Sally screwed the top onto the thermos and reached down to the floor of the car and picked Rebecca up and placed her in her lap.

"Rebecca's happy too, aren't you?" Sally cooed, rubbing the little dog's silky ears. "She's been downright morose for the last couple of months. I guess we've both been fighting off cabin fever. My social life has been about as active as a Carmelite nun's."

"You were the one who decided to break it off with George."

"George certainly couldn't be thought of as a social life. All he ever did was turn up an hour late every week for a dinner I'd cooked and spend most of the evening telling me how much he loved his ex-wife. Listening to some guy moaning about alimony payments isn't my idea of really exciting foreplay, even if I do have a charter membership in Masochists Anonymous. Nope. It's time I faced the facts—I got no talent where men are concerned. God knows I've tried a cross-section of the population and I never thought I'd live to say it, but I'm bored with the whole scene."

Jesa looked over to her right and changed lanes on the highway. She caught a glimpse of Sally's face. Its expression was not one of boredom: the features had sagged slightly into a look of hurt questioning, which made her appear older and terribly young at the same time. Jesa had often wondered why her friend hadn't connected in any lasting relationship with anyone. None of the psychological constructions seemed to apply. No one could accuse Sally of avoiding men or of having rigidly high standards about their qualifications. If she erred it was always on the side of quick emotions and generosity. There was nothing of the coquette in her and, at least in the eyes of her best friend, she seemed to have a great deal to offer to any relationship. Jesa searched for an understanding of Sally's disappointments and desertions and could find none. It wounded her to see Sal's vivacity harden to boisterousness, to hear her quick tongue become cynical, to watch the increasing dependence on alcohol that Jesa dared not mention.

"You'll never guess who I heard from," Sally said. Her face brightened into its mischievous grin.

"I give up, who?"

"Señor José Rodriguez himself. I sent his kids a copy of the last book and he wrote to thank me."

"Now there was one that shouldn't have gotten away."

"Don't be ridiculous. Can you just imagine me sitting in some hacienda chewing on my mantilla and waiting for him to come home from his factory so we could have his mother over for the evening rosary? I would've been so bored I'd have joined the guerrillas in the hills and taken up making Molotov cocktails. That is if Mama hadn't put a tarantula in my bed and finished me off first. But we did have a wonderful summer together. Hey, remember the night when Ed was learning to play the guitar and José taught all of us to sing 'I've Been Working on the Railroad' in Spanish?"

Sally broke into a chorus of the song and Jesa hummed along. Then Sally went through her repertoire of old favorites until Jesa made the turn off the highway. They drove for another twenty minutes through the still-gray, rolling hills and meandering streams of the countryside until Jesa saw the weather-beaten mailbox that she had painted with bright flowers. The dirt drive wound in and out through the woods for another quarter of a mile until the house finally came into view. It was an impressive old place. It had been built almost a hundred years ago and much of the original structure still remained. Ed had added a studio with a fine skylight, but Jesa had insisted that it go at the rear of the house, so as not to destroy the original lines. She had been up here only once since Ed's death, and that had been in the company of her brother-in-law, who wanted to get a look at the place in order to make his own assessment of its value. He had advised Jesa to put it on the market. As she walked up onto the old porch and unlocked the heavy door, Jesa was glad that she had resisted his suggestion. More than any of her material possessions in New York, Jesa considered the country place hers. She had felt a special pride when she had decided to buy it. In fact it was one of the very few decisions she had made on impulse and without Ed's prior approval.

She had driven up to the area to visit some friends and happened to see the "For Sale" sign out on the road. In a rare moment of private adventure, she had driven up the road, walked around the house and garden for more than an hour. The house was situated on a little hill, but the woods were thick and it had a feeling of privacy. There was an old mill pond further back on the property and a neglected apple orchard. She peeked through all the downstairs windows to try to get a look at the interior of the house. And when the frustration of not being able to see was too much for her, she drove ten miles into the nearest town and called the realtor. He met her that afternoon and showed her the place. The former owners had painted over much of the woodwork, but the exposed interior oak supports that resembled the inside of a ship had not been destroyed. There were several open fireplaces and the kitchen was floored with flagstones. Jesa fell in love with it. She'd decided that she would invest the small annuity from her aunt in this house. Ed had, of course, come up and looked it over before the final purchase.

Soon after they bought the place, Ed was in Atlanta working on a project, so Jesa had ventured up alone. She felt that Ed was humoring her decision to buy the house, so she labored long and hard to show him that her vision of its possibilities was not unfounded. She had stripped and spackled and caulked until she had callouses on her well-manicured hands. She had yelped with happiness when she finally scraped through five layers of paint and reached the original white pine board in the living room. And she had fallen into bed in such a state of exhaustion that she hardly missed Ed. When he called and suggested that she hire workmen to help her, she'd said no, this was her baby.

She stepped into the hallway and looked into the living room. Except for the dust cloths covering the furniture and a damp, woody smell, she might have been here yesterday. She paused for a moment and a tiny smile of satisfaction creased the corners of her mouth. Then she heard a rumble of thunder and Sally's curses as she struggled to unload the car.

"Hurry, Jesa, or we're gonna be in a real downpour," Sally shouted. Rebecca ran about, yapping excitedly. They managed to unload their bags and carry in the groceries and Sally's painting equipment just before the rain began.

"Home sweet et cetera," Sally sighed as she plopped herself down on the couch. "Thank goodness we have that load of logs there. It'll be chilly enough to have a fire in a while and there's nothing like a warm fireplace and a hot toddy."

Jesa unpacked the groceries and ran down into the basement to turn on the electricity and light the gas pilots. Sally came to the top of the basement stairs and yelled down, "You're really super around here. So self-sufficient. I remember the one time I came up here alone I was rooting around down there in the dark for a couple of hours trying to figure out how to turn things on. I was afraid I'd blow the whole place up. I'm such a city girl I always figured you'd have to have a janitor in residence to figure out a fuse box."

Jesa came up from the basement, put the flashlight on the hook by the door, and started to light the pilot in the oven. She was content to putter around, taking the chores in order, feeling simple and useful. Sally, having mixed up a pitcher of martinis, was planted at the sink, washing and peeling vegetables, singing in an off-key alto and taking sips of her drink.

"I'm gonna make us a barrel of ratatouille. My grandmother used to say that you add the garlic according to conscience and social engagements, so unless you've got a hot date tonight, I'm gonna smother this stuff with it until we're breathing like dragons."

"Shall I set the dining room table?"

"Lord, no. How long do I have to know you to break you of your blue-blood affectations? It doesn't taste as good unless you eat it in the kitchen."

While Sally cooked the dinner, Jesa walked into the living room and started a fire. Then she went to the window and looked out at her garden. The rain was still coming down, making it a dreary sight. She wondered if she would ever have the strength to plant again. Maybe she'd just come up here and lock herself in like a Gothic madwoman, and let the natural vegetation claim the house. She pressed her forehead to the cool glass and shut her eyes and remained in that position until Sally called her in to dinner.

They were just about to sit down at the kitchen table when they heard the old pewter bell that served as a door chime.

"Who in the world can that be?" Jesa asked. She put down her napkin and went to the front door, turning on the porch light and peering out of one of the glass panels. There was a very tall man standing there in an old mackintosh. The porch light shone down on his head, which seemed to be white. When Jesa opened the door and looked into his face, she was surprised to see that he was a much younger man. The hair and beard were actually blond, streaked with a good deal of premature silver. He had a ruddy complexion and a pair of bright blue eyes with pleasant crinkles around them, showing that he must spend a lot of time outdoors.

"I'm sorry to disturb you. Are you Mrs. Mallick?"

"Yes, I am."

"I'm Josh Graham. I bought the property next to yours. I didn't mean to be nosy but I noticed that there was some smoke coming from your chimney and I just wanted to make sure that everything was all right. The Barneses' place up the road was broken into a couple of weeks ago and I wanted to make sure that you weren't the victim of squatters."

"Thank you very much. That's kind of you. Won't you come in for a moment?"

He paused slightly and gave a deferential smile.

"I don't mean to intrude."

"Who is it?" Sally bellowed from the kitchen.

"It's a neighbor," Jesa replied. "Won't you come in out of the rain, Mr. Graham?"

The man wiped his Frye boots on the mat outside the door and threw his mackintosh on one of the wicker chairs on the porch.

"Really smells good in here," he said at he stepped into the hallway.

"My friend is cooking some marvelous Italian dish. Would you care to join us for dinner?"

"Thanks very much but I've already had dinner."

He followed Jesa down the hallway into the kitchen. Sally looked up from the pots, her face flushed with the heat of the stove, wiped her hands on a towel, and extended one to him.

"This is Mr. Graham, Sally."

"Josh."

"Sally, meet Josh. He's the new neighbor. When did you move in?"

"I'm still in the process. I bought the farm about six

months ago and I've been camping out there on and off since then."

"Pleasure to meet you," Sally said as they shook hands. "There's a pitcher of martinis here, could we talk you into one?"

"I wouldn't mind a bit. I've been working since early morning but I had to quit because of the rain."

"Working on a Saturday. You must be one of those conscience-stricken New England types," Sally smiled as she handed him a drink.

"I am from New England, yes. And I do suffer from time to time with the pangs of conscience—but really I work because I enjoy it. I had a desk job with the Department of Agriculture for about ten years and I've decided to go back to school and do some research in soil science."

"That's quite a switch. How'd you get into that?" Sally asked directly.

Josh looked a bit uncomfortable and sat down at the table and pulled his lanky legs up to rest on the rung of the chair.

"That's a long story."

"Nothing like a long story on a rainy evening," Sally persisted. "Besides, I'm always fascinated by people who turn their lives around in midstream . . . you know, Gauguin running off to the South Seas to be a painter after all those dreary years as a banker. . . . Zelda Fitzgerald taking up ballet . . . that sort of thing."

"I'm afraid my changes aren't quite that dramatic," Josh replied.

Jesa marveled yet again at Sally's easy familiarity. She had watched Sally extract entire life histories from people within the first fifteen minutes of meeting them. Jesa could see that Josh was somewhat reticent, but she couldn't find an opening in the conversation to return it to less personal topics. Sally's eyes were dancing with curiosity and her questions just kept coming. Josh gave way, accepted a refill, and started to talk. It turned out that he had gone into his family's wholesale produce business shortly after college, though he'd really wanted to be a scientist. Then he was called to Washington during the Kennedy administration and had remained there ever since.

"But what made you get up and quit all that?" Sally continued.

"Would you believe that I want to grow a bigger and better blueberry?" he chuckled.

"Sure I'd believe it. I guess lots of people want a bigger blueberry. But to quit being a big mucka-muck and actually go out and dig the dirt with your own hands? No. I don't think many people would actually do that. And being a student again? Sitting in classes with people who still have acne problems?"

"Most of the grad students are past the acne stage. Besides, being a student means you want to learn something. It doesn't mean that you are a particular age."

"I think you're right about that, at least theoretically," Jesa finally put in. "But it does take a bit of courage. Sally talked me into teaching an art class, and I must say that the kids overwhelmed me completely."

"So you're an artist?" he asked, turning his eyes to her.

"Well, not really . . ."

"Of course she is, and a fine one too," Sally said. "There's lots of her stuff here in the house."

"I don't really paint anymore," Jesa said quietly.

Josh finished his drink and placed the glass carefully on the table and got up.

"I'll make a deal with you. You show me your paintings one day and I'll be happy to introduce you to the joys of blueberry cultivation. In fact, why don't you ladies drop by tomorrow?"

"That's a wonderful idea," Sally enthused.

"I'll expect you in the early afternoon. And since it sounds as though the rain has let up, I think I'll be going. Thanks again for your hospitality."

He shook hands with both of them and Jesa walked him to the front door. When she returned to the kitchen, Sally was putting the food on the table.

"Not much for me, Sal. I'm not terribly hungry."

"Bet you'd take a slice of blueberry pie. Now there is an interesting man. The fact that he looks like Kris Kristofferson doesn't hurt either."

"You're too much, Sally. You really are."

Jesa sat down and placed her napkin neatly in her lap and promptly forgot about Josh. She lifted her fork listlessly and tried to enjoy the meal so as not to disappoint Sally. Sally chatted on about recipes and diets and slipped morsels under the table to Rebecca. After doing the dishes together, Jesa went upstairs to bathe, and Sally sat in front of the fire and listened to old records from Ed's collection and sipped her drink and talked to Rebecca in low, sad tones.

The next morning Jesa woke with the rays of the sun shining through the bedroom window. Dressing quickly, she passed the door to the guest room where Sally and Rebecca were still sleeping and crept out of the house. She wanted to inspect her garden, and walked alone amid the flat, tilled earth, where only a few weeds had the strength to sprout in the still chilly weather. She was wondering if she should go down to the local hardware store and pick up some seeds, but the thought of planting was too much for her. She was content to walk through the ruins of past labors, and finally sat down on the damp earth under her favorite tree and plucked at a few early shoots of grass. A gust of wind came up and shook the branches of the tree and blew her hair into her face. She pushed it back behind her ears, and her hand rested on the nape of her neck. That was the spot where Severio had kissed her. She saw his face above hers, remembered the smell of him, though she had no memory of having sensed it at the time of the embrace. Her fingers caressed the pulse in her neck and she lay back against the trunk of the tree. So strange that she should remember that slight touch. Sometimes lately she had no feeling of sensation in her body at all, and yet that spot still seemed to throb whenever she thought of the embrace.

She looked up at the sky, relishing the beauty of its many hues. She could see the sky from her apartment in the city, but somehow never really looked at it except to guess at the weather. Here in the country she could sit for ages and marvel at its changing colors. She was feeling very peaceful when Sally's voice trumpeted from the porch.

"Jesa? Are you out there?"

"Yes, I'm here," she called out and got up and walked to the house.

"My God, it's after twelve already. There wasn't a clock in my room, so I didn't notice what time it was. I'm just going to fix some coffee and then I'm going right to work."

"What about Kris Kristofferson? We promised him we'd come over and see his place, remember?"

"You'll have to go it alone, lovey. Now that I finally have my ass in gear I'm going to use that studio and get started on some real painting."

"I don't know if I want to go over there alone."

"Sure you do. It'll be interesting. You don't have any aspirin around the place, do you?"

"I think there's some in the upstairs bathroom."

Jesa watched Sally trudge up the stairs. She had noticed that Sally's face was blotchy and that her eyes were swollen, but asking for aspirin was the closest she got to admitting a hangover. Not that she made any secret of drinking. She was always ready with a joke about boozing. And the quips were a fine defense, because once she had started joking about it, it was almost impossible to have a serious discussion. But Jesa remembered their early days, when Sally had woken her up before dawn so that they could go down to the pier and paint the sunrise, when Sally was clear-eyed and always enthusiastic. It was Ed who had first noticed that Sally was more than a social drinker, but Jesa had told him that he was being a puritan and that Sally just loved to party. Now the evidence was irrefutable, but Jesa still couldn't bring herself to talk about it. She had an abhorrence for meddling in people's private lives, and since Sally seemed to be functioning in her work, Jesa felt that she should not interfere.

She decided not to take the car over to Josh's place, and instead walked down the dirt drive to the main road and up the half mile to his property. The long walk made her warm and she took off her woolen sweater and tied it around her hips. She was approaching his house when she saw Josh coming toward her. He walked with a long, easy gait, his head thrown back and squinting at the sky. In his left hand he carried a book. He stopped and read something in the book and as he looked up, noticed Jesa walking toward him.

"Do you always walk and read at the same time?" she yelled.

"You caught me. I was supposed to be doing some planting today, but I'm exploring again. Every time I walk the property I find something new," he said as he approached her. His arms went up involuntarily as if to embrace her in greeting, but he handed her the book instead.

"*Report on Geology in the State of Connecticut.* That looks like heavy reading."

"It's fascinating. Written in 1843 and the Geological

73

Survey still uses it. God, it's great to be here! I guess that sounds rather strange, but this time last year I was going to my umpteenth cocktail party in D.C. and filing my umpteenth report about international trade agreements. Being out here makes me feel as though I'm eighteen again."

As I recall, my eighteenth year was quite unbearable. My aunt insisted that I make my debut and I broke out in hives, but she still insisted. I was the only girl there who looked as if she had a case of measles and I spent most of the evening in the ladies' room, dabbing my chest with powder and crying."

"I'm sure you looked beautiful all the same."

Josh looked at Jesa in her white painter pants and checked shirt. Her hair, which had been tied back last night, was flowing over her shoulders and the tendrils around her face were curling with perspiration. He longed to lean forward and touch one of the delicate golden strands in the same way that he would touch a beautiful flower. Instead he looked at the bright blue sky and squinted his eyes against the sunlight.

"My eighteenth year was pretty unbearable too, now that I come to think of it. I guess what I mean is that I feel open to a lot of possibilities, but now I can make my own decisions about them. By the way, do you know this property?"

"No. We were over here a couple of times but I've never really seen it."

"Let's walk over to that old stone fence. That shows where the original division was, maybe a couple of hundred years ago."

They cut off from the road and walked through the woods. Josh pointed out various things about the vegetation and the soil. Jesa was attentive. She'd visited this country for almost a decade, but she realized that she knew nothing about it, and Josh's enthusiasm for its history communicated itself to her.

Finally they reached the remains of the stone fence. Josh reached for her hand and helped her over it, and they sat down.

"Can you imagine all the backbreaking work that it took to build these walls? Of course the fields were full of stones, so the materials were right at hand, but sometimes they dug down over two feet to provide a solid foundation. Right over there near those trees was the first old post road. They actually brought the mail by horse. Can you imagine. . . ." he broke off in a laugh. "Boy I must be boring. I just go on and on like some doddering teacher."

"No, it's interesting."

"You say that, but I bet you don't mean it."

"I do. I'm not very good at appearing enthusiastic when I don't feel it. That may have had something to do with my lack of success at debutante balls."

"That and the hives," he smiled.

"Perhaps that grew out of the other. I don't mean to sound precious, but I am a quiet person and lately . . ." Jesa paused in confusion, not wanting to discuss the problems of the last year.

"I know about your husband," Josh said in a low voice. "The Barneses told me about it when they went through the list of neighbors. In fact, they thought you might sell your place now."

"I was advised to sell it. I just couldn't bring myself to part with it."

"I'm glad you didn't."

They sat in the warm afternoon sun and Jesa's hand caressed the old stones she was sitting on. A silence followed but it was in no way tense. Finally Jesa turned to him. She was so relieved that he didn't gush with sympathy and the usual words of condolence.

"Sally asked you last night about making such a change in your life. It does take a lot of courage to leave a good job and go back to school and live out here by yourself."

He looked at the ground for a moment and seemed to be weighing whether or not to take her into his confidence.

"It wasn't that courageous. In fact I didn't just decide to do it . . . it was a whole constellation of circumstances. For one thing, my marriage fell apart. My kids are out of the nest and it didn't seem important to keep it together when we had so little in common. I guess I'd been living a life I hadn't really chosen ever since I was twenty years old. You see I always wanted to be a scientist or a farmer, but when my father died there was a lot of pressure for me to take over the family. And Nancy, my wife, doesn't really like the country much, so she was all for my going into business. I don't blame her. It was my own decision. Then it was on to Washington. . . . I guess the real catalyst was when a friend of mine died at his desk. Then I knew that I'd best spend the rest of my life in work that meant something to me. The old job is still there in Washington and there are lots of people who think that this farming thing is some sort of male change-of-life—and they're right. I'll never go back to the martinis and the wheelin' and dealin'. Not a day goes by when I wake up to the sun instead of the alarm clock that I don't say to myself that I'm very, very lucky."

"I was always begging Ed to ease up, but he wouldn't listen to me. Perhaps I should've been more insistent about it. I guess we had fallen into a groove and we just kept on without examining anything. I've had plenty of time for examination in the last year, but I don't feel any clearer about anything. In fact I feel more confused than ever."

"It's natural that you should think about what you might have done to prevent his death. But you know we all lead our own lives no matter how much other people love us."

He got up and brushed the dirt from his jeans and held out his hand to help her up. "Let's walk over to the greenhouse and I'll show you some of the things I've been doing."

While Jesa and Josh were talking about the problems of blueberry cultivation, Sally stood at the kitchen window sipping some vodka and juice. She had set up a canvas in Jesa's studio and had every intention of getting down to some serious work. She had even taken out Rebecca's leash, which she seldom needed, and tied the dog to a post on the porch. But when she'd looked at all of her equipment, lined up and ready for use, her mind went as blank as the waiting canvas. Just yesterday she had envisioned the painting in its entirety, but now she had no ability to recall it. She had left the studio and walked through the house to the kitchen, where she prepared a pitcher of drinks. Now she looked out the window and wondered how Jesa was doing. Josh seemed like such a likely prospect, and Jesa, Sally was sure, would never get through life without another marriage.

Public opinion to the contrary, Sally had never really thought of the married state as being desirable for herself. But Jesa was another matter. Whatever minimal sense of independence Jesa possessed had, Sally was sure, been stifled by Ed. It wasn't exactly that he discouraged Jesa from anything. His sins had rather been those of omission. There could be no doubt that he loved Jesa deeply, but his love was based on thinking of her as a wife and helpmate, not as a separate individual with her own talents. And Jesa had conformed to his vision, so that now he was gone she had neither career nor family to fall back on. Sally felt a catch in her throat when she thought of her friend's predicament. None of her own affairs had lasted longer than a couple of years. She tried to imagine what it would be like to be alone after sharing most of your adult life with one person. "Like losing your own legs, it was, when he died," her grandmother had said about her grandfather. Sally was about seven years old when she heard that and it struck her as a funny thing to say. "How could another person be like your own leg?" she had giggled, and her grandmother had given her a quick slap and labeled her "fresh." Sally never confused her lovers with an appendage of her own body. The first time she was deserted she had felt rage rather than loss.

She had set up housekeeping with Hugo Bridgeman, first love of her life, when she was barely twenty years old. This had severed her already strained relations with her family. They had pronounced her an "oddball" when she left home to live in Manhattan and go to art school, but living with a man without a license to do so marked her once and for all as a creature beyond the pale. Her mother still visited her in secret, worried about the neighborhood she lived in, and slipped her the odd twenty dollars for a new pair of shoes. For the rest of the family she became an object of gossip rather than concern. She'd covered her hurt feelings and defiantly predicted that when she had earned fame as an artist they'd repent their evil ways and put her back on the guest list for holiday dinners. In the meantime she worked at various jobs to help support herself and Hugo, who was going through graduate school in psychology.

Dear Hugo! How could she ever forget that wonderful body, that keen intelligence, that easy betrayal. She was so much in love with him that she accepted his pronouncements on everything from the nature of the universe to the ripeness of cantaloupe. And of course he had very firm ideas about the role of women. Hugo often remarked that while it was true that Sally had talent as an artist, the real creative joy of womanhood must come from home and maternity. So Sally bought cookbooks along with her art supplies and tried to measure up to Hugo's notion of a home-maker. They had lived together for almost a year when she became pregnant. She was genuinely amazed when he suggested that she have an abortion. Her mind struggled with his previous declarations about women's roles, but he explained that she must develop the thinking side of her nature as well as the instinc-tual, and surely she must agree that neither of them was in a position to support a child. She had tearfully agreed that she wasn't being practical and the opera-tion had been performed.

Hugo had enjoyed Sally's bed and bank account for almost two years when Inge appeared on the scene. Hugo claimed to be interested in Inge's knowledge of Jungian psychology, in which she was pursuing a degree. Sally thought that the Swedish girl's excep-tionally long legs might have had something to do with the attraction, but Hugo claimed not to have noticed any of Inge's physical attributes. Inge visited the apart-ment often. Sally cooked and refilled the wine glasses and listened to cryptic conversations about the collec-tive unconscious and fought her base suspicions. The only time she ever mentioned her fears to Hugo, he scorned her as being a victim of paranoid delusions and bourgeois mentality. Since she was determined to be neither neurotic nor middle class, she accepted Hugo's analysis of the situation.

One night after finishing the late shift at the restau-rant where she was working, she'd returned to the tiny apartment above the grocery store which she and Hugo shared. She had barely kicked off the shoes from her swollen feet before she sensed that something was different about the apartment. She could not remember if she had first noticed the half-empty bookshelves or the envelope lying on her worktable. She did remember the note: "Dearest, dearest Sal," it began, "You were right about Inge and me. I didn't think that it would be productive to discuss . . ." She had never finished reading it.

For six months after Hugo's disappearance she lived in moping celibacy. Going to work at the restaurant and talking to Jesa were the only things she managed to do. When spring came she had a ritual burning of all the things that Hugo had left behind and she began to paint the canvases she now referred to as her "red period." She took them to all of the art fairs on the streets of Greenwich Village and magically sold the lot of them. Then she quit her job and vowed that she would never again work at anything except her painting.

After the catharsis of the "red period," there was a steady line of suitors. While her face could never be spoken of as pretty, she did have an infectious energy as well as an attractive body and she attracted admirers of all sorts. Some even made offers of marriage, but Sally was now firmly fixed on her career. No man, she vowed, would ever be in a position to tell her what she was feeling or thinking ever again in her life. Sink or swim, she was on her own.

For the first five or six years after Hugo, it seemed as though it was going to be sink. She worked hard. She sold some paintings. When her work was reviewed it received some critical acclaim. But there was a constant financial struggle and more than once Jesa and Ed came to her rescue with loans. Finally she started to get some commercial work—first greeting cards and then illustrations of children's books, After the first couple of books in the Troillina series she was quite well known and making a lot of money, but she never considered the illustrations as her "real work."

The fact that she lived alone didn't matter, she told herself, as she walked back into the studio. The real love of her life—art—was still there for her. Her happiest times had not been with her lovers, but in front of an easel. She had experienced moments when her mind was lucid and bold, when she had seen the finished painting blaze in her imagination before she had even taken up the brush.

Now she stood in front of the canvas fearful, expectant. There was no surge of adrenaline. No imagination. Maybe she'd just dried up. She'd prepped the canvas a few days before and now she noticed that she'd missed a tiny spot. There it was—white, porous, unprepared—how had she missed it? She concentrated all of her energies on this little spot. She put down her brush and took another drink.

Jesa came back in the late afternoon. She untied Rebecca's leash and carried her into the house. She called Sally's name, but there was no response. Finally she went into the studio. The late afternoon shadows loomed on the whitewashed walls. Then she saw Sally curled up on the old couch.

"Sal, are you asleep?" she whispered.

Sally rolled over and blinked her eyes and tried to focus them.

"Yeah, I musta dropped off," she slurred.

Jesa sat down on the edge of the couch and rubbed her friend's back. She noticed that the canvas next to them was blank.

"Guess the work didn't go well, huh?"

"Watta y' mean—that's a masterpiece. I think I'll call it 'Portrait of the Artist's Mind.' How'd your little jaunt turn out?"

"I'm glad I went. He's an awfully nice man. He told me things about the country that I'd never heard before. Then we went to his greenhouse and he explained all about the soil problems up here."

"Mealy bugs and earthworms, huh . . . well, whatever turns you on."

"I invited him over for dinner. I hope you don't mind. I'll cook."

"That's good, 'cause I'm gonna need a crane to hoist me off this couch. God, do I have a headache."

"Just rest here for a while. I'll get things going."

Sally rolled over and shut her eyes again. Rebecca tried to crawl up with her, but Sally pushed the little dog aside. Jesa tiptoed out. She had seen Sally in her cups before, but this was somehow different. She'd seen her with a morning hangover, and now she had passed out by the late afternoon. Worse than that, it had been an afternoon when Sal had said she was going to work. Jesa knew that she must find a way to make Sally confront her problem, but she was at a loss to know how.

Josh arrived at seven with a bottle of wine and a book on organic gardening which he presented to Jesa. Sally noticed that his eyes turned to Jesa with interest and pleasure whenever she spoke, but Jesa seemed oblivious. She talked to Josh in a very relaxed and disinterested manner. Sometimes her hand would go up to the nape of her neck and she would smile. She was enjoying Josh's company, but her inner thoughts were on Severio.

Josh left early in the evening, saying that he had to go to early classes at the university the next day. When Jesa walked him to the door and shook his hand, he said he hoped that she would be coming up again soon because the earth would be ready for spring planting in a couple of weeks. As he walked home across the moonlit fields, he cursed himself for being so matter of fact with her and wished that he'd had the courage to ask for her number in the city.

A year ago, when he was first divorced, he hadn't really thought much about women. His colleagues made the usual jokes about his new-found freedom and kidded him about the boundless supply of eager women that would now be available to him. But sexual conquest was the last thing on his mind. He was intent on changing the course of his life in midstream and didn't have time for dalliance. But as the spring thaw came he realized one day that he had spent almost an hour just sitting in the quad at the university and looking at women. It was such a delight to see the legs and arms appear again after the winter when all bodies had been swathed in cumbersome boots and mufflers and coats. He satisfied himself that his interest, was aesthetic until a particularly bouncy student with lovely legs walked by. Then he felt the desire to touch as well as look, and he blushed up to his hairline.

His appetite was healthy enough, but he couldn't bear the thought of waking up with someone to whom he had nothing to say. When he'd expressed this feeling to one of his friends, the man had stared at him and said that Josh needed to have his head examined, that the only distance between hunger and gratification was a simple statement of need. "A guy your age and with your looks—are you kiddin' me?—it's a buyer's market." Josh felt even more at sea when he was referred to as a "buyer," but finally scruples gave way to biology.

There was a student who had a part-time job washing out equipment in the labs. She took a little longer than efficiency would dictate to finish her work and would often wander into Josh's office and talk. She made it very obvious that she was ready to go to bed with him and he was attracted by her firm flesh and easygoing attitude. He made a point of telling her that he wasn't in love with her. She, too, looked at him blankly and told him that it wasn't necessary. But after bedding her down, Josh reaffirmed that it was necessary for him. He still slept with her occasionally and was still excited by her physically, but he felt no real tenderness toward her, no commonality of interest. Jesamine was the first woman he'd met in ages for whom he felt both sexual attraction and a desire for companionship. Next time he saw her, he would be bolder, he told himself.

That night after Sally had gone to bed, Jesa stood at her bedroom window. There was a light patter of rain and she had gone to shut the window. She put her hand out and caught some of the drops, feeling the same sensation in her hand as she had felt in her neck when Severio had kissed her—a tingling, a surge of blood, a hint of joy. She decided to leave the window open so that she could feel the gentle dampness. She crawled into the bed and instead of moving over to "her side" spread herself out in the middle of it, luxuriating in the pleasure of sleeping alone.

The next morning they had packed up their things and set off quite early. Sally explained that she had to meet with her publisher, who should have had a chance to look over the final Troillina drawings during the weekend.

"He used to bitch at me about everything—wanted pastels when I'd use primaries and vice versa. But now that Troillina's hit the big time, I swear I could have Rebecca do the drawings and he'd still love 'em. That's the price of success—no one to criticize you anymore," she groaned.

"The work is good. That's why he doesn't criticize," Jesa said.

"Oh, bat pucky, as my cousin Lenny used to say. Did I tell you that they want me to do a coffee-table book of Troillina for adults? This country's crazier than I thought if grown-ups are gonna plunk down $14.95 for a bunch of elf drawings. But what do I care? My aunt in the Bronx who hasn't spoken to me for fifteen years called me up and asked me to come to a wedding, so I guess I've finally made it."

The drive back to the city was unusually silent. Sally gazed out the window and smoked far too many cigarettes and was even grouchy with Rebecca. She was embarrassed that Jesa had seen her in such boozy depression the day before. She had vowed that she wouldn't drink today, but when she went into the studio to pack up her painting equipment, she felt such a wave of hopelessness that she headed for the kitchen and took a swift belt. She wanted to talk to Jesa, to ask her advice, but she was afraid that such a discussion would leave her even more depressed. So she turned on the car radio and pretended to be asleep.

After dropping Sally off and parking the car, Jesa walked toward her apartment feeling expectant. Perhaps Severio had called her. She debated if she would return the call or wait for him to call again. She was struggling with her overnight bag when O'Hara opened the door with a flourish.

"Welcome back, Mrs. Mallick. Did you have a nice time in the country?"

"Yes, thank you."

She had barely stepped into the lobby before she saw Sophie Moss.

"You're back! My dear, I was worried about you. I came up to your apartment just last night because I had some tickets to a show and my friend Ruth couldn't go because one of her grandchildren was having a birthday. I just hated to see the ticket go to

87

waste, so of course I thought of you."

"That's very kind of you," Jesa replied politely, "but I was up in the country with a friend."

"A male friend, I hope," Sophie winked.

"No, an old girl friend," Jesa answered tiredly. She resented her weakness giving Sophie further fuel for conversation, but she could never seem to find a way to cut the woman off without seeming to be unmannerly.

"Oh, too bad," Sophie sighed, "Still, as Abbie used to say, 'company is company.' "

Jesa wondered if Sophie lurked in the lobby twenty-four hours a day or if it was just some evil curse that she was always there when Jesa came in. Perhaps perforated eardrums had been the cause of dear Abbie's demise.

"Well, my dear, the show was really something—there was even nudity. I guess that's the usual thing these days. If they aren't showing their you-know-what, they're putting designer labels on it. And speaking of labels . . . I have a friend, well, actually a friend of Abbie's, who has a shop and I'd love you to come down there with me because you have such good taste in clothes. I never buy at Saks anymore since Sylvia told me that they slant the mirrors in the dressing rooms to make you look slimmer. I always go to . . ."

Jesa listened and nodded and prayed for the elevator. O'Hara's weather report saved her for once.

"Says the clouds are going to disperse and that we can expect a temperature in the low fifties with variable pressure centers," he said to no one in particular.

"Hasn't it been the most awful winter?" Sophie continued, nodding toward O'Hara. "You know Abbie bought me my first mink way back in '53 and I said to the cleaners just last week that I wasn't going to put it away in storage until at least the end of the month."

The elevator doors opened and Jesa stepped quickly inside.

"Goodbye, Sophie. I'm really very tired from the drive back and . . ."

"My dear, I forgot to tell you the most exciting thing. I met your cleaning lady in the lobby today and O'Hara was giving her a little surprise for you, and don't tell me that it came from a girl friend."

Jesa had no idea what Sophie was talking about. The elevator doors started to close and Sophie wandered over to share her concerns about fur storage with O'Hara.

As Jesa walked into the living room she saw a huge bunch of white peonies on the piano. There was a note attached.

"Dear Jesamine," the heavy scrawl began, "I trust that your days in the country have refreshed you enough to accept an invitation for Tuesday evening. Some old friends, the Hartmans, are having a small dinner party and I'd love to take you. . . . Please call, Severio."

She reached for the phone without pausing.

When the phone rang in Severio's apartment, he removed his arm from under his head and quickly reached for the receiver. The girl beside him groaned something about goddamn telephones and rolled over onto her side and curled up like a cat.

Severio had met Melinda the previous evening at Bettina and O.W. Fanshaw's. The girl was introduced as the daughter of one of O.W.'s business associates. She was a sexy-looking kid who seemed to have done everything to disguise her good looks. She wore a secondhand, transparent bed jacket, embroidered jeans, and ankle socks, and her mouth was painted a vivid carmine. Severio recognized the rag-bag attire as the uniform of a certain set of wealthy teenagers. He also guessed that Melinda's rebellion went no further than mocking the manners of her elders and spending her sizable clothing allowance on dope. She attached herself to him within moments of being introduced. Bettina gave her a withering look when she had refused to sit down with the other guests and had planted herself, cross-legged, on the antique rug in front of Severio and dropped ashes from her cigarette on the floor.

It had been a terrible evening for Bettina. She had set her sights on Severio the moment she had met him, but her behavior in front of O.W. required at least a modicum of restraint, and she could not ignore her social obligations to at least appear cordial to Melinda, when she wanted nothing more than to slap the little beast.

Severio was well aware of all these currents. He walked a tight-wire, sharing his attentions with Melinda, but being careful not to neglect Bettina. Bettina had, after all, volunteered to help with his gallery opening, and she knew a great many people who

90

might be prospective buyers for his work.

Around midnight when most of the guests were departing, Melinda announced that she was not in the least bit tired, and suggested that they all go dancing at Regine's. Bettina didn't want to let Severio drift into the clutches of this scruffy teenybopper. But O.W. rolled his eyes to heaven, snuffed out the last of his cigar, and said that he and Bettina would have to call it a night.

Severio had little choice but to offer himself as an escort. He watched Bettina's thinly disguised rage as she kissed both him and Melinda on the cheek and said goodnight.

As soon as they were inside the taxi, Melinda had rubbed her leg against him and admitted that she didn't really want to go dancing, but would be interested in seeing his studio. Severio smiled inwardly at Melinda's rather clumsy variation on the "show me your etchings" routine. He placed his hand on her thigh and gave the driver directions to his apartment.

Once he had made a rudimentary effort of showing her his studio, he drew her to the floor and made love to her quickly and violently. He had little interest or patience with women who made themselves so quickly available. In fact he regarded them with contempt, and this was manifest in his lovemaking.

Melinda, though very young, was not inexperienced, and Severio's indifference seemed to act as an aphrodisiac instead of a turn-off. She made no attempt to dress after they had sex. Severio had rolled away from her, feeling rather tired, and had sought the comfort of his bed. She had stripped off the socks which he hadn't bothered to remove and joined him, unbidden, amid the fur pillows. She touched his back and murmured that it had been "too much." When that received no response she said she knew that he would make love the same way he painted, a remark that Severio answered with a feigned snore.

But Severio did not sleep as Melinda curled her limbs around him in a cuddly fashion that he found particularly odious. He thought about Jesamine Mallick. He had been pondering the best way to woo that lady for several days when a dinner invitation arrived from the Hartmans. Instantly he knew that this was the ideal circumstance for a first evening with Jesa. He guessed that she had some reservations about being alone with him. The dinner party would pose no threat to her. Since the party was to celebrate Loretta Hartman's purchase of one of his paintings, he was sure to be the center of attention. Jesa would see him to advantage, and he would have the pleasure of showing her off.

"Hello, Severio?" Jesa's well-modulated voice sounded at the end of the wire. "Am I disturbing you?"

"Not at all. I was just working, but I picked up because I thought it might be you. How was your weekend in the country?"

"Much more pleasant than I thought it would be, despite the rain."

"I'm happy to hear it. Will you be able to come to dinner tomorrow night?"

"Yes, that would be nice. And thank you for the flowers. They're really lovely."

"I'm glad that you liked them. Will seven o'clock be all right?"

"Fine."

There was an awkward pause while Jesa thought of what else to say.

"I'd best let you get back to your work. Goodbye."

"Goodbye, Jesamine. Thank you for calling."

Melinda squinted her eyes and rolled over toward him.

She had a mischievous little smirk on her face.

"Do you really think of this as working, Severio?" she asked.

He threw back the covers and started to get out of bed.

"As soon as I shower and shave I have every intention of working, Melinda. I'm sure that you must have plans for the day as well."

"Not particularly," she yawned, and stroked her hands over her breasts.

"Then I suggest that you make some."

"Actually I have," she said in a seductive voice. "I thought we might spend the afternoon in bed."

Severio stared down at her naked body as she continued to fondle herself.

"I noticed last evening, Melinda, that for a young lady of your background, you had extremely poor manners. I was hoping that your lack of manners would not extend to the bedroom."

"I think your talk about manners is bullshit. I just

93

try to be honest with people and I guess you don't."

"Honesty, my dear, has its limitations, which you are undoubtedly too spoiled and inexperienced to realize. But if it's honesty you want you may have it. Get out of my bed and go home."

Melinda's eyes narrowed and her hands were still. She reached out to touch Severio, but he knocked her hand away, and walked into the bathroom. She was alternately shocked and excited by his brutality. She had never experienced sexual rejection before, and she sat on the side of the bed and breathed heavily, her mind searching around for some means of revenge. When Severio had finished a very long shower and come back into the room, it was empty.

Chapter 4

*T*esa dressed with great care the following evening. As she went through her wardrobe she realized that it had been a long time since she had bought anything new. She made a note to call Sally and ask her if she'd go shopping with her. Finally she selected a black woolen dress with classic lines and a matching pair of silk pumps. As she checked herself in the mirror she was dissatisfied. Ed had always liked this dress, she recollected, but it seemed somehow dowdy. Ed was so conservative about everything. Her hands paused as she was about to clasp a string of pearls around her neck.

She'd never actually thought of Ed as being conventional before, but of course he had been. He disliked ostentation of any kind. Shortly after they had started dating, he'd expressed disgust with the free-wheeling artsy crowd that Sally had pulled Jesa into, so she'd stopped accepting invitations to their parties. And while Ed had never directly chosen her clothes, he had dropped a few hints that perhaps her peasant skirts and colored stockings and loose hair were not as appropriate for dinners with his business associates as he would like. She had abandoned the colorful clothing of the young artists' crowd and adopted a well-tailored, conservative chic. The only time she had deviated from this style and bought an evening dress with a slightly daring décolletage, Ed had smiled ruefully and said that while she looked delightful, he didn't want to spend the evening protecting his wife's bosom from the stares of admirers. She had changed the outfit without a second thought. He had always inspected her before they went out for the evening, and always complimented her. She missed their little ritual of examination and approval. She had mentioned this to her psychiatrist once and he had suggested that Ed was playing a paternal role. Jesa replied that Ed was in no way paternal, besides they were the same age. What a silly and naïve remark that had been! It occurred to her now that she had always welcomed Ed's suggestions not just because she loved him and wanted to please him, but because she'd had so little experience in forming her own image. After her parents had been killed in the auto accident, she had no one to help her to develop her own sense, her ability to choose. She had been packed off to a variety of schools for young ladies where a uniform was mandatory. Her holiday clothes were always selected by her aunt.

I've never really chosen much of anything for myself, she thought, as she sat at her dressing table and pressed a bit of translucent powder to her face. She leaned forward and looked at herself in the mirror: black dress, double string of pearls, hair slicked back in a chignon. She would please both her aunt and her husband, but did she please herself? She was still staring at herself when she heard the intercom buzz. She had let Maggie go home early because she wanted to be alone when Severio arrived. O'Hara announced that Mr. Euzielli was on his way up. She dashed back into the bedroom, dabbed some Chanel on her wrists, and walked slowly to the front door. She waited for the buzzer but he knocked instead. She counted to ten and opened the door.

Severio was wearing a dark gray suit and a black turtleneck sweater. Instead of making him look staid and respectable, the suit somehow emphasized the wildness of his dark hair and the exotic look of his eyes.

"Hello, Jesamine. You look wonderful." He stared at her with appreciation.

"Won't you please come in and have a drink?"

He followed her into the living room and walked over to the bar.

"Please allow me," he said, "I used to work as a bartender when I was in art school. I know every drink known to man."

"Would it disappoint you if I asked for a simple martini?"

"There's nothing simple about a really good martini," he joked and began to fix the drinks with a flourish.

Jesa sat on the couch and watched his performance with amusement. After he had finished mixing the drinks, he brought them over to her and touched his glass to hers.

"*Primavera.*"

"What?"

"The great painting you remind me of, Jesamine. It also means spring."

"*Primavera* then."

She moved aside slightly to make room for him on the couch, but his eyes held hers for a moment longer and then he walked over to the easy chair. He sipped his drink, deciding if a mention of their first meeting was the best way to open her up emotionally or if it would scare her off.

"It really is a pleasure to see you looking so well. The other night . . ."

"I really don't want to talk about the other night. I was very depressed. It was such an inauspicious meeting," she replied.

"Not really. We managed to end it on a more positive note, didn't we?"

"Yes, we did. I want to thank you again for all of your kindness."

"I didn't bring it up to solicit your gratitude, but to express mine. I've thought of you a great deal since then."

"How has your work been going?" she asked, wanting to change the focus.

"That's right, you've never seen any of it, have you? Well tonight you shall have an opportunity. The Hartmans just bought a canvas and my show isn't even going to open for another couple of weeks. I could hardly turn down an invitation to see my own work, could I? I hope that the critics' response will be favorable and that I'll sell out. Ellman seems to think that it will be well received."

"Do you mean Ellman Smith?"

"Yes, so you know him?"

"For many years. His gallery has a splendid reputation. Last year he had a marvelous retrospective of . . ."

Jesa kept up the small talk out of nervousness. She really had no desire to speak at all. She wanted only to look at Severio, to see if the pictures that she had kept in her mind since their first meeting were accurate. He was as handsome and full of pride as she'd remembered him. Was there a touch of cruelty about that full mouth? When he caught her looking at his mouth, she dropped her gaze and the conversation stopped. She put her hand up to her neck. The sexual tension between them was palpable. He savored it a moment longer, until he saw her slender hand grip the couch. What a delicious combination she was, he thought: the veneer of poise and beauty and money with that almost childish innocence just beneath the surface. He rose from the chair and came over and stood in front of her. He must let her know that he wanted her without moving too quickly.

"I'm feeling . . . restless. Would you care to walk for a while before we go to the Hartman's?"

"I'd love to walk," she breathed gratefully.

She fetched her fur coat from the hall closet. He was right behind her and took it from her and draped it over her shoulders. The touch was casual, a polite gesture, but she shivered ever so slightly when his fingers grazed her shoulders.

Once out of doors it was much easier to talk to him. They walked alongside the park and chatted about their student days.

"Whatever became of that red-headed girl you always used to hang around with? You two were inseparable."

"You must mean Sally Gold. Believe it or not we are still the best of friends. In fact she was with me last week when you saw me at Friends of Young Artists."

"I know it sounds like an old song, Jesamine, but I only had eyes for you that day." He slowed his pace and reached out to touch her cheek. She stood perfectly still in the chilly evening air, the wind ruffling her hair, and allowed his fingers to trace the outline of her lips. Her eyelids drooped involuntarily. She thought he was about to kiss her, but he pulled the fur closer to her face and said, "It will be exciting when spring is really here and you don't have to cover up your loveliness. I think you're shivering, my dear. I'll get us a cab."

He stepped out into the street and raised his hand for a taxi.

The Hartmans were the kind of couple with which Jesa had been familiar for years. In fact Fred Hartman, who was a real estate mogul, claimed to have met Jesa many years ago at the opening of a building that Ed had designed. Loretta Hartman was a typical New York society matron—fond of charity, fashion, and the arts in equal proportion; given to occasional ripples of ennui which she could always overcome with a binge of spending or redecorating. She counted herself extremely fortunate in having discovered Severio Euzielli before he had become the celebrity of the hour. She had taken pains to make this dinner party a success. Fred had been a bit peeved with her when he found out the price of the painting she'd purchased. She had done her best to convince him that even though he didn't like it, he should look upon it as "an investment." She was sure that this evening would convince him of Severio's imminent success and was pleased that Severio had chosen such a lovely woman to accompany him. Now Fred, whose appreciation of art was sorely lacking, would have something pleasant to look at, and that would put him in a receptive mood.

They were introduced to the three other couples, two of which were carbon copies of the Hartmans. The third pair—a former actress named Lisa and a gay interior designer—had been included on the guest list because Loretta was sure that Fred and his cronies would get into their inevitable discussion of stocks and bonds, and she wanted the group to have an injection of "artistic ambiance." Lisa wore half of Tiffany's and her hair was tinted a shade brighter than good taste would die rate. She fixed a hungry gaze upon Severio as soon as they were introduced; her companion did likewise. Fred Hartman took Jesa under his wing and began a discussion about his hobby: the collection of fine wines.

Severio observed Jesa across the room. She sipped the Bâtard-Montrachet that Fred had been telling her about and commented on its fine bouquet. She seemed as placid as a professional model at a long sitting. Only the occasional flutter of her eyelids hinted that she might not be thoroughly content. But her mind was racing. She wished that she had remembered to renew her prescription for the tranquilizers. She felt claustrophobic and rebellious. She was fed up with measuring out her life in spoonfuls. She wanted to dance, to shout, to clutch at Severio—anything that would give her a sense of being alive. She longed for the parties of her art school days, where people sat on the floor and drank cheap wine and flirted and argued and joked with each other. But she sipped and smiled and feigned interest in Fred's descriptions of vineyards in the south of France.

When they were taken into the dining room, Jesa was seated across the table from Severio. She couldn't help but notice the facility with which he charmed the women on either side of him. To Loretta, nervous about the beef Wellington because she had just employed a new cook, he was attentive and reassuring. He displayed equal ease with Lisa, admiring her diamonds and chatting about recent theatrical productions. Lisa hung on his every word and was several minutes behind the other guests in finishing each course, which caused Loretta more anguish about the quality of the cuisine. Severio turned from one to the other with the gracefulness of a ballet dancer executing a *pas de trois*. His glances across the candlelit table hinted that he was supremely bored and wanted only to look at Jesa.

She watched him with curiosity. Ed was always reserved with other women. He had no sense of flirtation. Women had often commented to Jesa that Ed didn't seem to like them. What they really meant was that he failed to give them the flattering attention that attractive women considered their due. Jesa turned her large gray eyes to Fred Hartman and decided that she would indulge in a little flirtation herself. She remembered something Sally had said about flirting with a homely man being an act of kindness. Fred was more than pleased. He was a highly intelligent man when it came to business and he dreaded these soirées that Loretta put together because he knew that he couldn't discuss his own area of expertise and would wind up looking like a boob if he tried to discuss anyone else's.

After the meal, Loretta got up and announced that liqueurs would be served in the study. She touched Severio's arm with a girlish giggle and said *sotto voce,* "This is the closest thing to an unveiling that I could devise, maestro." They dutifully followed her into the study where a large canvas had been mounted on the wall. It was painted in great swaths of earth tones. The main form seemed to be the bulk of a great bull with his head down for the charge.

"Oh, it's so *forceful*," Lisa gushed. Then fearing that her remark had sounded too suggestive, she began a more technical discussion of its merits. "Of course the central mass has such a sense of movement. It's easy to see that you've been influenced by your adopted countrymen. It's rather like a Siqueiros, isn't it?"

"It's rather like itself", Severio replied.

"Of course," she flustered, "every work of art is complete unto itself."

"I think she means that it possesses the sweep and passion of an abstraction, yet it does have a certain primitive quality," her companion piped in.

There were "oohs" and "aahs" from the ladies and grunts of approval from the men. Fred Hartman struggled to understand what the conversation was about and was innocent enough to think that he was the only one present who didn't. Loretta kept signaling him with her eyes that he should join in.

"I only hope that it won't overwhelm my powers of concentration too much," he said finally.

"Don't be such a Philistine, darling," Loretta said as she pinched his arm as though he were a naughty child. "He loves it, Severio, he really does. He told me so this morning."

"You've been rather silent, Mrs. Mallick," Fred said to Jesa. "What's your opinion?"

"I like it very much," she answered quietly.

She was impressed by the painting. She was not good at pretending, and had she not respected Sev-

103

erio's work, would have made future conversation difficult. But the work did have great technical expertise as well as strong individuality. Lisa was not far off the mark when she'd described it as "forceful."

Severio caught Jesa's eye and winked at her. She had no idea what it meant—was he making fun of the fawning company or was it to let her know that he was pleased with her? Whatever its message it was a signal of intimacy that made her feel better. She turned again to Fred Hartman and gave an insouciant smile.

"I think it's a wonderful investment, Fred."

Fred visibly expanded. She had taken him off the hook in the conversation and assured him of his investment at the same time. God, she was a fine woman, he thought. Beautiful, of course, but more than that. She seemed intelligent, but didn't have much to say, which was Fred's ideal. He searched his brain to give her just the right compliment.

"You're a very aesthetic woman, Mrs. Mallick."

Jesa nodded and smiled again. Loretta announced another round of drinks and Severio, looking regretful, said that he must go home to work.

Once they were out of the building and walking along the quiet side street, Severio stretched his body and exhaled a huge sigh.

"I hope that wasn't as tedious for you as it was for me, Jesa. Now where would you like to go?"

"So you don't have to go home to work?"

"Of course not. I want to be with you. I thought if I had to listen to those tedious people go on about 'art' and 'passion' for another minute I'd do something desperate. Respectable people always make me claustrophobic."

"So you think that's what makes *you* claustrophobic," she asked, thinking about her own feelings of suffocation and rebellion earlier in the evening.

"They are always so eager to talk about 'passion' while their minds are really on their bank accounts."

"I think that's a bit harsh. People can't show who they really are or what they're really thinking when they are in a social situation."

"Then to hell with social situations," Severio scoffed. "I go because it's important to sell my work, and in order to do that I must play the game. Artistic success, as you must know, doesn't have much to do with quality. What if poor Van Gogh had had enough savvy to charm people into buying his work?"

"Perhaps you have a more alluring physical presence than poor Mr. Van Gogh," she said archly.

"*Touché*, Jesamine," he laughed. "I had no idea that you had a sharp tongue. But don't wriggle out of this—you know what I mean about the claustrophobia, don't you?"

"Yes. I do. Though it is a recent thing with me. You see I was brought up in a highly respectable, even repressive environment. It wasn't until after Ed's death that I began to feel my social graces fall apart. Now I feel a sort of impatience about life. I know that it should be precious, but I don't really know how to enjoy it. I just have these feelings of depression and . . . I don't know . . . a strange thought of rebellion."

Severio looked directly into Jesa's face. There was a

tiny questioning furrow between her pale brows. He had a simultaneous desire to nurture and protect her and an impatient, almost cruel impulse to see her stripped and vulnerable.

"And what would you rebel against, Jesamine?"

"That's just it. I don't know. Maybe just myself . . . or the self I've been for most of my life." She stopped short, confused and exposed.

"Perhaps you should just take me home," she suggested.

"No. Let me take you to a little place to hear a singer that I've discovered. It'll be crowded, but not with anyone who is trying to be respectable, so I promise that you won't become claustrophobic."

Jesa nodded dumbly.

An hour later she found herself slightly tipsy and humming along with a large black woman in a low-cut dress who was singing "Mean to Me" as though she meant it. When the last low note had sounded, Jesa started to applaud and realized that her hands didn't have their usual coordination. Her hair had loosened from the chignon and several strands wisped about her face, which was flushed pink from the wine she had been drinking. For the first time in her recent memory, she was having what is known as a good time.

"I used to think you looked like Princess Grace, but now you look more like Jean Harlow," Severio laughed.

"Princess Grace, Jean Harlow, Botticelli! Always the comparison. 'It is rather like itself,' as a famous man once said," she teased.

The singer's eyes fanned around the audience as they shouted for more. "Thank y'all. Thank you. I can tell you're all down-home folk, so you won't mind if I sit down."

She hoisted her bulk up onto the piano with ease.

"I usually sound my best notes when I'm sittin' in my bathrobe sippin' gin and feelin' sorry for myself, so I'm gonna do my best to give this next one to you with that same recipe."

The audience chuckled and applauded some more. The singer waited until they had settled down to an almost religious silence and then she began. Her eyes filled with tears, yet she controlled her voice expertly and worked in perfect communion with her accompanist. The plaintive melody of "Goodmorning Heartache" wailed through the tiny smoke-filled room. Jesa sat perfectly still. She had a sense of shared suffering that she had never experienced in church. Tears began to form in her own eyes. When the song was over, she felt a great sense of relief. She rose to her feet and whispered "Brava" then became self-conscious and sat down again. When she turned to Severio her eyes were flashing.

"Now that's art," she breathed.

"I'm glad you like her. I thought you would."

"No, no," she talked on, surprised at her volubility. "I mean she takes her emotion and she gives it back to other people. She *uses* what she feels. How I envy that talent."

The waiter pushed his way through the throngs of people and set another round of drinks on the table.

Severio tipped him and reached for Jesa's coat. The time was ripe to be alone with her. Some of the reserve had slipped and here was a different Jesa—easy, spirited. He was, if possible, even more desirous of her now that he'd seen this side of her.

"Do you want to wait for the next set?" he asked, even though he was already putting the coat around her shoulders, "or are you tired?"

"I guess I should be tired," she said, slumping back into the booth and assessing her feelings. "But I don't feel just tired. Sort of mellow. Isn't that the word for it?"

"Yes, Jesamine, mellow."

He took her arm and helped her up. She was not really drunk, but a bit wobbly on her feet. She leaned against him, gave him a drowsy smile, and said, "Thank you for bringing me here" like a dutiful child.

In the cab on the way back to her apartment, he pulled her to him. She averted her face but nuzzled her head into a comfortable position on his shoulder. It had started to rain again and the sound of the puddles splashing as they drove through them and the smell of the damp, cool air from the open window gave her a delicious feeling of well-being. He took her hand from her lap and placed it on his chest. She sniffed the scent of perspiration that mingled with his cologne and her fingers could feel the hair on his chest beneath his sweater. She could feel the beat of his heart and it filled her with a sense of mystery and vitality. When she lifted her face to his to say something, his lips were instantly on hers—insistent, skillful. He pulled her body into his. She felt as though she had dived into a deep pool and was trying to surface. She pulled away gasping. How could she be necking in a car as though she were a teenager? She turned her face to the window and inhaled the cool air. She glanced at the cab driver, who seemed to be oblivious to anything but the road.

"Shall we go to your place?" Severio whispered.

That suggestion sobered her completely. How could she take this man, no matter how much she wanted him, to Ed's apartment to sleep in the same bed that they had shared for years?

"No. It's very late," she muttered as the cab drew up to the curb. She could see O'Hara standing at the doors peering out into the misty street. "I'd best go in alone."

Severio was bitterly annoyed with himself. He had allowed the desire of the moment to make him thoughtless. He knew instantly that he had blundered in suggesting her apartment. He got out of the cab and walked around to open the door for her. When she extended her hand he laughed.

"Refuse me, Jesamine, but don't shake my hand. We're past that surely."

Jesa withdrew her offending hand. She wanted to apologize, to explain. But she could see that it would only muddle the situation further. She said thank you yet again and walked toward the doors alone.

Bettina Fanshaw put down her coffee cup with a clatter and leaned across the linen tablecloth. She fixed her companion with a steely glance.

"But how do you know that?" she queried.

Lisa shook her many bangles and stared back at Bettina incredulously. In all the years of their acquaintance Bettina had never questioned her veracity. Lisa would be the first to admit that she indulged in gossip, but it was always reliable gossip.

"Everyone knows it," she replied coolly. "I myself was at a dinner party at Loretta Hartman's and, my dear, they could hardly take their eyes off each other. Left early, presumably so that Severio could go to work."

She gave Bettina a knowing smirk and speared another shrimp into her mouth. Bettina pushed her plate aside and waved at someone at an adjoining table before returning her gaze to her companion. Lisa pressed the napkin to her carefully painted lips and lowered her voice.

"All I can say is, he must've been working pretty hard to crack Jesamine Mallick. She looks like the most frigid woman I've ever met."

"I introduced them, you know," Bettina replied casually, not wanting to appear to be left out.

She was more than a trifle miffed at Severio. He had been absent from her company for the last couple of weeks, but she had accepted his excuses of getting ready for the opening of his show. She had volunteered a good deal of her time to make the show a success and taken a pile of invitations from Ellman Smith so that she might scrawl a personal note urging some top people to attend. She had even asked a friend of O.W.'s who was in the liquor business to donate all of the refreshments and made sure that the major art critics would attend. And now she felt cheated out of the rewards of her labors. Despite her best efforts to insinuate herself into the role of Severio's indispensable companion and part of his success, that mealy-mouthed Jesamine Mallick was going to walk off with the honors. It was just too much.

"It's possible that he's only being kind to her," Bettina continued as she motioned the waiter to remove her barely touched luncheon plate. "After all she is a widow."

"And a rich one at that," her companion slipped in.

"But I think that she's far too conventional to attract a really vital man like Severio."

"Just wait until you see them together. That'll tell you a thing or two. As someone who has been on the stage, I can tell you that physical attraction is one of the hardest things to fake. I remember when I was playing *Design for Living* with this perfect pip-squeak of a leading man. Had to look at his ears to get any sort of feeling going, if you know what I mean."

Bettina didn't know what she meant and didn't care. She looked thoughtfully past the potted plants and out the restaurant window at the people scurrying down the avenue. She wondered where she had misplayed her hand.

"What was that about ears?" she asked.

"I looked at his ears because they were rather like an old lover's. It was a sense-memory. It turned me on."

"Oh, of course," Bettina replied absently, her mind reverting to her own concerns.

It wasn't really that she wanted Severio as her lover. But she wanted to be the object of desire and spicy gossip, to have him at her feet, ultimately to reject him after a lengthy public dalliance. Her friends conjectured that Bettina must have a real attachment to her husband, but this was not what kept her faithful. Despite her seductive appearance, she generally found the act of love both messy and inconvenient. O.W. presumably found his pleasures elsewhere, and that was none of Bettina's concern so long as he was discreet and didn't disrupt her life with a scandal. But the image of the siren was planted firmly in her ego, and she was greatly annoyed to think that she could be bested in any competitive situation. She brought her attention back to her companion.

". . . to wear to the opening? I haven't really made up my mind yet. I saw a nice chiffon at Persephone the other day."

Perhaps she'd been too helpful, she mused. Too worldly wise. Perhaps Severio was actually attracted to the retiring type. He certainly hadn't been enthused about tacky little Melinda's advances, that she knew.

"I've made up my mind," Bettina continued, "I'll wear a sweet up-to-the-neck batiste."

"That sounds a bit ingenue for you, my dear. . . . I don't mean age-wise. I mean the style."

"Don't worry," Bettina smiled, "I know what I'm doing."

"You always seem to, don't you?" Lisa replied as she reached for the check. Receiving no reply, she too turned her attention to the street. The crowds were enjoying one of the first warm days of spring. Con-struction workers, denied their favorite pastime for so many months, whistled at passing female forms. The flower stalls seemed to be doing a lively business in lilacs and daffodils. The trees and shrubs were showing their first shoots of greenery. A group of tourists clustered around a street musician. It was too nice a day to waste on Bettina, she decided. She checked her diamond watch, feigned alarm at being late for a hairdresser's appointment, kissed Bettina on both cheeks, and left the restaurant.

The news that had caused Bettina such alarm had an entirely different effect on Sally. She was delighted to find out that Jesa was going out with someone. She had yet to meet Severio, but from all reports he seemed to be made to order for Jesa. After her first date with Severio, Jesa could contain herself no longer. She now called Sally with almost daily reports about her engagements with the handsome painter. They had gone to such and such a nightclub, attended this concert or that, had dinner at Tavern-on-the-Green or Le Périgord, taken in an exhibit at the Frick. It seemed to be a "whirlwind" romance. Whether or not it had been consummated, Sally did not ask. Jesa was not the sort to give details about her sex life, not even to her closest friend. Sally simply assumed that they had become lovers and waited for the chance remark that would confirm her assumptions.

Sometimes Jesa's descriptions of her evenings with Severio served to make Sally more aware of her own loneliness and she missed having Jesa's company for an occasional dinner or movie. She quickly repressed such thoughts as being unworthy. She was glad to see Jesa exhibit some exuberance and interest in life again, she told herself, and if credit for that flowering went to Severio Euzielli, then she should be more than happy to give it to him. But she was eager to meet Severio and form her own impressions of his character. Jesa was, after all, so naïve and inexperienced in these matters.

She'd agreed to meet Jesa to go shopping and was pleased to see that it was a lovely day. Jesa had said that she wanted to buy a new dress for Severio's opening and Sally also wanted to buy something new. She had been nominated as "Illustrator of the Year" in the children's book division of the American Book Awards and the awards ceremony was to take place the following week. The only other time she'd accepted an award, as "Most Promising Student Artist," she'd made a complete ass of herself. She knew she'd need a stabilizing influence at the dinner and wanted to ask Jesa to go with her but realized that it would be inappropriate.

"Goes to show we haven't really come a long way, baby," she complained to Rebecca. "I mean, all I need is someone to give me moral support, but it's an unwritten law that it has to be someone of the opposite sex."

She made a mental note to invite Ellman. He'd taken her to dinner several times in recent weeks and she knew she could count on him.

"Lucky Jesa," she said, as she threw things into her bag and searched around for her keys, "she doesn't have these escort problems anymore. She's got a real lover."

But even though she was now possessed by daily fantasies of being in his bed, Jesa still felt an impenetrable barrier to the satisfaction of her desire. She was aware of the quickly shifting sexual mores of society. One could hardly open a newspaper or turn on the television without being told about research on female orgasm or statistics on marital infidelity. But to Jesa it was all "out there." She heard the gossip of her set. There was certainly more discussion of sexual activity and maybe there was even more of it, but these conversations always seemed to Jesa to be in questionable taste.

Sally had asked her once how she managed to be faithful to Ed for all those years when there were so many men who were attracted to her. Jesa had replied that though it gave her some ego satisfaction to know that men found her desirable, it had never entered her mind to act upon it. Their lovemaking had, of course, been less frequent over the years, but it was still satisfying. More than that, she somehow thought of her body as belonging to Ed. Sally had rolled her eyes to heaven on that one. Jesa tried to explain that it wasn't that she felt servile or possessed by Ed. It was that sex was a special bond between them.

"Sure," Sally had replied, "but what if you met someone who really turned you on and you had a glorious afternoon with him and Ed never found out? What's the difference?"

115

"There would be a difference. I'd have to hide it from him. I would have violated our contract."

Sally answered that she didn't think that love was a contractual agreement. Jesa said of course she didn't think of it that way, but was at a loss to express just how she did think of it.

"Well, there's love and there's sex," said Sally. "If you're lucky they go together, but most times they don't. A man doesn't have to be honorable or have a good character to get your juices going."

Jesa was not aware of such a split between the physical and the emotional. She couldn't imagine going to bed with a man for whom she did not feel affection and respect. Sally assured her that there was no such unity in the world of the senses, but everything in Jesa's character and experience cried out against such a schism.

"I'm not just saying this out of my own crazy life," Sally added. "Lots of psychologists say the same thing. Even the Greeks recognized the split between the Apollonian and the Dionysian."

"But you'd be the first to point out that all that stuff was written by men," Jesa countered.

"True. And they had their hang-ups," Sally acknowledged, "but they still weren't dummies."

Jesa still wasn't sure if she was in love with Severio, but she could not deny that she wanted to have him make love to her. They had had countless conversations about all sorts of topics, but never about sex. She wondered if he shared her feelings that it was a special bond, but even she knew that a discussion would not reveal his true sentiments. She could find out only by

116

being his lover, and that involved considerable risk.

Since that first evening together, Severio had been very cool with her physically. In fact, the last time she had seen him he had not even kissed her goodnight. She wondered if his desire for her had been quenched with that first rejection. But all the evidence of her senses denied this. He still looked at her in a way that made her blood race. The most casual brush of the hand created a powerful current between them, and she was forced to avert her eyes when their glance held for more than a few moments. The trouble was that no matter how much she prepared herself in her mind, she still backed away from those opportunities when they might have come together in a wild embrace. She needed time. And still more time. Severio, she feared, might be too impatient to wait.

Severio Euzielli was not experiencing the impatience that Jesa feared. He had taken her measure and knew that if she had not succumbed that first evening, he would have to wait. It was a delicious period of cat and mouse. It had been years since any woman had resisted him for so long, and he knew that the prize would be worth the race. His fantasies about Jesa had now taken another turn. He had purposely restrained himself and avoided any physical overtures. It was not enough that he should possess her. It would have to be at her request.

In the meanwhile he amused himself with Melinda. She had appeared on his doorstep a few days after he had kicked her out of bed. At first he had been annoyed to see the rich little teenager in her ragged attire, but she had walked straight into his studio and had begun to take off her clothes without even saying good afternoon. He guessed that this was Melinda's pathetic gesture to show that she was using him as a sort of stud. Severio was convinced that this was a game that women could not play to win, and he could see no reason why he shouldn't indulge his appetite. So he took her nubile body again, sure that he was the one who was doing the using. It was usually after sex with Melinda that his desire for Jesa was greatest.

On this particular afternoon, Melinda had appeared again. They had no conversation, except Melinda's requests that he try certain things with her that she supposed were novel to the act. Severio artfully obliged when the solicitations agreed with his own tastes. He had finally disengaged himself from her frenetic embrace and was walking into the bathroom to shower, when she announced that she was going to be present at his opening the following evening.

"Anyone can come, right?" she asked with a touch of malice.

"I believe that invitations have been sent out," he said, frozen in his tracks.

"I even have one of those. Madame Bettina Fanshaw sent one to my daddy, so that includes me. In fact I'm going with Daddy and if you're very lucky I'll tell him to buy something. Or maybe he'll commission you to do a nude of me."

She lolled back into an artful pose and winked at him.

"Mainly I want to get a look at what's-her-name—that society dame you've been playing footsy with."

For a moment he thought that perhaps the little vixen had the power to read his mind. His body became tense with rage, but he could think of nothing to say that would dissuade her.

"Do what you like, Melinda. I really don't care," he said casually.

"That's what everyone always says to me," she replied as she pulled on her panties. "I'd hoped you'd be a restraining influence."

"Let yourself out," he said as he closed the bathroom door.

Chapter 5

Jesa stood in the dressing room at Saks clad only in her slip. Sally and Jesa shooed away the blue-haired saleslady, who was still lurking just outside the dressing room nursing her wounded pride. Sally dashed back into the showroom to find another dress for Jesa to try on. She pulled back the curtain of the dressing room and dropped her voice to a Mae West growl.

"Take it off, baby. Take it all off. Here's the bustle for you."

She held out a slinky backless dress in a pale gold crêpe de chine.

"C'mon, Jesa. Down to the buff and don't look at the price tag."

"Oh, Sal, I don't think so," Jesa shook her head.

"That's too . . . too everything. I don't think it's me at all."

"How do you know what's you? You've been kvetching all week about how dowdy you are, so let's just push this little identity crisis along. Put the damn thing on, then tell me if I'm wrong."

Jesa reluctantly took the dress and slipped it over her head. Then she unhooked her brassiere, wriggled out of her slip, and drew the dress down over her body. Sally started to laugh.

"You know the first time you ever stayed the night at my place, way back when I lived on MacDougal Street, I watched you get undressed for bed and I said to myself, 'Now there's a kid who's been to the best boarding schools.' You're the only person I've ever seen who can do a complete change of clothes without showing more than an inch of flesh."

"I know it's silly. Ed always kidded me about it. It took me years to be able to strip down. But this dress? Sally, it's too . . . it's . . ."

"Terrific on you."

When Jesa looked at her reflection in the mirror she had to agree. Though the dress was far more daring than anything she had ever worn, it was more than becoming. It slithered over her lean thighs and curved almost to the waist in the back to expose her creamy skin.

There was a tiny knock outside the curtain.

"Would Madame be wanting any assistance?" the blue-haired lady inquired.

"Come on in here," Sally said, throwing back the

curtain. "Now let's have your objective opinion. What do you think of my friend in this dress?"

The saleslady patted her bun and did her best to ignore Sally's behavior. She was determined to regain her rightful position as fashion consultant even at the price of a sale. She wanted to find the dress unsuitable, but Jesa looked so obviously attractive in it that she was compelled to mutter a compliment.

"But what about the front of it?" Jesa questioned, touching her breasts lightly. "I've never gone without a brassiere before. I'm afraid I'd be self-conscious."

"I don't believe that the gown was designed with an undergarment in mind, however if Madame feels self-conscious . . ."

"Self-conscious? With those boobs? You've got to be kidding," Sally put in. She looked around for support of her statement, but the last remark had forced the blue-haired lady to withdraw. "Take it Jesa, please. It's a knockout."

Jesa drew a deep breath and looked at herself in the mirror again.

"I'll take it."

"That's the spirit. I'll go tell Mother Superior she's made a sale."

They trailed around the shops for another hour. Jesa bought some matching shoes and splurged on a bottle of Joy. Whenever she found something she thought Sally should try on, Sally said she was too tired to undress and called herself a blimp.

"That's nonsense. You're no more than ten pounds heavier than you were when I first met you."

121

"Then I must've been chubby then too. And as the famous stripper once said, 'It's all there, it's just lower than it used to be.' "

"Oh, stop it," Jesa said firmly.

"Listen, Jesa, all I want to buy is another pair of support hose and a stiff drink. Now stop bossing me around and let's have lunch like proper ladies do. You can tell me more about Severio. The next best thing to being in love is to talk about it. And this time I want the straight poop."

They walked a few blocks to a little French restaurant and asked for a table in the rear.

"Just how serious is this thing?" Sally asked when she'd gulped her first Bloody Mary.

"Serious? You sound like something out of Dear Abby."

"Watch your mouth. I happen to be a fan of Dear Abby."

"Well," Jesa began tentatively, "he's an exceptional man. Not only in talent but in sensitivity. I've been able to talk to him, really talk to him, about all sorts of things. About my feelings about myself."

"So he's a good listener, but does he give you the flutters?"

"He's . . ." Jesa searched for the right description. The little smile appeared on her lips and her eyes danced with excitement. "He's very strong-willed. Very proud. His work is really impressive. We went by the gallery the other day and I saw most of the exhibit. He has the most wonderful eyes . . ."

"Got it bad, huh?"

"I didn't say that."

"You don't have to. It's as obvious as measles."

"Oh, Sal. It's just like you to think of it as a disease."

"If you'd been infected as many times as I have, you'd recognize the symptoms. But a couple of weeks in bed should bring some relief. Then you'll be able to judge just how bad the case is."

Jesa wouldn't rise to the bait. She didn't want to discuss her feelings for Severio with anybody. She touched the package from Saks and hoped that Severio would like the dress.

"Ellman says that Bettina Fanshaw's been stomping around the gallery like Napoleon organizing the troops," Sally continued.

"Well, she is interested in art."

"Art my ass. She just loves to boss people around and Ellman's such a Mr. Nice Guy that he won't push her out of the way. Still, she knows everyone in town, so it should really be a big bash. I'm looking forward to it about as much as a trip to the dentist's, but at least I'll get to have a look at the fabulous Mr. Euzielli."

"And you'll be crazy about him, Sal. I promise."

After lunch Sally set off to teach her art class for disadvantaged kids. Wanting to be fresh for the evening, Jesa went home to take a nap. But she was too excited to sleep and got up again to try on the dress. Maybe it wasn't right for her after all and she'd just accepted Sally's notions. She surveyed herself in the full-length mirrors of her closet. "To hell with all these doubts," she said out loud. She felt sexy, so why shouldn't she look sexy? She would push aside her inhibitions. She would enjoy herself with her lover.

Sally arrived at the gallery as the caterers were setting up the bar. Ellman, who was rearranging some large potted plants, came over and took her hands in his.

"Thank goodness you came early, Sal."

He held her at arm's length and looked at her. She had taken more time with her grooming than was characteristic with her and looked quite fetching in a green velveteen suit. It was strange, Ellman thought, how much one's feelings for a person affected one's perception of their looks. He had always thought that Bettina was handsome enough to grace the cover of *Vogue*, but after seeing her at close range during the last couple of weeks, he had developed an antipathy for her appearance. With Sally it was quite the opposite. He had always found her only passingly attractive and a bit slatternly, but since he had started to see her more often, he had developed an affection for her inquisitive brown eyes and her diminutive, curvy figure. Sally didn't think much about her feelings about Ellman, but they too had undergone a change. Whereas she had always thought of him as being very ordinary, she was now fond of his bearish body and the preoccupied but intelligent eyes that were hidden behind his thick glasses.

"Take a look at the exhibit and tell me what you think, before the herd arrives," lie said.

"I'd like a drink first," Sally replied and started to walk toward the bar.

"No drink. Look at it first."

"Are you kiddin'? You know if I have to face that bunch of yahoos, I'd better be fortified."

Ellman relented and went to the bartender and had him open a bottle of vodka and pour a neat shot into one of the glasses.

"There's an ocean of champagne here but I didn't think you'd want that," Ellman said, returning with her drink.

"Right you are. Now don't be nervous, Ellman. Half the people here will be charmed and the other half will wait for the reviews to tell them what they think." She patted his arm and gave him a hug.

"But I am glad you came early, because I value your opinion."

She walked around the gallery. Ellman had made sure that all of the canvases were shown to maximum advantage. He had taken special care with the lighting. The later paintings, which showed a South American influence, were surrounded by plants and trees that created an exotic, junglelike atmosphere. Sally was most impressed by the early canvases. She found them both passionate and well-executed. There was one portrait that particularly caught her attention. It wasn't exactly a madonna, for the girl in the portrait did not cradle a child, but was well along in her pregnancy. Her arms were loosely but protectively held around her swollen abdomen. The face was neither full of celestial concerns nor simpering. It was anxious and enduring yet full of tenderness. The artist clearly had great feeling for his subject.

The later works, though increasing in size and skill,

displayed no such emotional attitude. They aped the style of the great Mexican painters and lacked originality. Sally walked to the back of the gallery and found Ellman seated in his office.

"First off, darling, I don't think that you'll have any trouble selling the lot. . . ."

"I know that, Sal. I wouldn't have done the show as an act of kindness. Severio doesn't exactly tickle my sense of humanity. I expect he does that better with women. I want to know what you think of him as an artist."

"I think he's very good, but I wonder where he's going. The early stuff had lots of life, but the later work seems so facile and imitative. Of course you know that I have a limited tolerance for complete abstractions, so you take my prejudice into consideration."

"I agree with what you say. I have wondered. . . ."

But their tête-à-tête was interrupted by sounds at the front of the gallery. Ellman did not get up to greet the first comers, but the privacy of the conversation had been interrupted. Sally wished that she and Ellman had been sitting over the remains of a nice dinner so that they might have continued their discussion.

"Here come the clowns," Sally said and walked out to the bar for a refill.

By the time she was on her third drink, the gallery was almost full. Some had really come to look at the paintings and edged through the crowd, craning their necks to get a better view of the canvases. But most were there to enjoy a social event. The assemblage was certainly diverse: there were artist types in open-necked work shirts and jeans, young women with masses of frizzled hair and sequined eyelids, a slew of females sporting the latest haute couture, and men who looked as though they had lifetime subscriptions to *Fortune* magazine. There was a frail dowager who was supported on either side by a pair of albino twins. A famous Russian dancer on the arm of a burly-looking bodyguard.

Ellman introduced Sally to a bespectacled young man who seemed to be on the verge of nervous collapse. He turned out to be the art critic for a national magazine. Sally tried to talk to him about the exhibit. He nodded his head and said, "I know what you mean," in response to everything. She searched around for a topic that might inspire him to speech. When she was reduced to talking about the weather and he still bobbed his face in front of hers and mumbled, "I know what you mean," she concluded that his visual orientation had robbed him of the most rudimentary verbal skills, and excused herself to go to the ladies' room.

The moment she returned to the gallery, Ellman came up to her again with a portly man who looked like a parish priest. Ellman introduced him as a bishop who had authored a book entitled *The Moral Ambiguity of Modern Art*. Sally was afraid she was out of her depth, but the bishop announced that he wanted to meet her because he was a Troillina fan.

"You'll be happy to know that I used one of your little books as an example in my sermon the other week. For Troillina there are no moral ambiguities. It's a simple case of encountering good and evil in an imaginary context."

"Yeah . . . well, it's for kids," Sally said.

"Precisely, and when our Lord said, 'Suffer the little children to come unto me,' I contend that he was speaking not only to our junior citizens, but in a metaphor that challenges all of us. Your work, Miss Gold, illustrates that point."

"Could be," Sally nodded. Her eyes ranged around the room, frantically searching for Ellman. "Listen, your eminence . . . could you excuse me for just a moment while I go to the ladies' room?"

"Oh, you're such a natural person," he smiled benignly, "just as I imagined you would be. A pleasure."

Sally hid in the bathroom for a discreet five minutes and then stationed herself at the bar with a firm decision not to move from that spot. She chatted with the youngest bartender, who was an unemployed dancer from Iowa. He was about to take out his wallet and show her pictures of the family's farm when a sad-looking teenage girl came up to the bar and asked for "a slow comfortable screw." The bartender noticed Sally's surprised look and whispered, "It's a real drink. It's sloe gin, Southern Comfort, vodka, and juice."

Sally turned to the young woman in alarm.

"That combo will make you sick, honey."

"I'm sick already," the girl replied, pursing her carmine lips insolently.

"Okay, so it'll make you sicker. Take a word of

advice from an old hand: if you're gonna drink, drink straight."

The girl looked at Sally incredulously.

"Just thought I'd put in a word," Sally smiled.

"No, that's all right. I mean it's nice of you to be concerned."

Her face, which was almost obscured behind a mask of trendy makeup, softened. She put the syrupy drink back on the counter and asked Sally what she should order.

"I'd say a Shirley Temple. But that's probably because I'm feeling very old and therefore you look very young."

The girl laughed when Sally told the bartender to chuck out the concoction and give her a glass of white wine.

"You're very funny," the girl said without malice. "So you think I should drink white wine?"

"I don't mean to be maternal."

"I don't mind advice. And I wouldn't even know if it's maternal because my mother never gave me any advice at all."

"She must've been an unusual mother," Sally said.

"They were divorced when I was five. Mom got the stocks, the country house, and the pets, and Daddy got me. It was one of the first paternal custody fights in the state. I guess I was a good investment, 'cause Daddy's law firm gets a lot of cases like that now.

"Poor baby," Sally winced. "I guess I'd better get my shot in fast. One, stay away from egotistical men and two, order a plain drink, not an obscenity."

They clinked glasses. The young woman said, "To sisterhood," with a very solemn look on her face.

"Whatever . . . to life," Sally toasted and drained her glass.

She was interested in the girl and since she'd been given the green light in advice giving, she was about to ask why she'd covered her face with that absurd makeup and was wearing such bizarre clothes, when someone touched her arm. She spun around to see Jesa, resplendent in her pale gold dress.

"Jesa, you're here at last," she cried and leaned forward to embrace her friend.

"I've been here for about ten minutes but it's so crowded I couldn't locate you," Jesa replied breathlessly. "Isn't it wonderful! All these people."

"To me it's like the subway only with more perfume. Let me introduce you. Jesa this is . . oh dear," she said to the waiflike girl, "I didn't get your name.

"Melinda Laird," the girl replied meekly. "That's my dad, George Laird, over there talking to Severio."

Sally introduced her to Jesa and was about to ask her how she knew Severio, but the girl was looking at Jesa as though she were transfixed.

"Please excuse us," Jesa said to Melinda. "I want to introduce Sally to Mr. Euzielli."

"See you later, kid. And stick to the white wine," Sally called over her shoulder as Jesa took her through the throng.

"I thought that kid's eyes were going to pop out," Sally said. She noticed that everyone had their eyes on Jesa. She looked so radiant and sexy that the crowd actually seemed to part to make way for her. "You do look terrific."

"I met my neighbor Sophie in the lobby—you know the one I told you is my nemesis. She told me I looked like a sun god, so I immediately thought that I must look flat-chested," Jesa laughed.

When Severio saw Jesa approaching with Sally in tow, he excused himself from the knot of admirers and stepped toward them, extending his hand to Sally.

"A great pleasure to meet you at last, Miss Gold. Jesa has told me that you are quite an artist yourself."

"It pays the rent," Sally said. "I'd like to congratulate you, Mr. Euzielli. The show is really very good."

"You flatter me," he smiled, and raised her hand to his lips. "And please call me Severio."

Hand-kissing seemed to be such an affectation, Sally thought, but if anyone could get away with it, it was a man like Severio. She remembered now that she had caught a glimpse of him at Bettina's apartment. She felt slightly embarrassed that he fixed her with such a seductive gaze. But then men like this looked at all women with the same alluring expression. He was the type that would have made her heart race ten years ago. Now she found the style a bit off-putting. But there was no denying that he was extremely charming.

"I'm glad that you enjoy my work," he went on. "I expect that I would have some trouble convincing Jesa of my worth, if you didn't find me satisfactory."

"I particularly like the madonna portrait. My taste tends toward the human form. You must have known the model well to give it that particular sensitivity."

131

"That's very old," he replied. "It almost goes back to my student days. But Ellman convinced me that I should show a retrospective. The girl in the portrait is my sister."

For some reason Sally was not sure of the veracity of that remark.

"We should all get together and talk about art and life over a bottle of cheap Chianti—just like our student days," Jesa said enthusiastically.

"If it would please you, my dear," Severio assented.

"Shall we say Tuesday next?" Sally asked. "I'll cook and I'll invite Ellman too."

"Very well, next Tuesday. I'm eager to hear the opinions of what Jesa tells me is an acutely critical mind," Severio smiled, exposing his fine teeth.

For some reason that she couldn't put her finger on, Sally felt that the smile was unctuous rather than sincere. She wanted very much to like Severio and fought against what she thought was a prejudice about people who had such social ease. There was no denying that he was smooth.

Jesa was beaming with happiness as she watched the two people she cared about most in the world talking with each other. She was making arrangements for the upcoming dinner when a voice cried, "Severio," from across the room. Bettina Fanshaw, wearing a white lace Victorian dress, was pushing toward them. O.W. was bringing up the rear and moving through the crowd, trying not to burn any unsuspecting bystanders with his cigar. Sally wondered why Bettina, who was usually slinky, had decked her glossy black hair with tiny roses and was wearing a gown that was more appropriate to a prom queen. She thought she could detect just a flicker of shocked surprise when Bettina reached them and saw Jesa's dress. Bettina regained her composure and leaned forward to kiss Jesa on both cheeks.

"Jesa, my darling—lovely to see you—and you too, Sally."

She barely glanced in Sally's direction, but O.W. shook Sally's hand good-naturedly and looked at her in a way that said he had not forgotten the incompleted pass he had made at her some time ago.

Well, I certainly think that *everyone* is here," Bettina rushed on.

"Soup to *nuts*," Sally said, putting special emphasis on the last word.

Severio took Bettina's hand and started to kiss her, but she drew back and fanned her face with her hand.

"The place is so packed that we may all pass out from heat prostration," she laughed. "All except Jesa. She's already *un*dressed for summer . . . and such a lovely gown, dear. Wherever did you find it?"

The slightest look of embarrassment crossed Jesa's face. Sally felt a rush of hostility. She was so tired of Bettina's bitchy remarks. Both of the men seemed to be oblivious to the insult, but Sally guessed that Severio was far too savvy to have missed it.

"Bettina, my dear," he put in quickly, "let me thank you for all that you've done. If the evening's a success it's due in large part to your efforts. And I see that you don't even have a drink, so let me toast you with some champagne."

"That would be divine," Bettina cooed. "I do want to introduce you to Lyman Reims. He's the new curator of a museum down in Dallas. I see that he's about to leave and I know that you two should meet each other. You will excuse us, won't you?" she said as an afterthougbt to Jesa and O.W. as she took Severio's arm and steered him through the crowd.

Sally, O.W., and Jesa adjusted themselves into a closer circle, smiling aimlessly at each other. The general babble of the crowd was now reaching such a decibel level that it was difficult to hear normal conversation.

"Great that your kids' books are getting so much publicity," O.W. bellowed.

"I can hardly hear you, O.W. This place is like the zoo at feeding time," Sally said.

O.W. took his cigar out of his mouth long enough to guffaw. "Oh, Sally! If I were stranded on a desert island I'd rather have you than a good book."

"Fortunately, we're in mid-Manhattan," Sally replied dryly, which made O.W. crack up all over again. His laughter was interrupted by the appearance of Loretta and Fred Hartman. Loretta clutched Jesa's hand and shook it vigorously.

"Guess if we can't reach the man of the hour, we'd best give our congratulations to his consort. Isn't it a wonderful opening?" Loretta enthused.

"Pleasure to see you, Jesa," Fred put in soberly, "and I mean it."

There was another round of introductions. Jesa

responded to the warm glow of appreciation in Fred's eyes. She was not put out by Severio's disappearance. She had been to far too many gatherings with Ed to take it amiss when her partner had business priorities, and she was genuinely enjoying the huge gathering. Sally was not so forgiving. The fact that Severio had put himself in a position of being grateful to Bettina told her that either he was a poor judge of character, or else he was as adept at games of mutual usage as Bettina herself. Neither possibility appealed.

Loretta Hartman babbled on about the exhibit and said that an she was thinking of redesigning her living room to accommodate one of Severio's larger canvases. Her husband looked as though he was an advertisement for indigestion pills.

"I've already got a raging bull in my study, now I 'spose I'll have another one in the living room. Why don't you show me around, Jesa? Tell me what you like," Fred begged.

"Yes, yes, please show him around," Loretta urged.

Jesa took a grateful Fred by the hand and excused herself from the group. When Loretta turned her attention to O.W., Sally walked back to the bar hoping to find Melinda, but the girl was nowhere in sight. The bartender from Iowa asked her how she was doing and filled her glass again. She thanked him and searched the room for a corner in which to hide. Finally she sat balancing herself on the rim of a planter, partially obscured by the foliage of the tree-sized growth. She pushed back some leaves and looked around trying to find Ellman, but he was nowhere in sight.

She saw Bettina and Severio head for the spot where she was sitting. She started to get up, but apparently they hadn't noticed her, for they turned their backs to the plants and stood a little distance from her, but still within earshot.

"I can see that Lyman Reims is most impressed," Bettina said softly. "You'll have a canvas in that new museum as fast as you can paint one."

"Ah, Bettina, what would I do without you?" Severio said.

"What you've been doing, I presume," she replied, her lower lip distending in a pout.

"Now, now, don't spoil the evening by being pettish."

He spoke to her in the same manner that would be used to chastise a child or a naughty pet. Sally was amazed to see that this treatment worked, and Bettina, instead of being infuriated, dimpled her cheeks in a demure smile.

"Jesa's looking well," she said innocently after a slight pause.

"Yes, she is," Severio replied with equal simplicity.

"I've known her for many years, and I've never seen her display so much flesh in public."

"If you'd been in the shackles of boring monogamy for fifteen years, you might want to break out a bit yourself."

"I wouldn't know. I've only been married for twelve," Bettina countered, fluttering her eyelashes.

"Then your time is about to come," he said smoothly, taking a rose from her hair and sniffing it.

They laughed together for a moment and then moved back into the crowd.

Sally was so annoyed that she was shaking slightly and spilled some of her drink on her skirt. How could Severio flirt with that terrible woman? How could he act in collusion with her to denigrate Jesa? How could they suggest that the gown she had helped to pick was in questionable taste? She determined to overcome her inhibitions against meddling in Jesa's life. Her friend was clearly too infatuated with this man to see that he was a womanizer and a creep. She would tell Jesa what she thought of Severio, even at the risk of hurting her feelings.

She stumbled through the throng of people preparing the speech she would give to Jesa. She pushed open the door to the ladies' room and started to blot the stain on her skirt when she heard retching noises followed by the flushing of a toilet. Melinda came out of one of the stalls, her face an even whiter shade than the layer of powder that covered it.

"Hi, kid. I told you to stick to the white wine," Sally said, reaching out to steady the girl.

"It isn't the booze," Melinda breathed. "It's him. God, how I hate him. I'm gonna get even with him if it's the last thing I do."

"Oh, man trouble," Sally sighed. "Too bad you started so young, 'cause believe me it doesn't get any better."

She moistened a towel and pressed it gently to Melinda's forehead. Melinda was muttering something incoherently and clutching the rim of the sink.

Sally wanted to go and find Jesa, but felt she couldn't leave the girl alone. She shushed Melinda's invective and mopped her brow.

When Severio walked back to Jesa he ran his hand gently down her spine. She excused herself from the Hartmans and turned to him slowly.

"How did you know it was me?" he asked softly.

"Oh, I knew it was you," she whispered, and arched her back ever so slightly so that the nipples of her small breasts showed through the dress.

"And what do you think of the opening?"

"I think it's a great success. I think you're wonderful. And . . ."

She paused and swallowed. Her face flushed and her lips parted. She looked straight into his eyes and held the gaze.

"And?"

"And . . . how soon can we go home?"

"Now," he whispered, and led her toward the door.

Chapter 6

Severio's apartment was in darkness, except for the silvery rays of the moon that spilled through the skylight at the far end of the loft. In all the weeks of their courtship, Jesa had never been to his place. As she leaned against the wall and tried to adjust her eyes, she heard him turn the lock in the door behind her. The sound startled her. She froze and waited for him to turn on the lights.

They had rushed out of the gallery, nodding and smiling to the throng of guests, but not pausing to say goodbye to anyone. He had held her arm firmly as he guided her out onto the street. Once inside the taxi he had given the driver the address of his studio. Clearly she'd decided to let him make love to her and he didn't want to run the risk of having her amorous mood destroyed by going back to her apartment, which, he perceived, she still considered to be her husband's territory. She had been mildly surprised when she heard him give his address, but she had said nothing. Her emotions were far too tumultuous to bother with such details. They sat silently, intent and expectant, not daring to look at each other or even touch. The cab sped through the almost deserted city streets which glistened from the spring rain.

She waited for him to turn on the lights, but he was next to her immediately, pulling her body to his, his warm mouth on her neck. As much as she wanted him to make love to her, had consciously decided that tonight was to be the night, her body tensed as she felt his powerful arms tighten around her. She was annoyed with herself because she couldn't let go. Why should she feel trapped when she had come here with him voluntarily? She wanted to talk to him. She wanted to somehow explain the importance of what she was about to do. The words caught in her throat and came out as a stifled, aching sound. She needed to see him. To know that it was Severio, a man she cared about and longed for, not just a powerful, faceless male.

As if divining her thoughts, he reached for her hand and led her over toward the skylight.

"I want to see you," he whispered as he slipped the fur coat from her shoulders. She shivered slightly as the cool air hit her naked back. His hands moved over the flesh of her arms and shoulders as if to warm it. He slid the straps of her dress down, so that her breasts were exposed, and stood back to look at her. She took a deep breath, flung her head back and closed her eyes. Even though he had promised himself that he would wait until she begged for his embrace, the sight of her there, half-naked but still reserved, drove him into a frenzy. He brought his mouth to hers with demanding urgency. Her teeth clenched and her lips closed. She wanted to yield to the raw, anonymous sexuality, but her body stiffened when she felt him against her. She felt as though she were on a roller coaster that was approaching the top of the first big dip, every muscle tensed in fear and expectation.

"I love you, Jesa," he murmured, his voice almost angry.

The words pushed her over the top. No matter how confused her feelings, no matter how incapable of spontaneity she felt, she could not refuse this encounter. She went limp in his arms. He gathered her up and carried her over to the bed. She could barely make out the features of his face as he loomed above her. It blotted out everything else in the world.

Afterward they lay together silently. She could hear the sounds coming up from the street. A car cruised by swooshing through the puddles. There was the distant night cry of a siren. The moments ticked away. She listened to Severio's breathing. It changed from the labored, excited gasps to a more regular rhythm. The world was trickling back into her consciousness. How strange it was that this had been the realization of so many fantasies. She felt only the calm of a task completed, the exhaustion of physical exertion, as though she had run a race.

She opened her eyes, propped herself up on her elbow and turned to look at Severio's face. It had softened with the release of his passion. It seemed younger and more open. She was not annoyed that she had seen him absorbed in such a single-minded pursuit of his own gratification. It made her feel that she knew him that much better. She reached out tentatively, tracing the line of his dark brows, her fingers straying over his face and down onto the matted hair of his chest. He stirred slightly and smiled up at her, welcoming her exploration. They moved closer together then shifted apart, touching with a languid, sensual calm. The cocoonlike warmth of the bed lulled her into a drifting dream state, but she was alive with curiosity about the flesh and blood reality of the body she had imagined so many times. He tossed back the covers and then relaxed back, stroking her.

"I'll be glad when it's summer," he whispered. "I like to make love best in the summer."

For the slightest moment his remark disturbed her. She realized that his sexuality was an independent thing, not exclusively connected to her. She thought of all the other women he must have had. But he had mentioned the summer. Her imagination leaped forward. She thought of enjoying him over and over, under all sorts of conditions and circumstances. She nuzzled her head into his neck, breathing the sweet odor of his fresh perspiration. Her vision had become more acute in the semidarkness. She could see the silvery outline of his body, feel his eyes on her as she touched him. All her senses were filled with his presence.

Miraculously the languid sensuality began to change. The playfulness took on all the urgency that she had felt before but had been unable to express. The wildness of her passion surprised him. He had already had the satisfaction of taking her and indulging his own desires and thought that possession of her passive body would be the chief element in their lovemaking. Now she clutched at him and moved on to him, moaning, knowing that this time she would experience all of the joy of release that she had resisted before. He toyed with her, seeking out all the nuances of her desire, amazed at her abandoned response. They thrashed about in a free, unifying gratification.

"You amaze me, Jesa," he whispered finally when they had rolled away from each other.

"Why do you say that?"

"You know," he answered in a husky voice. "I feel as though it's a secret you've kept just for me."

He brushed the hair back from her flushed face and pulled her closer to him. Her response had been even more of a surprise to her than it had been to him. As she snuggled up next to him, she searched her memory for another instance of such unrestrained, demanding lovemaking. When she had met Ed she had been a virgin, ignorant of the pleasures of her own body. Because she adored and trusted him, she had let Ed guide her into sexual expression of their love. He had "taught" her. His desires had been regular and healthy, never erratic. It had been rare that she had ever initiated the act. She had always found comfort and satisfaction in bed with him, but it was not like the wrenching emotional experience of mutual abandon that she had just felt.

It was true, she mused, that she had been alone for a long time, but that was not the major difference. With Ed she had always remained, at least in part, what she had been at the onset of their affair—a trusting girl. The girlishness had less to do with age than with a psychic mind set. Now, for the first time, she had come to a man as a woman. One day, she thought as she adjusted the covers around them, I will tell Severio all about this. But not now. It would be almost sacrilegious to talk about sex now. It would be like dissecting a work of art instead of experiencing it.

"You've got that special little smile on your face, St. Jesamine. I thought that when we finally became lovers, I'd be able to penetrate all your mysteries."

"No mysteries, just a private thought."

"I'm not complaining. It's boring to be with a woman who can be easily read. This way, I'll find you endlessly fascinating."

She laughed slightly. Then a troubled expression came onto her face.

"What is it?"

"I just remembered that we didn't say goodnight to anyone. Not even Sally or Ellman. I hope they won't be angry with us."

"You're so conventional," he said, tickling her. "Ellman will understand that I couldn't have talked business last night. And the state your friend Sally was in, I doubt if she'd not we left."

"You mustn't be too hard on Sally. She's really one of the kindest people I know. And she's kept me going during these last months. There really wasn't anyone I could rely on except her."

"But now you have me," he said simply. "Darling, I'm parched. Will you join me in a glass of champagne?"

"Champagne? It's almost morning!"

"Then we'll toast the new dawn."

He threw on a robe and disappeared into the kitchen. She sat up and looked over at the skylight. Streaks of coral were beginning to appear in the morning sky. It would be a fine day, filled with warmth and sunshine. A few moments later Severio came back with a bottle of champagne and two glasses. As he popped the cork, the fizzy liquid spilled onto the fur coverlet. Jesa immediately started to mop it up with a sheet.

"Leave it," he cried. "I'll never have it cleaned. It'll be a memento of the happiest night of my life."

He filled the glasses and touched his to the rim of hers. She looked into his face. His dark hair was tousled and his eyes were glowing with exhilaration. They held the gaze for so long that she could feel the stir-rings of desire all over again.

"To the most beautiful woman I know."

"To your gallery opening," she smiled.

"To success!" he cried, tossing his head back and draining the contents of the glass with a single gulp.

He put the glass on the floor and took off his robe. She sipped her champagne and admired his body as he slid in next to her. Then, as he took the glass from her and his lips touched her cheek, she whispered, "To love."

The midmorning sunlight shone into the cluttered living room. Sally shifted herself on the couch, groaned, and staggered over to yank the draperies shut.

"It can't be morning already. Feels like I only went to sleep ten minutes ago," she grunted to Rebecca. The little dog wagged her tail and trotted over to the front door.

"Not a chance," Sally said, as she unzipped her vel-veteen skirt and let it drop to the floor. "I may be up, but it's only temporary and we're not going out."

She walked slowly into the bathroom, flung a robe over her slip, and fumbled with the toothpaste. She was brushing her teeth with careful, slow strokes when the fog in her mind lifted and the details of the pre-vious evening came back to her in minute detail.

"It may not have been one of the worst nights in your life," she muttered to her own reflection, "but I think we can put it on the runner-up list."

She had been stranded in the ladies' room with the retching and slightly hysterical Melinda for at least twenty minutes. Whenever she thought she had succeeded in calming the girl down, Melinda would launch into another tirade about "that man" and spew out threats of vengeance. Sally tried to get a picture of what was bothering her, but the girl was so busy hiccuping and cursing that it was impossible to get her story straight. When Sally had soothed her into a sullen calm, she made her promise to stay in the bathroom until she could find her father and tell him that Melinda wanted to go home.

She walked back into the gallery. Jesa was nowhere in sight. Putting aside her own concerns, she tried to remember which man Melinda had pointed out as her father. There was a silver-haired, carefully groomed gentleman standing near the entrance engaged in conversation with O.W. and Bettina. He seemed to be a likely candidate. She approached them and inquired politely if he was Mr. Laird. When he answered yes, she told him that his daughter was in the ladies' room, didn't feel well, and would like to be taken home. He was immediately solicitous and asked Sally to go and bring her out.

"I'd better go myself," Bettina sighed with the look of a martyred saint. "God knows what Sally has been giving her to drink."

Sally opened her mouth with an angry reproach, then checked herself. No use trying to plead her case with the likes of Bettina. O.W. patted her on the back and said she was a fine babysitter. Bettina swept past them and headed for the ladies' room. Sally stood still and accepted O.W.'s bumbling attempts at good fellowship and scanned the room for a sight of Jesa. Mr. Laird covered his embarrassment by ranting on about the incompetence of all the psychiatrists to whom he'd sent his wayward daughter.

"Maybe she just needs a mother," O.W. put in. "Kids that age go through all sorts of crazy phases. 'Course my kids were already off in college when I married Bettina, but I remember all the problems I had with 'em during their teenage years. But don't worry, they straighten themselves out in their twenties."

"I'm not sure I have the patience to endure that long," Mr. Laird replied shortly.

Melinda was being led through the throng by a grim-faced Bettina.

"I suppose we'll have to go home now," she sighed heavily. "And I don't seem to be able to find Severio."

O.W. was sent off to get their coats and the girl stood, shamefaced, in front of Sally.

"Thanks for being so nice to me."

"Don't mention it. I hope you feel better."

"Could I have your phone number? I'd really like to talk to you some time."

"We have to get going," Bettina interjected quickly.

Sally found a bitten-off pencil in her purse and jotted her number down on a cocktail napkin.

"Perhaps I'd better have it too," Mr. Laird said. "You might be wanting to send me the bill for your sessions."

"Oh, Daddy," Melinda spat out, "not everybody

does things just for money."

"You say that because you've got so much of it," he replied tartly.

Sally patted the girl's hand and excused herself as quickly as possible. It looked like the beginnings of a nasty family argument. She spied Ellman standing near the door of his office talking with the bespectacled art critic.

"I'm sure that Mr. Euzielli would like to meet you personally. Unfortunately he was called away on an emergency just a few minutes ago, so we'll have to arrange a meeting for another time."

The young man bobbed his head, poked his glasses back onto the bridge of his nose, and wandered off.

"What emergency?" Sally demanded.

"Shush. No emergency. He and Jesa just took off. The call of passion, I suppose. He should have stayed and met a few of these people. Still, everyone seems to be so impressed that he'll be forgiven. Severio knows how to play the impulsive artist role to a tee."

"How much longer before this wing-ding is over?" she asked impatiently. The crowd had thinned out, and those who remained had given up all pretense of viewing the paintings. They clustered about the bar chattering to each other or sat amid Ellman's jungle foliage nibbling the leftover hors d'oeuvres.

"They look like a bunch of monkeys at the city zoo," Sally said.

"And what's put you into such an acid mood?"

"Quite a few things. I'll tell you as soon as we're alone."

"Why don't you take the key to my apartment? I'll be over in a half hour or so."

"You're on," Sally sighed, putting out her hand for the key.

As she trudged the few blocks to Ellman's place she thought of how to warn Jesa about Severio. She would be diplomatic, of course. She would have to work her way through the miasma of Jesa's infatuation. But she would be firm, too. She would counsel her friend carefully.

The discreet order of Ellman's apartment had a settling affect on her nerves. When she'd first visited his place she'd been a bit nervous that she might spill something or knock over one of the carefully arranged objets d'art with which he surrounded himself. But Ellman lived comfortably with his treasures and now she was beginning to relax around them. He wasn't really the stuffy bachelor that he seemed to be; he just put great value on a tranquil and beautiful environment. She poured herself a drink and walked around the apartment. She even peeked into the bedroom. The opalescent bedside lamp cast a warm glow on the carefully turned down bedcovers. It looked very peaceful and inviting.

She was fixing Ellman a pot of herb tea when she heard his key in the door. He came up behind her and gave her a hug and thanked her for making the tea.

"It's so pleasant to walk into the house and have someone here doing for you," he smiled as he settled onto the couch and took off his shoes.

"I guess that's why men like to have wives," she said

sarcastically.

"It's not just being a wife, Sally. I try to anticipate your needs, too."

"I'm sorry. I guess I'm just down on men tonight. Meeting Severio didn't exactly increase my regard for the opposite sex." She sat down next to him and he put his arm around her affectionately.

"So tell me what you think about him and why."

She had been waiting for an opportunity to unburden herself. He listened attentively, reaching out every now and then to touch her hand or chuckle appreciatively at her turn of phrase. In a last effort to convince him of the seriousness of the situation, she told him about the conversation she had overheard between Bettina and Severio. She put down her glass with a "so there" punctuation and waited for his response. He shrugged his shoulders.

"It doesn't surprise me. Severio is a smooth one with the ladies."

"It's more than that. He was disloyal to Jesa. He's just toying with her. You don't know her the way I do, Ellman. She's not emotionally secure enough to weather a disastrous affair."

"But she's old enough to find that out for herself. It's best not to interfere in affairs of the heart."

"Oh, come off it. You're just so busy counting all the money you made tonight that you don't even care what I'm talking about."

He took off his glasses and rubbed his eyes. A contented smile came over his face as he reached out for her again. "I'll admit it went even better than I'd anticipated. That means that Severio will be able to pay back the money he owes me. Maybe when you're finished with the book we can take a vacation together."

"You loaned him money?" she said. "That's another thing. I knew he was irresponsible."

"For God's sake calm down. He's good for it."

She disengaged herself from his embrace and walked to the bar to fix herself another drink. She could feel his eyes on her as she poured a stiff shot of cognac into a snifter.

"Don't look at me like that."

He sat up straight on the couch and stared at her.

"I thought if you came up to the apartment I might have the pleasure of looking at you. I even thought that we might have the pleasure of . . ."

He paused. He had almost said "the pleasure of staying the night with each other." It was not a plan that he had formulated in his mind. But he was glad of her company there at the gallery and when he had walked in and saw her fixing tea for him, he felt a desire to hold her, nurture her until her snappishness was eased away and she became the fun-loving woman he had come to care for. He stirred his tea, grunted and censored his words. ". . . have the pleasure of talking with you. But if you're going to be in such a snippy mood . . ."

"Then I'd best go home."

She put her coat on quickly and searched around for her purse. He rebuttoned his vest and started to put on his shoes.

"It's all right. I can get a cab for myself," she said,

fixing a bright smile on her face. "I'll talk to you soon."

The moment she was out the door she was full of remorse. She wished that she could have been more friendly to him. She might at least have congratulated him on the success of the opening instead of being so rude. Nothing had gone right for her lately. Neither her work nor her private life. And now this thing with Jesa and Severio. She could feel her spirits sinking. Even though she wanted to go back in and apologize, she made it a point never to let anyone see her when she was in a real slump. She would go home to Rebecca, have a nightcap, and tune out the world.

When she walked into her own apartment, she groaned at the cluttered mess. She automatically turned on the television, tuning the volume down to the hum of background noise. Pulling Rebecca onto her lap, she curled up on the couch with her drink. When the test pattern appeared on the television screen, she had drifted off into oblivion.

The ringing of the phone startled Jesa out of a deep sleep. Severio moved his arm from under her head, waited for the ringing to stop, then groped for the phone and yanked the receiver off the hook without even opening his eyes. He reached out for her and readjusted her body to fit his position, turning her back to him and cupping one of her breasts in his hand. He fell back to sleep immediately. She stayed awake, marveling at the pleasure of waking up with him next to her. It was all so strange and new. She shifted her head slightly so that she could look at him.

She wanted to kiss him into wakefulness. To tell him how much she loved him. He slowly opened his eyes and looked at her.

"Damn it! Anyone who knows me wouldn't dare call before noon."

"I hate to tell you, but I think it must be noon already. See how beautiful the sunlight looks coming in through the skylight? Monet captures those soft dappled tones so well in the waterlily series."

"You're the one with the artist's eye, Jesa. When are you going to start painting again?"

"Believe it or not, I was thinking of it just now."

"I hope it won't sound too unromantic if I say that I was thinking about eating. I'm ravenously hungry."

"Would you like me to fix you something?"

"I think I have the usual bachelor's larder: half a dozen eggs, some moldy cheese, and a couple of bottles of booze. I'd offer to take you out for lunch, but I don't think you could get by wearing that slinky number you had on last night even in this neighborhood."

"Oh goodness, I'd forgotten about that completely. How am I ever going to get home in that?"

He ruffled her hair and put an expression of mock concern on his face.

"You'll just have to stay till nightfall and sneak out. Otherwise the neighbors will think I'm supporting a high-class call girl."

She threw a pillow at him. He dodged it, pushed her back down onto the bed and kissed her. Then he went to the closet and pulled out a sweater and a pair of jeans.

"I'm off to bring home the bacon. There's an espresso machine in the kitchen if you know how to use it."

"Sure I do. I'll make us some."

She inched her way out of bed, carefully wrapping a sheet around her nakedness. As she walked past him, he playfully took hold of the end of the sheet and started to unwrap her.

"None of your prudery here, Miss. I want to see you naked all the time. That way I can do a nude from memory."

He held her at arm's length and admired her. She did feel languid and beautiful, but the goosebumps were popping out over her pale skin.

"I have lousy circulation. Sometimes I even wear socks to bed."

"That's the title: 'Nude with Socks.'"

He held out his robe and slipped it around her, tugging the sashes tightly around her waist. Guiding her into the kitchen, he showed her where the coffee was, She had been afraid that there might be embarrassment between them the next day, that they would be remorseful, or clumsy with each other. But here they were teasing and embracing and talking about trivial domestic things like making a cup of coffee.

"I'd better get going before I decide not to go out at all. I'll be back as soon as I can."

She hummed softly to herself as she fooled with the espresso machine. She opened the cupboards. They were indeed bare. The whole loft had a feeling of spareness, of bold yet minimal style. It was so different from her apartment. As soon as she opened her eyes when she was at home, she felt weighted down with memories. Every nook and cranny had had the benefit of years of careful decoration. And every object had associations that wedded her to the past.

She wandered into the massive room where the spring sunlight now drenched the wooden floor. She touched the brushes and vacant canvases lovingly. Though the fur bedspread, the fine mahogany work-table, and the expensive clothes that were tossed about the floor were not exactly signs of a Spartan existence, the spaciousness of the loft gave her a sense of unencumbered living. Severio's style wouldn't permit him to clutter up his life with an accumulation of objects. She wondered now that she had ever found such satisfaction in collecting and arranging. She supposed that it had made her feel secure. It was a sort of substitute caring, taking the energy that she might have spent on a child, or even on her own career. She brushed aside such contemplations and spun around the room, feeling so light and free that she was almost dancing. When she heard the door open she rushed forward to help him.

"Whatever did you buy?" she asked, eyeing the overflowing bags of groceries.

"Caviar, croissants, shrimp—you name it. This neighborhood may not look like it, but there are some people with very expensive tastes living in these old warehouses. Someone has been smart enough to build one of New York's best-stocked delis just down the block."

They unwrapped the purchases, nibbling and

testing each thing as they opened it. Severio suggested that they take a shower before they really got down to fixing the meal.

They stood in the shower together, allowing the warm spray of the water to play over their bodies. Severio turned her back to him and began to soap her, massaging her shoulders with slow circular movements. She couldn't remember how long it had been since she had been the beneficiary of such pampered attention. She felt the sense of deep gratitude that was so much a part of her character whenever the slightest kindness was bestowed on her. Her shoulders began to shake and she felt the tears welling in her eyes.

"You're not crying, are you?" he asked as he turned her around to face him. "You're not unhappy?"

"No. I know it's silly of me to cry. It's just that . . ."

She swallowed hard and tried to suppress the tears. He turned off the water and stepped out, taking a bath towel and wrapping her up in it. He led her back to the bed and asked her to tell him what was the matter.

"Kindness . . . little attentions . . . they always make me so ridiculously sentimental. Once when I was in boarding school, oh, I must've been quite young, seven or eight at the most . . . I was new there and very frightened. When the housemother was turning out the lights in the dormitory, she came over and patted my head and tucked me in. I was amazed."

"Why?"

"Because I knew that she thought I was asleep. Even at that age, I was surprised that someone would do something affectionate when there was no audience to applaud them. I started crying then, too. Strange, I haven't thought about that in years."

"It sounds as though you had a pretty rotten child-hood."

"I don't like to talk about it. I don't want anyone to think that I'm making a plea for sympathy. I've never really discussed it with anyone except Ed. I talked about it for a bit with the psychiatrist, but I never felt really comfortable with that."

He took a corner of a sheet and dabbed her cheeks.

"I intend to pay you a thousand little attentions, so don't tell me that you'll be crying all the time."

"I won't. I promise."

She smiled contentedly as he pulled the covers over her.

"Don't worry. Everything will be all right now."

Melinda pushed aside the dinner tray that the maid had brought up to her room. She took a joint out of her little gold cigarette case, put a record on the turntable and sat down on the floor to think.

The night before her father had given her a terrible tongue lashing. He told her that she was a disgrace to his reputation and that if she did not mend her ways he would turn her over to her mother, custody fight or no. He simply wouldn't believe her when she said that she wasn't drunk at the opening, just emotionally upset. When he asked her why she was unhappy, she couldn't bring herself to tell him about the affair with Severio. She sat, mute and hostile, while he searched around for a suitable punishment for embarrassing him in front of his friends.

"If you're too immature to know how to conduct yourself at an art gallery, then you're certainly too immature to go to Spain alone next month."

"But, Daddy, you promised," she wailed.

"And you promised me that you would start behaving yourself. I just don't know what's gotten into you. I should probably take Bettina's advice and pack you off to boarding school again."

"I graduated in January, remember?" she hissed.

"Then, damn it, I'll send you to a college where they keep the doors locked."

"Why don't you just send me to a nunnery? That's what rich people did in the old days when they didn't want to be bothered with their daughters."

George Laird's face was livid with anger and too many martinis. He had followed the advice of Melinda's psychiatrist to spend more time with his daughter, and this was the result of his effort. The first time he took her out in company she'd made a fool out of him. He recalled how sweet and loving Melinda had been when she was a little girl. How much he'd looked forward to coming home from the office and having one of the servants present Melinda, all clean and sweet-smelling from her bath, her face shining with anticipation of his embrace. He couldn't remember when the little girl in the ruffled nightdress had turned into this truculent, painted creature sitting in front of him. She looked more like one of the tarts he might discreetly pick up on an overseas business trip than his own child. He bent forward and touched her cheek, trying to wipe away some of the rouge.

"Now what is it, baby girl?" he said softly.

"I'm not a child," she answered emphatically, pushing away his hand.

Frustrated by her rejection, he walked away and paced the room. He had no idea how to talk to her. No notion of what was going on in her head. Having failed at being the solicitous daddy, be resumed the role of stern disciplinarian.

"You are a child, Melinda. As long as I'm paying the bills you'll listen to me. You are not going to Spain. You are grounded for a week, and you are not, under any circumstance . . ." He fumbled around for another suitable punishment. "You are not to disturb the quiet of this apartment by playing your damn records at full blast at any hour of the day and night. Do you under-stand me?"

"I understand you perfectly, George," she said icily as she started to leave the room. "You're the one who doesn't understand anything."

"Melinda," he screamed, as she started up the stairs, "Melinda! You will stay here and talk to me!"

She kept walking up the stairs to her room.

Once she was alone, she threw herself onto the canopied bed and cried into the ruffled pillows. It just wasn't fair. They all treated her so badly. Not just her father, but the servants as well. They were always nice to her when he was around, but when he was out of sight they dropped the polite guard and she could see in their eyes that they thought she was a spoiled brat. She didn't feel spoiled. Just terribly misunderstood and neglected. And Severio had behaved worse than any of them. She knew that he didn't love her, even though she'd tried to be sexy and do everything she could to let him know that she adored him. When he'd seen her at the opening, he had pretended that he barely remembered meeting her. When she'd looked directly into his eyes, hoping for at least a signal of recognition, he had asked her how her school work was going, when he knew very well that she wasn't even in school anymore. He had patted her as though she were a puppy or something and then walked over and put his arm around that Mrs. Mallick as though Melinda didn't even exist. She sobbed for hour remembering the rejection. Despite her threats the last time she was in his studio, she didn't have any real plan to make trouble for him at the opening. She had just wanted to be near him. To have him show her with a look or gesture that he knew she was in the world, that they had had sex together.

The next morning when she woke up she'd decided that she would apologize to her father. She hadn't really meant to embarrass him. She was just mixed up. Maybe the vacation in Spain would help her to get away from it all and think things out. She had scrubbed her face clean and even put on a dress so that she would appear cute and ladylike, the way she knew he liked to see her. Daddy would agree with her and they would make up.

But when she got down to the dining room, the cook told her that Mr. Laird had already left to go to the coast on business. He had left strict instructions that Melinda was not to go out and could not play her records too loudly. She went back to her room and called her shrink, asking if she could see him for an extra session. He said that he was sorry he was over-booked. Unless it was a real emergency, he would have to see bet at her regular appointment.

She sulked in her room all morning, trying on different outfits and playing with her makeup. Around midday, she tried to call Severio. She was afraid to talk to him, but the desire to simply hear his voice was unbearable. She would just wait until he said "Hello" and hang up, she told herself as she dialed. The phone rang for a long time but there was no answer. When she tried again, just a few minutes later, the line was busy. By late afternoon the operator informed her that there was no trouble on the line, but the number she had called had probably been taken off the hook. She knew that must mean he was in bed with someone, probably that Mrs. Mallick.

"It's such an awful frustration,
No one understands my situation,"

the song on the record player screamed out to her. She turned the volume dial tip to maximum. So what if some servant knocked on the door and told her to turn it down? Whose house was it anyway? She knew how to deal with her custodians. She had witnessed an unending procession of nannies, cooks, tutors, and maids ever since her infancy. They needed to have her on their side because if she didn't like them she would carry tales of unkindness or sloppiness to Daddy and they would be dismissed. If she did like them, she could be depended upon to intercede with Daddy for special days off and other favors for them. Besides, Daddy would probably have forgotten what he'd forbidden her to do by the time he got home from his trip.

There was a knock on the door. The maid, who was new, from the Phillipines and barely spoke English, put her head in.

"Mister Laird say not too much noise, Miss," she said quietly, barely audible over the scream of the stereo.

"That's okay. I know. Please leave me alone now."

When the woman looked at her uncomprehendingly, Melinda shouted, "I need it. I need the music to think."

The woman nodded and shut the door. Melinda rocked back and forth to the music, taking in its message.

"It's such an awful frustration,
No one understands my situation,
But I'm gonna get what I want, yeah, yeah
I'm gonna get what I want."

She would get what she wanted. She would go to Spain and she would fix Severio real good before she left.

Chapter 7

*I*t was early evening when Jesa finally put on the gold backless dress again. Severio covered her shoulders with her fur coat and they walked out onto the street to look for a taxi. He wanted to escort her back to her apartment, but she said that was foolish. Exhaustion had finally caught up with her. She felt a gritty sensation in her eyes and her limbs were pleasantly aching. She longed for a good night's sleep. He admitted that he was ready to collapse himself, kissed her lightly as he opened the door of the taxi for her, and promised to call her the next day.

The street lights had come on early, illuminating the vivid new foliage of the trees. She opened the window and breathed in the moist spring air. She could see children playing underneath the lamps. Young people lounged about the corners, laughing and teasing each other in an age-old ritual of adolescent courtship. Even old people, still holding their cardigans about their chests, walked in the open air enjoying that lift of spirit that comes with the end of a seemingly endless winter. She asked the driver to go through the park and not to hurry. She was awash in ebullient good will, experiencing the joy of living in a way she thought she was past feeling. She even thought of taking up the paintbrush again and trying to capture all of the light and beauty that surrounded her.

She swept into the lobby of her building. O'Hara rushed forward to help her with the door, but she had already opened it for herself.

"Glorious weather, isn't it, Mr. O'Hara?" she said blithely.

"Saw your picture in the paper, Mrs. Mallick," O'Hara smiled sheepishly. He noted her dress and reasoned that she must have been out all night.

"What picture?"

He fumbled with the *Post* and finally found the page that he'd circled in red and presented it to her. She had been vaguely aware of photographers at the opening, but didn't realize that her picture had been taken. Here she was, her face in profile and her almost nude back to the camera as she leaned into a smiling Severio. Bettina and O.W. were standing next to them. The photographer had caught Bettina at a bad moment: her eyes were closed and her mouth was open. "Bettina won't like that," she thought as she scanned the copy.

"**Bettina Fanshaw** and hubby O.W. were among the well-wishers at wing-ding opening for artist-about-town **Severio Euzielli**. **Mr. Euzielli's** date for the evening was **Jesamine Smythe Mallick**—she's blond as the sun and lean as a whippet. Congrats Severio."

She grimaced slightly, laughed, and handed the paper back to O'Hara. As she moved past him to the elevator, she glanced about the lobby admiring a display of irises on one of the marble tables that stood in the foyer.

"Who's responsible for those lovely flowers?"

"That's Mrs. Moss. She's in charge of the Tenants' Beautification Committee, y'know."

164

"What a dear thoughtful woman Sophie is. I must remember to thank her when I see her," she said sincerely.

She picked up the hem of her gown and disappeared into the elevator, leaving the befuddled O'Hara to sort out his newspaper.

She was running a bath and humming quietly to herself when the telephone began to ring.

"Jesa? Thank God you're finally home. I've been worried about you."

"No need to worry, Sally. I'm just fine. How are you?"

"Can I come over for a while? I've been wanting to talk to you ever since last night."

Though she was hoping for a quiet evening alone, Jesa hated to turn down Sally's request. She thought what a pleasure it would be to finally be able to tell someone about her love for Severio.

"Come on over. I should warn you that I'm absolutely bushed. I have to make it an early night. But I have some really wonderful news to tell you."

By the time Sally arrived she had bathed, shampooed her hair, and was feeling very sleepy. She noticed that Sally was in an agitated state, but then Sally often was. Ed had always joked about her friend's mood swings, asking if Sally was "passionate purple" or "bruised blue." Tonight was definitely blue. She fixed Sally a drink, poured herself a thimbleful, and curled up on the couch, toweling her hair dry and ready for a rehash of the opening.

"I tried to call you all day long," Sally said, "I

couldn't imagine where you were."

"I was down at Severio's. You'll have to come down to Soho sometime, Sal. He has such a wonderful place. Right down to the essentials—you know the way we lived in the student days."

Sally stirred her drink with her finger and said nothing.

"What did you think of the opening?" Jesa bubbled on. "Did Ellman think it went well? I never thought I'd see myself in a gossip column. Did you see that squib in the *Post*?"

"That must've been Bettina's doing," Sally replied without smiling. "She's such an egomaniac she thinks it's a news event when she goes to the bathroom."

"You're probably right," Jesa conceded. "Still, it can't hurt Severio to have his name in the papers."

"Yeah, he seems to have a nose for publicity. I know the show will be a big commercial success."

The inflection that Sally put on "commercial" was distinctly unpleasant. It had never occurred to Jesa before that Sally might have some professional envy of Severio. Perhaps she was over deadline on Troillina again and that accounted for her mood. Jesa was feeling very generous. She decided to cheer Sally up with a little attention.

"What happened to you after we left?"

"I was stuck in the bathroom with a hippy teenager who kept throwing up and crying about some man who'd done her wrong. Then I went to Ellman's— then I came home. It was a helluva night."

"Ellman really seems fond of you. I want the two of

166

you to come to Severio's sometime next week."

Sally was silent. She poked at the ice cubes in her glass and stared absently around the room. Jesa stayed still, eyeing her. She knew that Sally was incapable of suppressing her emotions or opinions for very long. She would blurt out what was bothering her if Jesa just gave her time. Finally, Sally raised her eyes and stared Jesa in the face. Her large brown eyes were serious and sad.

"I don't think that Ellman and I will go out with you. In fact, I guess I may as well tell you right now. I don't trust Severio."

"But you hardly know him," Jesa said incredulously. "How could you possibly form an opinion in a couple of minutes?"

"I've been around a lot more than you have, Jesa. I hope that experience has sharpened my intuition to some degree. I think Severio's a playboy. If you're just wanting to have a good time, then all's well and good. But if you're starting to be emotionally involved with him—and knowing you, you probably are—then I think you'd better take a closer look at him."

Jesa tried to keep the testiness out of her voice as she got up and refilled Sally's glass. She couldn't imagine why Sally, who had been pumping her for details of the affair only a few days ago, had suddenly done an about-face.

"I don't see how you can be so opinionated about someone you've hardly met, Sally."

"If you must know, I heard him talking to Bettina last night and . . ."

"Is that all? I know, Severio's an inveterate flirt. I know you don't have any fond feelings for Bettina. I don't particularly like her myself. But she has been awfully nice to Severio. He's just appreciative of it."

"Naturally they'd get along. They're both a couple of users."

Jesa left Sally's drink on the bar and walked back to the couch. She was annoyed that Sally was picking away at the first joyous mood that she'd experienced in almost a year. There was a long pause in the conversation. Sally got up and retrieved her replenished drink. Jesa pretended to be absorbed in combing the tangles out of her hair.

"I know it's a real downer to have me say all of this, Jesa. But I know how you are. You always want to see the best in everyone. You know you're naïve."

"Sally," Jesa said with a finality that surprised her, "I've always considered you to be my closest friend. But I don't look to you for maternal guidance. I'm perfectly capable of making my own decisions."

"You mean, 'My mind is made up, don't confuse me with facts.'"

"But you're not giving me facts," Jesa replied impatiently. "You're ranting on about some vague intuition that happens to be insulting to . . . my lover."

"Oh, God. You're not thinking of marrying him," Sally said with genuine horror in her voice.

"We haven't discussed anything like that yet."

"Yet?" Sally cried, sinking back onto the couch. "Oh, my God, Jesa. The first man you go to bed with after Ed's gone and you naturally think that you're wildly in love. I've warned you about confusing sexual attraction with the real thing."

"I hardly think that you're the person to talk about confusion in sexual attraction," Jesa blurted out.

The moment the words had left her lips she wanted to retract them. It was so unlike her to aim below the belt. She wasn't the sort of friend who used someone's personal life against them. Her hand started up to her mouth in an incomplete gesture. She looked at Sally, her eyes begging forgiveness.

"I'm not put out by your saying that," Sally said, denying the hurt she felt. "I'd be the first one to admit that I mess things up. But that doesn't mean that I don't know what I'm talking about when it comes to you."

She took another slug of her drink and stared at Jesa evenly. She knew that the conversation wouldn't be pleasant but she was prepared to tough it out.

"Look, Sal, I know I haven't been spending much time with you since I started to see Severio."

"If you're hinting that I'm jealous, you're way off the track," Sally answered with vehemence.

"It wouldn't be unnatural if you were," Jesa continued solicitously. "After all, you've been with me almost constantly since Ed's death; and you don't have anyone in your own life now."

The words cut Sally to the quick. Without waiting to weigh anything that Jesa suggested, she was on her feet. "Why the hell are you talking to me as though you were Lady Bountiful?" she demanded. "I come over to tell you I think this guy's a womanizer and you

169

don't even take the trouble to listen to what I'm saying."

"You're the one who isn't listening. And since you're telling me how much you know about my character I'll make an observation about yours: when you start to tie one on, you seem to lose the capacity to judge things."

Sally put her glass down on the coffee table with a crash and gathered up her purse. Jesa rose and crossed to her, touching her arm to stop her from leaving.

"I don't mean to be unkind. I'm in love with Severio and he's in love with me. He's made me extremely happy. I won't listen to his being berated. And that's that."

Sally stood for a moment, her lips pursed to suppress a quiver, her eyes angry.

"Lots of luck, Jesa," she said. She walked to the entrance hall and left without looking back.

Had she not been dressed for bed, Jesa might have run after her. She hated fights and disagreements. She couldn't understand her friend's distrust of Severio. Sally was usually free of both professional and personal jealousy. But Sally had been having a rough time lately. As she washed up the glasses and walked through the apartment turning out the lights, Jesa chided herself for not being more understanding. On another evening she might have jollied Sally out of her suspicions, but as it was the timing was so bad. She was caught up in the euphoria of her love affair and resented being brought down from a rare mood of hope. And she didn't need Sally's advice. She had only recently begun to realize how confined she was by the opinions and expectations of others. Now that she was beginning to feel a new sense of individuality and freedom, she wouldn't go back to running her life according to other people's notions, no matter how sincerely concerned they might be. "I'll give her a couple of days to cool off, and then I'll call her and we'll patch it up," she thought as she slipped out of her robe and pulled back the sheets.

As she settled down into the center of the bed, her thoughts were again filled with Severio, her body tingling with the memory of their lovemaking. She envisioned all the blissful times they would spend together. She would get out the cookbooks and arrange quiet dinners at home. She would take Severio up to the Connecticut place and show him the house she loved. She might even get out the paintbrushes again and dabble around by herself while he was working. Though her body was throbbing with fatigue, her mind was darting about, turning over one image and the next, shaping the future, coloring the world as though it waited for her like a clean canvas. It had been a long time since she'd felt this free play of her imagination. After the tremendous upheaval of Ed's death, she seemed to be too numb to think or feel much of anything. Now images drifted, floated, and metamorphosized in her mind with the same ease that sensual pleasure had come to her body.

She pulled the covers up to her chin and turned her head on the pillow so that she could see out the window. As a child she was always staring out the window. In fact she had such a habit of "going off" as her teachers called it, that she was punished several times. But there was one teacher who had been kind to her, who had placed her hand on Jesa's shoulder and whispered, "It's all right to daydream, Jesamine. The mind playing freely is the beginning of all new things." Strange that she should have such vivid recall of childhood memories now, when she had struggled unsuccessfully to remember anything while she was in therapy. But loving Severio had brought everything to the surface. There was something else that teacher had said to her that she must remember. She tried to recall it as she drifted off to sleep. Oh, yes. "Don't forget to pay attention to what's going on around you."

During the next few weeks Jesa had no time to pay attention to anything. The reviews of Severio's showing had been favorable, his prospects for future sales even better. Thanks to Bettina's interest, he had become not only an up-and-coming artist, but a social figure as well. He was in demand for every gathering— from stodgy sit-down dinners in the Park Avenue apartments of wealthy collectors to overcrowded, artsy happenings in lofts of old factory buildings. Jesa worried that such an active social life took him away from his work, but Severio explained how important it was to capitalize on his publicity and promised to get down to some real work as soon as all the shouting was over. Jesa acquiesced. She accompanied him on the almost nightly social obligations he felt were necessary to insure his future success. They didn't have time for the quiet evenings at home that she had envisioned. But there were always the afternoons, filled with hours of intimacy and lovemaking.

She had woken up quite late, still feeling exhausted from the previous evening's entertainments. She exercised and gave herself a facial before wandering out into the kitchen to get her morning coffee.

"Thank goodness you're up, Miz Mallick. I was wanting to run the vacuum, but I was afraid I'd wake you," Maggie said.

She turned the gas on underneath the coffee pot and watched Jesa sit at the kitchen table and run her hands through her loose hair. Mrs. Mallick was sure busy these days. Running around like a chicken without a head. Maggie hardly ever saw her, but she had to admit that she looked better than she used to. Even though she was out most nights, she had a certain bounciness that Maggie hadn't seen since the first years she'd worked for her. It must be that Mr. Euzielli. Like the song said, "Love makes you crazy." 'Course this Mr. Euzielli couldn't hold a candle to Mr. Mallick. He was just about the kindest man Maggie had ever worked for. She mourned him when he passed on, and still remembered him in her prayers. Still, your real concern had to be with the living, and it was a pleasure to see Mrs. Mallick take a new lease on life.

"What time is it anyway?" Jesa asked as she stirred the sugar into her cup.

"It's about noon," Maggie replied, taking a bite of a sandwich and looking at Jesa more closely. If memory served her right, Mrs. Mallick's hair was just a shade

173

lighter than it used to be. "Your hair sure looks nice like that."

"Do you really like it?" Jesa asked, pulling a golden strand around and looking at it. "Severio said it would look good, but I'm still not sure. Well, too late now."

"It looks just fine. just fine. Oh, I forgot to tell you, a package arrived from Bloomingdale's and another one from some store I don't remember the name of. I put them on the dining room table."

"Oh thanks," Jesa smiled and jumped up. "That's my new dress."

She took the packages into her bedroom and opened them with the excitement of a four-year-old pulling apart a Christmas present. She wanted to try on the diaphanous ice-blue caftan Severio had persuaded her to buy the other day. Once they'd started to go out so often, she realized that her wardrobe was in need of replenishment. Severio offered to come with her on a shopping trip. At first she thought he was just being considerate and that he would be bored out of his mind. It turned out that he actually enjoyed shopping and had a wonderful eye for what would look best on her. She no longer protested "It isn't me" as she had done when Sally had encouraged her to be more daring in her dress. She accepted any and all suggestions. As long as they came from Severio.

She swirled about in front of the mirror, happy to see that the alterations had been done so well. Then she folded the dress neatly and put it back into the box. She would take it down to Severio's and wear it tonight. She now kept a robe, makeup, and a few extra clothes at his loft and could get ready to go out from there. Severio rarely came up to her apartment, unless it was to pick her up.

Slipping into a poncho, jeans, and loafers, she quickly tied a scarf around her hair and started to leave. Maggie waved at her over the roar of the vacuum cleaner. She dashed back from the front door, yelling, "I forgot the dress!" and reappeared a moment later, saying goodbye again.

When she reached the lobby, Sophie Moss was standing near the marble table. It was strewn with several dozen carnations, ferns, a frog, and a book.

"Oh, Jesa, be a darling and come over here for a minute. I know you have such artistic taste. I got this book," she held up a volume titled *Zen and the Art of Flower Arrangement*, "but I think it's about religion, not flowers."

Even though she was in a hurry to get to Severio's for their afternoon rendezvous, Jesa was in such a good mood that she couldn't ignore Sophie. She put down her packages and picked up the carnations and started putting them into the frog.

"Thank you, darling. It's so good to see you! It seems as though you just visit the building lately. But I told the people at the Tenants' Beautification Committee that you were with us in spirit if not in body. An old friend of Abbie's is in the flower business, and he keeps sending me all these flowers, and I just thought, 'Why not share them with my neighbors? Make the place look more like spring.'"

"I think that's very nice of you, Sophie."

"Look, a woman my age does what she can to keep busy. What else am I going to do to celebrate the spring? Walk in the park and hold hands?"

She paused for the slightest moment, snapped the stem off a carnation and looked at Jesa with a wicked smile on her face.

"So come on, darling, you can tell an old friend like me, when's the wedding?"

"What wedding?" Jesa asked, genuinely confused for a moment.

"Come on. You and Mr. Euzielli. When are you going to tie the knot?"

"I . . . we don't have any marriage plans, Sophie."

"That's not what it looks like from where I sit. You should marry him soon, Jesa. Don't let this one slip through the net."

Jesa planted the ferns in the centerpiece with increasing speed, saying nothing. Sophie intuited that she'd used the wrong words in describing marriage as entrapment.

"I guess I shouldn't be so nosy, dear. Regardless of what crazy ideas are going on today, because I don't think that new couple on the fourth floor are actually married, the one sure road to happiness is to be with a man who's devoted, a good provider, and interested in a healthy physical relationship."

Jesa could feel a blush rising to her temples. The relief doorman, a young Puerto Rican named Juan, stared out at the street with such intense interest that Jesa knew he was listening.

"Of course in my day," Sophie went on without

inhibition, "there wasn't much talk about sex, but believe me, we knew it was there. As a woman who was happily married for over forty years, I can swear by it. Dear crazy Abbie always used to say, 'I don't mind if you burn the food or if your hair isn't curly, as long as you like to cuddle.' "

Jesa cleared her throat and fished around for another sprig of fern. The thought of Abbie and Sophie "cuddling" caused her cheeks to dimple.

"See there, you know what I mean," Sophie laughed.

She glanced over her shoulder, saw Juan, and continued in a whisper that was loud enough to be heard across the lobby.

"And you know what they say about buying the cow when there's free milk."

Jesa was so amazed at Sophie's Rabelaisian turn of mind that she broke into laughter.

"I wouldn't worry about that, Sophie."

"Well, not just yet. Now you're having fun. But keep it in mind. And darling, I kept that picture of you from the paper. All the girls were so impressed to find out I know you. 'Blond and lean as a whippet'—that's what it said about you. I was so proud you are my neighbor."

"Thank you, Sophie. Thank you," Jesa got out between giggles. "I really have to be going now."

"Sure, sure, I understand. Thanks for putting this together, Jesa. And *mazeltov*."

Jesa picked up her packages, let Sophie kiss her on the cheek, and said goodbye. As soon as Jesa was out

177

of the door, an expression of deep befuddlement came over Sophie's face. "What *is* a whippet?" she wondered out loud.

Jesa smiled to herself all the way down in the taxi. She tried to remember Sophie's conversation verbatim so that she could tell Severio about it. Sophie's unabashed nosiness and forthright manner, though touched with the ridiculous, were a relief after all the people she'd been meeting lately. Their style of communication reminded her of a hip debutante ball— there was more booze, some drugs, lots of loose language, but underneath it all, it was still a group of people sizing each other up for credentials. She would be relieved when Severio had drifted from center stage and they had more time together.

She tipped the cab driver too much and ran up the stairs to Severio's. She felt so glad to be alive that her body had a new lightness. She had been almost ashamed to survive after Ed's death. Afraid somehow that her enjoyment of anything was a betrayal of him. The conscious knowledge that he would want her to be happy didn't seem to alter matters. Now the weight was lifted, and she moved with buoyancy.

"Whew, I feel like Ginger Rogers," she panted as Severio opened the door.

"I have no idea what you're talking about," he said in a low voice as he drew her into the room.

Before she could explain, he was kissing her. She returned his embrace as eagerly as if they had been the victims of a long separation, instead of having seen each other only the night before. And here it was again, the effortless renewal of desire, the satisfaction that increased appetite. She was crazy about the man. The only times she wanted to be away from him were to prepare herself to be with him again. Silly Sophie had been right: the road to happiness was to be with someone you loved deeply with the future stretching before you. She clutched him more tightly as they lay down on the bed together.

The colors from the skylight changed from the clear, brightness of springtime afternoon to the vivid blue of early evening.

"Jesa?"

"Oh, don't wake me up," she crooned, wrapping her arms about him lazily.

"I think it must be after six. We'd better get dressed."

"I don't want to. Why don't we start a rumor that you have mononucleosis? Then we won't have to go out for months."

"I'd love to stay home too, but that guy from Dallas is in town again. Of course, if you really don't feel like it . . ."

"No. No. No sacrifice is too great. We'll go."

After they'd showered, Severio leaned against the bathroom door and watched her put on her makeup.

"Doesn't this ruin the final effect for you?" she asked and she patted a touch of pale blue shadow on her lids.

He shook his head. The possession of the kind of woman he had coveted for so long was still with him. He enjoyed watching Jesa transform herself from the passionate bedmate into the graceful, reserved lady be could take into society.

"Really, Severio," she said, as she ran the brush through her hair a final time, "I don't think I can keep up this pace much longer."

"I know. It's a drag."

"You're just saying that. I've watched you. You get a kick out of all the crowds, you dissolute artist type. I want us to have more peace and quiet. More time to talk."

"Talk? Do you really want to talk?" he asked, his eyelids drooping into the sleepy, seductive look she knew so well.

"Believe it or not I do. There are so many things I don't know about you. I know nothing about your ex-wife, or your family."

"My family spoiled me rotten."

"But you weren't an only child?"

"No. But I was the only boy. I had a helluva lot of aunts, cousins, not to mention three sisters."

"So that's how you developed the strongest ego on the eastern seaboard. They must be awfully proud of you now."

"I don't know. I never see them."

"I suppose I'm idealizing it because I never had a family, except Ed. I think if I did I'd see them all the time."

"You are idealizing it. But then you're an idealist. My lifestyle is so different from theirs. I have no reason to go back. It wasn't just the poverty and the overcrowding and the overbearing affection. It was the damn sameness of it all: work, eat, sleep, and work again. I knew I wasn't going to live like that from the time I was a kid."

"So now we play, eat, sleep, and play again," she teased.

"Don't get on my case, Jesa. Believe me, you're lucky when you have only yourself to think about."

He held her at arm's length and surveyed her, touching her hair into place and straightening the pendant around her neck.

"You look fine," he said approvingly. "Now let's get going. We don't want to keep Lyman waiting."

Lyman Reims, the curator from Dallas, was already seated at their table at the Coach House. Jesa soothed away his impatience with a few gracious words. Severio watched her as she chatted with Lyman. He loved to show her off. She was such an asset in any social situation, her natural gentility the perfect foil for his aggressiveness. After the meal they were supposed to go to a gallery to see some "Living Art," but Jesa suggested that Lyman might want to walk through Washington Square. The trees, she pointed out, were starting to sprout and the crowds of young people and musicians who frequented the park in warmer weather were bound to be there. Lyman thanked her for wanting to show him around.

"Guess there's plenty of things wrong with the city of New York, Mrs. Mallick, but you're not one of 'em."

Jesa was enjoying the stroll so much that she hated to think of going indoors. She didn't have much idea what "Living Art" might be, and when they finally got to the gallery she was even more at sea. Great swatches of parachute silk had been dyed various brilliant colors and hung from the ceiling and the walls. If she craned her neck over the crowd she could see a young man sitting in his underwear and sucking spaghetti into his mouth in slow motion. The neon sign next to him proclaimed "Eater." In another area of the room, a nude young woman sat in the classic pose of Rodin's "Thinker" against a backdrop of computer readouts. Jesa didn't have much stomach for pushing through the assemblage to view "Sleeper." She had a pretty good idea what that would be already.

"I think I'd have to do a real snow job to sell this in Dallas," Lyman whispered to her.

"Only in New York," she whispered back.

"Jesa's a traditionalist. She doesn't like anything past Impressionism," Severio said.

"That's not entirely true," she answered. "But this does look rather like a college hazing."

"Betcha didn't like Andy Warhol either," Lyman grinned.

"Not enough to want to buy him. I already have soup cans at home and they only cost me 49 cents."

"Just between you and me and the lamp post, Mrs. Mallick, I couldn't agree with you more. Now that I've seen *Eating, Thinking, and Sleeping,* I guess I'll go into the other room and see if they have a more lascivious activity on display. I'll rejoin you in a little while."

Jesa smiled as Lyman took his leave. She turned to Severio, took his hand, and rolled her eyes to the ceiling.

"Patience, Jesa. Do you mind if I ask a few people back to the loft for drinks?"

"I guess not."

"You don't sound very enthused."

By way of an answer she looked into his eyes. Surely he could tell that she had no interest in anything but being with him, and that she was just put off by all these shenanigans around her. "This just seems so worthless," she said, *sotto voce.*

"Relax. Don't take it seriously."

Once they were back at his place she fell into the familiar role of hostess, arranging glasses and ice cubes and digging around for a plate of snacks. Lyman hoisted himself up onto one of the counter tops and watched her bustle around, talking nonstop about all the new developments in the Southwest and encouraging her to come out for a visit. The buzzer rang a few minutes afterward and Severio went to the door and let in half a dozen people, none of whom Jesa had any recollection of meeting before. He pulled several over-sized pillows from their bed and tossed them onto the floor near the skylight.

"Oh, my God, a skylight! I didn't even think they existed anymore," squeaked a woman with close-cropped hair, whose face was slashed with streaks of "punk" makeup.

Jesa thought she looked vaguely familiar, but couldn't place her. Severio introduced her and Lyman to the others. She could only remember the name of one of them, David something or other, who had put the "Living Art" show together. Jesa extended her hand. She had disliked the show so much that she couldn't think of a single complimentary thing to say. As she looked into his sallow face, which could have been an utterly wasted twenty-five or a well-preserved forty, she fell back on her hostess role.

"Would you like something to drink?"

"Whatcha got? Some kinda juice will be fine. Oh boy, do I have the munchies! Anything to eat around here?"

Jesa handed him a plate of cheeses without replying.

"Did you see the way she did that?" he yelped, turning and gesturing to the others. "Did you see that? Hey, Jesa, you've got this great fluidity of movement. How'd y'like to be in my next show? I'm gonna get into more and more rarefied forms of activity—y'know 'Handing Plate to Guest,' 'Cleaning the Ear With Q-Tip.' Whoa! What an idea!"

"What are you talking about? It was my idea to make 'Thinker' a woman. If I hadn't come up with that, no one would have been interested in the show," the woman with the crew cut snapped.

"Oh," Jesa said, "you were the woman in the show. I didn't recognize you with your clothes on."

"I've heard that line before," the woman sneered.

This brought a peal of laughter from the others that was all out of proportion to the humor of the statement. Even to Jesa's untrained eye, it was obvious that they were high on something. She looked around for Severio. He was standing over near his worktable listening to one of the young women.

"So who do you think has more class? Pace or

184

Castelli? My old teacher at Pratt says I'm not ready to show yet, but what the hell, he's so ancient he thinks working in acrylics is revolutionary."

"I'll . . . get some more cheese," Jesa muttered to no one in particular. She walked back into the kitchen and leaned her head against the refrigerator door. It was so cool and bare. It was stark and comforting, the way Severio's loft was when it wasn't invaded by all these freaky people. Why was it so important for Severio to be with them? With the exception of Lyman, who had some trace of an outdated gentlemanliness, they were such a bunch of louts. But perhaps she was being unfair. They were mostly younger than she. Perhaps she'd led such a quiet life that she judged things by old standards like manners, instead of looking at the "whole" person.

"Don't jump, darling. It's me," Severio said as he put his arms around her from behind. She turned around, nuzzling her head into his chest for a moment. He took her chin in his hands and turned her face up to his.

"They won't stay too long. Wanna stay the night?" he joked.

"They're so . . . so . . . rude," she whispered.

"And you're so uptight, darling. Just relax. Go along with things."

He bent down and took a playful bite out of her cheek. She was instantly reassured, just by his physical presence. The voices from the other room were becoming more strident. She slipped out from his embrace and put some more food on the plates.

185

"If they don't leave in twenty minutes, could you tell them I have a migraine?" She grinned as she walked past him back into the studio.

David was now standing in the middle of the room with the others sitting around him, as though he were a famous guru. Lyman had withdrawn from the group and was sprawled out on the bed, sipping bourbon, and watching the proceedings.

"Let's face it, there were never any really great women artists," David said emphatically, punctuating his statement with little jerks and leaps.

"You're full of it," Marisa shrieked back. The other voices joined her in cacophonous dispute.

"There have been some fine women artists," a soft voice said.

Jesa felt the room grow quiet around her and realized that the last pronouncement had been hers. She didn't know why she had spoken out. It was so unlike her. Perhaps it was just a general annoyance with the shouting.

"Wow! Support from unexpected quarters," Marisa cried.

"I just mean that I do like the work of Mary Cassatt, and Georgia O'Keefe, and more recently Nevelson, Frankenthaler, Agnes Martin and . . ." she ran out of names ". . . others."

The room was quiet and since she had the floor she continued in a soft, reasonable voice.

"Perhaps we should ask what we mean by great. Perhaps pushing for acclaim may not have much to do with greatness."

She hadn't heard that "let's go back to basics" voice come out of her since she'd been eighteen years old. Surprisingly, no one seemed to notice that there was a sophomoric tinge to what she was saying. They started up with cross-interrogations and accusations. She settled herself down on a pillow, declined a joint that Marisa held out to her, and sipped her wine. Severio was sitting on the bed next to Lyman, refilling his glass. He nodded his head intently to whatever it was that Lyman was saying, but paused long enough to turn to her and shape his fingers into a "V" sign.

"Here I thought this Jesa was some establishment type, and she turns out to be really wild, really Fauvist," David beamed.

If they're not going to leave, I might as well go with it as Severio says, Jesa thought, sipping her wine. Marisa caught her looking at Severio.

"He's really something, isn't he? There's lots of chicks who'd like to be in your shoes. What are you anyway, a collector?"

"Not really. I own some paintings. And I paint a little bit," Jesa said shyly.

"What do you mean paint a little bit? You mean you do miniatures or you mean you dabble?"

"I guess I dabble. That is to say, I take the work seriously, but I'm not that talented. I don't really pursue it day to day. I've never really tried to sell."

"Yeah," Marisa said conspiratorily, "You know, I'm not really connected to David here. I just needed some extra bread. I'm pretty good at illustrations, though."

"You should meet my friend Sally. She makes a

good living doing children's books. Maybe she could give you some advice."

It wasn't the first time that evening that Jesa had thought of Sally. Indeed she'd made it through the show at the gallery by imagining what Sally's comments might have been. She couldn't wait to call her old friend on the phone and tell her all about the evening. Sally would howl. She would understand how Jesa felt. She'd been meaning to call Sally for weeks. Now she had the excuse of asking advice for a young artist. Jesa knew that Sally was always receptive to such requests and made a mental note to call her the following day.

She was feeling very mellow and sleepy after her third glass of wine. She lay back on the pillows and watched Marisa dance with one of the nameless young men who were part of David's entourage. David had shifted over to Lyman and was trying to make points with him. It was after two in the morning when they finally left, shouting and energetic, bumping their way down the stairs in various states of inebriation. Luckily Lyman had been persuaded to go with them.

"I thought they'd never go," she gasped as she slipped the caftan from her shoulders and went into the bathroom to brush her teeth.

"You were great, Jesa. You ought to have been a politician's wife," Severio called out to her as he took off his clothes and stretched out in the bed.

She pulled on her robe and walked back into the studio, disgusted at the disarray. She picked up glasses and ashtrays and started to carry them into the kitchen.

"Forget the clutter and come give me a nice toothpasty kiss," Severio yawned.

She put down the glasses and took off her robe. He threw back the covers and moved over, making a place for her. The comfort of being received by him like this wiped away her grouchiness. If she were going to have the heady experience of a private affair with a very public man, she reasoned, she would have to pay the price. It wasn't as though he were neglecting her for the company of other women. She could see that he did have to take advantage of his recent success. She turned her face to him and smiled. It might be a bit bumpy just now, but they would work it out.

"Severio, I wish you could come up to the country with me. It's so beautiful up there now. You could work and . . ."

"You know Lyman commissioned me to do something for him, so I guess I'll have to get to work."

"That's marvelous! Why didn't you tell me?"

"I just found out tonight. I think you helped to swing the deal. He really likes you. So, if you want to, we can go up to your precious house in Connecticut this Friday and stay for four or five days."

"Oh, thank you! I know you'll love it. The house is so special and private. And the woods. Oh, the woods just make you feel like a kid again."

"You make me feel like a kid again," he answered huskily.

He turned his body away from hers long enough to

switch out the bedside lamp. Then he was in her arms again.

Friday was particularly busy. She stayed home and helped Maggie to clean out the old maid's room. She'd used it for storage for several years and now thought of turning it into a workroom. Severio had encouraged her to start painting again. He said she had a keen eye and needed an activity. She drove down to Pearl Paint on Canal Street and purchased some supplies. On her way back to the apartment, she dashed into Zabar's and bought bags full of special delicacies to take with them. When she got home she arranged them in the wicker hamper, wrapped some wine glasses in napkins, and added a bottle of good rosé. If the weather held fine, they would picnic on the hill behind the house tomorrow; if not, they would lunch in bed together. "Solitude and fresh air," she smiled to herself as she packed up everything and loaded it into the car. She was waiting for him to arrive when the phone rang.

"Darling, it's me."

"It doesn't matter if you're going to be late. We can still get away before the really awful traffic starts."

"That's what I called to tell you. I can't come."

Jesa took the phone away from her ear and held it to her heart. She mustn't burden him with her disappointment.

"Bettina just called me up and reminded me that she's having a dinner party for Lyman before he goes back to Dallas. She told me about it weeks ago, but it just slipped my mind," she heard when she'd slowly brought the receiver back to her ear.

"Couldn't you tell her that you've made other plans?" she asked tentatively.

"Now, Jesa, you of all people know that wouldn't be polite. She's still miffed because we disappeared the night of the opening. And she has been helpful to me. I just hate to let her down."

He sounded so contrite that she almost forgot her own feeling of being let down.

"Shall we put Connecticut off 'til next weekend?" she asked.

"No. No, darling. You go on alone. I know you've been straining at the bit to get up there. Let's face it, I don't get much work done when I have the distraction of your beautiful body around. I will go to Bettina's. But I'll also barricade myself in the studio and get started on the painting for Lyman."

"All right," she answered half-heartedly.

"When will you be back?"

"I guess I'll come back on Tuesday," she answered, not fully realizing that the decision to go had more or less been made for her.

"Would you like me to come up and help you pack the car? Give you a goodbye kiss?"

"That's not practical. But it's sweet of you to ask. If I'm going to miss the traffic, I guess I should go pretty soon."

"Darling, do you forgive me?"

"There's nothing to forgive. But I'll miss you."

"I'll miss you too. Give me a call as soon as you get

back. I love you. Enjoy the house."

As soon as she'd hung up, she felt all the disappointment return. She hated the idea of being away from him, even for a few days. Besides, she didn't like to drive alone. Sally. She would give her that call she'd been postponing. She really had missed her friend's company. A nice weekend in the country would be the best setting to have the long talks that could put their relationship back on the old footing. She dialed the number by rote, thinking that she wouldn't even mention the argument. They were both big enough to forget it. She would simply tell Sally that she missed her and wanted her company. There was no answer on the other end of the line.

Chapter 8

"Really, Miss Gold, if you'd come more often I'd at least have your hair in a shape I could work with," Mr. Ralph sighed. "As it is . . ."

He picked up a lock of Sally's hair and let it fall, wagging his head sorrowfully. Sally stared straight ahead into the mirror, avoiding the glance of regular customers who would never allow themselves to degenerate into such a state of disrepair. Mr. Ralph worked valiantly for over an hour, but when he swiveled the chair around and handed her a mirror so that she could see the back of her hair, it was obvious that he was not happy with his work.

"Perhaps if you bought a little top-knot of curls it might help," he suggested half-heartedly.

192

"Sure. I mean, if you think it'll help."

She might have known it was a mistake to try to glamorize herself for the awards dinner. Glamor just wasn't in her repertoire. Whenever she tried, it only made it more obvious. Mr. Ralph found a cluster of curls that matched her hair almost perfectly and spent another fifteen minutes anchoring it to the crown of her head. She struggled to think of a compliment that might reward his efforts. When she couldn't think of anything to say, she left a large tip on the counter and walked home, conscious that every breeze might dislodge her sculpted curls. As soon as she settled into her apartment, she reached for the phone to call Jesa.

She had tried to make the call several times during the last weeks, but the bitterness of the exchange between them always stopped her. She still felt she was right about Severio and couldn't force herself to make an apology. She had gone over Jesa's accusations again and again. What if she were interfering and jealous, when she prided herself on being solicitous? The self-doubt made her miserable. And Jesa had certainly been right about one thing: Sally's life was no model of happiness. She would just tell Jesa that she was sorry and that she wanted them to make it up.

When there was no answer at the other end of the line, she turned back to the task of fixing herself up for the evening. She bathed, took her green velveteen suit out of the dry cleaner's bag, and started to dress. Ellman would be at her apartment in another fifteen minutes and here she was, totally unprepared though she'd devoted all of the afternoon to remodeling herself. She poured herself a drink and carried it back to the bathroom, balancing it on the rim of the sink. She pulled out all the makeup paraphernalia she'd kept for ages but never used. False eyelashes were too much, but she might take a look at an article titled "Minimizing Your Liabilities" that she'd kept in the cosmetic bag. She struggled for about twenty minutes, sipping as she tried to shade her upturned nose. By the time the doorbell sounded, she was cursing and accusing Rebecca of having hidden the face powder.

She rushed to the door, still in her slip, flung it back, and told Ellman to come in and make himself comfortable.

"Help yourself to a drink," she yelled, racing back into the bathroom. "I'll be ready in about five minutes if I don't decide to drown myself in the tub."

When she came into the living room, buttoning up her blouse, Ellman was sitting on the couch reading the paper with Rebecca in his lap. He walked over to her, pecked her on the cheek, and smiled at her.

"You look very nice, Sally."

"I look horrible. Don't make it worse by flattering me."

"As you will."

"So you do think I look horrible?"

"I can't win with you. I give you a compliment and you accuse me of insincerity. If I say nothing, you act as though I'm insulting you."

"I'm sorry, Ellman. Really I am. I just get so damn nervous. I'm supposed to give some sort of acceptance speech and I haven't even thought about what I'm going to say."

"Just say thank you and that you're honored."

"Sure. Sure. You make it sound very simple."

"It is simple, my dear. Now calm down."

He put his arms around her shoulders and gently massaged the back of her neck. His eyes peered out from behind his glasses, affectionate and friendly. She bit her lip and looked up at him.

"I just feel such a wreck," she sighed forlornly. "Everything has me so upset. I haven't done any work for about three days. And I've been so worried to think that Jesa is angry with me."

Her voice trailed off. She disengaged herself and walked over to the bar.

"Don't worry about it. You have years of friendship behind you. You'll make it up."

"It's noble of you not to say, 'I told you so,' " she said, as she poured another vodka. "But you did tell me so. I shouldn't have opened my big mouth."

Gazing at her reflection in the mirror over the bar, she gingerly touched the top knot. It was all wrong. She took a sip of her drink and reached up, pulling the pins that secured the hairpiece. She yanked it free and threw it on the floor. Rebecca trotted over and sniffed at it suspiciously.

"I'll be with you in a minute," she cried, rushing into the bathroom and grabbing the brush. "I just can't go like that. I feel like Marie Antoinette or something. With my luck it'd fall off into the soup."

She pulled the brush through her hair violently, screwed on her best pair of gold earrings, and turned

195

out the light. Ellman was waiting in the hallway. He handed her a small box. She opened it hurriedly to see two perfect sprigs of lily of the valley nestled in the tissue.

"Oh, Ellman, this is damn nice of you. I was in such a flap that I didn't even notice you'd brought them."

"I thought of getting a corsage, but I guess that's not done anymore," he said, pinning the delicate flowers onto the lapel of her suit.

"You couldn't tell by me. I stopped having what people would call a normal social life when I didn't get asked to the senior prom. But they are lovely. It's so thoughtful of you."

She kissed him impulsively. He put his big arms around her and pulled her to him, returning the kiss. He was certainly putting more than brotherly affection into it this time. The thought flitted across her mind that she might want to go to bed with him. But that meant risking their present relationship. She couldn't bear the thought of losing him as her friend. Still, it would be nice to cuddle up to that bearish body, to know that there was real feeling between them and that she never had to pretend she was something she wasn't. And she knew from experience that these quiet types were often a pleasant surprise.

"Do you feel better now?" he asked, as he released her.

"Yes. I think I'm fine."

She felt very organized and hopeful as she flicked off the lights and told Rebecca to be a good dog until they got home. She would put her anxieties behind her, at

196

least for the next couple of hours. She would be gracious and friendly. Afterward, she and Ellman could be alone together and she would tell him just how much she appreciated him.

They chatted and joked all the way to the hotel where the dinner was being held. They were so relaxed and convivial with each other that the cabbie sized them up as a long-married couple who still have the good fortune to really enjoy each other's company. As they pulled up to the entrance of the Waldorf, she clutched his hand one last time and gave him her bravest smile.

"Sorry I was so crazy. I'm okay now."

"I knew you would be," he assured her, helping her out of the cab.

A sign in the lobby announced that the Children's Book Awards would be held in the Empire Room. It was a huge place, with vivid blue carpets and gold and white decorations. There was a small dance floor and a decent-sounding combo that pounded out old favorites for those who were energetic enough to dance. As they moved through the throng, several people came forward to shake Sally's hand and congratulate her. Some of them she recognized, but most she didn't. She whispered to Ellman that she felt like the Queen Mother on a tour of the colonies. The hostess directed them to their table, which was up toward the dais where the awards would be presented.

"Yoo hoo! Over here," she heard a familiar voice cry.

It was Joan Carlton Webster, Sally's collaborator. Joan had had a moderate success as the author of many children's books, but it wasn't until the publisher has teamed her up with Sally that they had skyrocketed to the top of the kiddie-book market. Though their names were linked because of the Troillina series, they barely knew each other. They had met a couple of times at the publisher's and for luncheons. The only time Joan had visited Sally's apartment, she had referred to it as "a quaint pad." Mostly they communicated by telephone. Sally could always hear squeals, TV sets, dogs, and servants in the background, for Joan was the mother of five in addition to her career.

"It's so good to see you," Joan cried, as Sally introduced Ellman to Joan's husband Arthur. "It was really quite a day. I was up at six to get the kids off to school, then I had to make an eleven o'clock meeting and chair the Citizens' Committee for a Better Environment. After that I ran to the beauty parlor, took Dennis to the orthodontist, and put in a couple of hours writing before tucking them all in."

Just listening to her made Sally feel tired. She couldn't imagine how Joannie had actually fashioned her life into a replica of one of those modern, integrated women in the TV commercials. She was perpetually bouncy and positive, dispensing maternal concern and unwavering cheerfulness to anything that crossed her path.

"Isn't it exciting!" Joan bubbled on. "It's such an honor."

"And you deserve it, sweetie," Arthur smiled.

Sally thought they looked like cloned Cheshire cats, purring and oozing charm all over the place.

"Yeah, it's nice that we've been chosen. Who are the judges? Did you have to pay them off, Arthur?" Sally asked.

The creases in Arthur's face, formed by a perpetual show of goodwill, were drawn down temporarily. He let go of Joan's hand and fingered his bow tie.

"Just a joke," Ellman put in. "Sally's always joking."

"Of course," Arthur replied, regaining his composure. "Now that balding gentleman at the head table is from some sort of publishers' association. A Mr. Johnston, I think."

"Yes, honey, it's Richard Johnston," Joan said, always ready with an assist. "He said his grandchildren just love the books."

"And that man sitting next to him is a very well-known psychiatrist. He's the representative of the Children's Mental Health Association. I think his name is Hugo Bridgeman."

Sally felt the muscles in her throat constrict. She turned her head as casually as she could. It was Hugo Bridgeman all right. She hadn't seen him in over fifteen years. The face had settled a bit, so that the square jaw was now just a little jowly. The hair had thinned slightly around the forehead. But the eyes were the same. She turned her head back to Joan quickly. At the same time she clutched Ellman's knee under the table.

"Isn't he cute?" Joannie inquired.

"I'd like a drink," Sally said quickly.

Joannie and Arthur exchanged a glance.

"Aren't you going to ask me to dance, sweetie?"

Joannie said. Without waiting for an answer, she took Arthur's arm, helped him out of his seat, and steered him onto the dance floor.

"What the matter?" Ellman wanted to know.

"That man. That Hugo Bridgeman. I used to live with him. Years and years ago. Oh, my God."

"Don't get upset, Sally."

"You don't understand. He was . . ."

"What?"

"True love. Ruined my maiden faith. All that stuff."

While Sally told the waiter that she wanted a vodka on the rocks, Ellman reached for an olive, craning his head ever so slightly to get a better view of the head table.

"He's very handsome," he said, trying to make it sound like a simple statement of fact.

They were silent as the waiter placed the drink in front of the little name card with "Ms. Sally Gold" engraved on it. She reached for the glass.

"Bonsai!"

"I think you'd better go easy. You've got a whole dinner between now and the presentations. I don't mean to get on your case. . . ."

It wasn't like Ellman to use slang expression. He hoped that lingo would make his warning sound casual. He knew Sally couldn't abide lecturing. She nodded and put the glass back down.

"Right. Thanks, Ellman. You're right."

The music had stopped playing. Sally could see Joannie's paisley ruffled dress coming through the crowd.

"Oh, I can't face rare roast beef and Joannie. Dance with me."

"I can't dance a step. I'd only embarrass you."

"Then let's go downstairs to the lobby and look at the luggage shops. Anything,"

But it was too late. The waiters were busy putting down the salads. Joan adjusted the flounces of her dress and leaned over to talk to Ellman. Arthur, who had apparently been told to keep Sally occupied, started to discuss property values in Westchester.

By the time the entrée was served Arthur had given her all the details of future mortgage rates. Their publisher came over and shook hands with everyone and drew up a chair. He'd been approached by a toy company that wanted to make Troillina dolls. Sally pushed aside her plate and munched on a celery stick while he told them of increased sales and profits. Joan shrieked with enthusiasm. They agreed to meet with lawyers and discuss the deal later in the week. Sally tried to pay attention, but the hairs on the back of her neck were standing up. She was sure that Hugo Bridgeman was looking at her, but she couldn't turn around.

Despite her promise of restraint, she kept drinking steadily. By the end of the meal she felt removed from everything. The room buzzed around her. The first speaker stood up and went to the rostrum. He checked his notes, adjusted the microphone, and boomed out a series of unsuccessful jokes. He was followed by a lean, no-nonsense woman from some educational group who introduced the judges and gave a long-winded speech on literary habits of grammar school children. Then Hugo took the microphone.

Sally gazed at the ice cream that was slowly melting in the silver bowl. Ellman motioned one of the waiters to fill her coffee cup. He patted her hand and turned around to listen to the handsome Dr. Bridgeman.

". . . and Troillina has captured the heart of America's youth, not just because it is colorful and entertaining, but because it probes the fundamental traumas of the child's experience. As that master in our field, Dr. Bruno Bettelheim, has often pointed out . . ."

Sally blinked and shuddered. Hugo's voice rang out authoritatively. He had used just that tone when he spoke to her in their tiny apartment so many years ago. She turned in her chair and looked at the guests at the head table. She could see that Hugo's mouth was still moving, but she couldn't make out his words. "No bitterness," she told herself, "it's all in the past." But rational injunctions failed her. She could feel a tide of hostility sweeping through her. Here were all these people hanging on Hugo's words, swallowing his sage advice as she had so many years ago. When he'd concluded his speech a wave of enthusiastic applause broke out. He acknowledged the audience with suave humility and started back to his seat. A tall, blond woman wearing a sleek dress that exposed her rather athletic arms and shoulders moved toward Hugo. He embraced her and smiled again. It was Inge. Now, presumably, Mrs. Hugo Bridgeman. Sally couldn't imagine why she hadn't spotted her before. Her hand trembled as she pushed the coffee cup aside and finished off another vodka.

"I think we're next," Joan whispered in her ear.

The master of ceremonies cleared his throat several times and tapped the microphone until there was quiet in the room.

"And now the ladies you've been waiting to meet and applaud: Ms. Joan Carlton Webster and Ms. Sally Gold."

Joan gave Sally a gentle kick under the table, and rose to acknowledge the ovation. The minute Sally started to get up she realized that she hadn't gauged her drinking capacity as well as she'd thought. The room seemed to tilt with her and the faces of the crowd overlapped and melted into each other. Joan started toward the dais, flinging her hand back for Sally. Sally reached for the hand, knocking over a glass of water. Ellman quickly put a napkin over the mess and gave her an encouraging smile. She clung to Joan's hand and was led up to the main table, behind the judges and speakers. As she passed Hugo, their eyes met for the slightest moment, but neither of them said anything.

"I have always considered writing for children to be a special trust," Joan began, dewy-eyed. "Being the mother of several little ones myself, I know just how important books can be in child development."

Sally couldn't concentrate on the rest of it, because she was frantically trying to come up with something to say. She pulled in her stomach muscles and tried to look erect and serious when she saw Inge smiling at her. Joan piped on in the vein of motherhood and apple pie. The audience nodded their heads and whispered appreciative comments to each other. When she'd concluded her speech, they gave her a very warm hand. She backed away from the microphone and motioned Sally toward it. As she gripped the microphone, Sally realized that her hands were sweating.

"I guess I want to say thank you to everyone," she began uncertainly. "To Joan especially, and to our publisher . . ."

She searched frantically for another thought, another sentence. The audience was deathly still.

"To the panel of judges . . ." She saw Hugo and Inge's eyes, acknowledged the smiles that were plastered on their faces with a tentative smile of her own.

"When I was a kid, I loved to read. I never thought it was educational. I just thought it was a real good escape."

She paused again, knowing that she'd said the wrong thing.

"I loved to draw and paint too, 'cause beautiful colors are even more of an escape than words."

The lady from the educational association was now looking at her sternly. The attentive looks on the faces in the audience were melting into the immobile, rigid stares of mannequins.

"When I grew up, I found out that escaping was an expensive thing to do. Y'see, I wanted to be a real artist . . ."

Her eyes flitted back to Hugo. Didn't he remember how she used to be?

"I guess I've had just about every crappy job I could

get the minimum wage for. . . ."

The nights she'd climbed the stairs to their dingy apartment, her feet so tired and swollen from working the late shift at the restaurant that she was beyond pain and only wanted to giggle. The nights she'd sat at the kitchen table quietly (so as not to disturb his sleep) arranging the coins the customers had left for her in neat piles. Didn't he remember?

Hugo's face had the look of hypnotic boredom of a late-night TV watcher. She wanted nothing more than for the ground to open and swallow her up.

"I don't really know why you're giving me this award. I sure don't think Troillina is educational or uplifting or anything like that. But I guess she sells. It means I don't have to . . . Oh, screw it. It pays the rent. So thanks."

There was a rustle of laughter. A small minority of the audience clapped enthusiastically, but most barely put their hands together. The master of ceremonies grabbed the microphone and encouraged the audience to "give these talented ladies a hand."

Sally staggered back to the table, where Ellman was congratulating Joan and already gathering Sally's purse up for a quick departure.

They drove back to her apartment in absolute silence. Sally wanted to go upstairs alone, but Ellman was right behind her. As soon as she'd thrown off her wrap, she collapsed on the couch and broke into tears. Rebecca whined and jumped around her crumpled form in confusion. Ellman picked the little dog up and took her to the bedroom and closed the door.

"Why'd you do that?" Sally cried.

"Because I want to have a serious talk with you without any interference."

"Oh, please. Not now. I feel just dreadful."

"And you'll feel dreadful tomorrow morning and the morning after that. It has to stop, Sally."

His voice had a tone she'd never heard before, hurt and angry. She started to tell him that she was sorry if she'd caused him any embarrassment, but he raised his hand to cut her off.

"There's no point in excuses or recriminations. You may think that I'm a very conventional person, but I don't really give a damn what other people think. I care about you. You aren't capable of handling this alone. You must get some help. I know a place you can go. My sister-in-law dried out there last year. It's a good quiet place with a reliable staff."

"What are you talking about? I can't do that! If you think I'm crazy now . . . well, I'd just crack up completely if I did that."

"You have to, Sally. You just have to. I really care about you, but I can't keep seeing you if it's going to be like this."

"If you're threatening to leave because you don't like the way I am, then go ahead," she yelled, her voice out of control.

"No. Because *you* don't like the way you are," he shouted back at her.

"Ellman, I had no idea that you could be this emotional about anything," she said sarcastically.

"That's because, for all your wit and intelligence,

you've been alone so damn long that you don't really see anyone clearly any more. And in another couple of years you will have destroyed so many brain cells that you won't ever have a chance of seeing anyone. Seeing that they care about you."

"I don't want a lecture. If you want to say goodbye, then just say it and leave!"

She had risen to her feet and was staring at him defiantly, daring him to walk out. He looked at her squarely, then shrugged his big shoulders and started to button up his vest. Rebecca could be heard whining in the bedroom. He couldn't bear to utter a goodbye, but walked toward the front door, shaking his head and feeling hopeless. Sally plunked herself down on the couch again and stared straight ahead, apparently oblivious to his departure. When he closed the door behind him and she heard the lock click, she let out a great wail. She was on her feet instantly, running after him, flinging the door back.

"Ellman!"

He turned in the hallway, walked back to her and took her in his arms. He pulled her head into his chest and made shushing sounds, comforting her as one would a small child who has fallen and hurt itself.

"I'm just so scared," she sobbed, clutching at him.

"I know, Sal. I know," he soothed. "It'll be all right, you'll see. It'll be all right. Trust me."

Chapter 9

She stirred in her sleep toward dawn and automatically reached out for Severio. Before she could open her eyes, the chilly fresh air of the room reminded her that she was in the country. When she realized that Severio was not next to her she sighed and rolled over, clutching the pillow to her breast. The disappointment was almost overcome by her pleasure at being back in the little bedroom with the spare antique furniture and the windows that gave her a view of the budding trees.

Tossing the patchwork quilt aside, she crawled out of the old oak bed. She had gone to sleep in a tee shirt and a pair of heavy woolen socks. "Just as well Severio can't see me now," she thought as she caught a glimpse of herself in the wardrobe mirror, "I look like a waterboy on a high school baseball team."

She pulled on a pair of dungarees and a sweater, then padded down the carpeted stairs, braiding her hair as she went. Even though she'd planned to catch up on some much-needed sleep, she was glad that she'd woken up early. Now she could inspect the garden as the sun came up.

She hummed softly to herself as she fixed a cup of tea. Balancing the cup in her hand, she walked outside onto the veranda. The birds were chirping away. The air was moist and still a trifle chilly. She sipped the hot tea and walked around the flower beds surveying all the work that had to be done. It would take many hours of toil to bring the garden back to its former beauty, but here and there nature had come up with a few surprises that didn't require cultivation. A cluster of snowdrops and a clump of narcissus had pushed themselves up through the earth. The narcissus were particularly beautiful. She set her tea cup on the cold ground and knelt down to inhale their fragrance. She touched their bright green stems, turgid from the recent rains, and looked at the flowers which were still glistening with morning dew. The idea of this fragile blossom pushing through the dark, crusted earth and seeking the warmth of the sun brought a catch into her throat. What an incredible effort it took to be alive, even for a plant. How hardy and powerful all this translucent delicacy really was. It reminded her of her own struggles over the bitter emotional chill she had felt all last winter. She wanted to capture its victory.

Without even bothering to fix herself any breakfast, she went straight into the studio. Hurriedly unpacking the supplies she'd dumped on the floor the night before, she set up the easel. She squeezed the paint out onto the palette. Her hands moved quickly, mixing the glowing orange-yellow that was the heart of the narcissus and stroking it onto the canvas. She worked on feverishly, eager to put the feelings she had into the painting.

Then she paused, suddenly fearful. What about the composition? She hadn't given any thought to all the things she'd learned in art school. Perhaps she'd blunder and make a mess of it if she didn't plan it with more deliberation. She stood transfixed for an unaccountable amount of time. Then her hands started to move involuntarily, swirling the paint in bright free colors. Again she was stopped, overtaken by a paralyzing caution. Again she felt a spurt of instinctive creativity, a sense that the painting was flowing through her, requiring no act of the will.

The work went on in this fashion—gushes of ease and freedom in counterpoint with crippling caution. Finally she stood back and looked at it.

It was unlike anything she had ever done before. The line where the stems broke through the dark, crusted earth had a primitive, painful quality. The blooms themselves were triumphant with a delicate sensuality, their centers a vibrant mixture of gold and coral. The entire painting had a boldness and simplicity that she didn't associate with her own work. As she cleaned the brushes she superstitiously averted her eyes from the canvas. She suspected that it might be very good, but felt she couldn't evaluate it.

"I'll just walk away and not think about it," she determined.

She left the studio and walked past the grandfather clock that she'd remembered to wind the night before. One o'clock. It couldn't be right. Five hours had gone by as though with the snap of her fingers. And she'd been so worried that she'd have trouble getting through the day without being consumed with loneliness for Severio. She felt famished and decided to reward herself by taking the picnic lunch she'd already packed for them up onto the hill behind the house. She retied her sneakers, washed her hands, and walked out of the back door into the woods.

It had warmed into a balmy day full of sweet smells and glorious colors. After hiking to the top of the hill, she unfurled the blanket onto the sweet spring grass. If I were in the city now, I'd probably be on my way down to Severio's studio, she thought. She rolled up her sweater and put it under her head and stretched out, staring up at the serene blue sky and reminiscing about their lovemaking. What a shame he wasn't by her side at this very moment instead of being imprisoned by work and social obligations. She closed her eyes and drifted off into a pleasant reverie of their future together, imagining all of the simple, intimate pleasures they would share. She would show him how understanding and patient she was. She would help him to be productive. She heard some twigs crackle underfoot and jumped up, startled. Someone was coming through the woods.

She shaded her eyes and stared at the tall masculine figure that was making its way through the trees. The dappled light fell on the blond silvery hair and beard and picked up the bright colors of the checked shirt and jeans that covered a long, sinuous body.

"Hey there. I didn't mean to startle you."

It was Josh Graham. He walked toward her with long, easy strides, his lips parted in a welcoming smile.

"Oh, Josh. Hello. I was just lying up here daydreaming."

"This is really a pleasant surprise. I was wondering when you'd be coming up here again," he said, sounding almost boyish in his enthusiasm.

She moved over to make room for him on the

blanket. He shook her hand and then sat down, drawing his lanky limbs into a cross-legged position. "Isn't it beautiful this time of year? I spent all morning painting some narcissus I saw in the garden instead of doing any work."

"So you're playing hooky. That's what I'm doing. I should be driving over to the university to check on an experiment, but it's just too good a day to be indoors."

"You can share my picnic. I brought too much for one person."

She began to take the food out of the hamper, chattering on about the weather and the garden. He had thought of her often since he'd last seen her, and found himself walking or driving by her house, looking for a sign of life. He had even been on the verge of asking a neighbor for Jesa's number in the city, but since he couldn't phrase what he would say to her when he called, he had put it off. And now he had come upon her, lying in the grass on top of the hill. It was almost like a surprise gift. She looked even more beautiful than he had remembered her. Her hair had begun to loosen from the single braid that hung down her back. The sunlight shone in her large gray eyes and caressed the tips of her lashes. The palest freckles dotted her nose and there was a smudge of green paint on her chin.

"You're looking very fit," he said, wishing that he could tell her how much he'd longed to see her again.

"It's kind of you to say so. I'm really a mess today. I don't even think I stopped long enough to run a brush through my hair."

"I don't put a high priority on glamour. I always think ladies who do themselves up are kinda like Christmas trees."

"What's wrong with Christmas trees?" she laughed.

"Nothing. I like to see them once a year. I meant that most attempts to improve on nature impress me less than the real thing."

"Aren't your bigger and better blueberries an attempt to improve on nature?"

"I'd rather think of them as finding the conditions that suit her best."

"How has the work been going?" she asked. She handed him a plate piled high with roasted chicken, cheeses, and marinated mushrooms, glad to share her fancy picnic with someone, even if it weren't Severio.

"Really well. I'm going to get a grant to do further research next year. That means I can hire another grad student to work with me, so I'll be able to publish my results sooner than I thought. That is, if I can keep my nose to the grindstone and not be seduced into playing hooky on beautiful days."

"Congratulations. I think that calls for a toast. I've got a bottle of wine somewhere here."

She reached into the hamper and came up with the bottle. He unwrapped the wine glasses from the linen napkins, while she uncorked the bottle and poured the rosy liquid into them. As they touched glasses, he cleared his throat and proposed a toast to springtime. She leaned over and pecked him on the cheek. It was an impulsive, friendly gesture, more an expression of good will than a flirtation. When he felt her soft lips

213

brush his beard, be wanted to pull her to him and kiss her back.

"You seem to be so much happier than you were the last time I saw you," he said, placing the glass on the grass and picking up his plate.

"Believe me, I am. For so long there it was as though I were moving in a perpetual fog. No matter what I tried to do, I just couldn't feel much of anything."

They sat in silence, listening to the call of the birds, respectful of each other's solitude. It was a great comfort for him to be with a woman close to his own age. Whenever he'd taken out any of the younger women at the university, he always felt that he had to keep the conversation going, and while he relished nothing more than an exchange of thoughts and feelings, it became awkward when he felt that he had to keep talking. Jesa didn't have to go on about her tragedies and disappointments. He could intuit them and trust that she understood his silence. He saw the furrow in her brow and the tiny lines about her eyes. She had experienced loss and bereavement and had somehow emerged the stronger for her pain. He thought how resilient she seemed, sitting there, shaking off her unpleasant memories and turning her face up to the sun.

"I'm glad you're feeling better," he said finally.

"Better isn't the word for it. I'm reborn."

She wanted to tell him about Severio. Being in love with him had changed her life, given her a new sense of hope and liberation. She remembered what an attentive listener Josh had been when she'd spoken to him about Ed. She had only rarely felt such ease with a man so quickly. Perhaps because she guessed that he was the sort who was not afraid to talk about feelings. But her old reticence crept back in. She was afraid that she might be overstepping the bounds of taste if she started to wax enthusiastic about her lover.

"How've your kids been?"

"Pretty well, I guess. My fifteen-year-old, Janet, is going through a difficult spot just now. My wife arranged for her to spend the summer at camp, but now Janet's getting cold feet and wants to come and stay with me instead. It isn't that I'd mind having her. Hell, I love the kid. But she's so withdrawn and shy that I think she needs to be with kids her own age."

"What did you tell her?"

"I told her to screw up her courage and go to camp. But if she discovers that she's really miserable, she can come here. You see, she looks like the model teenager, but I know she's been hiding behind her scholarship. I guess she takes after her old man. Now my son Kevin's another matter. You have to threaten him with horrible deprivation, like not being allowed to go to a rock concert, to get him to crack a book."

"It sounds as though you miss them a lot."

"I do. Kevin's already been away at college for a year. I probably see him as much as I did when we were all living together. And I'm not sure how much help I could really be to Janet if I were at home. When they're going through the teenage blues I guess all you can do is lurk in the background and let them know that the support is there when they need it. Basically,

I think they're both good kids. I'd like them to meet you the next time they come up."

"Do you miss your wife, too?"

"I don't really think miss is the right word. You see, I've been with Nancy since I was eighteen. And it's still painful to think that we didn't walk off into the sunset together as a nice old couple. I think about her a lot. Funny, I always remember her birthday now, and I confess I often forgot it when we were together. I do worry whether the new life she's chosen for herself will give her all that she expects of it. But I give her credit for having the gumption to try. You see, she wanted me to rise in Washington politics and I just didn't want it. I think she's much happier now that she's doing the scene herself. That's really what she wanted in the first place, but she wasn't bought up to think that she could do it. And she was grounded when the kids were small. If I hadn't been so damn tied up with my job, I might have been more sensitive to the changes she was going through. Still, I think we're both relieved now that we've made the break."

"And you're happy in the solitude of the laboratory?"

"Not entirely, As you know, I love the work. And I do have a couple of friends I trust and enjoy. The only thing I'm really missing to make my life complete is . . ."

"A wife?"

"No. A mate. She would of course have the option of being my wife."

"Yes," she answered reflectively. "Being in love is one of the great joys in life."

216

"Not just being in love," he corrected her. "That's exciting and wonderful. That's like spring itself. But if you're going to make a life together, you have to have some of the same values, don't you think? I don't mean being crazy about the same movies or playing chess. I mean an attitude toward what's rewarding in life."

They stayed on for another hour, exchanging stories from their past, telling anecdotes, questioning and listening and laughing. Jesa offered to refill his glass. He looked up at the position of the sun and said he judged it to be close to three.

"We've been so busy talking that I haven't noticed the time. I really do have to go now," she said reluctantly. "I should have been working in the garden myself. Somehow this whole day has just spun itself out. I haven't done any of the things I'd planned to do."

"You said you were painting. That's getting something done."

"It's really all right. I don't feel that the day's gotten away from me. It's just presented itself as a special kind of surprise."

"That it has," he answered, helping her to gather up the picnic things. "Let me help you carry this stuff back to the house. Then we'll both get on with our work."

As they walked back through the woods, he tried to think of how he could ask to be with her again. He couldn't think of asking her out on a date. They were both too mature to think of their companionship in social terms. Their hours of conversation had put them on another level of familiarity.

"How'd you like to come with me to a town meeting tonight?" he asked as he placed the hamper on the veranda of her house.

"There's a big hotel corporation that wants to buy the land up near the lake and turn it into a luxury resort. I don't know how you feel about these things, but I'm opposed to private development of that spot. Some of us are trying to get the council to vote it down."

Damn, he cursed himself. First he'd talked his head off about his kids and now he was inviting her to a town meeting. Hardly a romantic approach to a desirable woman, especially one who must have a glamorous social life in New York.

"I guess that doesn't sound too exciting," he apologized before she'd had an opportunity to reply, "but I promised to go. Maybe we could get a bite to eat afterward at the Inn."

"I don't imagine I'll be tilling the soil after dark and I hate to cook for myself. It sounds fine to me."

"Then I'll pick you up around seven," he grinned, reaching out to shake her hand.

"Seven it is," she agreed.

He started off down the driveway, kicking a stone and stuffing his hands into his pockets. Jesa had been so gracious that she didn't even seem to notice that he'd bungled all of the preliminaries. But that didn't matter. Once he took her in his arms she would know that he had the soul of a lover.

Shortly after seven she heard a car in the driveway. She stopped examining the tiny callous that the afternoon's gardening had given her right hand, ran the brush through her hair again, and went to the front door. Through the leaded glass she spied a racy convertible sports car. Josh didn't even open the door of the car, but bounded out of the seat over the side and raced up to the door. He was wearing a loose corduroy jacket and slacks and his hair shone in the porch light. She thought that he looked very handsome and wondered how it was that some attractive neighbor or a student at the university hadn't managed to catch his eye.

"I never would have guessed you'd be the type to own a fancy sports car," she said, as he helped her on with her jacket and gently pulled her hair out from the collar.

"That was another mid-life crisis idiocy," he joked. "About two years ago when I was really feeling dissatisfied with myself, I thought that if I started to enjoy the fruits of my labors, that is become a real consumer, I'd feel better about my life in Washington. To tell you the truth, I'm not sorry I bought it. I race up and down these country roads like a maniac James Bond."

He was true to his word. He gunned the car into reverse and they were soon bumping down the road at an exhilarating speed. Jesa laughed out loud as he turned up the tape deck and started singing at the top of his voice. The night breeze ruffled her hair and she started to sing along too, feeling as though she was finally having one of the joy rides she'd heard other girls talk about when she was a teenager. It wasn't until they saw the lights of the village that Josh slowed down to a respectable speed.

They hopped out of the car and walked toward the old courthouse. The place was packed. People had started to spill out into the lobby. He took her hand and steered her through the crowd to the front of the courtroom, where a man was beckoning to Josh that he'd saved a place. They'd just squeezed into their seats when a portly man rose at the front table and banged a gavel for silence. When they stood up to say the pledge of allegiance, Josh whispered that the chubby fellow was the head of the town council.

He introduced a representative of the hotel corporation who painted a glowing picture of the future development of the area. He was followed by the head of the Chamber of Commerce, who talked about the new business that a resort could bring to the community. Josh leaned forward, intent on the proceedings, his bright blue eyes concentrated and intelligent. When it was his turn to speak, he strode to the microphone in the aisle, bending his tall body slightly so that he could speak into the mouthpiece.

He introduced himself quietly, omitting any of his more impressive credits with the Department of Agriculture and stating simply that he was a resident who was concerned about preserving the environment in which they all lived. He began with a short history of the area, then marshalled his facts to point out the traffic and pollution problems of other communities that had scurried into the arms of land developers.

Jesa had been listening to arguments from both sides with impartiality, but Josh's speech won her over completely. She was amazed at his eloquence and strength. When he concluded his talk with an impassioned plea for maintaining the lake area in its natural state, there was a burst of applause from the audience.

"You were very convincing," she whispered as he took his place beside her again. He glanced at her and nodded, but turned his attention back to the next speaker. The pro and con arguments went on for another hour before the head of the town council banged the gavel in a flustered manner and concluded the meeting.

"You mean they aren't going to vote on it tonight?"

"Nothing takes longer than local politics. This'll be a cause célèbre for the rest of the year," he told her as he gathered up their jackets and led the way up the aisle.

Several people came up and complimented him on his speech, but now that he'd concluded his public performance he was his usual deferential self, ducking his head in embarrassment whenever he was praised. Once they reached the lobby, a girl selling Sierra Club posters plucked at his arm and started to talk to him. Jesa stood to one side, amused to watch the star-struck girl batting her eyes at the oblivious Josh. Then a perky middle-aged woman with crisp gray hair and huge gold earrings asked Jesa to sign a "Save the Lake" petition.

"Aren't you Jesamine Mallick?" the woman asked, as Jesa scribbled her signature. "I'm Flor Marcal. I met you a couple of years ago at a Fourth of July party."

"I'm not sure if I remember. I haven't been up here much during the last year."

"Well, it's great to see you again," Flor went on enthusiastically. "I didn't know you were interested in local politics, but we're really glad to have your support."

Her eyes flitted from Jesa to Josh. Next to local politics, conjecture about the lives of her more attractive neighbors was Flor's main interest in life. She wondered how Josh Graham had managed to survive on that old farm alone, and she knew that just about every local woman between the ages of eighteen and fifty had a similar question. Some of them, she knew, had dropped by his place to offer more than neighborly hospitality. They all swore that Josh was a confirmed loner, a fact that made him seem even more desirable. Flor thought that any man who was that sexy had to have a woman hidden away somewhere. Now her mind turned on the possibility that it was the lovely Mrs. Mallick.

"Listen," Flor went on, pushing the petition under the nose of another bystander, "we're having some people over to the house for a caucus and a couple of drinks. Won't you come along? We'd all like to congratulate you, Josh. You were really something tonight."

Jesa had been enjoying herself much more than she thought she would, but she still didn't want to spend the evening with a group of people. She'd had nothing but socializing lately. She'd enjoyed her conversation with Josh so much that she was looking forward to finding out more about him. But she didn't dare indicate that she wasn't interested in going to Flor's place. Josh might have friendships with these people and choose to be in their company.

"That's really kind of you, Flor, but I think I'll take a raincheck. I'll be at the regular meeting next Friday," Josh said politely.

"Okay. See you then. We'll have lots more signatures and we can talk about the next step of the campaign. You come too, Jesa. It's good to see your face again."

She was soliciting another signature for the petition when Josh guided Jesa toward the side door.

"I hope you didn't mind my turning down an invitation without asking you," he said as they strolled back to the car. "I felt like being alone. Could you go for some lobster at the Inn?"

"That sounds perfect. Flor was right, though. You really did give an impressive speech."

"The first time I had to testify in front of a congressional committee I thought I had laryngitis. But I've had more experience at it now. Besides, this is something I really care about. Not that caring always makes me articulate," he added meaningfully. "Sometimes just the opposite."

He looked directly at her, hoping that she would know what he was struggling to say. Either the remark went over her head or she chose to ignore it, he could not be sure which. She started asking him more questions about "Save the Lake," saying that she might like to work with them during the summer. She did love the countryside around her home and thought it was high time she got out of her shell and started to be involved with more people. The psychiatrist had told her that she had structured her life around Ed to the exclusion of all else. He had urged her to become more involved with groups, cultivate her outside interests. At the time it had had all the appeal of an advertisement on a bus, but now she felt that she might actually enjoy doing it. Besides, Severio would be busy with his work. So she should find something to do with her time so that she wouldn't be underfoot.

Josh pulled the car into the yard of the Inn and helped her out. He put his arm around her casually as he walked her over to the stream and offered her a penny to throw into the mill pond. She squeezed her eyes shut and made a wish that she would be happy with Severio forever.

"We'd better hurry up. You know this is the country. They close the kitchen at eleven."

He had reserved a table near the window. They ordered the lobster and settled back into their leather chairs, listening to the steady splash of the water wheel just outside. The flickering light of the fireplace played on her face. She had a tiny smile on her lips and her eyes were misty and far away.

"I'm going to take some of the kids from the university up to the lake next week. Try to inspire them about joining the campaign."

"I'd think that anyone who was studying soil science would automatically be a conservationist," she answered, turning her attention back to him.

"Not necessarily true. Lots of them will go on to lucrative jobs keeping golf courses green or planning manicured lawns for super rich people who don't like to get their hands dirty. You're really an idealist, Jesa."

"That's not the first time that's been said to me. I guess I do have a tendency to romanticize things."

"I didn't mean it as a put-down. I think it's an appealing aspect of your character. There are enough hard-nosed realists in the world. Idealists dream and lots of interesting things come out of dreaming."

"On the other hand I might be looking at the sky and trip into a puddle of mud."

"That's all right too. As long as you can pick yourself up after you've fallen. You seem to be able to do that. You've come through some bad times and you've started to live again. That takes some spirit."

"You're giving me too much credit. I could never have done it alone."

Again she almost told him about Severio, but the waiter came with their lobsters.

When they had finished the meal, he sat and looked at her, feeling the warm glow of contentment. He couldn't remember a day in recent memory when he'd been happier. Even when he discovered that one of his assistants had neglected to alter the thermostat in the laboratory and had thereby ruined an experiment he was doing on the effects of temperature on seedlings, he had merely shrugged his shoulders and set the whole thing up again. He was usually bad-tempered when people around him did not display the same

225

degree of professionalism that he did, but today he was able to overlook anyone's misdemeanors.

"I'm really feeling sleepy," Jesa said softly as they drove through the moonlit countryside.

He let up on the accelerator and drove more slowly. Jesa tried to keep her eyes open, but her lids drooped and she cuddled up on the seat, her head nodding toward his shoulder. He put his arm around her as she dozed off, smelling the sweet perfume of her hair. How wonderful it would be to wake up in the mornings and have her soft, sleeping form beside him.

When he pulled the car into the driveway, she jerked into wakefulness. "Won't you come in and have a cup of coffee? It isn't really very late and now that I've had my catnap I feel completely refreshed. Maybe I'll even have a go at finishing the painting. It's been lurking in the back of my mind all day long."

"Can I see it?"

"It's not finished yet. Oh, what the heck. Come have a look at it anyway."

She took him into the studio, turning on the lights and walking slowly over to the canvas. She was afraid that her burst of creativity that morning had not been as wonderful as she'd originally thought. He stood and studied it for several minutes.

"My God, it's really fine. When you said you painted a narcissus, I thought that it was going to look like something from a greeting card, but this is incredibly beautiful. And strong. It makes you feel the effort that it takes for the flower to break through the ground."

"I'm so glad that you see that. That's exactly what I

wanted to capture. I've never done anything quite like it before. Most of my other stuff really is like pretty little greeting cards."

"And it has a tremendous feeling of hopefulness. I'm not an art critic but it seems that you're very talented. Why didn't you ever pursue your career in it?"

"I could give you a hundred and one reasons, but I suppose the real reason was that I was scared. I was afraid that I didn't have the gift for it, and I knew that I didn't have the drive to compete. I know it sounds strange, especially for a woman who had no children to care for, but I devoted everything to my marriage. Now that I look back on it, I actually wonder what I did with my time. I don't mean that I was lazy. I was up at seven fixing breakfast and all of that. I ran the house, kept Ed's schedule together. I was always busy. But I guess that there's really nothing to show for it."

"There's nothing to 'show' for sitting on the hill in the sunlight and talking, but what would life be like if we didn't enjoy such things? Maybe you're a late bloomer, like me. Now is the right time for you to use some of your energy to develop your own talents."

She turned from him and looked back at the painting. He knew that she couldn't quite believe that it had come out of her. But he had no question about it. The pushing through and coming into bloom was quintessentially her. As he moved behind her and placed his hands on her shoulders, he felt a desire prompted not only by her physical beauty but by his respect and tenderness for her whole personality. Damn the torpedoes. He was going to kiss her and tell her that she was the most desirable woman he'd ever met. How could she reject him? She was so ripe for everything he had to offer. She spun around to look at him, her face radiant.

"Oh, Josh. I'm so happy. I could never have done anything like this if it hadn't been for Severio. He's the one who's made the difference in my life."

His hands fell to his side. He stepped back from her, unable to speak. Jesa was talking so animatedly that she did not seem to notice the look of shock that he was trying to control.

"I really don't think I would have been able to start to paint again if it weren't for him. My relationship with him has made me feel so hopeful about everything."

She paused briefly, running her hands through her hair and laughing self-consciously.

"I've been wanting to tell you about him all day, but I guess I'm still inhibited about discussing things like this. You've been so open with me about your life and even though we haven't really known each other long, I know you're the sort of friend who can appreciate my feelings."

He stood very still, and not being able to face her, turned his eyes back to the canvas again. Thank God he hadn't actually taken her in his arms. That would have been an incredible fiasco. Not only because of his personal embarrassment, but because it might have caused a wedge in their friendship. When he'd arranged his features, he turned back to her, trying to make his voice sound casual.

"What's he like?"

"What's he like? I can't really tell you. When you're in love, it's hard to give an accurate description."

He was sorry he'd asked the question. The last thing in the world he wanted to hear was an enraptured account of his "rival's" sterling qualities.

"Whatever he's like, he must be something. Congratulations."

"I knew you'd understand," she smiled. "As I said on the hill today, I'm reborn."

He wanted nothing more than to be out of her presence. Apparently she was so caught up in her discussion that she hadn't noticed that he was about to make a declaration of love. But he was no good at camouflaging his emotions. If he didn't get out of there soon, she would detect his hurt and embarrassment.

"You deserve to have someone in your life, Jesa. I only hope he realizes what a lucky bastard he is to have you," he said as evenly as he could. "Hey listen, I don't think I'll wait for that coffee. I've already played hooky enough for one day. I'd best make it an early night and get up bright and early tomorrow."

"Thanks so much for coming by. I can't tell you what a pleasure it's been to share some time with you."

She started to take his hand as they walked out of the studio, but he disengaged it. He was afraid that she might reach up and give him a sisterly goodnight kiss. He walked quickly to the front door and out onto the porch. There was no light there so she couldn't see his face. When he reached out to shake her hand, she brought his palm up and placed it on her cheek.

"Thanks again."

"Goodbye," he muttered tersely as he rushed down the steps and out into the night.

"I'll see you soon," she called after him. But he had already gunned the car into reverse and was speeding out of the driveway.

Chapter 10

Severio had not been strictly honest when he told Jesa that he was honoring a dinner invitation at Bettina's. It was true that he had called Bettina up and made plans to see her, but not at one of the crowded soirées at her apartment. He intended to take her out alone and be charming enough to make up for his many weeks of neglect. After all, Bettina had helped to launch him in the city. He had no real feelings of gratitude toward her because he knew that she promoted new talent less for her interest in the arts than for a desire to keep herself in the limelight. Still, it was only good sense to make payment where favors had been tendered. Especially when the payment required so little from him. He had only to pay court to her, patronize her whims, show attention without intention. Flirting publicly with a glamorous woman could hardly he considered a chore. He had invited her to dinner on Saturday night.

When Saturday morning rolled around, Severio was feeling so dissipated that the prospect of an evening with Bettina seemed more burdensome. Lyman had let it be known that he was interested in seeing some of the sleazier night spots in the city, so once Jesa had left for the country, Severio had called up the Texas curator and suggested that they have a "men only" night on the town. He had even contacted a friend to get some cocaine in case Lyman really wanted to let it rip.

They had gone pub crawling to every hole-in-the-wall topless joint that Severio knew of, and a few he'd never heard of before. When he dropped Lyman off at his hotel in the early morning hours, Lyman assured him that he'd had the best time in his life since he'd gone on shore leave in Tokyo when he was eighteen. He told Severio that he'd be in touch about the canvas he'd commissioned for the cultural center. Severio slept most of the day. When he did wake up in the late afternoon he felt sluggish and vaguely depressed. The quiet evening at home that Jesa was always talking about seemed very appealing. He would have liked nothing better than to relax the company of a beautiful woman who loved him and wanted to attend to his needs. Instead he was going to have to be scintillating and witty with Bettina. And with Bettina one always had to be on guard.

He went to the gym for a steam bath and massage but lethargy persisted. As he walked back to the loft through Washington Square, the street lamps were just beginning to come on. Underneath one of them he saw a young couple. The boy was playing a guitar and the girl sat on one of the rails that guarded the sprouts of new grass and listened to him, her upturned face glowing with adoration. Jesa often had that same expression: the open admiration that belonged to the very young. At least the very young of another generation. Even though the first elation of his conquest of her had died down, he still counted himself lucky to have her. In fact he considered her an ideal possibility for a wife. She was compliant enough to put up with all the wheeling and dealing he would have to go through to reach the dangling golden apple of success that was almost within his reach. There was no question that she would remain faithful to him, even if he strayed occasionally. And her income guaranteed that they could live with some style, even when his own fortunes were rocky. He didn't particularly enjoy the marital state, feeling that it cramped his social style, but just now, when he was feeling fatigued and lonesome, it did hold some attraction.

He groomed himself carefully and started out to the restaurant. He knew that he was going to be late, but he was sure that Bettina would turn up at least twenty minutes after the appointed meeting time. She usually planned things so that people were waiting for her. One good thing about dealing with Bettina was that he understood her psychology so well. She never slipped into pensive, private moods as Jesa did. As long as be watched his step, he could have a fine relationship with Bettina. There was an exchange of benefits that both of them were too tasteful to openly admit. He felt sorry when he thought about old O.W. trying to get any affection from his wife. Too bad that some men were so busy with business that they didn't know how to choose a wife who could really be helpful to them.

He ordered a bourbon and sat back, erasing all thoughts of Bettina and Jesa from his mind, enjoying the pleasure of looking and being looked at by all the wealthy people around him.

Bettina paused in the lobby of the restaurant and quickly assessed her image in the mirrors. She had had such a terrible day that the tiny frown line between her brows was quite marked, even though she'd given herself a facial before putting on her makeup. O.W. had been getting ready to go out of the country on an extended business trip. She had quite forgotten that he was leaving and had scheduled a luncheon appointment. But O.W. was in an uproar because the new maid didn't know how to pack his suitcase properly, so she had had to cancel her own plans and supervise his departure. She'd smoothed out all of these boring domestic problems and retired to her bedroom for a late afternoon nap when she heard a little tap on the door.

O.W. had bustled into the bedroom without even waiting for her to call out that it was all right for him to enter. She was overtired from a very busy week of entertaining and wanted to rest before she saw Severio. And here was O.W. taking off his shoes and slipping the lock onto the door. She was sure that since he was going to be away for several weeks, he was coming to demand his conjugal right. He had an annoying practice of wanting to have sex with her whenever he left or returned home from a trip.

He sat on the edge of the bed and hoisted off his undershirt, muttering about his flight schedule and

233

asking if she'd been sure to see that his pills were put into his carrying case. She was so relieved at the prospect of being without him for several weeks that she consented to his initial embrace passively. But when he slipped in beside her and started to remove her dressing gown, her annoyance at having been disturbed came back with full force. O.W. didn't seem to mind her indifference. At least he huffed and puffed his way through in his usual fashion. But afterward he lay there in the oncoming darkness, making no attempt to get up and not speaking to her at all. She decided that she would go and bathe. When she started to turn on the bedside lamp, he reached over and took her hand and held it fast.

"Why do you sleep with me when you don't enjoy it?" he asked softly.

It wasn't like O.W. to want to have postcoital discussions. She paused a moment, shook her hand free, and flicked on the lamp.

"It was you who came into my bedroom."

"I'm going away," he moaned, turning his face from the light. "I thought you'd want to."

"If you'd been paying any attention to my reactions you might have known that I wasn't in the mood," she snapped.

"It's hard to pay attention to your reactions when I haven't been able to go to bed with you for ages."

"My God, O.W., you're not eighteen years old. Don't make it sound as though your life is one of sexual deprivation. I know that you have other women to comfort you."

"Have you ever thought that might be because I get so little from you?"

"Please don't raise your voice to me," she said imperiously. "If you don't mind, I have a dinner engagement and I'm going to be late."

She strode off into her bathroom slamming the door behind her. As she tossed the bath salts into the sunken tub, she felt extremely sorry for herself. She didn't mind going to bed with O.W. occasionally, but she really couldn't stand it when he seemed dissatisfied afterward and carped at her as though he were a child who hadn't gotten his share of the birthday goodies.

As she settled herself into the perfumed water and washed her well-exercised body, the self-pity turned into anger. She was still young and damned attractive. Only last month her picture had appeared in a leading fashion magazine. She had been described as "the essence of chic." Why should she be burdened with a paunchy husband who invaded her territory without so much as a by-your-leave? Why didn't she have a real lover to appreciate her looks while she still had them? A man whose eyes would give back her reflection with the adoration she craved?

She lingered in the tub allowing her facial to dry until she heard O.W. slam the bedroom door. Then she got out, lathered her body with lotions and returned to her bedroom, flinging back the door of the huge clothes closet. She tossed the clothes about the room trying to decide what would be the best thing to wear. Since she'd seen Jesa make such a hit wearing that revealing gown at Severio's opening, she decided that she would not pursue the demure image. She chose a pair of white and gold evening pajamas that slithered over her trim figure. She took more time than usual with her makeup and fastened on her best jewelry. When she surveyed herself in the full-length mirrors, she was quite satisfied.

But now that she looked at herself in the restaurant lobby she saw that damn little frown line that wouldn't seem to go away. It was O.W.'s fault, she told herself. No matter how much effort one put into a toilette, one's emotional state still had something to do with looking well. She could always guess when one of her friends had a new lover because the woman had a special bloom. That was what she needed. She smoothed her dark hair back into the chignon, touched the emerald choker and wafted into the dining room.

The headwaiter ushered her to the table and pulled out the chair for her. She inclined her head toward Severio as he rose from his seat and allowed him to kiss her on the cheek. She thought he looked particularly handsome, but then she'd spotted him as the kind of man who would bask in success.

"Terribly sorry to have kept you waiting, darling," she whispered as she settled into her seat.

"It just piqued my pleasure in seeing you again," he answered smoothly.

"Aren't you the sly one? If you were really so interested in seeing me, why haven't you called?"

"You of all people can understand, Bettina. Sometimes one gets so swept up with all the obligations that there isn't time to see anyone."

"Spare me the excuses and order me a dry martini."

He had only to raise his eyes to the obsequious waiter to have him instantly at his side. He ordered the martini and a Perrier while Bettina cast her glance around, checking out the other people in the room.

"Don't tell me you're on the wagon."

"I've already had a drink."

"I thought we'd celebrate our reunion."

"I overindulged last night with Lyman. I'm still trying to recover."

"So you two did hit it off. I was sure you would."

"Yes, we did. He's commissioned a canvas for the cultural center down there. It was good of you to introduce us."

"Nonsense. If I can get people who have something to offer together with people who have the taste and money to buy, that's reward enough for me. I can't wait to see your new paintings."

Severio felt a tiny stab of guilt. He had been doing so little work lately that he had nothing new to show. Jesa had probably been right when she'd urged him to come up to the country. He signaled the waiter again and told him to change the Perrier to another bourbon.

"I'm afraid that it's a bit premature to be looking at my new stuff. I've been trying out some ideas that aren't really jelling yet. Perhaps in another couple of weeks you could come down to the studio."

"Don't tell me it's going to be that long before I see you again. O.W. is off on a trip to Europe and I'll be quite at loose ends," she said seductively.

He sipped his drink and looked closely at her. Was it possible that she was really coming on to him? He knew that she liked to flirt with him, but there was a new quality of seriousness in her tone that he had never seen before. She held his gaze for so long that he broke eye contact with her and stared down at his drink.

"Of course I know that you're busy, Severio. And not just with your work."

"I don't know what you mean."

She tossed her head back and laughed, exposing her brilliant white teeth. "Severio! It wouldn't be too original of me to point out that it's a small world, especially *our* world. The whole town is talking about you and Jesa."

"And what is the whole town saying?"

"That you're having a hot affair. With Jesa that probably means marriage."

"People don't know what's going on in my private life," he answered, trying to keep his voice under control. He could feel the effects of the bourbon on his empty stomach and knew that he'd sounded too curt. He had no intention of discussing Jesa with Bettina. He opened the menu and pretended to be studying it. She slicked back her hair again and turned ever so slightly to acknowledge the admiring glance of a man at another table.

"I suppose there's no understanding the affairs of the heart," she went on. "I mean, who would have believed that Ellman Smith would ever have taken up with someone as crazy as Sally Gold?"

"I didn't know they were an item," he said offhandedly, relieved that the conversation had shifted away from Jesa.

"God, yes. I guess no one picked up on it at the beginning because it was so unthinkable. Not that Ellman is so good-looking or anything, but he does have money and reputation. I know lots of beautiful women who find him acceptable. And Sally is such a . . . well, I suppose eccentric would be the kindest thing to say."

"I don't really know her well."

"I'm surprised. She and Jesa are like two peas in a pod. There was even some talk about the . . . closeness of their friendship, if you know what I mean."

Severio couldn't help himself from laughing out loud.

Bettina instantly knew that she'd hit the wrong note in trying to gossip about Jesa. If Severio seemed unwilling to talk about her then she would just have to let it go, even though she was dying to find out how intense their affair was. She simply couldn't believe that a man like Severio could actually be in love with a woman like Jesa—she was so passive, such a doormat. She contented herself with her veal and fleeting glances from her admirer across the room.

Severio suffered through another hour of desultory conversation, picking at his food and sneaking glances at his watch. Bettina went on about a benefit auction for Friends of Young Artists of which she was the chief organizer, drifted into a discussion of her vacation plans, then shifted gears to talk about some paintings she was thinking of buying.

"What is your opinion of Kasimir Malevich? Have you seen his work? They say that Russian Constructivist paintings aren't a bad investment now."

"I'm sorry, Bettina. I really wasn't listening. Who?"

"Never mind," she said acidly, as she motioned to have her plate removed. "If I wanted to be ignored I could have spent the evening with O.W."

"I'm sorry. It's just that I'm very tired."

"But I was hoping that we could go out to that new disco 'Vibrations.' Everyone's talking about it and I really do feel like dancing."

"If you like. But I should warn you that I'm in no shape to stay up all night again."

They lingered over coffee and brandy. Severio could see that she was beginning to pout and made a renewed effort to listen to her chatter. He had known the evening might be a strain, but he hadn't anticipated just how much energy it would take to appear attentive. When he picked up the check from the silver tray, he was upset to see that it was over one hundred fifty dollars. He was reminded of his dwindling capital and felt resentment that he was having to spend so much on a woman whose fortunes so far exceeded his own. Jesa had worried that he was spending too much money and had offered to loan him some until he got payment for his recent sales. That had been out of the question while he was still wooing her, but now they were lovers it was a different matter.

In the taxi driving up to the disco, Bettina rested her head on his shoulder. She began to tell him how misunderstood she was. O.W. was so much older than she

240

that she felt he was incapable of satisfying her needs. Severio couldn't tell if he was feeling sick because the strong aroma of her perfume was bothering him, or because he knew from experience that when women started to talk about their marital dissatisfactions, they were usually looking for more than a confidante. He disengaged himself and rolled down the window. She snuggled up to him again and went into a more detailed explanation of her discontents.

He was vastly relieved when they reached the disco. A wispy young man with pale ginger hair pushed his way through the snake pit of twisting bodies and made a great show of hugging and kissing Bettina.

"This is Jacques," Bettina yelled over the blaring thrump-thrump of the music. "He's a divine designer."

"So why aren't you wearing something I created?" he brayed.

"Don't be such a nag, darling, or I won't introduce you to Severio."

"Then I won't introduce you to Ralph."

The burly man dressed in leather standing at Jacques's side offered his hand to Severio. When Jacques motioned Bettina out into the crush of gyrating bodies, Ralph led the way to a small table. Severio was too annoyed to be amused by the exhibitionism of the dancing. He rubbed his hands over his eyes as the strobe lights flashed on and off and longed to be home. Ralph sat next to him, stony faced.

"You've picked yourself a real hunk of man there," Jacques yelled to Bettina as he circled around her.

"Oh Jacques, stop teasing."

"C'mon, don't tell me you're just friends."

"A little more than that," she shouted back as she rotated her pelvis and tossed her hands in the air in imitation of Jacques's movements. She was feeling confident and in control of the situation again. She had flirted with Severio for so long that he probably hadn't picked up on the fact that she was offering herself to him now. She was sure he wouldn't reject her once he knew that she was serious. When she took Jacques's hand and led him back to the tiny table where Severio and Ralph were sitting, she was already plotting her next move.

Severio rose from the table as she approached him. She collapsed into his arms, holding her body tightly against his.

"Won't you dance with me, Severio?"

"Sorry. I really don't feel like it."

"Maybe you like slow dancing better. We could go back to my house, turn on the stereo. O.W.'s gone and all the servants will be in bed."

"I'm very sorry, but I'm really bushed. You seem to be having such a good time with Jacques. Maybe you'd like to stay."

"But darling, it's not even one o'clock yet," she persisted.

"I hate to say 'no' to a lovely lady, but I really must go," he said firmly, stepping back from her.

Jacques looked from one to the other, sizing up the situation. He leapt in to save Bettina from further embarrassment.

"We're certainly not going home yet, are we, Ralph? We know this really kinky little after-hours place. Come on, Bettina, let's make a night of it."

Jacques motioned to Ralph, who was immediately on his feet offering to take Bettina onto the dance floor again. She looked him up and down appraisingly, gave Severio one piercing glance and pushed her way back onto the dance floor. Jacques was fumbling in his pocket to give his name card to Severio, but the handsome painter was already heading toward the door.

For the rest of the night Jacques did his best to entertain Bettina, taking in a frenzied round of the "in" night spots. But her angry mood only got worse. When they left her at the door of her town house at four in the morning, she barely said goodbye. She was sure that by tomorrow Jacques would have blabbed it all over town that Severio had treated her rudely. Clearly she'd made a mistake to put in so much time promoting Severio. He was an egotistical ingrate, she swore to herself as she kicked off her shoes. She would just have to show him that there were certain rules of behavior that he could not violate with impunity. There must be a way to give him his comeuppance, to send him back to the ranks of unknown social climbers. As she pulled off her earrings and tossed them onto her dressing table, she glanced at the list of messages her secretary had left there. One item caught her attention:

"Mr. George Laird called twice. He said it was important. About his daughter Melinda."

Sally leaned forward to use the lighter on the dashboard of Ellman's Bentley. She knew she must have gone through half a pack of cigarettes since they'd left the city, but she didn't care. She puffed on another one, turning her head to blow the smoke out of the window.

"Just up here on the left there's a nice little stream. We could stop the car and take a look at it if you'd like."

"Ellman, please spare me your running commentary on the beauties of nature. You've been sounding like a tour guide for the last half hour."

"It's just that you're so quiet. I've never known you to go so long without talking."

"Look, I know it's a beautiful day. I know spring is busting out all over. I know the fields are green and the air is clear and the birds are singing. I just don't give a damn. It's hard to be blissful about the scenery when you're being carted away to the loony bin."

"First of all you aren't being carted away. You agreed to come. Second of all, it isn't a loony bin."

"Okay. Sanitarium. Drying-out hole. Drunk farm. Whatever you wanna call it. And don't bother to give me the sales pitch again. You can hardly expect me to be overjoyed at the prospect of spending a month with a bunch of people I have nothing in common with except that we all like to get pickled. How close are we anyway?"

"I think it's about another thirty minutes."

"Dear God in heaven," she groaned and scrunched herself down in the seat.

"Would you like to stop for a while?"

244

"I'd like to turn around and drive toward the Mexican border. Hey, I don't mean to bitch. It's damn nice of you to take the time to drive me up here. And all those phone calls you made to get me into the place. I just wouldn't have been able to handle that, you know."

"If I've been a bore talking about the scenery, you've been twice as tedious telling me thank you every five minutes."

He reached over and took her hand. They rode on in silence for another few miles until they saw the orange roof of a Howard Johnson's.

"I personally think these places are a scourge on the face of America, but since we missed the turn-off to the stream it's the last place we can stop before we get to Rolling Hills."

"Anything to delay the execution."

They parked the car and walked through the lobby full of vending machines. Ellman started to walk toward the coffee shop but Sally plucked at his blazer.

"I'd really love one last drink," she whispered, her big brown eyes looking up to him imploringly.

He nodded, took her arm and turned toward the pink neon sign saying "Cocktail Lounge." Inside it was dark and musty-smelling. The bartender was leaning on the counter, munching pretzels and watching a soap opera on the TV set that hung above the bar. The two or three customers didn't even look up when Sally and Ellman walked past them and took a back booth. They sat in silence until a commercial came on the television and the bartender stuffed one last pretzel into his mouth and wandered over to them.

"What'll it be?" he croaked.

"A glass of club soda and a straight shot of vodka for the lady. Make that a double shot."

Sally laughed softly and took Ellman's hand again. "You're really pretty wonderful, Mr. Smith."

The waiter hurriedly poured the drinks and dashed back to plunk them down on the table before the commercials were finished.

"To you," Sally said, as she clinked her glass to his. "And now you have twenty minutes to tell me all the wicked secrets of your life before they put me away. Do you know, all this time we've become friends I've been blabbing out my life history and you've hardly told me anything about yourself."

"That's not true. You're always drawing me out. You know more about me than almost anyone else does."

"I know you're a pretty weird duck."

"Why do you say that?"

"Why else would you take up with me?"

"I'll pass over the fact that you have such poor regard for yourself, Sally. Let's just say that you have certain qualities that I find attractive in a woman."

"Such as?"

"You're honest. Sometimes to the point of lacking all diplomacy. But still, you're honest. And you're talented. And you make me laugh. And you were never hungry to snatch me up because you thought I was an eligible bachelor. That's been a great relief."

"I never thought that you were eligible if you want

to know the truth. I thought you were a confirmed and kinda stodgy loner."

He peered at her through the gloom, then took her hand and patted it.

"Maybe it is time to tell you the story of my life. My love life. I've been having an affair with a married woman for the past ten years."

"Ten years!"

"Yes. I have the persistence of a St. Bernard and just about as much intelligence. You see, I really did love her. I suppose in a way I always will. She kept talking about leaving her husband. Several times I actually thought she was on the brink of it. But there was always something. First she wasn't sure whether or not she still loved him. That took about four years to decide. Then she was convinced that she didn't love him, but she felt obliged to stay with him because her children did. Last year her youngest started college and she finally decided to get a divorce."

"So?"

"She ended up marrying her dentist."

"You're kidding me."

"I know it's a pathetic story. Unfortunately it's true. I suppose lots of people would say that I was neurotic to stay in a relationship for that long. But I was in love with her. I kept telling myself that if I were persevering it would come out all right in the end. I suppose I must have seen too many Walt Disney movies when I was a child—all those happy deer mating for life. But promiscuity is just alien to my nature. The few times I tried to go to bed with other women I just felt miserable. I always thought of Helen."

Sally nodded glumly, ignoring her drink, waiting for him to continue his story.

"Throughout the ten years we always managed to meet regularly. I had my business and an active social life. Women like Bettina were always glad to have me on their guest list as an acceptable, if unexciting, extra man. I knew that people thought of me as you would say, a weird duck, but I've never been particularly interested in the opinions of others unless I respected them. Unfortunately there are very few people in that category. You're one of them. You aren't drinking your vodka, Sally, and it's going to be a long time between drinks."

"I think I'm in shock. I mean, when I started to get interested enough to wonder about your private life I just couldn't put it together. It sure would have been impossible for me to come up with this one."

She sipped her drink. His face was quite impassive, but through his glasses she could see that his eyes were sad and contemplative.

"I'm sorry," she said softly.

"About what?"

"About Helen. I know how it feels to love someone and have them walk out on you. And I was never hooked up with anyone for ten long years."

"It has been a time of reassessment."

"Reassessment, hell. I think I'd probably want to murder her."

"I suppose that I knew a couple of years ago that we weren't going to get together in a marriage. But you know the force of habit. There are so many memories that connect us to the past that we forget how to live in the present. I could see that Jesa was having that same problem. Ed died just about the time that Helen told me it was all over between us."

"I knew that you were attracted to Jesa."

"Jesa's a very attractive woman. But it wasn't her beauty that made me want to see her. It was because I knew something about her sense of loss. I was never able to find the words to communicate that to her. And you're the first person I've ever been able to talk to about Helen."

"You can always talk to me, Ellman. I don't gossip about important things."

"I know that. It's good to trust someone."

"Nothing like it in the world."

They had drawn closer together during the conversation so that their heads were almost touching. He put his arm around her and held her close to him.

"We must look pretty strange," she sighed. "Mooning over past loves in a dinky bar at Howard Johnson's is okay for my style, but it's a helluva comedown to your sense of form."

He sat up straight and pushed his glasses back onto the bridge of his nose.

"If you're finished with your drink we really should go. I told the doctor you'd be there by three."

"Those who are about to die salute you," she said as she drained the glass and replaced it firmly on the table.

When they reached the winding driveway of Rolling

Hills, they were holding hands so tightly that it stopped the circulation in her hand. She thanked him again for taking care of Rebecca during her absence.

"I really couldn't have come here if it meant putting her into a kennel, you know. If you walk her once in the morning and once at night she'll be good and won't mess up your fancy carpets. And could you please call Jesa and tell her where I am. I still feel sick about that damned argument. She knows I love her. Maybe when I get straightened out I'll learn to keep my mouth shut."

"They help people here, Sal. They don't perform miracles," he said slyly.

"See what's happened to you? Since you've been around me you've started to get a mouth on you too. Tell her . . . oh, you'll know what to tell her. I . . ."

She could see a young black man dressed in an orderly's uniform walking over to the car to collect her luggage. She gulped and leaned over to kiss Ellman goodbye.

"I'll be all right. I'll be all right," she whispered to herself. She opened the car door and stepped out, flashing a smile.

"Hi, I'm Sally Gold. I guess you're expecting me. I've come to dry out."

Chapter 11

ad it not been for Severio's seductive midnight phone call, Jesa might have stayed in the country longer than she'd anticipated.

Of course she daydreamed about him constantly as she puttered about the house or planted in the garden and in the evenings when she slipped in between the bed covers, she had a strong desire to find his body there. But most of the time she was active and content even though alone.

As soon as she'd completed the painting of the narcissus, she conceived the idea of an entire series showing the first germination of a seed into its blossom and eventual decay. After looking at the original painting as objectively as she could and deciding that it did have merit, she energetically began a series of sketches for the series. Though there were still bouts of fear and trembling the intervals between them decreased. She longed to share the news of her breakthrough with Severio, to show him her work and hear his opinion of it. She had usually been at loose ends whenever she was away from Ed. Now she had a feeling of personal strength that she had lacked throughout her years of marriage. It pleased her to know that she was not a clinging vine who would wilt without the constant companionship of the man in her life. She tried to call Severio several times; but not finding him at home, she felt only a momentary pang of loneliness before going back to her work.

On the evening of her fourth day alone, she had settled into bed dressed in her old tee shirt and woolen socks. She was happy that she seemed to have broken her dependency on sleeping pills. Now she could drift off into a peaceful slumber without them. Snuggling down beneath the coverlet, she felt like one of the seedlings that she had been painting. She thought she might call Josh tomorrow and ask if he'd like to come over and see what she'd been up to. No matter how secure she was feeling, it wouldn't hurt to have a word of encouragement and she was eager to see him again.

The ringing of the phone jarred her out of the warm, drifting sensation she had just before dropping off. The moment she heard Severio's voice on the phone, she was wide awake. He told her that he'd missed her terribly. Couldn't she drive back to the city the next day? Overjoyed by the prospect of being in his arms again, she instantly agreed. She would leave early the next morning so they could meet at his studio at their usual time.

After she'd hung up the phone and nestled down into the covers again, she was sorry she hadn't had the presence of mind to ask him to join her. It seemed ridiculous to pack up all of her equipment, especially when she knew that she never seemed to have the time to get any work done while she was in the city. And she would have to call Flor Marcal and tell her that she wouldn't be at the "Save the Lake" meeting on Friday. But nothing could be as important as being with Severio if he needed her.

The next morning she put the house in order, reluctantly closed the studio door and started back toward New York. Ordinarily a cautious driver, her desire to be with him again was so great that she had to watch herself and not exceed the speed limit. She planned to stop by her apartment first to bathe and change her clothes, but by the time she saw the George Washington Bridge, she knew that she couldn't pause to do anything. She drove straight down to Soho and pulled the car into a garage with exorbitant parking rates. Ed would have wanted me to drive around looking for a place on the street, she thought as she grabbed her purse and the bunch of flowers she had brought for Severio.

"Hey lady, where's the fire? You forgot to get your ticket."

"I'm sorry," she said as she rushed back and grabbed the ticket from the attendant.

"If it weren't the middle of the day, I'd think you had a hot date," he winked.

She raced down the street, dodging a crowd of tourists who had paused on the sidewalk to examine a map of the Soho galleries. Skipping up the htairs to his studio, she pushed the buzzer and stood back, wiping the tendrils of hair from her perspiring forehead.

When Severio came to the door he was wearing his bathrobe, his heavy-lidded eyes still drowsy with sleep.

"Darling, I'm so glad to see you. Did I wake you up?"

"Yeah. I don't know what's wrong with me. I just seem to have gotten into a crazy schedule where I can only sleep during the day."

"You shouldn't stay up so late working."

She noticed that the studio was in complete disarray. Morning-after-the-party clutter disfigured the minimal furnishings, making it look much worse than a conventionally decorated room. Glasses, half-empty bottles, and various articles of clothing were strewn over the floor and the air was heavy with old cigarette smoke.

"The place looks like it's been invaded," she said lightly.

"Some people dropped by last night and stayed way too late. I was already wasted from Bettina's dinner party and an evening with Lyman, but I just couldn't seem to get rid of them."

"You're not feeling sick, are you?"

"Now that you're here, no."

"I've missed you so much," she breathed. "I didn't even realize just how much until now."

"That's good. I wouldn't want you to get the crazy idea that you can get along without me."

"I have so much to tell you. I don't know which I want more: to kiss you or to talk with you."

"Let me help you decide," he whispered into her ear. He crushed her in such a hungry embrace that she dropped the little bouquet on the floor.

An hour later when the muffled sounds of the city brought her back to the world beyond the bed, she propped herself up on her elbow and smiled at him.

"Now may I talk to you?"

"As long as you only expect me to listen," he replied languidly. "Why do women always want to talk after sex?"

"It's just that I'm so excited. I can't wait for you to see the painting I did. And I've started on a series of sketches. You know, all my life I've been so worried about following the rules. When ever I tried to paint I always felt as though someone was standing behind me waiting for me to make a mistake. This time I didn't feel that at all. I just felt the need to do it. And you know what? It turned out really well. It's much more abstract that anything I've ever attempted, but I think it has a content that people can understand. I showed it to my neighbor and he understood immediately what I was trying to do."

"You mean some of your hayseed neighbors really know some thing about art?"

"I don't know how much he knows about art, but Josh Graham's a highly intelligent person." She faltered, feeling that she had to give an account of Josh's qualifications. The old doubt that she was really capable of doing anything worthwhile crept back.

"As long as you found something to occupy your time, dear," he said casually.

"It's more than that. You make it sound as though I was watching a TV show or doing a crossword puzzle. I really felt good about it."

"Listen, I'm sure it's just fine. I guess I have other things on my mind just now."

While they were making love, she had guessed that he was preoccupied. He was as masterful as ever and she felt a great physical satisfaction when they were finished, but somehow he had been almost impersonal. He had barely opened his eyes. He had seemed intent upon his gratification, but she had dismissed her slight feeling of isolation by telling herself that it was natural that he should be so single-minded after they had been separated.

"What's bothering you?" she asked solicitously.

"I don't know. I just feet blocked."

She stroked the dark hair back from his face and looked at him, waiting for him to go on with whatever it was that was disturbing him. He sighed deeply, ran his hands over his face, and looked out of the skylight.

"It's hard to work under financial pressure."

"But I thought that some of the commissions from the sales at the show would have started to come in by now."

"Yeah, and Ellman's getting his cut."

"But darling, every gallery owner gets a cut. Ellman's is more modest than most and you know he's honest."

"Sure. I know. But I have a lot of expenses. Lyman did commission a painting for that damn cultural center, but I want it to be really good. I don't want to rush it."

"Please don't worry about money. You know I'll be more than glad to loan you whatever you need."

He threw back the covers and started to get out of bed. She was afraid that her offer might have offended him. "I don't really mean loan," she added quickly. "I mean give. Please don't be silly about it," she went on, touching his arm and drawing him back to her. "You'd help me out if I needed it."

"But you're not likely to need it, are you? Ed left you pretty well fixed."

"Yes. But it wasn't always like that. I know it sounds corny, but we struggled a lot during our early years. I'm not an extravagant person. You'd be surprised how minimal my needs really are."

He turned to face her, giving her his most ingen-
uous smile.

"You're really very sweet, Jesa."

"If you'd come up to the country, it would really cut
your expenses. It's just glorious up there this time of
year. And the people are so nice. All my life I've
thought that I was a shy person, but now I realize that
there's a certain kind of socializing that I just don't
enjoy. It's not just because I'm no good at it, I'm really
happier working in some community group that I'll
ever be at some chic party."

"You are a little bourgeois housewife, aren't you?"
he laughed as be ruffled her hair.

"I wish you wouldn't make it sound like a disease."

"I didn't mean to. I think it's amusing."

"Oh, Severio, give it a try. Just come up with me and
see if you like it. I know that you could work up there,"
she pleaded.

"We'll see. Right now it's just not possible for me to
get away. I promised Bettina that I'd donate a sketch
to some damned fund raiser she's getting together.
That's next Friday, so I'll have to throw something
together by then."

He rose from the bed and kicked some clothes out
of his way. As the phone rang, he cursed and told her
not to answer it. Putting his bathrobe back on, he
walked out into the kitchen.

"Do you want a drink?" he called out.

"Perhaps a glass of wine."

She couldn't understand how the warm glow of
their lovemaking could be so quickly dissipated. She

could have spent the next half hour with him, touching and talking. But she'd been married long enough to know that even lovers' moods did not always coincide. She would have to make allowances.

He came back from the kitchen carrying a glass of bourbon for himself and one of chablis for her. He still had a scowl on his face as he gulped his drink and looked around the room distractedly.

"Don't you want to come back to bed?" she asked, moving to make room for him.

"We've just been to bed. You are insatiable."

"I didn't mean to make love again. I just meant that we could lie here together. Cuddle and talk."

"Cuddle? Jesa, sometimes I think you have a case of arrested development."

"I know you're not feeling well," she went on tentatively. "I'm sorry that making love didn't comfort you."

"I don't look to sex for comfort."

"Don't you?" she asked, genuinely amazed.

"No. Excitement. Release. But not comfort. And don't tell me that comfort is what you're seeking. You enjoy the excitement as much as I do."

"Of course I do. But making love makes me feel closer to you as well. That's comfort."

"If you, say so, my dear. Personally I'd rather do it than talk about it. And just now I'd rather take a shower."

He drained the last of his bourbon, placed the glass on the floor, and walked into the bathroom. Jesa stayed in the bed, pulling the sheets up to her chin and staring at the ceiling. She had never seen him in such a mood before. He seemed so impatient with everything she had to say, and each new attempt at communication seemed to lead to more misunderstanding between them. It certainly wasn't the reunion she'd fantasized. But if she were going to make the relationship work she couldn't expect him to remain the dashing cavalier he'd been throughout their courtship. Perhaps this was even an opportunity for them to draw closer together. He was dropping the mask of ardent lover and letting her see some of his real problems. If she really loved him, she would have to make allowances for the rough spots, soothe him when he was disturbed and support him in any way that she could. After all, he had been understanding to her when he had first met her. He had been patient when she had been fearful.

"Jesa," she heard him shout from the bathroom, "I forgot to get a clean towel. Could you bring me one, please?"

The simple request for a domestic service rang an old chord. She jumped out of bed, found a fresh towel, and handed it in to him. When he came out of the bathroom a little later, she was picking up the mess in the apartment, humming softly to herself. He watched her going about her chores, the little secret smile playing on her lips. Yes, there was definitely something to be said for widows, at least those who had loved their husbands. He vowed to make an effort to be more pleasant to her.

"Don't bother yourself with that. Why don't you go

home and change and I'll pick you up and take you to dinner?"

"All right. That is, if you're not too pressured with your work."

"I am pretty busy," he faltered. "But I don't want to disappoint you."

"I don't mind. We're going out tomorrow night, aren't we?"

"Yes. Another dreary dinner party at the Hartmans'. Thank God you'll be along to help entertain those drones. Would you like to come down here in the afternoon or shall I pick you up?"

"Whichever you prefer."

"I prefer that you come down here. I know I was too grouchy today to really pay attention to you," he said softly as he pulled her into his arms. "I am glad to have you back."

She surrendered to his embrace, relieved.

Back at her apartment, she hoped that there would be a message from Sally waiting for her. She really missed having an intimate friend to talk to, someone who would listen and question not just out of politeness, but out of real concern. All these years Sally bad been encouraging her to paint. Now she would be able to tell her about what she'd done. She also longed to talk about Severio with someone she trusted. Even if Sally had thought he was a poor choice to begin with, she knew her friend enough to guess that Sally would cool down and come to an acceptance of him once she really explained how in love with him she was.

There was no message.

She fixed herself some scrambled eggs and watched the sky darken over Central Park. The old feelings of loneliness came back to her again. She was about to look in the medicine chest for the last cache of sleeping pills and retire for an early night when the phone rang. Ellman went through all of his polite preliminaries before asking if he could drop by and talk with her.

A half-hour later when she went to the door to let him in, she was surprised to hear the yapping of a dog. She opened the door to see Ellman with a struggling Rebecca cradled in his arms.

"Whatever are you doing with Rebecca?" she asked as the tiny dog strained toward her and she took her in her arms.

"That's one of the things I wanted to tell you. Sally's gone away. Don't be alarmed. I don't mean she's disappeared. I drove her up to Rolling Hills the day before yesterday."

"Where?"

"It's a sanitarium. Or in Sally's more colorful language, a drunk farm."

"I don't understand."

She started to usher him into the living room, but he said he'd prefer to sit in the kitchen with a cup of tea. She could see that his association with Sally had already altered his habits. It wasn't like uptight Ellman to suggest sitting in the kitchen. He seemed more relaxed and friendly as he loosened the buttons on the vest of his three-piece suit, took Rebecca back onto his lap, and stroked her ears as Jesa prepared the tea. He

261

gave a long monologue relating the events that had led up to Sally's decision, including the debacle at the awards dinner.

"I have to tell you that I'm really amazed," she said finally. "I've wanted to talk to Sally about her drinking for years, but I've never have the courage or the tact to know how to broach it. How did you ever manage to talk her into it?"

"You know Sally well enough to know that she wasn't talked into anything. But we've become . . ." he cleared his throat, the old sense of propriety returning, "we've become close. I know that it seems to be an unlikely alliance. To tell you the truth it's a bit of a surprise to me. You know I've always admired her, but she has so many defenses that it's difficult to really be intimate with her, especially for a man. I can't claim to take credit for her seeking professional help. Perhaps I was just around at the right time. I think that the falling out with you probably triggered her into some self-examination. The awards thing just tipped the scales."

"I feel just terrible about our argument. I've been wanting to make it up with her."

"You can rest easy, because she feels exactly the same way. In fact, she asked me to call you and tell you where she is."

"Can we go up and see her?"

"Not for a while. It's part of the regimen that the patients be cut off from their environment. I can tell you that I miss her already."

"I suppose she told you what the argument was about."

262

"Yes, she did."

Ellman shifted uncomfortably in his chair. He had warned Sally against discussing Severio with Jesa, and was not about to go against his own advice. While he didn't share Sally's violently negative opinion of Severio, he did find him feckless and egotistical, certainly not a love-match for a woman of Jesa's character.

"I only wish that Sally had a chance to really know Severio."

"He's a very talented man," Ellman answered, hoping to tread the thin line between fact and opinion.

"I don't just mean his talent."

"I don't consider that I really know him. I've dealt with him in a business capacity. And of course I've met him socially many times. You see him with the eyes of love, and that's an entirely different proposition. '*Le coeur a ses raisons que le raison ne connait pas.*' "

"Ellman," she laughed, "it's just like you to obscure a discussion by quoting something in French."

"It means, 'The heart has its reasons, which reason knows not.' I wasn't trying to be obscure. I only meant that I don't think any outsider can really judge a relationship between a man and a woman. I might, upon meeting someone, guess her political preference or even her taste in art, but I wouldn't presume to guess what she would find desirable in the opposite sex. Love is still rather mysterious, no matter what the psychologists or sex researchers tell us, don't you think?"

"Yes, it is mysterious," she answered with a dreamy half smile. "I used to think I knew exactly what love was, but now I'm beginning to think I have to reevaluate my notions."

He stirred the remains of his tea and lifted Rebecca's paws from the table. If Sally was right about Jesa's trusting nature, he felt an obligation to inject a few words of caution. "I do hope that you'll take the time to really get to know Severio before you make any long term commitments," he began. "One can hardly be in a mood of serious evaluation during the first blush of an affair . . ."

Conscious that he sounded awkward and condescending instead of smoothly diplomatic, he swallowed the remains of his tea and looked about the kitchen. "May I please have another cup?" he asked politely.

She was relieved that Ellman wasn't going to say anymore about Severio. He had admitted that he didn't know him well, but be had undoubtedly heard an earful from Sally and that had colored his opinion. Besides, it seemed disloyal to be discussing her lover with anyone who wasn't favorably disposed toward him. She turned the conversation back to Sally, a topic which Ellman was only too happy to discuss. He asked about their student days together, listening so attentively to Jesa's reminiscences that she guessed the depth of his affection for her friend for the first time. When Rebecca started to get restless, they went downstairs together and strolled along near the park.

As she started back toward the apartment alone, she looked at all the couples walking together enjoying the balmy spring night. Though she tried to comfort herself with the thought that she was with someone, even though he wasn't physically present, the old loneliness and isolation were still there.

Chapter 12

*I*t had taken all of Bettina's tact and diplomacy to pacify poor George Laird when he came to her with the news of what he supposed was his daughter's deflowering. According to Melinda's report, Bettina had introduced her to Severio and had allowed them to go off together in the middle of the night. George felt that Bettina, as an older woman, should have been more protective of his innocent child, and he somehow held her responsible for allowing his little girl to be seduced by a perfidious man.

Bettina swallowed hard and resisted the temptation to tell George that anyone but a doting father could instantly see that Melinda was neither innocent nor a victim. Instead she expressed her shock at finding out that Severio was a philanderer. She commiserated with him about the difficulties of raising a daughter alone and poured him a large tumbler of scotch. She urged him to abandon his plan to prosecute Severio, insisting that a scandal would only make it more difficult for Melinda to get over her trauma. By the time she had refilled his glass, she had talked him out of going down to the painter's studio and confronting him. When he mentioned that Melinda wanted to go on a trip to Spain, which he had denied her, Bettina guessed that this might have something to do with Melinda's confession of sexual abuse. She told him that he should give the kid a chance to get away from it all. George accepted her advice and apologized for being angry with her. After accepting the name of yet another psychiatrist who specialized in teenage problems, he wobbled unsteadily toward the door.

She motioned the maid to remove the decanter of scotch and sank back in her chair, staring up at the ceiling. So Severio had been stupid enough to take up with that trashy little Melinda. She wouldn't have guessed that he'd be capable of such a lapse of taste. But her surprise was nothing compared to what Jesamine Mallick's would be. She asked her secretary to get Mr. Euzielli on the phone.

"Severio? It's Bettina. I'm awfully sorry if I've interrupted your work."

"That's quite all right, Bettina. I was meaning to call you and apologize about the other night. I was so damned tired that I'm afraid I was a horrible bore."

"No, darling. I'm the one who should apologize. I just felt like a night on the town because I'd had such a dreadful day getting O.W. off on his trip."

Her voice was crisp and matter-of-fact, with no hint of her usual seductive tone. It was the first time he'd ever heard Bettina say she was sorry for anything. Perhaps she was embarrassed for hurling herself at him. The relief of not having to kowtow to her injured feelings threw him off guard.

"I've gone through my things and I've come up with a sketch you can have for that auction on Friday. It's not much, but you ought to be able to raise something on it."

"I knew you wouldn't fail me. I'll send a messenger down to collect it. I'm so looking forward to seeing you on Friday night."

"I'm not sure if I can be there."

"Oh, Severio, please don't disappoint me. I've already told scads of people that you'll be there. And I want to see Jesa again. Please bring her. It's been ages since I've had a chance to talk to her."

Friday was the first day to give a hint of the summer heat. Jesa rose early in the morning and went for a walk in the park to clear her head. It had taken several days after her return to the city to get back into her painting and she was not pleased with the results. Whenever she settled down to work she was deluged with interruptions: people called with invitations, Sophie Moss wanted to enlist her on a committee to redecorate the lobby, Severio needed her to find a maid to clean up his apartment. She had spent most of the previous day picking up supplies that he needed but was too busy to buy for himself. Now she told Maggie to please take all calls except those from Severio and retired to the little back room she had turned into a "studio" to try to pick up her work.

When Severio called to remind her about the auction for Friends of Young Artists she tried to beg off. She was just getting going again, she explained. He told her how much he needed to be with her and promised that they would only put in a brief appearance.

She was coifed, perfumed, and wearing a light off-the-shoulder summer dress when he arrived to pick her up. He gave her an appraising look, complimented her on her appearance, and sank down onto the couch. She went over to the bar and fixed him a bourbon.

"I'd have gotten here ten minutes earlier if I hadn't met that old bag of a neighbor of yours in the lobby."

"I guess you mean Sophie. Please don't call her an old bag. I know she's nosy and talkative, but she's just lonely."

"Is that supposed to justify her chewing my ear off?" he grumbled.

"No. I know she can be a pest. But we have to make allowances."

"I'll leave the role of understanding friend to you. You can put up with anyone."

"I put up with people you know that I don't like. I'll never forget that pretentious bunch that did the Living Art exhibition," she laughed as she came and sat next to him.

"I didn't ask you to like them. I know they're phonies. But you never know when a contact like that will come in handy."

"How did the work go today?"

"All right, I guess. Damn phone kept ringing off the hook."

"That's what I keep telling you about the country, love. Blissful quiet with no interruptions. Ed always used to say that he could get more done up there than he could in his office. He designed all the plans for that complex in Arizona while we were up there."

"I'm not Ed."

"I didn't mean to compare you," she apologized.

"God, Jesa. Sometimes I think that you belong in India. Isn't that where the widow casts herself on her husband's pyre and gets cremated with him?"

She pulled away from him, stung. Even though it was true that he was under a lot of pressure and she'd vowed to be sympathetic to his needs, she was annoyed at his insensitivity. She bit her lip, determined not to start another argument between them.

"I'm sorry," he said after a moment, pulling her back toward him. "I guess I can't help my jealous nature. It was a stupid remark and I apologize. I just can't bear to think that you loved anyone as much as you say you love me."

"I do love you. And I loved Ed. It's not comparable. Do you want me to deny my past life?"

"Darling, I said I was sorry. We're just feeling tense with each other because we didn't have a chance to make love this afternoon."

"I don't want to turn to sex as an answer to everything. We have to be able to talk sometime."

"I think all those exploratory conversations about feelings and misunderstandings are a waste of time. We know how we feel about each other, don't we? Please look at me, Jesa."

She turned her face up to his. Instantly she was drawn into those dark, heavy-lidded eyes. They never failed to banish questions, arguments, explanations. Her body stiffened slightly as though an invisible current passed between them. It wasn't even necessary

269

for them to touch each other. Not now. Not yet. Now that the connection had been made, whatever happened during the evening would be inconsequential—marking time with a hidden pulse until they could consummate their desire.

"Shall we go now?" he asked, almost inaudibly.

Her secret anticipation carried her through the evening. Even when they moved through the crush of bodies and took their seats in the Fanshaw library, all she thought was that this was the room in which she'd seen him for the first time and had been too distraught to notice his presence. As the auctioneer started the bidding, she rested her arm on his, gazed into the mid-distance and remembered the chronology of their affair. She was momentarily alert when his sketch was being bid on, but mostly the whispered congratulations and laughter eddied about her without touching her.

There was a rush of applause when Bettina took the auctioneer's mallet and announced the total that had been raised. A pretty young woman, her hair chopped in a 1920s bob and wearing a man's tuxedo, walked to the dais and gave a speech of thanks on behalf of the Students' League. The guests then pressed unceremoniously toward the buffet table. Jesa glanced at Severio, hoping that he was going to signal their departure, but the girl in the tuxedo had rushed down from the platform and introduced herself.

Jesa stood politely to one side and watched them together. The girl seemed remarkably self-contained for her age. She stood erect, discussing her future ambitions in a clear, confident voice. Despite the compliments she was heaping on Severio, there was something in her manner that suggested that she considered herself his equal. Her self-possession made Jesa feel rather old. She couldn't remember any of her female colleagues of fifteen years back who had been so "together." Yes, that was the word for it. "Together" used to mean that you were with someone else. Now it meant that you had mastered yourself. At the moment Jesa felt neither. When it appeared that she was not going to be included in the conversation, she walked over to the corner near the windows and found a chair. She could see Bettina, still up on the dais, talking to the auctioneer and surveying the room at the same time. The moment she spotted Jesa she excused herself and came down to her.

"Jesa, my darling! It's been positively ages since I've seen you. My, aren't you looking well!" She touched Jesa's cheeks with both of her own, then pulled up another of the gilt chairs to sit beside her.

"Where is Severio?" she asked, though Jesa was sure she'd seen Bettina wave to him only minutes before. "Oh, yes, I see him. Over there talking to . . . what is *her* name?"

"I don't know. I wasn't introduced."

"Do you want to meet her?"

"Not particularly. I think we're going to have to leave soon. We haven't had dinner yet."

"My dear," Bettina continued in a lower voice, "I think it's absolutely wonderful. You and Severio, I mean. He's such a high-strung man. I suppose most really creative men are. But you have provided him

271

with the kind of stabilizing influence that he really needs. No matter how attractive all that youthful adoration seems—not to mention that youthful flesh," she paused long enough to give Jesa a knowing wink, "it's only an experienced woman who can nurture a man's ego and be wise enough to overlook his little peccadilloes. Believe me, I've had to ignore some of O.W.'s dalliances, but I think that sort of forgiveness is just part of a mature relationship, don't you?"

Jesa couldn't quite figure out why Bettina was taking such a dear-old-friends tone with her and making such a fuss over Severio's conversation with the girl. She focused on Severio, hoping that he would turn around so she could signal him that she wanted to leave. Bettina kept talking in conspiratorial whispers. Jesa listened with divided attention, stopping one of the maids to ask for a glass of punch.

". . . so I explained to George that he was making far too much out of it. Melinda has that poor man so twisted around her little finger that he'd believe anything the minx said."

Jesa thanked the maid for the punch and turned back to Bettina, who had an expression of deep concern mixed with impatience.

"Forgive me, Bettina. Who were you talking about?"

"Why, George Laird. He was so angry that he was threatening Severio with physical violence. Of course I knew what must have really happened. I could see Melinda throwing herself at Severio the first night they met. That was way back, when he'd first started dating you. I suppose it was only natural that he should have succumbed to her. Most men don't have the willpower to reject anything that easy no matter how good things are at home. And I'm sure he had no idea how young Melinda is."

"Melinda," Jesa said, trying not to make it sound like a question.

"I should have suspected what was happening that night of Severio's opening. She threw such a tantrum when she saw the two of you together, I think it was very cool of you to just walk out like that. Of course she didn't tell her darling daddy about it until last week. I'm sure she made it sound as though Severio had robbed her of her maiden virtue, but it's obvious that she was tripping down to his studio of her own free will."

Bettina now had her full attention. Jesa nodded automatically, desperately trying to control herself. There had been some disturbance with a girl at Severio's opening, but she couldn't remember the details. Perhaps Bettina was lying. But no. Bettina wouldn't make up a story that she knew Jesa would check with Severio. Her facial muscles were immobile, but her right hand began to shake. She gripped the punch glass firmly in both hands as Bettina went on with her steady flow of information.

"I can tell you, dear, it was quite a mess when George confronted me with it. I'm only glad that I was able to talk some sense into him and save the two of you from any embarrassment. But you do have to consider all the complications that might arise. A pregnancy . . ."

"What?" Jesa whispered, as she felt some of the punch spill over the rim of her glass onto her hand.

"No. No. Of course she's not pregnant, but what if she *were?* An underage girl with an insane father? Well. I cringe to think of the consequences."

Without pausing, Bettina reached over and took a napkin from a passing tray and handed it to Jesa. She could see that the blood had drained from Jesa's face and that her eyes had turned back toward Severio.

"But now that we have it all under control there's certainly no need to dwell on it. I didn't really mean to gossip about it at all. I just wanted to let you know, in case news of George Laird's hysteria had reached you, that it's all firmly under control. What I really wanted to say," and now she raised her voice to a normal level, "was that I'm so glad you could take the time out to come to my little gathering tonight. It was so generous of Severio to donate that sketch of his. It's so good of an artist who is already achieving some recognition to be concerned with those who are struggling. I was saying just the other day to the new chairman of the committee. . . ."

Jesa sat stock still. Her hand had stopped shaking. In fact she thought that her entire body might have been turned to stone. Her mind was frantically trying to assimilate what had happened. She knew there was not a shred of concern in Bettina's revelations. She knew what Bettina was doing, but she couldn't understand why. Deliberate cruelty was a mystery to her. She felt a stab of pain, not only at Severio's betrayal, but at her own inability to cope with the world. Would she always remain an innocent, a dupe, no matter how old she was? No matter how much she went through? And here was irrefutable evidence of her stupidity: Severio had been sleeping with this girl Melinda at the same time he was making love to her. Her heart constricted in agony.

She felt her body rise from the chair. She had to get out of the room before she entirely lost control and the cry of anguish that was welling in her throat came screaming out of her.

". . . so I think that you've handled the whole thing with the utmost intelligence, Jesa. After all Jesa, is something the matter?"

"I'm sorry, I have to go," she muttered.

She walked a few paces, then realized that she still had the punch glass in her hand. She stumbled back to deposit it on a table, bumping into Bettina, who reached out and steadied her.

"Aren't you feeling well?"

"I'm sorry, I have to go."

She wandered through the crowd and out onto the street. She was raising her hand to hail a taxi when Severio rushed to her side.

"Jesa, what the hell's going on?"

A cab pulled up to the curb. She reached for the handle of the taxi door, jerking it, but unable to open it. He pushed her hand away and yanked the door open. He gave the driver her address as she sat trembling beside him, unable to speak. When he reached out to touch her, she shrank from him.

"What's wrong with you?" he demanded. "Did Bettina upset you? Why did you just walk out like that?" When he saw that his questions were getting him nowhere, he pulled her to him and told the driver to hurry up.

She sank down onto the couch in her living room, still trying to control her shaking. Severio kept interrogating her, but her throat seemed to be too constricted to speak. He poured her a glass of brandy and tried to put it to her lips. When he said that he was going to call her psychiatrist, she managed to get out a single word.

"Melinda," he repeated blankly. "I don't know what you're talking about."

She looked directly at him, her eyes which had been so full of love now commanded him not to compound his infidelity with a lie. A trapped expression seemed to melt the features of his strong face. Then his jaw tightened in rage.

"Goddamn that meddling bitch!" he shouted, hurling the brandy glass across the room and shattering it against the fireplace.

"Do you know why she's telling you that muck? Do you? It's because she made a pass at me and I turned her down. That's why she's trying to poison you with all this dirty gossip."

She watched the brandy trickle down the mantelpiece. When one rivulet had reached the floor and started to form a tiny puddle, she turned to see his trembling body. Her voice came out calmly.

"I don't know what Bettina's motives are. I can't understand a woman like that. But that's not the point. It's true about the girl, isn't it?"

He turned away from her and stood staring out the window. His mute posture was the only confirmation she needed.

"I don't suppose I understand you any better than I understand Bettina. You told me that you loved me."

"I do love you," he said fiercely.

"Then how could you be sleeping with this girl at the same time we . . ."

"It wasn't at the same time. I met her when I first came back to New York, before we'd started up together. And I don't think my behavior is so difficult to understand. I was lonely and she was there. I never had any feeling for her. In fact I dislike her."

"Then why did you take her to bed?"

"Because when a man who likes sex is offered sex he doesn't say no.

"Bettina says the girl is only seventeen. Even if she did throw herself at you, her age might have stopped you."

"You sound like a prosecuting attorney," he yelled.

"I'm sorry," she said in a quiet voice. "You're right. There's no point in getting into any of that now. It's just that when I think of you with her, there in the bed we've shared, I . . ."

And now the image of it was too strong to tolerate. A great wracking sob came up from her chest. The sounds of hurt hurled themselves out of her body in an uncontrollable torrent. He came over to the couch swiftly and knelt down next to her.

"Jesa, please don't cry. We'll go away from all this.

We'll go up to the country. That's what you want, isn't it? We'll go away from all of it, just the two of us."

He took her in his arms, rocking her and smoothing the hair back from her tear-stained face. But she wouldn't stop crying. Nothing in the world made him feel so helpless as seeing a wronged woman weep out her soul. It made him feel as though he were drowning. He had to make her stop.

"Jesa, forgive me. I want to marry you. Please. Tell me that you'll be my wife."

Chapter 13

Even though a breeze was rippling the surface of the lake, the summer heat was oppressive. Jesa put her sketchpad on the grass, pulled the cotton shirt away from her perspiring back, and reached for the thermos of iced tea. The sound of laughter came from the opposite side of the lake. She shaded her eyes to see a young couple running through the woods toward the pier. They stripped down to their bathing suits and dove into the water, shouting and splashing each other. She watched them for a while, thinking how vibrant and happy they looked, then forced her attention back to the sketchpad.

Flor Marcal had asked her to do a poster for the "Save the Lake" campaign. At first she'd begged off, saying that graphic design wasn't her long suit. But Flor had insisted she give it a try, and she'd accepted, thinking that it would give her something to do while

Severio was painting. She still had dreams of doing the series of paintings she'd started with the narcissus, but somehow she couldn't seem to motivate herself. Besides, she had turned the studio over to Severio, reasoning that he had priority.

After struggling with the sketch for another half hour, she slipped off her sandals and walked toward the water's edge. When she looked across the lake again, she thought the young couple had disappeared. Then she made out their figures lying on the pier, hands and feet touching, faces turned toward the sun. She waded out until the cool water lapped at the hem of her denim skirt, still staring at them. The young man propped himself up, slipped the straps from the girl's shoulders and started to massage some oil into her back. Even at a distance Jesa could see the erotic tenderness of his touch. She quickly cast her eyes down to the water and pretended to be picking up a stone. She hoped they hadn't seen her looking at them. She waded back toward the shore and strolled off in the opposite direction. As she cast a quick glance over her shoulder, she realized that they were far too engrossed with each other to be aware of anyone else.

"I'll end up like Sophie Moss yet," she thought. "By the time I'm sixty I'll be bursting into tears when I hear a chorus of 'Hello, Young Lovers.' "

It wasn't that she envied them. Quite the opposite. She felt sad and protective about the changes that the years would undoubtedly bring them. That simple, all-consuming togetherness would be eroded as sure as death and taxes. They would stop being in love and start to struggle with a "working relationship." Compromises would be reached, allowances made, expectations sacrificed in the name of commitment. If they were lucky, the changes would be minor and gradual. The accumulation of time and the shared memories would counterbalance the loss of excitement and romance. But if there was a sudden violation of trust, they might suffer a test they were unprepared for, as she had with Severio.

She had been true to the promise she'd made the night he had proposed to her: she had never mentioned his affair with Melinda again. Sometimes when they were together, she believed that she could put it behind her, but when she was alone, it still tormented her. She told herself that she was unreasonable. After all, she believed his explanation of how the affair came about and she could hardly expect him to be faithful to her before they had even become lovers. She tried to take responsibility for her disappointment. She had been hurt because she'd constructed an idealized Severio in her mind—a man who didn't resemble a real human being with faults and failings. But she wasn't a girl of eighteen. She was a mature woman who must accept reality with grace, as she accepted the tiny lines that had formed around her eyes. Acceptance was a large part of any successful marriage. Yet she had made no real plans for the wedding and was relieved when Severio suggested they put it off until September so that they could prepare for a real social event.

She looked at the pebble she still had clasped in her hand and skipped it across the water. When she'd retraced her steps back to where she had left her things on the shore, she noticed that the young couple had gone. The pier was now occupied by two elderly women who were supervising a group of noisy children. Packing up her gear, she trudged up the path toward her car and decided to visit Flor.

It was always open house at the Marcals'. Whether Flor was arranging a sleep-over for her youngest child, cooking a dinner for eight, or mobilizing the community for "Save the Lake," she always had time to linger over a cup of coffee. "Housework is my last priority," Flor often said, and the Marcal homestead was testimony to that fact. Jesa pulled up to the three-storied wooden house, parked the car next to the overgrown garden, and knocked at the screen door. Flor's powerful voice yelled that she should come back to the kitchen. She walked past the skateboards, a bushel of tomatoes, and piles of magazines that had been left in the hallway.

"Your timing is perfect," Flor beamed as she came forward to hug her. Flor was barefoot, wearing a loose orange shift and her perennial gold-loop earrings. She pushed the crisp gray hair back from her forehead. "How'd you know that we were mixing up a batch of piña coladas? I just wanted to open a couple of cans, but you know what a perfectionist Josh is. He insisted we get a real coconut and a real pineapple."

Jesa looked past her into the kitchen, where Josh was standing at the sink chopping a pineapple with a large knife. He was wearing cut-offs and an open shirt that exposed his chest.

281

"Gosh, it's been ages since I've seen you, Josh," she exclaimed.

She had called him over six weeks ago when she and Severio had first come up to the house, inviting him to dinner. He had excused himself, saying that he was teaching in the summer session and was deluged with work. She hadn't heard from him since and was sorry that she hadn't run into him at any of the meetings that Flor organized.

"It's good to see you too, Jesa," he smiled, offering his hand.

Flor's eyes darted back and forth between them. The slight tension in Josh's voice fueled her suspicion that they had had an affair that had somehow gone awry. The first time she had ever seen them together, she'd had a strong vibration that they were more than just friends. And just last week she'd thought that Josh might be avoiding Jesa—he'd casually inquired if Jesa was going to attend a meeting and when Flor had answered in the affirmative, he'd said that he was too busy to come. She couldn't wait to get a look at Jesa's friend Severio. He would really have to be something to outclass a man like Josh Graham.

"This is no time to dally over old friendships," she said lightly, wanting to save them from any possible embarrassment. "Matt will be home soon and if I don't plan to meet him at the door wearing a flimsy negligée, the least I can do is to put a cold drink in his hand. Just let me find you the blender, Josh."

She scrounged around in the cabinets and unearthed the blender, then drew Jesa to the table to show her the new pile of petitions they'd accumulated. Josh went back to the sink and seemed to be absorbed in fixing the piña coladas. He noticed that Jesa did not look as well as the last time he had seen her. There was a listlessness in her body and her eyes betrayed the same sad expression they had worn when he'd first met her.

Over the last months he had convinced himself that he had gotten over his attraction to her. He had even started seeing a woman who was teaching a poetry course at the summer session. She was pleasant company and he had enjoyed sleeping with her, but he knew that when the session came to an end they would go their separate ways with no regrets. Now that he saw Jesa, sitting at the table and casually braiding her hair as she listened to Flor's steady chatter, he felt the old concern and desire return. He attacked the coconut rather angrily and drained the milk into the blender. When there was nothing else for him to do, he asked Flor for the rum.

"Oh my God, the rum! I forgot the rum. How can we have piña coladas without the rum? Will you dear people excuse me for about fifteen minutes? I'll just dash down to the village before the store closes." She pushed her feet into a pair of scuffs, grabbed her purse and rushed out of the front door.

"Mind if I steal a piece of pineapple?" Jesa asked, as she walked over to the sink.

He picked up a sliver and popped it into her mouth.

"So how have you been?" she asked when she had finished eating it.

"Fine," he answered noncommittally.

"I came over to your place a couple of weeks ago. I really wanted to talk with you."

"What did you want to talk to me about?"

"Nothing in particular. Just missed your company. I was having a blue day."

"I've thought of dropping by your place, too, but. . ." and now he shifted his eyes from hers and looked out the window.

"But what?"

"I was afraid I might be interrupting your painting. How's it going?"

"I'm ashamed to say that I haven't been painting. I was down in the city for several weeks and I thought I'd get into it when I came back, but somehow I can't seem to motivate myself,"

"That's a shame. You were so excited by it. What's the trouble?"

She shrugged her shoulders and sat down at the table, her delicate fingers playing with the ivy in the copper kettle. She looked so dejected that he thought he'd best not press her.

"I've been working on some rough drafts for the poster, but I don't think any of them are very good."

"Sounds like you're having a crisis of confidence. You'd better get a second opinion. Can I see what you've done sometime?"

"Oh, I have all my sketches out in the car."

They walked out to the car, brought the folder of sketches back into the kitchen, and sat down at the table to examine them. Josh's bright blue eyes narrowed critically as he went through the sheath of papers. Finally he selected one, placed it on the sideboard, and moved back to look at it from a distance.

"What's the matter with you, woman? This one is just fine. Where would you put the lettering?"

Her mind started to click again. She took up a pencil and showed him where she planned to put in the information about their organization. She trusted his objectivity and now that he'd given her some encouragement, she could see that the poster really was pretty good.

"I don't understand why you were so negative about what you've done. The last time we talked you really seemed to be getting on the track. What's been happening to make you feel insecure again?"

"Oh, I don't know. Sometimes I just lose all faith in my judgment. Not only about the painting—about everything. I just feel mopey and drained, even though there's nothing I can point to objectively as the cause."

"But there must be a reason," he prodded, putting his arm around her.

She looked up at him, wondering if she could or should divulge any of the problems that had been nagging her. But they all seemed so deeply personal that she didn't know where to begin.

"I don't mean to pry," he said, withdrawing his arm. "But I can tell you one thing: you did a helluva good job on this poster. You ought to be proud of yourself."

Just then Flor flew in the door, plunked the paper bag down on the table, and kicked off her scuffs.

"I made it," she panted. "They were just about to

close the store and . . . hey, the poster's finished. Why didn't you say so when you first came in, Jesa?"

"It's just a rough draft. But I can have it finished by tomorrow, if you think it's okay."

"It's terrific," Flor said enthusiastically. "Josh told me you were really talented, but I'd never seen any of your work. I should've known this man never lies. I don't know how he managed to stay in Washington as long as he did."

While Josh finished making the piña coladas, they sat at the table and discussed how many posters they'd put out in the first printing. Jesa's mood brightened considerably. When Josh had poured the foamy liquid into their glasses, he banged on the table and announced that he would like to propose a toast.

"To our resident artist, Jesamine Mallick. With this kind of talent behind us, we'll whip the whole community up and put those corporate boys back on their duffs."

"Here! Here!" Flor chimed in. "Hey, we can't break this up when we're all having such a wonderful time. Why don't you guys stay to dinner? I just have cold cuts—it's too damn hot to cook—but we'd love to have you."

"I really think I'd better be getting home," Jesa said.

"If you're worried about your friend, call him up and invite him. And you can call your lady friend and invite her, too," she added quickly to Josh.

Josh paused for a moment, then agreed that he'd try to give his friend a call. Jesa said she'd go on home and bathe, then call up to tell Flor when they'd be back.

The sun was just beginning to go down as she drove through the countryside. The intense heat of the day was waning and the plants gave off a satisfying, woodsy smell. As the car bumped along the road, Jesa felt refreshed and hopeful. It would be so pleasant to spend an evening in the company of people she enjoyed. And her curiosity was piqued at the prospect of meeting Josh's lady friend.

She called out Severio's name as she walked in the door. When there was no answer and she felt the quiet of the house, she crept upstairs and quietly opened the bedroom door. Severio was stretched out on the bed, a sheet partially draped over him. The deep coral tones of the sunset outlined his sleeping body. She put her folder of sketches down beside the bed and bent over to kiss him.

"Hello, darling. How did it go today?"

"Real good. I just showered and came in here for a nap. I wish you would put up some dark curtains in this room. It's hard to sleep with the sun blaring in," he answered groggily.

"I've always liked to look out at the trees. Besides, I hardly ever nap in the afternoon."

"But I do. There's not a helluva lot to do up here in the boonies but work and sleep."

"That's not true," she said as she sat down on the bed beside him. "As a matter of fact we've been asked out for the evening. I was just over at Flor's showing her my roughs on the poster and she's invited us back there for dinner. Flor and Matt will be there, and Josh and a friend of his."

"What did you say this guy Matt does?"

"I think he's in insurance."

"Oh, my God, Jesa. I can just imagine an evening with an insurance salesman and a farmer."

"They're very interesting, warm people," she protested.

"I still don't want to go. I might work some more tonight. You can go over if you like."

As much as she wanted to be with her friends again, the thought of going back there alone didn't appeal to her.

"Do you want to see the poster they picked?" she asked. "It's not half bad."

"Not now, darling," he murmured, undoing the top button of her blouse. "Look, Sally and Ellman are coming up tomorrow. You'll have all weekend to be with your friends. Why don't you just take a quick shower and hop into bed with me? I've been thinking about it all day."

"I'll have to call Flor and tell her we're not coming."

"Sure," he said, pulling her toward him and then releasing her. "But hurry."

When she came back to bed he sensed her disappointment at his refusal to visit the Marcals, and made a special effort to arouse her. He prided himself on being an expert lover and after so many months with her, he was completely attuned to the rhythms of her desire. She would not have thought it possible that she could achieve greater physical satisfaction than she had when they were first together, but she did. No matter what difficulties or tensions existed in their relationship, they rarely manifested themselves in the bedroom.

"Masters and Johnson could plug us up to their machines as an example of the quintessentially perfect sex act," she whispered afterwards, with a touch of irony in her voice. But Severio had already rolled away from her and seemed to have fallen back to sleep, though it was not like him to drift off after they'd had sex. She ran her hands over the damp flesh of his arms and played with the matted hair on his chest, hoping that he would stay awake and talk to her, but he grunted quietly and pulled the sheet up over his body. She slipped into a kimono, closed the windows lest the sudden change to evening air might chill him, picked up her sketches, and crept downstairs.

After soothing her parched throat with a tumbler of iced tea, she went into the studio to see what he'd been doing. The huge canvas made her feel uneasy. It wasn't that the technique was poor—far from it—Severio had a mechanical skill that would always put hers to shame. But the painting was almost a replica of the canvas of the charging bull that she had seen so many months ago at the Hartmans'. But many painters reworked the same subjects, she told herself. It was almost a mark of the artistic temperament that recurrent themes bedeviled or captivated the imagination. But there was no metamorphosis here, no progression. It was virtually the same canvas, only larger. If only he weren't so eager to dash off these commissioned works while he was "hot," she might be able to get him to relax and really explore his talents.

She wandered back into the living room, propped her poster up on the old oak desk, switched on the desk lamp, and moved back to the couch to get a better look at it. When she'd decided the changes she wanted to make, she was about to get up and take it into the kitchen to work on it again when a strong image came to her: she could see Ed sitting at the desk, his left hand twirling the forelock of his hair. This twisting of his hair was a gesture that he had whenever he withdrew into his private thoughts. He could sit like that, nodding as she spoke to him, so that the casual observer might think that he was listening to her. But she would know that he wasn't listening. He had drifted into some daydream. It might have been about anything from the destruction of the ozone layer to memories of the first girl he'd ever kissed. Whatever it was, he was unreachable. The gesture had always infuriated her. Now she remembered it fondly.

She rested her chin on the arm of the couch, still staring at the desk, conjuring up his presence. For months after his death that presence had appeared unbidden. It had scourged her memory; made her weep with the ache of her loss. She had cursed it, feared its appearance, tried to banish it altogether. Now it seemed almost comforting. During recent months she had come to take a more objective and even critical attitude toward her marriage. She realized that she had subjugated a great part of her personality to Ed's and knew that he had taken her for granted. She admitted that their sexual life had become comforting but unadventurous. She won-

dered what might have happened had she been consciously aware of these things while Ed was still alive.
"I guess we could have talked about them," she said
softly. "We were always great talkers."

Even in the beginning of their relationship, they had
stayed up until the wee hours talking. As the years
rolled on, when they no longer rushed into each
other's arms to declare their love, when he would
come home tired and grouchy and give her a perfunc-
tory peck on the cheek—even then, they had always
been eager to talk. She would reconstruct her day for
him. Whether she'd had a rough time at the doctor's
office or tried something new in her art class, she
would always find that in talking it out with him, she
understood her own experiences more fully. She
would chatter about bills and furniture, and even
though she knew that he didn't give a damn if the new
couch was beige or burgundy, he would put in his two
cents' worth. They had their running jokes about
mutual friends. They developed catch words and
phrases that would send them both into the instant
laughter of recognition.

He knew her so well. He had seen her retching from
the flu. He had held the ice pack to her puffy jaw when
she'd had her wisdom teeth out. He had sat by her side
when she'd lost the baby, weeping in mutual loss.
When all illusion was gone—when she had been
drained or bitchy or haggard—he had still been able to
tell her with a smile that she was the best woman on
earth for him.

"No matter what. No matter what, Ed. You were my

best friend."

She curled up on the couch and thought and thought. When the overhead light was turned on, she jerked her head to attention, startled.

"Why the hell are you sitting here in the dark?" Severio asked.

"I was just thinking."

"You are the moody one," he wagged his finger at her playfully. "What's bothering you? And whatever it is, can we talk about it over a meal? I'm starved."

"I'll fix something," she said quickly as she started up from the couch.

"Sorry I fell asleep on you, darling. Is this your poster? It's quite good."

She couldn't confess to her image of Ed. When they had first started seeing each other, Severio had been attentive, even encouraging when she wanted to talk about her husband. But lately he seemed to think that he was the victim of unfair comparison. He had told her that be thought that for the sake of her own mental health, she should suppress her remembrances. She only idealized Ed, he cautioned her, and that idealization was bound to make her melancholy. She didn't think that she could convince him that she was not being morbid now, only introspective. She asked him what sort of supper he would like, and hurried off to the kitchen to see if she had the ingredients.

As she washed the endive and tore the watercress into pieces for the salad, she was almost glad that she'd decided not to go down to the city with him this weekend. They'd received invitations to a black-tie affair at the Whitney, but they had already invited Sally and Ellman up for the weekend. It had been months since Jesa had seen Sally, because after she'd finally gotten out of Rolling Hills, Sally had flown off to Bermuda for a vacation. Jesa explained to Severio that her reunion with her friend had priority over any social event and tried to talk him into staying in the country. He asked her to give his apologies to Ellman, but said it was necessary for him to put in an appearance at the Whitney, which relieved her. She had no idea what the "new" Sally would be like, but dreaded the notion of any tension between her volatile friend and her lover. Besides, she wanted an opportunity to talk with Sally alone.

Severio was in fine spirits when she drove him to the train station the next morning. They were necking playfully in the car until he heard the train approach, then he grabbed his overnight bag and rushed up to the platform, calling out that he would telephone her late the following evening to give her the gossip from the Whitney. She went home and finished up the poster and took it over to Flor's. She was arranging some fresh-cut flowers in the guest room and wondering whether Sally and Ellman were sleeping together or if she would have to make up a bed for him on the couch, when she heard a car horn honk in the driveway.

She hurried to the veranda to see Sally fling back the passenger door to Ellman's Bentley and rush toward her. The change in Sally's appearance was radical: she was wearing a neatly tailored beige pantsuit that showed she'd lost weight, her hair was clipped and fluffy, and the old bounce was back in her step.

"I don't believe we're really here," she laughed as she ran up the steps and threw herself into Jesa's arms.

Ellman put the overnight bags down and gave Jesa a hug. Rebecca pranced around her feet, yapping for attention.

"Oh, my God, it's good to see both of you," Jesa cried. "You look wonderful. Both of you look wonderful."

"I look okay now, but this time last week I had more freckles than a turkey egg. I kept telling Ellman that my skin couldn't take the sun, but he insisted that I trudge around those damn golf courses with him."

"What's the point of being in Bermuda if you don't go out in the sun?" Ellman managed to get in. "I told her to wear a hat, but she's so stubborn. . . ."

"I got so badly burned we had to stay in the bungalow for three days straight. Had little blisters all over me."

"That wasn't so bad. You just hated it because I kept beating you at chess."

"Naturally you beat me at chess. Chess is for eggheads. Who else wants to sit for hours wondering what the other guy's tactical move will be? You can't even talk. But just tell Jesa how much I won from you when we switched to poker," she grinned with devilish satisfaction.

Jesa put her arm around Sally's waist and opened the screen door. "Come in, come in," she cried happily. "I'll fix us all a drink."

She stopped short. She'd promised herself that she was going to be politic and not mention liquor and now she'd violated her resolve in the first three minutes they were together. Sally squeezed her hand.

"It's okay. Don't get all flustered. I can talk about it. I just can't drink it. I do once in a while. Hell, you didn't think I was going to come out of the place as a latter-day Carry Nation, did you? I'd love a soda. This heat is about to melt me away."

Sally flopped on the couch, fanning herself with a magazine. Ellman inquired where their room was. Jesa pricked up her ears when she heard the singular of "room" and walked him back to the downstairs bedroom. Then she fixed a tray of cool drinks and they sat down to talk, Sally giving vivid descriptions of their holiday, Ellman filling her in on recent happenings in the art world. Jesa was relieved to see that Sally's mood seemed to fit with her improved appearance— she was as sassy and sarcastic as ever, punctuating Ellman's stories with her own observations and embroidering his descriptions. When Jesa brought up Sally's stay at Rolling Hills, Ellman excused himself, saying that he was going to drive into the village to have the radiator hose checked.

"He's so sensitive," Sally said, when she heard the Bentley leave the driveway. "There's nothing wrong with the radiator hose. He just knows that we want some time to talk alone."

"So tell me all about it," Jesa said, tucking her feet underneath her and pulling Rebecca into her lap.

"God, I don't know where to begin. 'The Rolling

Hills Saga' "—Sally threw her hands into the air as though she were announcing the title of an old-time melodrama. "It was dreadful. The first week I honestly didn't think I could survive it. I felt as though I were trapped in some damned story by Edgar Allan Poe. The doctor was nice enough, but there was this damn nurse who kept talking to me as though I were in nursery school. She'd come around to my room and talk about my being 'clean and dry'—I felt like she was going to check my diaper! But I knew I had to do it. I just had to. Ellman told me that he gave you the low-down on the awards episode. That was the clincher. I tell you, Jesa," and here her voice became gentle and reflective, "I really don't think I would have survived it if it hadn't been for Ellman. I always used to think that the word supportive had something to do with under-wear, but this man has really taught me what it can mean."

"So it's good between you?"

"Good isn't the word."

She drew a cigarette from her purse, leaning forward with a conspiratorial gleam in her eyes.

"I just know that Ellman would have me drawn and quartered for telling anyone this—you know how reserved he is—but when he picked me up from Rolling Hills, we stopped at this Howard Johnson's. We'd stopped there on my way to be committed and for some insane reason I wanted to stop there again. Well, we were sitting in the parking lot. I just threw my arms around him. I wanted to thank him and I just knew I couldn't find the words. Next thing you know, we were getting a room there. Can you imagine Ellman consummating an affair at Howard Johnson's? Bermuda was nothing after that! And the surprising thing is that I thought I was doing it as some sort of gesture of gratitude and it turned out to be absolutely terrific. The outside world will never know, but beneath those thick glasses, our mild-mannered Clark Kent is really you-know-who."

Sally doubled up in excited laughter. Jesa caught the enthusiasm and started to giggle.

"He'd just kill me if he knew I'd told you this," Sally grimaced and hit her hand in mock contrition.

"But don't you remember the first time I went to bed with Ed and I called you up at eight in the morning to tell you all about it?"

The laughter mounted until both women were rocking back and forth with tears in their eyes. Nothing they were saying was really that funny and they both knew it. The outburst was a sign that they had made it up without the apologies and forgiveness. The pleasure in each other's company was there as it had been for the last twenty years, giving them both a sense of relief and continuity.

"But I haven't told you the really big news," Sally said. "We're getting married."

"I don't believe it."

"Neither do I. I'm scared out of my mind. But I've already said 'I do.' "

The laughter stopped in Jesa's throat. She had said yes to Severio, but she didn't feel any of Sally's enthusiasm herself. Sally leaned forward and touched her hand.

"I've been gabbing about myself all this time. I want to bear what's been happening to you. I know you and Severio are living together and . . . I want to apologize for everything I said about him."

"You know you don't have to. That's all forgotten now."

"But I want to. You said that I was jealous. At the time I didn't think that was true. I thought I was glad that you'd found somebody. But in retrospect, I can see that I was feeling so lonely that anything that threatened to change the pattern with you—the one friend I knew I could rely on—scared me to death. I said terrible things about him and I don't even know him."

"But I didn't even listen to anything you were saying. I've never told you this, but that day when we had the argument, I'd just gone to bed with him for the first time. I wasn't in any mood to listen to anything you said. I was awful toward you."

"Forget it. I was out of bounds. Let's close the chapter," Sally insisted, stubbing out her cigarette. "How are you doing now? Do you think you'll marry him?"

"He has asked me, yes. And I've said I would. It seemed to be exactly what I wanted, but now . . . I have so many doubts."

"But you're a perfect candidate for marriage. Much more than I am. After all, you have been happily married. You're the sort of woman who should be with a man. I don't say that because I think you're dependent or conventional or any of that. I've always considered myself to be an independent woman, but now I know there's a big difference between independence and loneliness. I don't mean that everyone should be loaded onto Noah's Ark in some mindless coupling. But I do think that life is richer if you can share it."

"I want to share it. . . ." Jesa's voice trailed off.

She began to talk about some of her misgivings, though she couldn't mention Severio's affair with Melinda. That seemed disloyal to him, and though she was ashamed to admit it, it hurt her pride. Still there was some relief just trying to unravel her feelings as Sally sat listening and nodding. But there was no resolution. Despite the comfort and warmth of her reunification with her oldest friend, she knew that she would have to face her decision alone.

When Ellman returned from the village, they walked the property together and returned to the house for a leisurely dinner. Jesa had almost forgotten how much pleasure she took in entertaining people she cared about. She told them about the "Save the Lake" campaign and showed them the poster. When Sally asked if she'd been doing any other work, she decided to let them see the narcissus painting.

Sally took one long look at the canvas and let out a low whistle.

"It's fantastic, Jesa. So full of life. So . . . well, sexy. It's totally different from anything else you've ever done."

Ellman moved back and forth in front of the canvas, taking off his glasses, massaging the indentations on the side of his nose, replacing his glasses, and grunting softly.

"That's his appraiser's behavior," Sally explained. "The fifth grunt is the signal that we're about to hear the last judgment."

Ellman cast a patient glance at Sally, cleared his throat, put his arm around Jesa and said, "It's fine work. Best work I've ever seen you do. You finish the series and I'll give it a showing if you want me to."

"Coming from Ellman Smith, that's a superlative. Finish the series, Jesa. It's time you started thinking about making some money on your work."

"I'm glad you both like it," Jesa replied quietly. She wondered how Severio would take it if she actually started to have a professional career.

It was after midnight when they all said goodnight. As Sally slipped into the lacy cotton nightgown she had bought for their trip to Bermuda, she could hear Jesa padding around upstairs.

"So what do you think?" she asked, *sotto voce.*

"About what?"

"About Jesa, for God's sake."

"I think the painting is really excellent. Has a lot of verve, an almost primitive, and as you said, sensual . . ."

"I know that, darling," she said with forbearance. "I mean, what do you think about Jesa personally? How does she seem to you?"

"I'm not sure," he answered as he picked up the cream and started to massage it into her peeling back. "There's something, I don't know, something stiff-upper-lip about her demeanor. Is she getting along with Severio?"

"Well, they are living together and he's asked her to marry him, but she's unsure. She talked around the issue a lot. I don't really know what's making her so hesitant, but I'm certainly glad she's giving it some time. I still think he's a rotten choice for her, but I've learned my lesson. I'm going to keep my mouth shut."

"Good idea, love. Why don't you start to practice now? I'm bushed," he yawned, as he recapped the cream and patted her back.

"Ah, the first sign of cruel neglect," she sighed as she switched off the light and snuggled into his arms. Within minutes she could hear the rhythm of his gentle snoring. It was a comforting sound, but she stayed awake pondering her friend's life.

Chapter 14

*S*everio adjusted the headrest, leaned back, and listened to the steady clackety-clack of the train that was taking him back to Connecticut. Except for the burning sensation that lack of sleep had produced in his eyes, he had a delicious sense of well-being. He'd made a few contacts at the Whitney celebration and his brief encounter with the girl had given an unexpected flip to his weekend of freedom.

He would not have even recognized her had she not been wearing the same tuxedo she'd had on when they'd met at the Friends of Young Artists auction months before. He didn't remember her name, but he had reintroduced himself so skillfully that she'd never noticed his lapse of memory. He kidded her about her outfit, saying that she didn't have to take the "black tie" on the invitation literally. He offered to fetch her some more champagne and asked how her painting was going. After fifteen minutes of conversation, her eyes were giving him the green light. But it wasn't until he'd casually cross-examined her to make sure that they had no mutual acquaintances that he had offered to escort her home.

He knew that he had to be cautious. He had no intention of subjecting Jesa to the kind of upset that his affair with Melinda had caused her. Jesa had to be protected, because she would never understand that he needed these little flings to retain his sense of vitality. She would think that his dalliances reflected negatively on his relationship with her, whereas they really only made him feel more alive and therefore more loving. If she found out she would stare at him with that wounded expression, with the same martyred, accusing eyes that reminded him of his mother. He couldn't bear the notion of another scene. Guilt stultified him, made him feel trapped and ineffectual, destroyed his creative energies. And there was no real reason to feel guilty. It wasn't as though he had come into the city with the intention of seeking out female companionship. It had come to him. Therefore he was absolved of blame. If only he remembered to be careful.

This time there were no slip-ups. He had taken the girl to her West Side apartment and sat on the Salvation Army couch sipping cheap California wine and nodding sympathetically when she told him about her difficulties in breaking into the art world. He had even been mindful enough to ask for a phone where he could speak privately so that he could give Jesa the promised call. While he was telling Jesa about the evening at the Whitney, he eyed the loft bed above his head and thought about the logistics of climbing up the wooden stairs in a state of arousal. He decided to put in another half hour of conversation to make sure that the girl was willing, told Jesa he was exhausted, and bade her goodnight.

When he'd left the next morning, explaining that he had to rush to his studio and change clothes because he had a train to catch, he'd managed to make an escape without even an exchange of telephone numbers.

As he gazed out the window at the lush summer countryside, the memory of the encounter gave him a tingling sensation of pride. As the conductor announced that they were approaching the station, he roused himself from his reveries and picked up his bag. He was very eager to see Jesa again. There was nothing more satisfying than being greeted by a loving woman, driven off to a well-kept house where he could enjoy a calm evening meal and some quiet conversation. And soon she was going to be his wife. He marveled at his stupidity in not having asked her to marry him sooner. But in the beginning he had been so consumed with the desire to possess her that he had failed to really see her character.

He had thought her aloof when she was only shy. He

had believed she was unattainable because she was wealthy—in fact she had an almost childish naïveté about money and class and had probably never noticed the discrepancies in their bank accounts or backgrounds. He had wanted her as his mistress, when it was obvious that she had the personality of a perfect wife. She was devoted to him, but her gardening, her small-town politics, her Sunday painting, all provided her with enough outside interests to inhibit any choking demands on his time. She had her own income, so he was free of any economic responsibilities toward her. And she loved him sexually. He certainly had the best of both possible worlds: an environment where he could work and recuperate and a life of freedom and adventure away from it. He felt a gush of affection as he saw her standing on the station platform, her willowy suntanned legs exposed by the short cotton frock, her flowing hair neatly ordered by the white headband. She was the ideal young suburban matron.

Had he looked more closely at her when he jumped from the train and planted a feathery kiss on her cheek, he might have noticed that there was a strained expression about her mouth. Despite her beautifully normal appearance, she was seething with unresolved feelings. The easy familiarity with which Sally and Ellman listened to each other, anticipated each other's desires and joked, made her realize how lacking her relationship with Severio was. And if Sally had exhibited restraint in talking about Severio, she had absolutely let out all the stops when she'd found out that Jesa had given up her studio to him. She had been astonished to see the work Jesa had done on the canvas of the narcissus and found it tantamount to masochism to think that she'd relinquish her working space just when she'd started to do some really interesting painting. Of course Jesa thought Sally was exaggerating when she described giving up the studio as neurotic, but she was no longer able to satisfy herself by calling it an act of love. She knew that it was just one example of how she adjusted, compromised, and shifted her daily life so that she wouldn't rock the boat. After the freedom and growth that she'd felt just a few months ago, she had lapsed into a pattern of fear and compliance that was affecting her psyche as much as a low-grade fever could affect her body. But she couldn't blame Severio about their lack of communication when she'd failed to speak up. She determined to lay all of her doubts and disappointments before him and hoped they would explore them together.

He slipped his arm around her waist as they walked down the wooden stairs toward the car. She was pleased to see that he was in a good mood.

"Shall I drive, or would you like to?" he inquired as he opened the car door and tossed his overnight bag into the back seat.

"I'd like to. You know I realized something the other day. Even though I'm a pretty good driver, whenever there's a man in the car, I always end up as the passenger."

"I leave for three days and I come home to find rebellion," he laughed as he slid into the passenger seat. "I'd think that saving the lake from the greedy corporate boys would be the extent of your political involvement. Now you're probably going to tell me that you've joined some radical feminist group."

"Oh, I was just thinking that I'd enter myself in the Indy 500," she laughed as she turned the key in the ignition, backed up and negotiated the turn onto the highway in a single movement.

"God, it's hot," he breathed, punching on the air-conditioning and reaching over to squeeze her knee. "I hope you've got something cool to drink at home."

"Of course I do. Gazpacho and shrimp salad and a bottle of Pouilly-Fuissé on ice to go with it."

"That's my girl. How was the weekend with Sally and Ellman?"

"I loved having them here. It was just like old times. Well, not quite—Sally isn't nearly so rambunctious since she's been on the wagon. But the really big news is that they're going to get married."

"No kidding."

"I know it's amazing. But once you see them together it all seems so natural. They're really a wonderful pair—she loosens him up and he calms her down."

"You mean they're the reverse of our relationship," he joked.

"It's strange. You think you know someone. You think that you can predict what direction her life is going in, and then you're brought up short. I never credited Sally with the willpower to stop the boozing. I surely never thought that she'd get married at this late date, and to Ellman Smith of all people. But their relationship touched me more than any romance between dewy-eyed youngsters, because they really know each other. There's a lot of mutual help and trust and it doesn't seem to be based on any illusions . . ."

"Speaking of weddings, how about our plans for the big event? I'm not gonna let a fuddy-duddy like Ellman outdistance me. What do you say to September? Blonds look wonderful in autumn tones. You could wear something in gold and rust and carry a bouquet of leaves."

"I've never met a man who had such a feeling about dress and color. Ed wouldn't have known if I was wearing blue or red." She bit her lip as the mention of Ed slipped out. There was no sense in complicating their conversation with a subject that nettled him.

"I know Ed was a sensitive man," Severio said casually, "but he wasn't an artist. That's why he never noticed things like color."

"I don't think it's just because you're an artist. I think it's because you were brought up by so many women. You could probably tell mauve from lilac when you were six years old. And speaking about all the ladies in your family, when am I ever going to get to meet them?"

"I really don't want to invite them to the wedding," he said, cringing at the thought of the embarrassment they might cause him in the company of his new-found associates. "You're an orphan, so it's easy to idealize families, but my mother would probably turn up in a kerchief and start organizing the kitchen before you could turn around. Besides, they'd all be out of place. Our crowd isn't the social scene they're used to."

"But surely that doesn't matter."

"It would matter. I'm not trying to cut them out. I'll write and let them know about the wedding. Believe me, it isn't for my sake. I just wouldn't want to cause them any social embarrassment.

"I can't wait to get back to work," he said quickly, eager to change the subject. "You know, when you first wanted to come up here, I was against it. I know I can be pigheaded, but I'm going to tell you just this once that I was wrong. It's been great for me to have this place. I've gotten a helluva lot of work done. 'Course I'm still going to have to go down to the city a lot. I think I'm going to buy a car, so I can make trips down to the city more easily. I don't want to inconvenience you by borrowing yours. I'd like to pay cash for it, so I may have to borrow some money until my next commissions come in."

She nodded agreement as she turned off the main highway into the drive leading to the house. It pleased her that he was chatting with her so openly. He had spoken of Ed without any jealousy or recrimination. He'd praised her judgment and said that he was grateful that they were living in the country.

"And another thing," he whispered, when she had shut off the motor and turned toward him. "I know I've been neglecting you. I've been too wrapped up in myself to want to socialize. So, in keeping with my resolution to do anything to make my future wife happy,

308

I've accepted a dinner invitation for tomorrow night. Fellow called Tim Badhams I met at the Whitney. Seems he lives close by here. I thought you'd like an evening out."

"That's thoughtful," she replied.

He lifted her hair from the back of her neck and blew cool air onto it, then his lips brushed her shoulder. Certainly now wasn't the time to carp about any of her misgivings.

By the time they had supper, bathed, and went to bed, her doubts were pushed so far back in her consciousness that she nestled against his chest and kissed him goodnight, feeling relieved to have him by her side again.

She rose early the next morning and drove with Flor to the print shop to check out the first posters. In the afternoon she cleared out part of the garage so that she could move her painting equipment in there and make good on her promise to get down to some serious work. She was sad to see the rain clouds forming on the horizon as she closed up the garage and went to get ready for their dinner date at the Badhams. It had been such a warm, peaceful day.

She was putting on the ice blue caftan that Severio liked so much when he came into the bathroom. She paused with the dress over her head, surprised that he had come in on her without knocking. It seemed more an invasion of privacy than an intimate action for him to walk in like that. She slipped the dress down and started to brush her hair.

"You look fine," he said as he surveyed her. "Why

don't you wear those little pearl earrings?"

"Is this dress inspection? They used to do that to me in boarding school. My aunt thought she wasn't getting her money's worth if my seams weren't perfectly straight."

"You usually like me to check you out when we're going somewhere."

"It just surprised me when you barged in on me," she smiled.

"I expect to be barging in on you a lot, Mrs. Euzielli."

" 'Manners are even more important in close quarters.' That's a quote from my aunt. But I wouldn't come in without knocking if you were in the bathroom."

"You can't force a code of conduct on me by saying what you'd do, Jesa. Now hurry up and find those earrings. I don't want to be late. And this time, I'm driving because the faster we get there the sooner we come home and then I can give you the kind of greeting I was too tired for last night."

They almost missed the Badhams house because its roof, which served as a parking deck, was level with the road. As they climbed down the several flights of stairs on the outside of the building and reached a platform decorated with multicolored lights, Jesa couldn't help thinking that the house was what Ed would have called "Disneyland Modern." A middle-aged man wearing a jumpsuit that didn't do much to disguise his corpulent body appeared from behind the sliding glass doors and introduced himself as Tim Badhams. He led them back into the "living space"—a large room with banks of carpeted platforms and no furniture. Three women were lolling on the platforms at the far end of the room near a display of neon sculpture. Tim grasped Jesa's elbow and walked her toward a modular structure that protruded from the wall and served as a bar. While he was mixing their drinks he introduced them to the two other men. The man called Jake looked Jesa up and down with such obvious sexual appraisal that she turned away embarrassed. She didn't catch the other man's name because Tim was steering them over to the other side of the room.

The young woman with red hair and a bright purple halter struggled up from the platform and gave Severio something between a curtsy and bow.

"This is my wife," Tim explained, nodding in her direction. "Now you girls have a good time."

Jesa waited to hear the woman's name, but Tim apparently felt that his mate's marital status was enough of an introduction. He put his arm around Severio and led him back toward the bar.

"I'm Jill," the redhead said in a little-girl voice. "And this is Debbie, Jake's wife, and Irma, Kenneth's wife."

Jesa nodded a greeting and folded the skirts of her caftan around her, sitting down as gracefully as the level of the platform would permit. Debbie hoisted up the bodice of the strapless sarong she was wearing and resumed her conversation about hotel accommodations in St. Croix. Irma agreed that the quality of service at the hotels had gone down at an appalling rate. The discussion of hotels, coupled with the sterile

311

decor of the room, made Jesa feel as though she were in the waiting area of an airport. She glanced over at Severio. He was standing with his arm around Jake as though they were long-lost friends. She marveled again at his chameleon social graces. He had picked up the "good ol' boy" manner of the other men in no time, while she was still struggling to find an entrée into a banal conversation about resorts.

"Don't mind the boys cutting us out," Jill breathed. "They're probably just talking about business."

"When *aren't* they talking about business?" Irma sighed.

They all paused and looked toward the men, catching the last part of a conversation that seemed to be about the stock market.

"And speaking of bullish . . ." they heard Jake say before he dropped his voice. The men gathered closer to him as be whispered something, and then punctuated whatever he'd said with a burst of laughter.

"Oh, hell, they're just talking about sex," Debbie said petulantly.

Even though she had no desire to listen to the men's conversation or be the object of Jake's lascivious looks, it had been a long time since Jesa had been at a party that was segregated by sex and she thought it ill-mannered. She turned her attention back to Debbie, who struggled with the front of the sarong again and leaned into the circle conspiratorially.

"What's good for the gander is good for the goose, I say. I've put up with Jake's shenanigans for years, but last summer I wised up. We were down in Acapulco—

on business, naturally—and I'd gone shopping 'til there just wasn't anything left to buy. I mean, how many silver bracelets and serapes can you wear? I was going out of my mind with boredom. So one day I'm down in the cabana and I see this scrumptious-looking kid. Rippling muscles, blond hair—the works. Turns out he's a dropout from U.C.L.A. and he's goin' 'round the world surfing and looking for life experiences. I knew in the first couple of minutes that I was going to be one of his life experiences, but the question was, where? I couldn't take him back to the room, 'cause I had no idea when Jake would come back. And he's sleeping on the damn beach if you please, so . . ." Jill and Irma suppressed their giggles and leaned closer to Debbie as she went on with graphic details of her tryst with the surfer. Jesa stared down into her drink, unable to meet Debbie's eyes.

"So the next day Jake sees this scratch on my back and he asks me how it got there. I told him that the chaise lounge by the pool had a nail sticking out of it and I'd hurt myself. So then he gets on the phone and starts screaming at the manager that he's going to sue him because his wife has been wounded by hotel furniture and has to have tetanus shots. I thought I would die!"

"You're really brave," Irma whispered, shaking her head from side to side. Iif Kenny ever caught me doing something like that he'd have a contract taken out on me."

"The secret is not to get caught," Debbie winked.

"I just know I'd get caught. I got caught when I just

tried to hide the bill from Bloomie's."

Jill noticed for the first time that Jesa had remained silent throughout, and since Tim had cautioned her that they were moving up in the world and she must improve her skills as a hostess, she cast around for some topic that would include her.

"Have you ever been to Acapulco?" she asked lamely.

"No. I've been to Mexico City a few times."

"Now you can really have some wild times there, too," Debbie continued. "We went slumming there one night and I tell you I was so wiped out that I didn't think I'd see the light of day. What all did you do while you were there?"

"I spent a lot of time at the archeological museum . . . and I went to see the Rivera murals." She could think of nothing else to say.

"How about a refill on these drinks?" Debbie asked, waving her glass at Jill.

"Maybe if we turned on some music we could get the fellas to dance with us," Irma put in.

"I think we'd better have dinner first," Jill replied, rising unsteadily from the platform and going to the intercom on the wall.

She pushed a button and told the cook that she was ready to have the dinner served, then pushed another button that filled the room with Muzak. They drifted out onto the terrace while the houseboy carried platters of Hawaiian food to the table.

"I brought the cook back from Hawaii with us," Jill said.

"We made such a bundle on a construction project there that we could've brought three cooks back with us," Tim told Jesa with pride.

She nodded and took a piece of spiced shrimp from one of the trays, and remained silent.

"Cat got your tongue?" Jake teased, eyeing her décolletage.

"Jesa's the quiet type," Severio explained, putting his arm around her waist.

"Well, I hope you thank the Lord every day for your blessings," Jake guffawed.

Debbie shot him a hostile look as they sat down to the table. Jesa was relieved that she could put food in her mouth and be absolved from joining in the conversation. She had not felt so out of place since being shipped to her aunt's for interminable and agonizing holiday dinners. She knew that no one in the present company would be watching her manners, but she felt so constrained that she became excessively polite. Severio smiled at her across the table with a sleepy, indulgent grin. She wondered how many of Tim's mai tai's he'd imbibed.

After the meal Jill, anxious to fulfill her role as hostess and not knowing quite how to deal with Jesa's reserved manner, suggested that she show her guest the house. Jesa summoned all her social graces in order to be able to comment favorably on the minimalist decor and the inset track lighting. When they returned to the living room, the rest of the company was sprawled on the platforms, apparently talking about business.

"This is why I wanted you to meet Jake," she heard Tim say as he threw his arm around Severio's shoulder. "Next year when the hotel complex is completed, Jake wants to have some first-class art for the lobby."

"Sure enough, Sev," Jake responded, his eyes still on Jesa. "This is going to be an exclusive resort for an international executive clientele. We're putting in golf courses, swimming pools, a heliport—the works. The lake is just a scenic backdrop. 'Course we're still having some problems with the local yokels who don't want the hotel; they know they'll have to pay admission to use the lake once we build, but we've got some Wall Street lawyers on the case. I'd say we'll break ground no later than next spring. Then it's full speed ahead."

Jesa was very still. When she'd first been introduced to Jake, the wisp of a memory had floated into her consciousness. She'd thought that she'd recognized him, but swept the notion aside, reasoning that all men who looked at women with that peculiarly predatory gaze seemed similar. Now she remembered that she'd seen him at the town meeting she'd attended with Josh. She was in the camp of the enemy.

"Didn't Tim tell me that you folks live out near the lake?" Jake asked, between swallows of his drink.

"Yeah, we're about fifteen minutes from it," Severio drawled. "I don't have much time to get there myself."

"Great setting, isn't it? A really beautiful piece," his eyes flitted over to Jesa again, "of real estate. It'll be a multimillion-dollar business within the next two years."

"I don't think your plan for the hotel will go through," Jesa heard herself say.

The room fell silent. Irma's mouth fell open slightly, amazed that this previously silent woman had the nerve to inject herself into the men's conversation, while Jill frantically started to refill the brandy snifters.

"Why don't you think the plan will go through?" Tim asked.

"Because the local property owners will fight it."

"Yeah, and they have as much chance as a snowball in hell," Jake chuckled.

"I wouldn't be so sure," Jesa answered, feeling the blood rise to her cheeks. "I own property there and I'm opposed to it."

"Jesa's gotten some info over a coffee clatch that's probably turned her head," Severio jumped in, as though saving her from an incredible faux pas.

"You probably don't know all the factors involved in this project," Tim said sententiously.

"I think I do," she replied, pulling her eyes away from Severio and attempting to hold her ground. "I listened to both sides of the argument at first, but now I've made up my mind. You see, you gentlemen think of the lake in terms of exploitation and profit—I suppose that's only natural since it's your business to look at the land that way. But those of us who live here have a very different relationship to the lake. We care about it. We think of it as a place of beauty and calm. If we wanted heliports, highways, and swimming pools instead of a natural setting, we wouldn't have chosen to live here in the first place."

"And I thought she just wanted a place to putter in the garden," Severio said, disingenuously, flashing his most winning smile at the others.

"I'm committed to fighting it," she answered, hearing her voice rise though she was struggling to sound calm. "And I believe we'll win."

"Fighting," Jill giggled nervously. "Nobody's thinking of turning this party into a fight, are they?"

"Why, I love a woman who's a fighter," Jake grinned, seizing the opportunity to put his arm around Jesa's naked shoulder and giving her a squeeze.

"I'm afraid Jesa tends to get a bit emotional about things," Severio said apologetically.

She shrugged off Jake's hand and challenged Severio's warning glance. "If you mean to say that I care about it deeply, then I suppose you could say I'm emotional."

"Hey, we're not going to solve any of these problems here tonight," Tim said with, forced bonhomie. "How's about a little refill on these drinks, folks?"

There was a flurry of activity. Jill turned up the volume dial on the Muzak. Irma and Kenneth got up to look at the view. Jake rattled his ice cubes in the empty glass and followed Tim back to the bar, and Severio, after one piercing look in Jesa's direction, started to talk to Debbie about the neon sculpture. After she'd taken a few polite sips from the brandy snifter, Jesa excused herself to go to the bathroom.

She sat on the edge of the tub and pressed her fingertips to her temples, not wanting to look up and confront the image of her flushed and angry face in the mirrors that covered the walls. It wasn't that she wanted Severio to take her part—he'd made it clear to her for weeks that he had no interest in the controversy about the lake—it was that he had dismissed her opinion in such a condescending fashion. It wasn't the first time that he had treated something that was important to her as though it were inconsequential. He had the same patronizing attitude toward her painting. And if he felt that her opinions and her work were meaningless, then what was the nature of his love for her? Did it have any foundation in respect or understanding? And what was her relationship to him? For the sake of tranquillity, out of her fear of conflict, she had ignored all of her intuition. She had contented herself with sexual satisfaction and glossed over all frustrations and doubts. But this public humiliation was too much.

When Jill knocked on the door to ask if she had everything she needed, she pulled herself together and walked back into the living room. Severio was dancing cheek to cheek with Debbie, who cast defiant glances toward Jake, but it was clear that she had long since lost the ability to make him sweat over the possibility of another man exciting her. Jake was spread full length on one of the platforms, waving his hand as though conducting the music. Irma and Kenneth were nowhere to be seen. A burst of thunder threatened a summer storm and Tim yelled out to batten down the hatches. Jesa suggested that they leave so as not to be caught in the rain. After bidding the Badhams goodnight and dodging another hug from Jake, she finally helped Severio up the stairs on the outside of the house.

"I think I'd better drive. You've had more to drink than I have," she said, as they dashed toward the car.

They had no sooner slammed the doors than sheets of rain swept down. She backed up from the driveway, paying close attention to the road, her need to talk momentarily suppressed as she peered through the slapping windshield wipers. When she had found the road, she looked over at Severio. He had rolled down the window and was slumped against the door, his head half held out in the drenching rain. She couldn't tell if he was trying to sober up because he'd downed too many of Tim's stiff drinks, or if he was pretending to ignore the entire situation.

She took steady breaths, hoping to calm herself. She was so conscious of the unpleasant tone that could creep into her voice when she was trying to penetrate his heedlessness that she usually backed off, afraid of sounding like a shrew. If she lashed out at him he could charge her with emotionalism, just as he'd done in front of all those ill-mannered strangers. And it was so important that he understand her. She grappled with the best approach. How could she speak to him so that her arguments sounded reasonable and well-thought-out? But the memory of her humiliation was so strong that anger overcame her struggle to find the tactically correct way of talking to him. As a flash of lightning illuminated their faces, a voice full of hurt and questioning rushed from her.

"How could you treat me like that?"

Chapter 15

*A*s soon as they walked into the house and she had switched on the lights, she went to the downstairs bathroom and got a towel. When she came back to the living room, he was pouring himself another drink. He took the towel, dried his face and hair, threw the towel on the couch, and reached out for her.

"You look very sexy with that wet dress clinging to you."

"How could you do that to me?" she asked, moving away from him.

"Listen, I didn't know that Badhams was involved in that hotel project."

"That's not what I'm talking about. I'm not saying that you had to agree with me, but how could you undermine me like that? You made it sound as though I was thoughtless and silly."

"Well, be honest, darling, you probably don't understand all the aspects involved in this project. You've never had to deal with business."

"Don't understand? I've put in a lot of time trying to understand this. I've spoken to you about it countless times—if you were listening. What do you think I did the poster for? Because I wanted something to do with my hands? I'm committed to it. Do you even understand what the word 'commitment' means?"

"Look, I know they're not your class of people. I met the guy at the Whitney, I thought he might be in the market to throw some work my way. That Jake could provide me with a hefty commission next year. So I don't see any point in alienating them. You're turning this into some sort of ego thing."

"Ego!" she cried, feeling the adrenaline surge. "It's your ego that took us there in the first place. We didn't go because you wanted to have some social life with me, though that's what you told me. And you didn't want to go because you liked Tim or found him interesting. You just thought of it as another contact. You thought perhaps you could use him. It seems to me that that's your general way of looking at people. You don't have any real curiosity, any real desire to know, you just want to size people up to see if they have anything you want. Sometimes I think you've come to look at me in the same way."

He shook his head slowly, put his hands on his hips, and looked at her sadly. "You're turning this into something it isn't. Believe me, I didn't mean it as a put-down when I told them you were emotional. I like that in you. But in its proper place. You think you can talk to people openly, tell them what you're feeling and thinking. Believe me, Jesa, it isn't like that. You have to be on your guard all the time."

"But when does the guard come down? You get so used to telling other people what you think they want to hear, to manipulating them, that you never say what you feel. After a while you don't even *know* what *you* feel. You get habituated to that way of dealing with others and you can't even be honest with the people who are close to you. I mean, I'm thinking of spending the rest of my life with you and I don't even know who you are."

"You don't know who I am?" he said sarcastically, smiling at her. "Come on now, you know me pretty intimately."

"I know you have two dark moles on your left shoulder. I know you like bourbon. I know you're handsome and you know it too. I know you like success, with a capital 'S.' And," she added softly, "I know the way you breathe when you sleep. But I don't really know what makes you tick. And every time I try, make any sort of attempt to get closer, to really develop our understanding of each other, you cut me off."

"I'm not going to deal with your neurotic notions of how badly you've been treated. If you had a rotten time at the Badhams, it's your own fault. You should have been polite enough to keep your mouth shut."

"I was expressing who I am and what I believe. I don't see why that was treated as an embarrassment by you."

"It was an inappropriate time," he shouted. "You of all people should know that. Didn't they teach you anything at those damn boarding schools? I'd hoped that I was going to have a wife who was an asset, not a liability."

"This is not a discussion of social graces," she yelled back, "it's about us. But since you brought up my background I'll tell you 'yes' they taught me something at school: they taught me how to be repressed. I used to think that you didn't want me to be stifled and insecure. And I'll tell you something else: no matter how naïve you think I am, I'm not going through the rest of my life behaving the way another person wants me to. Not even if that person is you."

She sat down on the couch, amazed at the strength of her own voice, trembling with frustration.

"Now you make it sound as though I'm trying to dominate you! Christ! I've done everything to fit into your life. I even came up to the country because you wanted me to."

"You're twisting this," she said slowly, trying to understand the swift turns his argument was taking. "You told me you wanted to come up here. And we're not discussing our location. I'm trying to talk to you about things that are deeply disturbing to me about our relationship and you're racking up points trying to win an argument. Trying to make me feel guilty. You don't want to talk. You want to win! You want to win everything. Life is just a competition to you."

"I'm sick of your goddamn criticisms," he bellowed, bringing the glass down on the bar so forcefully that she thought it might shatter. She winced and sucked in her breath. If he went into a fit of rage as he had the night she'd found out about Melinda, all hope of a discussion would be dead.

"I guess this isn't the time to talk. You've had a lot to drink and . . ."

"Don't use that frigid lady tone with me, 'cause I know you better," he snarled.

"I wasn't using any special tone," she answered tiredly. "I was just trying to calm you down. We can't talk if you're going to stomp around having a temper tantrum."

"All right, what is it? What is it, baby?" he said, his voice seductive, all the rage he had exploded with a moment before seemingly dissipated.

"I just . . . I just don't know what's important to you," she shrugged helplessly.

"*You're* important to *me*. What else do you need?"

His eyes narrowed and shone brilliantly as he slithered over to her. His hands massaged the tense muscles at the back of her neck as he gathered her to him. Her body was so fatigued from emotion that she gave way, melting into the comfort of his body, anticipating the healing power of a tender touch. She and Ed had often overcome their differences in this way. There would be a moment when they both decided that whatever it was that was coming between them simply wasn't important enough to stop them from reaching out. Even if they didn't end up making love, the embrace would magically dissolve the tension—the wordless expression of mutual need allowing each of them to give ground without losing face when they finally discussed the problem the next morning. But somehow this was different. Severio was reaching inside her dress, whispering that she was beautiful. She could feel his breath on her neck, and when she tried to release herself so that she could look into his face he held her more tightly. There was no warmth of shared need or reconciliation in his touch, only the desire to subjugate her, to bend her to his will by making her admit her need for him.

"Please don't do this, Severio. I hate the idea that you want to shut up any argument, any challenge, by simply taking me to bed."

"Are you saying I can't take you to bed?" he murmured playfully, trying to undress her.

"You think I'm just conquered territory," she murmured slowly, taking in the truth of the words rather than speaking directly to him.

"What's that supposed to mean?" he yelled, roughly releasing her and throwing his hands in the air.

"It means you don't have to deal with me. You don't have to be curious about who I am or what I think, because I'm already yours. You found out what you needed to know about me to get me to love you. Just like you find out what you need to know about anybody so you can get what you want from them."

He stared at her for several minutes. He had never seen her be so assertive before. There was only one way to deal with her and that was to call her bluff. He knew how fearful she was of being alone, and she had already promised to marry him. If he withdrew himself she'd cool down and plead for him to come back.

"If that's the way you feel about me, then I guess our marriage is off. The best thing I can do is to give you some time alone so you can get over this neurotic persecution complex you've suddenly developed. I'll go down to the city tomorrow."

"Do we have to deal with each other like this?" she pleaded.

"You're the one who wants it this way. I'll sleep down here."

"Please, Severio, that's not necessary. Let's just go to sleep together. We can talk in the morning."

"I said I'll sleep down here," he said firmly, and turned his back on her.

As she turned and mounted the stairs, feeling so tired that she wanted to curl up on the landing, a hundred thoughts were warring within her. She undressed mechanically and threw herself on the bed, going over the argument in her mind, giving it more weight, then less, wondering when sex and rage had clouded the issues, examining her own failure to communicate with him. It was like adding up a bill one didn't have the money to pay: no matter how much the figures were juggled, the total was still unacceptable. Her mind, like the little mouse that goes 'round and 'round in its wheel, finally collapsed in exhaustion and as the first cool breeze of the dawn came, she drifted off to sleep.

When she heard the car in the driveway, she was instantly on her feet. Moving to the window, she saw the battered Buick that was the only automobile of Pat's Village Taxi Service and watched Pat get out and lumber toward the veranda. She froze listening to the muffled conversation coming from downstairs, but when she heard the front door slam, she grabbed her kimono, quickly pulled it onto her naked body and rushed downstairs. She reached the door in time to see the Buick back up over the border of pinks that edged the garden and take off down the drive. Running to the guest room, she flung back the closet door to see that the overnight bag and most of the clothes that Severio kept there were gone. She stumbled back to the veranda and wandered out to the place where the tires had flattened the flowers. The cool air was already seeping away from the summer morning, the garden buzzing with the insistent sound of insects. She had not expected that he would leave without speaking to her. Clutching the kimono about her, she sank down on the earth, feeling as dazed as though she had been the victim of an accident and knowing she must stay very still until she was calm enough to examine her injuries.

During the next few days she did everything she could think of to keep herself occupied. She stripped an old cabinet that had been sitting in the garage for years, shoveled and weeded the garden, waxed the car. Unearthing a long-forgotten language record, she drilled her Italian vocabulary. In the evenings, after a bath and an aspirin to soothe her aching muscles, she would swallow a Valium and drag herself to the corner of the studio where she'd set up her easel and work until she began to feel drowsy. There was little of the free flow she'd experienced when she'd created the narcissus painting, but she labored on. Sometimes, by sheer dint of will, she was able to concentrate on the tasks she set herself, but the few times the phone rang she jumped out of her skin with anticipation. But it would be Flor wondering where she was keeping herself, or Sally, running up the long-distance bill by asking her advice on wedding preparations. When Sally asked if the rupture with Severio was permanent, she said she didn't know. When asked if she was depressed, she replied that she was keeping herself busy.

When the phone rang on the fourth day, she was certain that it must be him. It was the manager of a moving company, asking when it would be convenient for his workers to come by and crate Mr. Euzielli's paintings. She was organized and efficient enough to oversee the entire operation. As she watched the sweating men carry the last of the things to the truck, she sneezed. That evening she came down with the first cold she'd had in years.

She slept, had horrible dreams which she couldn't remember, and slept again. She was groggy and listless, hardly knowing what hour of the day or night it might be. As much as she had used her conscious mind to force herself into the merry-go-round of tasks during the first days of his absence, she now drifted semiconscious in the nether world of her psyche.

She woke with a start when she heard the clang of the bell on the veranda. Fumbling for the table lamp, she pushed her feet into her slippers and stumbled over to the door, pulling her kimono around her. The silver-blond hair and beard came into focus, and she stepped aside to let Josh in. He hesitated, thinking for one awful moment that he had interrupted her with Severio, but then he gazed past her to see the pillow, carton of orange juice, and the wastebasket full of Kleenex next to the couch.

"Jesa, I'm sorry to bother you. I didn't know you were sick."

"Come on in. I know I must look like hell," she sniffled, thinking about her appearance for the first time in almost a week. "Damned summer cold."

"Your resistance must be low."

"You don't know the half of it," she chuckled as she took his arm and guided him into the living room.

"Maybe this isn't a good time to call. I did try to phone earlier but there was no answer."

"I must've been asleep. I feel as though I've been under water for days. But stay. I'm glad you're here."

She fixed him a glass of lemonade and sat in the armchair opposite the couch, explaining that she might still have some cold germs. Pushing her straggly hair back behind her ears, she curled her feet up underneath her and asked why he'd dropped by.

"I didn't really plan to come over, but as I came past your drive the car just seemed to have a will of its own. Guess I felt the need for a little feminine wisdom."

"Maybe you haven't come to the right place. I've been walking the planet for a long time, but I'm still taking baby steps."

"It's my daughter Janet. She did leave camp and came to stay with me last week. She's so damned miserable that whenever I look at her sideways she bursts into tears. I swear to God, Jesa, I've never felt so powerless in my life—not even when I was trying to map out farm policy to a panel of bleary-eyed senators who thought that getting plowed had something to do with drinking. I just don't know how to make Janet feel better. I don't even know what's wrong with her. I suspect that she's had a disastrous first love and of course she thinks I'm the last person in the world who could understand that. I probably don't understand it—at least not from a woman's point of view. And she is a woman now. I can't make her feel better by promising her a trip to the circus. And it hurts me. I don't like to see anyone in pain, especially someone I love. But that's not the only reason I'm disturbed. I think it really bothers me because I like to feel on top of things and seeing her miserable makes me feel powerless. When I drove her over to Matt and Flor's place to babysit tonight I found myself coming out with these boring platitudes. I told the kid, I mean Janet, 'Pain makes man think, thinking makes man wise, and wisdom makes life endurable.' Can you imagine me saying that with a straight face? I knew I was being pretentious when I said it, but I felt I had to say something."

"What did Janet say?"

"She said it didn't make much sense, since it didn't ask why people had to have pain in the first place."

"Smart kid," she said I softly, her mouth forming a wan smile.

"Yeah," he nodded, proud of his daughter's insight, "that's why I worry about her. Hell, there isn't much you can say to me when I bring you my problems either. But you and I are old enough to know that an attentive ear counts for a lot. But when you're sixteen the idea of understanding companionship sounds about as exciting as cold oatmeal."

They kept talking, wandering out to the kitchen to fix more lemonade, drifting back into the living room to sit on the couch together. When she'd staggered to the door to let him in, she'd felt incapable of communicating with anyone, but now, under the inquiring gaze of his clear blue eyes, she found herself opening up. At first she was tentative, choosing her words carefully, censoring her more emotional memories, then he took her hand and the touch of tender encouragement was all she needed to confirm her trust. She talked to him as she had to no one else, revealing the excitement, expectations, and disappointments of her affair with Severio.

". . . so when he left and I'd tried and tried to think it out and couldn't, I plunged into all sorts of activities—anything to stop my mind from going in those crazy circles. Then I got sick and locked myself up in the same old reclusive pattern."

"Maybe your body is smarter than your head. It knows when you need a rest."

"I'd been feeling so hopeful. After more than a year of aimlessness and depression, I thought I had some direction again. Now I feel that—I don't know—that I'm constitutionally incapable of understanding anything. Even myself."

"You may still work it out with him," he said offhandedly. As Jesa's friend he wanted her happiness, even if it meant seeing her with another man, but he certainly wasn't going to encourage her into a reconciliation with Severio. His feelings for her were not limited to unselfish friendship and there was always the possibility that if she really ended this affair, they might be able to explore their chances with each other. "But I certainly know what you mean when you talk about thinking you have a handle on things and then being brought up short. When I first bought the farm

I was euphoric for about a month. Then the heavy rains came and I noticed a bad leak in the bedroom ceiling. I just about went crazy. Got into a rotten mood, cursing myself for a sucker because I hadn't noticed it when I'd bought the place. Then I started to see all the things that had to be done to bring the place up to snuff and I felt like a real idiot for having given up a cushy job in Washington. Just as well I was alone at the time, 'cause I was such a mean bastard I don't think anyone could have put up with me."

"I can't imagine you being mean."

"Would I lie to you, lady?" he grinned. "Now I'm more in touch with myself, the real black moods don't last as long. What I'm trying to say, in my own inarticulate way, is that change is always hard. And you're hard on yourself to begin with. Give yourself some time. Baby yourself. Or since I'm here, let me baby you. If you feel well enough to get dressed, I'll take you out to dinner. How long since you've been out of the house?"

"About four days, I guess. I haven't even felt like working in the garden."

"Then let's go for a spin and a bite to eat. You'll feel better."

She was sure that she wouldn't, but she dragged herself upstairs and dressed. When she'd put on the peasant dress with the elaborate turquoise embroidery on the yoke, smoothed her hair back and put a tad of shadow on her lids, she was surprised to see that her appearance didn't bear much relationship to her emotional state. As they went out the door, Josh picked up the box of Kleenex.

"You'll probably need these. When I was a kid my mother made a special point of making sure I had a clean handkerchief whenever I went out. Handkerchiefs. That's something that slipped out of our lives, huh? Like Sunday dinners and dandelion wine and elections where you voted without knowing what the pollsters said first."

"You're sounding very old-fashioned for a rabble-rouser."

"I'm a radical conservative," he said as he helped her into the car. "That's what I was talking about inside: trying to keep the balance between what's desirable in the old patterns, but still being able to take a chance on the new."

After dinner they drove down to the lake. The full moon illuminated the trees and the water with a silvery sheen. The moist night air was full of the scents of plants and earth. She shivered a little as they strolled along the shore and he put his arm around her shoulder.

"I guess I'd better get you home."

"I'm feeling so much better than I was before you came. And I didn't even want to answer the door. You've actually pulled me out of it a bit."

"I hope I've helped, but you've pulled yourself out of it. I remember when you first showed me your painting. You told me that Severio was responsible for getting you to paint again. I'm not saying he didn't have a strong effect on you, but I thought it was strange at the time that you put it that way. You don't seem to have any trouble blaming yourself for things. Why don't you even it up and take a little credit? How's the painting going, by the way?"

"I've pushed myself to put in a certain number of hours every day, but I've been real short on inspiration."

"I've heard that only comes when you least expect it."

"Aren't you the hopeful one?"

When they reached the car, they turned simultaneously for one last look at the glorious vista of the lake. She relaxed against him, turning her eyes from the view and making out the strong, angular lines of his face in the moonlight. She reached up and touched his beard and her hands strayed into his hair. Before she knew what was happening he was pulling her to him, tilting her head with the pressure of his open mouth. His excitement took her by surprise. She'd had no sexual fantasies about him before, but now she knew in a flash how he would be as a lover. The eagerness, energy, ease of give and take—all the things she admired about his character would have sensual expression—surged toward her in smell, touch, and taste. The discovery amazed her. When she pulled away from him, he let her go, throwing his head back and staring up into the dark sky.

"I don't mean to take advantage of your feelings, Jesa, but . . ."

"No," she sniffled. "I had to pull away because my nose is so stuffed up that I couldn't breathe."

"Guess I'll have to wait till another night to take you

skinny dippin',", he laughed, putting his arms around her again and kissing the top of her head. He wanted to press his advantage. Now that she'd actually taken him into her arms—for some blessed and inexplicable reason, had actually initiated the embrace—he was sure that if he could just make love to her she'd realize how much they wanted one another. But as much as the idea sent the blood pounding through his body, he knew the timing was all wrong. The break with Severio did not sound permanent and even though he was sure that they could retain their friendship after sleeping together; if she took up with Severio again he might be relegated to a "just friends" status and that fall from grace could drive him crazy. He got into the car, handed her a Kleenex, and started up the motor. When they reached her house, she hesitated with her hand on the door handle. He could see that she was deliberating what she would say to him.

"Don't bother asking me in. I have to pick Janet up soon. Besides . . . it isn't the time."

"I was only going to ask you in for coffee," she said, half defensive, half flirtatious.

"Boy, am I glad I'm forty," he breathed, folding his arms over the steering wheel and resting his head on them.

"First you're going to tell me what's good about being forty. Next you're probably going to tell me there's a cure for the common cold."

"Patience."

"I'm listening."

"No. I mean patience is what's good. When I was

twenty, if I wanted something I had to have it. Had to have it fast. Felt that if I didn't grab it, it would disappear. The irony is that now I actually have less time in life, I know that when I want something, I can afford to wait. The blueberries taught me that. I can yell at them, curse them, pamper them—they still take their own sweet time."

He came around to her side of the car and helped her out. When they reached the veranda he shook her hand. The gesture pleased her more than a kiss.

"I'll call you tomorrow and see how the cold is doing. When you're feeling better, I'd like to have you meet Janet. And when you're really feeling better . . ."

"We'll talk some more. Thanks, Josh."

Chapter 16

It took several weeks for the importance of their fight to filter its way into Severio's consciousness. He'd anticipated that the separation would be a short one. He understood Jesa: it would only be a matter of days before loneliness and self-doubt overtook her and she would be contrite and eager to have him back. He brushed aside any questions of personal guilt and decided to enjoy another brief vacation from monogamy.

When the second day passed and he had no word from her, be had an impulse to go back to the country, make light of the argument, and admit that he'd been grandstanding when he'd walked out without saying goodbye. But he had no desire to set a precedent of apologizing, and thought the better of it. Instead be called the moving company and arranged for his things to be picked up, sure that this would jolt her into a reconciliation. When his things arrived in New York and there was still no word, he left the unpacked crates standing in the corner of the studio and plunged himself into a round of social activities. He reminded himself of how patient he'd been when he'd first gone after her. If she wanted to play games, he could outlast her.

By the third week he was in a foul mood, cursing the heat of late August and the dirt of the city, unable to work, too enervated to make his daily trips to the gym. His studio was in chaos and he wanted Jesa back, realizing how much he had come to depend on her to tidy up his daily life. Being accustomed to the quick gratification of his desires, it now seemed to him that she was being maliciously cruel in keeping herself from him. His pride prevented him from reaching out to her, but his confidence was badly shaken.

He'd accepted an invitation to a party in David Little's loft, thinking that a night out with the younger set might give him a lift. For the first twenty minutes he lounged in the corner of the dimly lit room, remembering that Jesa had once described the "Living Art" crowd as exhibitionistic louts. But after he'd had a few drinks and a couple of drags on the hash pipe that was being shoved under his nose, his concern with Jesa was momentarily relieved by the sight of the extraordinary amount of attractive womanflesh at the party. David sidled up to him and followed his gaze to the girl who was gyrating wildly in the center of the room.

"If they really wanted to up the tourist trade in the Big Apple, we could let the word out that the chicks here are the wildest and most willing in the world. And if you're in the arts and you're straight you've just added about fifty points to your competitive edge. Go get 'em, Euzielli. If you don't walk out that door with her in fifteen minutes, you owe me fifty bucks."

They were both high when they mounted the stairs to his studio. As he watched her buttocks move up the stairs in front of him, the old thrill of conquest went through him like an electric current. But even as she kicked off her sandals and lolled expectantly on the bed, he thought of Jesa. She pulled him down to her. He was seized with the fear that he might not be able to perform. The girl noticed he was preoccupied and went to new heights of forced abandon in an effort to involve him. He was able to function, but it was so joyless that it was almost a chore. As soon as they had rolled away from each other, she wiped the perspiration from her face on the sheet, switched on the bedside lamp and started to put on her clothes. He was relieved that she was leaving quickly and voluntarily, but there was something about the disinterested look on her face that made his ego shrivel. She took a pocket mirror out of her purse, repaired her eye makeup and slipped her feet back into her sandals.

"Perhaps we can see each other again some time," he said, as she started toward the door. She opened the door slightly and looked back at him over her shoulder, a quick smile twisting her lips. "Don't worry, baby. Even Casanova had a few off nights."

She was gone before he could think of anything to say. He sat up in the bed stunned. It had never occurred to him that his involvement with Jesa could affect his performance with other women. But it couldn't be that she had that much power over him. He was just troubled and a bit out of shape. The booze and the dope had thrown him off. And the girl—well, she was crude and vulgar. He went into the shower, determined to put the whole messy business out of his mind. He made a resolution to go to the gym the following day and to be more selective about the women he picked up.

But the idea of picking anyone up suddenly made him feel tired. He dried himself, noticing that another couple of his chest hairs had turned gray, and walked back into the studio. The unpacked crates, the litter of his hastily thrown-off clothes depressed him. He tried to sleep but couldn't. He flicked on the bedside lamp again, rifling through the clutter of unpaid bills and invitations that were scattered on the night table to find the book on contemporary English artists that Jesa had given him, but he couldn't concentrate enough to look at it. By the time the blue-black sky that always had the eerie tint of a million reflected city lights had paled to a watery blue-gray, he had had a couple of shots of bourbon and was doodling on an old scratch pad.

He remembered the first time Jesa had slept with

him how exuberant and awe-struck she had been by the beauty of the colors through the skylight. She was like a kid about things like that. He could see her curled up beside him. The thought of his life without her passion and devotion seemed intolerably bleak. How could she have abandoned him when he loved her so much? "I really do love her," he heard himself saying. He had told her so many times—to seduce her, to please her, to get around her—but he had never said it to himself. He grabbed the phone and dialed the Connecticut number. When there was no answer after the fifteenth ring, he became violently jealous. Could she be so perfidious as to be in bed with another man when he was waiting here wanting her? Not his Jesa. Not his wife-to-be. He tried the New York number so frantically that he mis-dialed and got an earful of invective from the irate man he'd woken up. Forcing himself to concentrate, he dialed again.

"Hello?" the soft, disoriented voice answered.

"Jesa. Thank God I got you. I didn't know you were in town. It's me."

There was a very long pause at the other end of the line.

"When can I see you?" he pressed.

"I . . . I don't know. I'm in town for Sally's wedding."

"When is it?"

"Tomorrow. I mean today."

"When will it be over?"

"The wedding is at Ellman's apartment, but the reception . . ."

"Then later. You can come down here. No. I'll come up there. I have to talk to you. Can I come at seven o'clock?"

"I don't think so. I . . ."

He could hear the tentativeness in her voice. He had to get her to agree while she was still off guard.

"All right. Eight. I'll be there at eight. I've missed you, darling. I've been wrong about a lot of things. Everything. I've missed you so much I thought I'd explode. Don't say anything now. I'll see you at eight."

"Thank God you're here," Sally said as she opened Ellman's bedroom door a crack and stuck her face out. "Is anyone else here yet?"

"The string quartet came up in the elevator with me. Otherwise the coast is clear. Oh, there's a fellow who looks a lot like Ellman only with less hair sitting in the living room."

"That's his brother Merlin. Their mother must've had a book on medieval curses when she named those kids. Come on in."

She opened the door far enough for Jesa to squeeze through and gave her a bone-crunching hug.

"You look more tense that I do," Sally said as she surveyed her face. "Now don't worry, it'll all be over soon."

"I didn't sleep very well."

"*You* didn't sleep well. I was like someone who was meeting the firing squad at dawn. Trust me to look bleary-eyed on my own wedding day."

"Hadn't you better get dressed?" Jesa asked, staring

at Sally in her slip and stocking feet.

"You're so conventional," Sally sighed, as she dashed into the bathroom.

"Don't rush. They can't start it without you."

"That's what my mother thought before they induced labor. Hey, there's a bottle of champagne in a bucket near the bed. Just struggle 'til you get it open, I have to put on my face."

Jesa grappled with the cork until it finally popped and rolled under the bed. Rebecca wriggled out, gave Jesa a pathetic look, and crawled back into her hiding place. As she steadied her hand and poured two glasses of the bubbly liquid she wondered bow Sally was doing with the drinking. She walked gingerly into the bathroom, where Sally was dabbing on foundation. They clinked glasses and a mischievous grin spread on Sally's face.

"Wait'll you see the crew that's coming. The minister is some old family friend of Ellman's mother. Looks like Cotton Mather. He was v-e-r-y upset when I asked him if we could change "love, honor, and obey" to "love, honor, and laugh." I don't think Ellman's mother liked the idea too much either, but she's so damned happy to think that Ellman's finally getting married. I don't think she even cares who to. If I can keep a low profile 'til she's shipped back to Maryland, all will be well. And my mother wouldn't care if Ellman were King Kong as long as he's willing to make an honest woman out of me."

They heard the string quartet tuning up. Sally grimaced, put the champagne glass on the shelf and dabbed some more foundation on her nose. Jesa wandered back into the bedroom, removed her suit jacket and walked over to the window as Sally chattered on.

". . . it's going to be a circus. We had to ask Ellman's brothers and their wives, so it was only natural to invite some of my clan. After that the guest list took on a life of its own. It was like watching some awful experiment with DNA—it just started doubling and tripling all by itself . . ."

She could see the tops of trees below on the avenue. The leaves had just started to turn color and trembled in the wind.

". . . so we put Ellman's second cousin, who is a kleptomaniac or something, next to my second cousin, who's a religious fanatic. . . ."

Early autumn days often had a melancholy effect on her. There was something about the leaves beginning to drop that made her throat catch, and the surprising gusts of chilly air made her shiver out of all proportion to the temperature. "You can be a romantic in the spring and a lover in the summer, but come autumn you need a mate," Ed had once said. She was a coward about the winter.

". . . oops, spilled some perfume on the floor. It's just as well that I've decided to keep my own apartment to work in. It's taken me months to feel comfortable here. At first I told Ellman he'd better put all the valuables up on the high shelves, like you do with a kid. And last night Rebecca was so nervous she had an accident on one of his antique carpets. I thought it was all over between us. . . ."

If only he hadn't called her. Caught her unaware. She'd been coping for a whole month now. She had been miserable, but she'd given herself a B+ for effort. The painting was going well and she had enjoyed some wonderful times with Josh. Had it not been for the presence of his daughter and her lingering feelings for Severio, she was sure that they would have been lovers by now. She was feeling an ever-growing attachment to him but was grateful that it was moving along at its own easy speed. If she started up with Josh, she knew that it would be a serious commitment. But Severio's voice had driven all these thoughts from her head. She found herself looking at her watch again, counting the hours until she would see him with anxiety but anticipation.

"I know what I haven't told you. Juiciest piece of gossip to come down the pike in ages: O.W. Fanshaw is going to ditch Bettina! She's telling everyone that she wants out, but I heard from Loretta Hartman that O.W. met some woman in Europe and he's the one who initiated the divorce. I hope he's got a slush fund stashed away because after Bettina gets through with him he'll be standing on Fifth Avenue in his undershirt."

The mention of Bettina reminded her of that dreadful night. She took off her watch and dropped it into her purse, determined to suppress all thoughts of the eight o'clock meeting. Sally ran from the bathroom in a sea-green chiffon dress.

"Zip me up, please. Ellman helped me pick this out so I know it must be tasteful."

She smoothed the dress over her hips and flounced the sleeves.

"How do I look? Say 'great' no matter what confronts you."

"You look lovely."

"Oh, Jesa. I don't know why I'm making jokes. I'm scared to death."

She sat down on the bed and bit her lower lip. Rebecca straggled out from underneath the bed and snuggled up to her feet. Jesa went and sat next to her, giving her a reassuring hug.

"Why do you feel that way? You want to marry Ellman, don't you?"

"Yes. But I'm scared of changing. Even when your life is bad, you know the old patterns. You're comfortable with it in a way that makes you settle into the dissatisfactions. After a certain age comfort seems to mean a great deal. Too much. And I've just gotten a handle on the drinking problem. Maybe I'm rushing things."

Jesa could hear the voices of the wedding guests from the other room, but Sally seemed oblivious. She took Jesa's hand and gripped it so firmly that her knuckles showed white.

"Remember when we first met each other, that day in the life study class? Oh, the energy we had then! We'd both kicked over our backgrounds and come to the city to be artists, too damned naïve to even imagine all the things that could derail us."

"Yes, I remember," Jesa said softly.

"I'd given up on the idea of getting married. I don't

even know why I'm doing it."

"Maybe you feel some of the energy toward Ellman that you used to feel about the painting."

"That's true," Sally said, her brown eyes going wide and surprised. "I'm going back to work on Troillina tomorrow. You know how I used to bitch about doing her, but lately I've actually started to miss her—and if my tender emotion isn't enough I've got Joan and the publisher breathing down my neck. But the real focus of my energy is on Ellman and myself. Because my mind and my heart tell me that he's the best risk I can take. I do feel, well, energetic about him. And it's not like that puppy love—the kind of rush I used to feel for Hugo that just rendered me helpless. I mean we're not even going on a honeymoon. Ellman wanted to take me to Japan but I talked him out of it. Right after the reception we're taking a cab across town to my apartment and we're just going to hole up for a couple of days. I'm going to be able to work and have a man that loves me by my side. What am I having second thoughts for? I'm the luckiest woman alive."

She jumped up and slipped her feet into the silk heels that matched her dress, checking out her appearance in the mirror again. Then she turned suddenly, her eyes thoughtful again.

"But what's been happening to you? I didn't even ask."

"You're absolved from the sin of self-absorption on your wedding day," Jesa laughed. "I've just been . . . painting mostly."

"How's it going?"

"It seems to be back on the track. I was able to work all during the breakup with Severio. In fact, it was the thing that really saved me. Remember how I used to be so careful? So pale and ladylike? Now I just let it rip. Some of it is actually looking good."

"If you say good then it must be terrific. You've always underrated yourself."

"I think it has a greater importance to me now. I mean, no matter whether I'm with a man or not, my painting is something I can do for myself and by myself."

"Talking about changes—I never thought I'd hear something like that coming out of you. You're really on the track."

"I'm trying. There are nights when I go to bed when I just lie there thinking about him. I . . ."

They had both been so absorbed in the conversation that they had barely noticed that the sounds from the living room had risen to a hubbub of many voices. There was a knock on the door. Jesa got up to open it while Sally rushed to the mirror for a last minute check. A stocky woman with a peasant face and lively brown eyes was tugging at the skirt of her cerise dress and looking at Jesa anxiously.

"I'm Mrs. Gold," she explained, bustling in. "Sally, are you ready yet? She's always been late. Even when she was a little kid, I had to struggle every morning to get her off to school."

Jesa had met Mrs. Gold once about fifteen years ago, but this was no time to remind her of their previous introduction. She picked up her suit jacket from

348

the bed, patted Rebecca, walked to Sally for one last hug, and started to leave the room.

"When they get to the part where they say, 'If anyone knows of any impediment to this union,' please don't jump up and say that the bride's a nut case," Sally cried as Jesa shut the door.

The lavish living room was now peopled with a strange assortment of faces that seemed to fall into two distinct genetic groups. A horse-faced woman with a silver pompadour and regal bearing, whom Jesa immediately pegged as Ellman's mother, was sitting in the front row of the chairs on the left side. The group behind her had acquired by nature or marriage, the same impeccably groomed, contained, and somewhat dour appearance. They waited politely, whispering among themselves and exchanging tentative smiles with the more motley crew sitting to their right. The bride's relatives, decked in their colorful Sunday best, eyes agog at the objets d'art, chattered boisterously and craned their necks toward the bedroom door, eager for Sally's entrance. The string quartet finished the selection. An anticipatory silence fell over the room as Mrs. Gold came out of the bedroom and bobbed her head in a nervous nod. The music started up again with Pachebel Kanon in D. Sally stepped into the room, her eyes. liquid and serious, her hands, which held a tiny bouquet of lily of the valley, trembling slightly as Ellman came over to meet her. He gave her one brief, triumphant smile and they moved up the aisle, stationing themselves between the lavish floral displays that bracketed the bay window. The stern-faced minister rose, nodded once in Mrs. Smith's direction, raised his eyes to the ceiling, and began:

"Dearly beloved . . ."

Throughout the ceremony Jesa felt the constriction in her throat that usually signaled tears, but she wasn't able to release them. She might have been standing before a minister now, dressed in the autumn colors that Severio found so becoming, waiting for him to slip the ring onto her finger and gather her into the embrace that would seal their union.

". . . in the holy state of matrimony . . ."

She recalled her own wedding to Ed: wanting to do the sensible thing and save what little money they had to furnish their first apartment, he had talked her into a rather bleak ceremony in a judge's chambers. She never let him know that she missed having all the trappings of a real bride. When she had heard "so long as you both shall live" then, it had been a romantic vow, holding no hint of the realities of death and widowhood.

". . . do you, Sally . . ."

As pleased as she was with her friend's happiness, she couldn't help but think of her own disappointment. The confidence she'd started to feel about living alone seemed to melt as she listened to the exchange of vows. It was true that she'd discovered satisfaction in her work, and the freedom to come and go at her own leisure, without worrying about anyone else's needs, was often exhilarating. She knew she could handle a solitary existence. After all, millions of women did it. There was no longer any social stigma attached to being unmarried. But it wasn't in her nature to fix a wonderful meal when she was the only one who would be eating it, and a pillow was no substitute for a lean, warm body. Lately she'd noticed that she often talked to herself out loud. Perhaps she should buy a pet for companionship. She locked her hands together in her lap and told herself that she mustn't give way to sentimentality.

She heard Mrs. Gold start to sniffle almost as soon as the ceremony had begun. By the middle of it, the spluttering had reached such a crescendo that it threatened to drown out the minister's inexpressive drone. Ellman's mother's ramrod back became even stiffer as the blubbering increased. When the vows were concluded and Ellman leaned over to embrace Sally, the string quartet struck up a joyful melody and Jesa moved back through the crowd, which was surging toward the newlyweds to offer their congratulations, and went up to Sally's mother.

"There, there," she said soothingly, patting the heaving cerise shoulders. "You should be very happy, Mrs. Gold. Ellman will be a fine husband."

"I can't believe it! My little girl finally getting married! I'd given up on it years ago. Even Father DeVito told me that I should stop praying, and when Father DeVito tells you to give up praying, you *know* it's a hopeless case. But I never gave up. I prayed to St. Jude—the patron saint of hopeless cases. And now my prayers have been answered. Somebody finally married her!"

"Yes . . . I'm sure you're very happy."

Sensing a presence at her side, Jesa turned to see Mrs. Smith.

"Now that we're relatives, Mrs. Gold, I wonder if you and your husband would care to join me. The chauffeur will take us to the Pierre. I believe that is where the reception is to take place."

"Why don't you do that, Mrs. Gold?" Jesa urged. "Where's Mr. Gold?"

"He must be here somewhere. I'll find him and we'll go with you, Mrs. Smith. And thanks. I mean with the price of taxis these days, it's always a treat to get a lift."

"I'll wait for you in the foyer," Mrs. Smith replied, creasing her lips into a replica of a smile and sailing off.

Once Mrs. Gold had gone off, Jesa searched through the milling crowd to find Sally and Ellman. She was told that they had already retired to the bedroom to change into their going-away clothes. She was about to leave and find a taxi for herself, when Ellman's brother Merlin introduced himself and suggested that she ride with him and his wife.

Despite Jesa's directions, Merlin managed to get lost on the way to the Pierre, so Sally and Ellman were already standing in the receiving line accepting kisses and handshakes from the growing multitude of guests by the time they arrived. Jesa excused herself and went into the ladies' room, grateful to find it unoccupied except for an attendant. She sat on one of the tufted chairs and stared into space for a long time, then, needing some activity to justify her stay, fumbled in her purse for a comb and pulled it through her hair in a absent-minded fashion. When other women started to come in, she pretended to be touching up her makeup, but as she heard the orchestra start up, she knew she'd have to go back.

Ellman and Sally were moving to the center of the floor for the ritual first dance. Ellman had all the grace of a hobbled bear and after a few bars of music, Sally flung back her arms, laughed and yelled, "Save me! Everybody up!" Merlin's wife, who bad spotted Jesa again, signaled to her husband to ask Jesa to dance, but Jesa said she was feeling a bit woozy and urged them to go on. The wife gave her one brief pitying glance as Merlin guided her through the crowd. If only people wouldn't give her that "you poor brave widow" look!

She forced herself to circulate, exchanging small talk with casual acquaintances and introducing herself to people she didn't know. When she'd registered two "poor brave widow" looks from women she knew and at least four "are you available?" looks from men she didn't, she retired to her table.

The free flow of champagne and general good-will seemed to be helping everyone, even the straight-laced Smith clan, to loosen up. Mrs. Gold was bouncing around chatting a mile a minute, regaling all of the guests with stories of her victorious novena to St. Jude. The serious-looking little man with dreamy eyes, who Jesa supposed must be Mr. Gold, had stationed himself near the bandstand and was getting quietly tipsy and waving one hand in time to the music. Through the ocean of faces, Jesa could make out Mrs. Smith's silver pompadour bobbing up and down as she led Ellman's assistant, who was a least a head shorter than she, around the floor in a surprisingly bouncy fox-trot.

"Oh, my God, I finally got to you," Sally cried as she sank down in the chair next to Jesa. "There can't be much more to do except cut the cake and then we can beat it out of here. You can be damned sure I'm not going to make any more of a spectacle of myself by throwing the bouquet, so here." She pushed the tiny bunch of lily of the valley into Jesa's hand as her eyes darted around the room. "Now cheer up, you're going to have fun at this party yet. I promise."

"I'm having a good time. Really I am."

"Why don't you dance? I've seen lots of guys ask you. Even Mother Smith is out there doing the hula."

"Stop being so bossy. You know me well enough to know that I actually enjoy being an observer. And there's enough going on here to entertain anybody."

"Ain't it the truth. It's starting to look like a block party. All we need is a raffle and a ferris wheel. Listen, are you going to stay in town or go back up to the country?"

"I don't know yet. I'm just taking it one day at a time."

"Well, I'll try you in both places in a couple of days. Hey, I see Ellman motioning me over to cut the cake. As many times as I've been a waitress, I'll probably forget myself and start stacking the dishes up on my arm and serving everyone. See you in a while."

Sally flitted across the room and Jesa rose to follow her, stationing herself on the fringes of the crowd that was gathering around the table. Feeling someone's eyes on her, she spun around to see an elegantly handsome man walking toward her. She turned quickly back toward the cake-cutting before doing a double take.

"Goodness," she gasped as he came up to her, "I didn't even recognize you."

"I hardly recognize myself. I had to get this monkey suit out of mothballs," Josh smiled.

"I had no idea you were going to be here. I thought you were still down in Washington."

"Sally asked me to come when they were up visiting. Then she called me last week to remind me."

Her initial surprise and pleasure in seeing him gave way to quick understanding. Her eyes shot over to Sally, who took in the accusing glance for a split second, smiled innocently and went on serving the cake.

"I didn't think I'd be able to come," Josh went on, noticing the dismay that had clouded Jesa's face, "but I got Janet squared away sooner than I'd expected, so I decided to drive through the city. Shall I dive into the crowd and get you a piece of cake?"

"No, thanks. I'm not hungry."

"Good. I know a little place called Louise's from my expense account days, maybe we could go there afterward."

"I'm terribly sorry, Josh. I . . ." There was no reason to play cat and mouse, but this wasn't the place to tell him that she was going to see Severio again.

He grabbed a glass of champagne from a passing tray and swallowed, checking out the men who were standing around them. He'd been so eager to see her that it hadn't even entered his head that she might have an escort. It was damned stupid of him to have come. It wasn't as though Sally and Ellman were close friends of his. It was patently obvious that he'd made the detour because he was chasing her. The minute she looked into his eyes he wouldn't be able to hide the fact that he'd been having vivid fantasies for the entire five-hour drive from Washington. And he proposed to give his daughter advice on how to handle the opposite sex!

"No problem," he said casually, looking past her. "It was just an idea. Say, I'd better go over and extend my congratulations. Come with me?"

He took her hand. As she locked her fingers through his and felt the tiny callouses on his warm palm, a wave of affection came over her. When his eyes met hers they stood, oblivious of the chattering merrymakers all around them.

"I'm so glad you could make it, Josh," she heard Ellman say.

"Yes, isn't it a hoot?" Sally put in.

Catching the hint of indignation in Jesa's eyes, Sally sheepishly licked a bit of frosting from her finger and put out her hand. "I've always wanted to dance at my own wedding, and you're probably my only chance. Will you give me a whirl, Josh?"

When they'd moved onto the dance floor, Jesa

turned to Ellman.

"I'll kill her," she whispered.

"I don't suppose it does much good to say that she always has the best intentions."

"I know that—it's just that the timing couldn't be worse."

Halfway through the song they were back. Sally hugged them both, said that she and Ellman were going to sneak out any minute now, but that they should stay and enjoy themselves.

"This swanky place is costing us an arm and a leg, somebody should use it 'til the time's up. C'mon Mr. Smith, Sally Gold Smith is going to teach you a thing or two about getting out the back way."

Josh slipped his arm around Jesa's waist and guided her onto the floor. Neither of them spoke. Whenever their bodies were pushed together by the crowd, they both pulled back, but the distance between them only made the sexual tension more obvious. The music stopped. They stood, silent, waiting for it to begin again. On the first note of the next number, they moved together simultaneously, no longer resisting the desire to cling to each other. By the time the third number was finished the bouquet of lily of the valley that Jesa had been holding was crushed into the vest of Josh's suit. When he pulled his flushed face back from her cheek and whispered in a low voice that he thought they'd better leave; she nodded and followed him through the crowd and out onto the chilly avenue.

They walked across the street directly into Central Park, still not saying a word. As soon as they were sheltered by the trees and out of sight of the street, he pulled her to him.

"Where shall we go?" he whispered hoarsely.

"I can't go anywhere. I've got to . . ."

"For Chrissake, Jesa, it can't be that important."

"I'm meeting Severio in a few hours," she confessed, sinking down onto a park bench.

"I see."

"No, you don't. He wanted me to see him and I just felt I had to because . . . Oh, I don't know what I felt."

"I'm going."

"Josh, please."

"Please what?"

"I don't know," she said lamely.

"I know you don't, Jesa," he replied, controlling the anger in his voice. "Look, I'm trying to be reasonable, but I can't be anymore. I don't think you're the kind of woman to lead me on, but I'm getting a helluva lot of conflicting signals from you. It's not big news to you that if you want me, I'm available. I guess that's not a very smooth way of putting it, but I never developed any seduction techniques. If you don't want me—hell, I don't know—I want to be friends with you, but I just don't think I can handle it. At least not for a while. I'm going back up to the country and I guess you're staying here, so that should make it easier. Easier!" he snorted.

She shivered, pulled the lapels of her suit up to her throat, and watched a solitary leaf twist in the wind, break off the branch, and float down to the ground. When he saw her quivering in the chilly twilight air,

358

the anger drained from him. He sat next to her put his arm around her.

"Sorry I yelled at you. You want my jacket?"

"No. I think I'd better be getting home."

"We can go back and get my car and drive you to your apartment if you like."

"Thanks, but no. I'd like to walk alone for a while."

"Well, I guess there's not much more to say."

He still waited for a moment, hoping that she'd reach out to him, say something tender that would give him a chance to retract the ultimatum he'd just given but wasn't really convinced about. Finally he stuffed his hands into the pockets of the expensive suit as though it were just another pair of his old dungarees, turned and walked away.

Letting herself into her apartment, she walked past the boxes she had brought back from the country which were still sitting, unpacked, in the hallway. She decided to take a bath. The ritual of bathing often calmed her and she wanted to look her best when he saw her again. Her pride would not allow him to think that she had gone to seed since his departure. Opening the bathroom cabinet to find her bath salts, she was momentarily drawn to the small plastic container of tranquilizers. She held them for a minute, then decided that she would do without them. She had overcome that dependency several months ago and had slipped back only briefly after he had left her. Immersing her body in the warm, perfumed water, she assured herself of the strength of her willpower and tried to relax. She had another forty-five minutes before he was due to arrive and she would meet him with a serene and confident demeanor. Coming out of the tub and wrapping herself in the apricot velour robe, she took up the brush and began to draw it through her hair, counting the strokes, soothed by the steady, rhythmic motion of her hand. She was about to go into the bedroom and get dressed when she heard the buzzer ring. The superficial calm drained from her body. She raced to the hallway and pushed the intercom button, expecting to hear O'Hara's voice. The buzzer rang again, and she realized that it was the front door.

She opened it slowly, their eyes met and held.

"Aren't you going to ask me in?"

"I wasn't expecting you until eight."

"I just couldn't wait to see you. I was walking around in the park and then I came over and O'Hara told me you'd already come up. I hope you don't mind."

She moved aside and they stood together in the hallway. He had been in a state of manic eagerness throughout the day, but it had also occurred to him that if he came early he might catch her off guard. Looking at her delicate hands clutching the opening of her robe, her freshly washed face with the wide, surprised eyes, be knew that he had calculated correctly, and some of his old confidence returned. He reached toward her, but she stepped aside and flicked on the hallway light.

"Can I fix you a drink?" she asked lamely, finally putting her feet in motion and moving into the living room.

"If you'll have one with me."

She concentrated on the many bottles that lined the bar as be unbuttoned his jacket and settled down on the couch. His movement had the same animal grace and self-assurance that always marked his motions, but she noticed that there was a puffiness under the magnetic dark eyes and a dissolute look around the full mouth.

"You look tired. Have you been working a lot?"

"You know the only time I really get down to work is when you encourage me," he said, warmed by her concern.

But you've never encouraged me, she thought as she dropped the ice cubes into the glasses.

"How's your painting been going?" he asked, as though reading her mind.

"Very well. I've missed being away from it even for these few days I've been in town."

"That's because you have such a sterling character," he said lightly but without sarcasm. "You have such a sense of dedication. I didn't realize how much I was dependent on your concern and inspiration until I was away from you. I guess the old cliché is right: behind every successful man, there's a great woman."

There was a time when nothing would have pleased her more than hearing such words, when the highest expression of her aspirations was to be the loving "woman behind the man." Now she felt the burden of supporting another ego while her own shriveled with neglect. She handed him the glass and started to move toward the armchair, but he gave her the briefest glance of questioning and hurt, and she moved back and sat beside him, feeling that it was contrived and phony that she should have to put space between them. That made it appear that she was out of control and she didn't want to give him that impression. As soon as she'd settled down next to him, he relaxed again.

"How was the wedding?"

"It was wonderful. You'll be glad that I didn't get overemotional and cry," she said archly.

"Were there many people there?" he began politely, then he ran his hand over his face impatiently. "Damn it, Jesa. I don't want to talk about other people. I'm not interested in them. I'm interested in us. I'm interested in you."

She turned her head away from his imploring eyes and started to get up from the couch. "There's no point . . ."

"But I love you. I really *love* you."

There was a tone in his voice that she had never heard before—an uncontrived honesty with a trace of amazement, as though he had discovered the emotion in himself for the first time. She turned back to him, taking in the expression of desire and contrition that brought a youthful look to his features for a moment. Her hand involuntarily reached up to the tangle of dark hair that she had dreamt about both sleeping and awake. Her lips parted and her eyes grew wide as his face came closer and she felt the heat radiating from his body. Then the full mouth was on hers and her body was drawn into the obliterating embrace. She

362

could feel the old delicious weakness flood through her, so that her legs turned to water. He had no trouble easing her back onto the couch and slipping his hand into the robe to caress her naked flesh. It would be so easy to give way to him, abandon herself to the time-destroying pleasure of his touch, he lost in that familiar whirlpool of the senses.

Suddenly she wrenched herself away from him, staggering to her feet, pulling the robe back around her nakedness and clutching the arm of the couch for support. He struggled up into a sitting position, his mouth agape, his face flushed with color, controlling the reflexive anger that flashed in him as he felt her pull away. Taking a deep breath, he forced his lips into a tolerant smile that wasn't reflected in his eyes.

"I know what you're going to say . . . we have to talk first."

"That isn't what I was going to say. I was going to ask you to leave."

"You can't mean that, Jesa! Don't deny that you want it."

"I wasn't going to deny it. I was only going to resist it."

"But why? It doesn't make sense. Just a moment ago you were lost in my arms . . ."

"That's the perfect word for it."

"What?" he muttered confusedly, still straining to regain his advantage, derailed by the quiet deliberate tone of her voice.

" 'Lost'—it's the perfect word. I can be 'lost' in you. I just don't want to lose myself anymore."

"I don't understand you."

"I don't want to marry you. I thought I did because loneliness and desire and a big streak of conventionality were all mixed up in my mind. If I misled you or hurt you by saying 'yes' then all I can do is tell you that I'm sorry. But I know now that it could never work out between us."

"But how can you say that?" he said unbelievingly. "I know you love me."

"If you mean that I still want you, then I suppose that you could say I do. You've been a wonderful lover. You've helped me to release things in myself that had been buried for so long that I didn't even know they were there."

"But I don't want any other women."

"That's beside the point."

"I want you to be my wife."

"Do you really know anything about me?" she pleaded, her voice rising in frustration. "You appeal to me as a lover. When I don't respond to that, you appeal to me as a wife. Do you have any idea who I might be if not in relationship to you?"

"What's wrong of thinking of you in relationship to me? How the hell am I supposed to think of you?"

"I couldn't explain that to you, Severio. And even if I could, I doubt if it would have much real meaning. For all those weeks after you first left me, I struggled to find a way that we might be able to salvage something out of the relationship. I even thought of calling you and being corny enough to ask if we could still be friends. Then I realized that that was the nub of the problem: we had never been friends to begin with."

"That's just typical of you modern women," he said, no longer able to control his annoyance, "you think you want a lover and then you try to emasculate the relationship by turning him into a friend."

"Does friendship mean a loss of manhood to you? Would looking at a woman with curiosity and affection, as a separate individual, really rob you of your virility? Because it doesn't threaten my womanhood. I can't settle for less anymore. I won't."

"You mean you've found somebody else," he said in a low voice.

"I mean I think I've found a self that I can live with—alone or with someone else. I may not be expressing myself very well. Lord knows it's taken me half of my life to even be able to open my mouth, and it's still not easy for me. But I know that if I lived with you, you'd force me back into being something that I've outgrown, that I don't respect anymore."

"Jesa, this isn't you. I know that I hurt you and now you're trying to get back at me, but this isn't you."

"There you go again—interpreting all of my actions as though they're reactions to you," she smiled helplessly.

"But I love you. I can't get along without you."

"I won't claim to know you better than you know yourself, my dear, but I truly think that you can and will. Now will you please leave?"

He rose slowly from the couch, picked up his jacket, and buttoned it with great deliberation. There was no point in talking to her now. But she would change her mind. Women were famous for changing their minds. It was only natural that she would have to reject him for a while, since he had wounded her by leaving. This was just a temporary burst of misguided independence. She would feel lonely and lost again. Then she would come back to him. His lips curled in a sad, indulgent smile.

"When you want to see me again . . ." he began.

She shook her head slowly from side to side. He studied her for a moment, then turned on his heel and walked to the door, conscious of the dramatic effect of pausing slightly before he flung it open, then leaving without looking back at her.

Alone in the elevator, his body sagged against the wall. What if she really meant it? What if she wouldn't come back to him? Was it really possible that she could have changed so much? He felt angry and abused. For the first time in his life he had humbled himself before a woman, confessing the depth of his feeling, even promising fidelity—and he had been rejected. How could she have been so nearly in his grasp and then have eluded him?

He clenched his right hand into a fist and rhythmically punched it into his left palm, the faces of the many women in his life flashing before him like a montage in an old movie: Angie, his first, who thought that because they'd lost their virginity together he should be signed to a lifetime contract; Betsy with that luscious bosom, who was already so single-minded about her career when they met in school that she didn't mind sharing him with her roommate, crazy Manuela, with her ancestors' priceless flatware and her rosary beads; Conchita and Barbara and Yvonne . . . He'd had so many already. He would have still more. After all he was in his prime. Even if he was starting to get a few gray hairs, he could make up for the loss of sheer animal energy in experience and technique.

But Jesa. She was another thing entirely. She might really have helped him to change his life. He'd actually grabbed the gold ring with Jesa, and then he'd fumbled and dropped it. He had a queasy premonition that everything afterward would be brass.

He wanted another drink. He wanted to sit quietly somewhere and think about his life. The same desperate need he had felt when he was a young man—to map out his future, to understand his existence—cried out in him. But he feared that indulging in that sort of soul-searching would only make him more depressed. If he took off the blinders that his frantic search for success and acceptance had forced him to put on, why he would be vulnerable, unable to survive, let alone advance. He unclenched his aching hand and pushed the lobby button on the elevator.

He ran down the list of people he might call, crossing off the first half-dozen possibilities before he hit on the right one. Why hadn't he thought of it before? She had all the qualifications. There was no question but that she wanted him as a lover. And once he'd established himself in that capacity, there was no telling where it might lead. Besides; they understood each other.

He straightened up, looking almost jaunty as he

crossed the lobby and went up to the doorman, asking for change of a dollar and the location of the nearest pay phone. "Keep the change," be called over his shoulder as he tossed the coin in the air, caught it and strode out onto the street. He was damned if he was going to let Jesamine Mallick get him down. Not when Bettina Fanshaw was only a dime away.

Jesa stood still for a long time, not quite able to believe that he had come and she had sent him away. There was no catharsis, no resolution of anguish just because she had brought all of her feelings to the surface and expressed them. She didn't even feel like crying.

She walked slowly back into the living room, wondering what she should do next. Passing the small handmade table that she had cherished throughout her marriage, she noticed that Severio had spilled part of his drink on it. Zombielike, she went into the kitchen, found the furniture polish, and crouched down on the floor next to the table. She rubbed the walnut oil into the grain of the wood for a very long time.

Finally getting up, she replaced the furniture polish in the cabinet, washed and dried the two glasses and put them back in the bar, and walked to the telephone with quiet deliberation. The phone rang for a long time at the other end of the line before he picked it up.

"Hello, Josh? It's Jesa."

Chapter 17

The next afternoon as she was preparing to leave, she opened the door to find a note. Before she even opened it, she guessed that the shocking pink stationery adorned with tiny hearts and flowers must belong to Sophie Moss.

Dear Mrs. Mallick:
I got it through the grapevine this morning that you're going to be leaving us again. Won't you please drop by for a cup of tea before you go?
Your neighbor,
Mrs. Abraham Moss

Jesa looked at her watch and decided that she could spare twenty minutes. She called the doorman, asked him to be kind enough to pick up the luggage in the hallway and transfer it to the lobby and be sure to have him ring Mrs. Moss's apartment when it was done.

"Darling, come in and sit down." Sophie opened the door with a flourish, and gestured toward the living room. In all the years she had lived in the building Jesa had never been in Sophie's apartment, yet it held no surprises for her. The cumbersome but enduring furniture of the '40s and '50s lined the walls. The dining-room table was covered with a very old, good quality lace tablecloth. The grand piano was decked with photographs—stiff, sepia-toned portraits of the generations that had preceded Sophie and Abbie as well as more colorful snapshots of grandchil-

369

dren making snowmen and accepting diplomas. The draperies were dusty rose brocade, as heavy as the curtains that Scarlett O'Hara had ripped down to make her dress. Above the fireplace, which now had quick-burning Presto logs, was the inevitable portrait of Abbie. He was erect and of serious mien, as becomes a great man of commerce, but the artist had been good enough to capture the look of benevolence and self-satisfaction in the eyes.

"Listen, darling, you just sit down here while I make us a cup of tea. When O'Hara told me that you were going up to your country place again, I said to myself, 'Sophie, something's going on with that lovely Mrs. Mallick.' "

"Please call me Jesa, Sophie."

"I'll try but I can't promise. You've always been my neighbor, so I've always thought of you as Mrs. Mallick. Anyway, I'm so glad that you took my little note to heart and decided to drop by, because, believe me, I'd feel really awful if you left without telling me. Are you really going to move up to Connecticut or what?"

"I haven't made up my mind. I had to be in the city when Ed was alive, but now that he's gone I think I'm happier up in the country. I've found some new friends there. And I seem to get a lot more painting done. . . ."

"Now you just take a load off your feet while I fix the tea."

Her voice piped over the clatter of kettle and cups, filling Jesa in on the most recent happenings in the building. She finally emerged from the kitchen, staggering under the weight of a large silver tray containing a tea pot, cups and saucers, and a plate of butter cookies arranged neatly on a doily. After pouring the tea with great ceremony, she popped a cookie into her mouth and leaned forward confidentially.

"So just between us, dear, are you up in the country alone?"

Jesa covered her smile by biting into a butter cookie that she didn't really want. There was no escaping the indomitable Sophie. She might as well relinquish all claims to privacy with good grace, because Sophie was obviously a better snoop than Sherlock Holmes and Miss Marple put together.

"I was seeing someone. . . ."

"That handsome Mr. Euzielli, I remember."

"Yes, him," Jesa said, still feeling a tremor at the mention of his name, ". . . but it didn't work out."

"Weren't you engaged?" Sophie pressed.

"Not exactly engaged," Jesa replied, starting to feel uncomfortable under the onslaught.

"I understand," Sophie said meaningfully.

Instead of the barrage of questioning that Jesa expected, Sophie picked up another butter cookie, munched it contemplatively and rose from the couch. She wandered over to the window, silent for a longer period of time than Jesa had ever remembered her being. Jesa watched her, thinking how much her feelings toward Sophie had changed. She recalled all the times she had avoided her, fearing somehow that eccentric widowhood might be catching. Then, during the early part of her affair with Severio, she had come to think of Sophie as a joke. Seeing her now, she felt neither aversion nor derision but a gentle affection. She forgave the incessant chatter, knowing it was Sophie's only relief from long hours spent at the window, munching cookies, looking at the New York skyline and contemplating Life's Great Mysteries.

"Look, darling," Sophie said finally, "one of my granddaughters is a Sociology professor. She just wrote this book which is all about marriage. From what I read in Sylvia's book, you don't have no reason to really need a husband. Sylvia says one, are you going to reproduce—you know, have babies. Two, do you have an independent income—like you shouldn't be worrying where the next meal is coming from. She says that if a woman isn't going to have babies and she can earn her own living, then marriage is a 'moribund institution.' Now Sylvia is a bright girl and I love her, but you know she's only twenty-six years old and she's spent most of her life in the library. You know and I know what it can be like to be married to someone— it can be a test of character. It can also be a heck of a lot of fun," her eyes shifted quickly to Abbie's portrait, as though waiting for confirmation and then went back to Jesa. "My opinion, not that you asked, is that you should just consider this Mr. Euzielli as a sort of fling. Because Sylvia is a very bright girl, and I'm a woman from another generation. All the time pushing you to get married again. What do I know?"

She nodded gently to herself and held out her arms.

Jesa moved toward her and allowed herself to be folded in the motherly embrace.

"Don't worry, darling. He may have disappointed you, but you'll get over it. You're a strong woman. To hell with Mr. Euzielli."

Jesa started to laugh. She laughed so much that the ache in her throat that she had not been able to get rid of was suddenly released and then she started to cry. Sophie pulled the beautiful head of pale blond hair to her pendulous bosom and reached into her pocket for a handkerchief. It had been so long since Jesa had seen anything but a Kleenex that the sight of the batiste hanky with its lace edging and hand-embroidered initials made her weep anew. Sophie patted and shushed her, dabbing the tears that streamed down her face. When her sobs had finally subsided, Sophie gave her a hug, sat her down on the couch again, and bustled back into the kitchen.

"So tell me, darling, how is the painting going? Juan, the new doorman, the Puerto Rican boy with the beautiful eyelashes, he told me that you were hauling all sorts of artsy stuff in and out."

"Yes," Jesa managed to get out, between great gasps of air. "I've been working on a series of paintings. They're all about flowers. Well, actually, they're about decay and rebirth and growth.

"A heavy theme," Sophie said, as she bustled back in with another steaming kettle. "You know heavy doesn't mean like it's too much to carry, anymore. It means like weighty, but in another way."

"Like 'together,' " Jesa offered. "You can be

'together' with another person, or just 'together' with yourself."

"I think that one should still mean both things," Sophie said philosophically.

"I do, too," Jesa smiled.

The buzzer interrupted further conversation and Jesa got up. "All my stuff is in the lobby now. I'd better get going."

"Have a good trip, darling. Don't drive too fast. Have you got enough change for the toll booths?"

"Yes. I'm fine. And thank you, Sophie."

"Don't mention it. And put a cap on your head. You know it's getting to be   out there again."

"I know. I used to be a coward about the winter, but I'm getting better about it now."

"That's because you wised up," Sophie smiled. "Now you know. It's followed by the spring."